WHEREER
YOU ARE

KRISTA & BECCA
RITCHIE

Cover Image ©iStock
Cover Design by Twin Cove Designs

ISBN: 978-1-950165-22-3

ALSO BY
KRISTA & BECCA RITCHIE

LIKE US SERIES

Damaged Like Us

Lovers Like Us

Alphas Like Us

Tangled Like Us

Sinful Like Us

Headstrong Like Us

ADDICTED SERIES

Addicted to You

Ricochet

Addicted for Now

Thrive

Addicted After All

CALLOWAY SISTERS SERIES

Kiss the Sky

Hothouse Flower

Fuel the Fire

Long Way Down

Some Kind of Perfect

STANDALONE ROMANCES

Amour Amour

Infini

A NOTE FROM THE AUTHORS

Wherever You Are is Book 2 in the Bad Reputation Duet. It should be read after Book 1, *Whatever It Takes.*

Wherever You Are contains mature language and graphic sexual content and is recommended for readers 18+

CONTENT WARNING

This book contains graphic scenes of physical abuse from older brothers to a younger brother and verbal abuse that may be upsetting to some readers.

"Broken souls are mended every day

by mended souls that were once broken."

CONNOR COBALT

(FUEL THE FIRE)

1

PRESENT DAY - January

Philadelphia, Pennsylvania

GARRISON ABBEY

Age 21

Heading into the first day of the new year, I try to be positive. *Don't fuck it up, Abbey.*

It's only been 48-hours since everything went down in London. But it's honestly felt like a millennium. Officially, I think I spent less than two hours in the country before flying back to Philly. It's pathetic on multiple levels, and embarrassed doesn't even cut it.

The only upside: it didn't end up on the internet. The students at Wakefield haven't really recognized Willow or just simply don't care. It's another big reason she needs to stay out there for school.

"I can come visit next week," Willow says, her soft voice echoing through my car speakers. I swivel the steering wheel and turn down a crowded street, traffic almost bumper-to-bumper.

Willow never got mad at me for punching her friend Salvatore. She wasn't even disappointed in me or sad. It makes me feel worse because she has every right to hate me.

She said that she understood I'm going through something. Her understanding is like air, helping me breathe. But I'm not sure I deserve my girlfriend's kind heart and empathy. I'm the bad boyfriend fucking with her perfect friends and her perfect London life.

I can't let her go.

I can't lose Willow, even if I'm the thing tarnishing the perfect world she's building.

She never even pushed me to reveal more of what happened in Philly. I've never pushed her past her limits either.

We've always been careful with each other, and that's something I appreciate. Because I don't want to lie, and I think if she asked point-blank—*did you see your brothers?*—I would've come up with some shitty excuse. Anything but admit that I was stupid enough to go home during the holidays, knowing they were there.

What she did ask: *Are you ready to talk about it?*

What I said: *Not yet.*

The moment she finds out I saw my brothers again, she's going to send in the cavalry to check up on me. Daisy. Ryke. Maybe even Lo. I don't need them to bombard me, especially when no one but Willow even knows that my brothers have hit me before.

I want to keep it that way.

"Garrison, did you hear me?" Willow asks over the phone.

I stop at a red light, hands tight on the steering wheel. "You don't need to visit. I'm fine, Willow." I take another breath, about to tell her something that might put her on edge. But *this*, I do want to be honest about. "I'm actually headed to my house. I have to apologize to my mom for bolting and pick up a hard drive on my old computer." It's got some stuff on it that I made back in prep school. It might be useful for the video game I'm creating.

"Wait—you're going home?" Willow's voice spikes with alarm.

"Yeah, but just for a second," I say quickly. "Davis, Hunter, and Mitchell already all left yesterday. They didn't want to spend New Year's Eve with my parents." I pull up to the gate at the neighborhood entrance. "So I'm not going to run into them. It's alright."

A security guard recognizes me and immediately presses a button to let me in. I wait as the gates slide open.

"Why don't you let Daisy pick it up for you?" Willow suggests.

Sweat builds, I lower the blasting heat and unzip my hooded jacket. "Because Daisy will ask questions. And like I said, my brothers aren't home." *It's safe.*

The line is quiet.

A lump lodges in my throat, but I want to say more… *I miss you. I'm sorry I fucked up.*

I love you.

Driving forward, all I say is, "You still there?"

"Yeah." She sounds concerned, but with a big breath, she layers on resolve. "Can you call me when you leave?"

I feel like I've already been calling Willow too much. We talk all night. Which is her entire morning.

Currently it's 9 a.m. for me, and I know she's not in class now. But Winter Break is almost over, and her business courses will be starting back up soon. This break is when she should be hanging with her college friends.

"I'll text you," I say.

"Right when you leave."

"Right when I leave," I agree.

4

We say *I love yous* and *goodbyes* as I park in the empty but plowed driveway of my parent's mansion. No other cars. It confirms what I already know: my brothers are gone.

I'll be quick.

Leaving my Mustang running, exhaust gurgling and visible in the cold morning, I take lengthy, fast steps up the front porch. The January chill barely touches me as I fumble for a house key. How my parents let me keep one—I don't know. They love me, I guess. Still after everything I put them through.

I unlock and enter. "Mom!" I call out in the posh foyer.

No one answers. Veering into the kitchen, I skid to a stop and locate my mom through the window. Towards the east side of the pool, she wears a pink pea coat and Burberry scarf, and while she's bent down, she shears thorns off rose bushes that surround a locked greenhouse.

I watch her brush snow off red petals. She's pretty meticulous about gardening. Don't get me wrong, we have gardeners, but no one except my mom is allowed to touch the flowers around the greenhouse and the plants inside.

It's her "calming" thing or whatever.

Maybe she needs calming after seeing me.

Great.

And this conversation is going to be happening *outside*. In the frigid ass cold. I'm not boiling hot anymore, and so I pull up my hood while I exit through the backdoor. My shoes slide on the icy patio, and I extend my arms for balance.

"Mom!" I call out again and catch myself from a face-plant.

Fuck, I hate the outdoors.

She lifts her head, brunette hair glossy and twisted in an intricate updo with diamond pins, and even though she looks like a rich housewife who'd have her fourth glass of pinot grigio by noon, I've never seen her drink more than a couple seltzers, and she's not too hands off or too overbearing. When my brothers and I played lacrosse in high school, she actually watched us and didn't just socialize with her PTA friends. She'd film the end for our dad who'd miss the action because of work.

So I'm not surprised that when she sees me now a genuine smile overtakes her face. "Garrison." She rises to her feet, brushing gloved hands on tweed pants. "What a surprise. Come here, sweetie."

I near the garden. "I just wanted to—" Words die in my throat as I see shadows through the frosted greenhouse windows. *People are in there.*

What if my brothers are home?

No.

No.

Fuck no…

"Garrison, what's wrong?" She touches my shoulder but I'm like the ice on the ground. Frozen. Only difference is that I break easier.

I need to go.

I need to *go.*

But I can't fucking move.

The greenhouse door swings open, and my pulse stops dead as Davis, Hunter, and Mitchell pool out together.

My oldest brother sets a glare on me. "Nice of you to show up when all the work is done," Davis says.

I feel my face crunch in confusion. "What are you talking about?"

"The greenhouse," Mitchell explains. "You didn't hear mom talk about how she needed help rearranging the plants and lights? You were at that dinner the other night."

I don't remember. Heat gathers again. Sweat caking my body and stifling me, but I can't unfreeze enough to unzip my jacket.

Our mom looks between them. "Boys, that conversation happened after your brother already left."

"Like he always does," Hunter adds, digging the knife in my back.

I drag my gaze across the snow.

Our mom lets out a sigh and says, "Be nice."

"He doesn't make it easy," Hunter snaps.

Likewise.

I swallow the retort and clear my throat to ask, "How did you all even get here? I didn't see your cars?"

"Uber," Davis says. "We were all still a little hungover from last night."

Right.

"We actually still need some help with the heaters and lights," Mitchell says to me. "You want to pitch in?" He nods towards the greenhouse and his eyes soften on me.

I think that Mitchell really believes he's giving me a lifeline to be in good graces with our parents and our brothers.

It's sad.

Because what I really need is for him to stick up for me. To keep our two older brothers from beating on me. But even if Mitchell tried now, he'd be twenty-one years too late.

"I left my car running," I say. "I wasn't staying long."

My mom squeezes my shoulder. "I'll shut it off for you." She holds out a palm so I can pass her the keys. "Go spend some time with your brothers."

I want to say *no*.

Deep in my gut, I don't want to be here, but it feels impossible to leave in this moment.

I nod tensely, and my brothers disappear back into the greenhouse while I search my pockets for car keys. My mom waits for me, patient.

I'm hot and I end up pulling off my jacket. Doing a piss-poor job, half my T-shirt rides up my waist in the process. As I clutch the keys and wad up my jacket, I look over at my mom.

Her eyes are unblinking and zeroed in on my bare abdomen. At the fresh welts that mar my cold skin. Ones from Hunter after he tackled me outside, the holiday dinner from hell. It wasn't even the first bad one I've had.

We're both motionless, except for our gazes that meet. Truths exposed and raw, and it's not like she hasn't known or seen before.

This just feels different. Maybe because I'm older. Maybe because she has the ability to protect me right here, right now, and I'm twenty-one and suffering under the belief that she won't.

She never has before.

My keys are cold in my hand.

She reaches out to stroke my cheek, and I stare down at the snow. Her soft touch feels as painful as the thorns she cut.

I glance at the greenhouse, then to my mom.

"Just give them a chance," she says in a pleading whisper.

I want to shake my head, but I can't. "They're not going to change."

She lets out this tiny breath and rubs my arm, and in her pitying gaze, I know that she's not waiting for them to change. She's always been waiting for *me* to change—to grow thicker skin. To be less sensitive.

More of a man, right?

I could make her a PowerPoint with all the evidence of their fucked-up deeds and she'll still claim I left the majority of their brotherly love off the slides.

I stick my arms back into my jacket sleeves, and once I shake off the snow from my hood, our eyes lock for another beat. *Protect me, Mom.*

Please.

I drop the car keys in her palm. Giving her my escape.

She has a choice to make, and she doesn't even hesitate. I watch her leave for the driveway. To shut off my running Mustang.

As soon as I walk into that greenhouse, I know for certain that I'm doomed.

IT HURTS TO BREATHE. PAIN SPLINTERS UP MY SIDE with each inhale.

How do I reach my apartment? I have no clue—the whole drive is a blur. Like a dusty Sega game, the TV screen crackling with static. But I remember the greenhouse.

I remember pushing Davis so hard that he fell into a stack of ceramic pots. They shattered. Dirt spilled. The door was finally clear.

And I left to the sound of my dad yelling at me. For destroying my mom's precious basil plants. They could've been parsley or spinach for all I know.

I didn't get a good look.

I didn't care, and I guess that's my fault, right?

Stupid, clumsy me.

Once I'm inside my Philly apartment, I hold onto my ribs and search my kitchen cupboards. Banging each one open. Trying to find some pain pills. When I was a teenager, one of my friends in the neighborhood dealt pills and gave me oxy. Her therapist would write her all kinds of prescriptions.

All I have now is ibuprofen.

With one hand, I place the bottle on the counter and twist the cap off, having perfected the one-handed twist on "child-proof" caps years ago. It pops. I purposefully knock the bottle and the pills spill on the granite countertop. I scoop a handful, not even counting and toss them back into my mouth.

As soon as they go down, I cough.

Sharp pain erupts in my ribs. They're broken.

I know they're broken.

Sinking onto my desk chair, I try to forget what happened. Maybe I can see the events from Hunter's fucked-up vantage. He just…he threw a bag of potting soil to me. It was heavy. I didn't see it coming. The bag slammed into my gut and knocked the wind out of my lungs.

I doubled over. Coughing. And the bag—it landed on a gardening hoe and tore open. Soil littered the floor.

Davis slapped me on the back of the head.

I tried to put distance between us, but I walked closer to Hunter. He shoved another bag at my back. As if I had hands connected to my spine to grab the damn thing.

He knew what he was doing.

The brunt force plowed me into a wooden shelf, and the corner jammed into my ribcage. I can still hear the *crack* in my ears. I can still feel my feet slipping beneath me and my legs buckling before I dropped to the ground.

"Come on, get up," Davis said. "Don't be such a pussy."

I blink back the images, and my fingers tremble as I type on my cell. I'm keeping my promise to Willow.

I text: Made it back home. All good.

I know—I'm not telling her the whole truth.

But she doesn't need to worry. I don't need to be the tumor in her life. Especially because this was the last time I'm *ever* confronting my brothers.

Before I left the greenhouse, I did something I never do.

I told them, "I'm never seeing you again." I choked out the seething words, and Hunter and Davis laughed. Like I'm some joke.

Mitchell got quiet. He looked between them and me, and his eyes fell to the floor in a daze.

I don't think any of them really believe me.

But it's true. I'm never going to see them again. Not even when I'm dead. I'd rather spend eternity in hell than come back as a ghost to haunt their asses. I refuse to let them have power over me anymore. The only problem…I forgot to grab my hard drive.

My stomach churns. It's either my hard drive or seeing them again. Fuck the hard drive, then.

I lean back, close my eyes, and wait to go numb.

PRESENT DAY

2

GARRISON ABBEY
Age 21

The next two days are a bigger blur. I bury myself in work and barely leave my desk at Cobalt Inc. Cans of Lightning Bolt! are piled in a tiny trashcan, and despite the fact that my ass hasn't left this chair for eight hours, my space is pretty organized.

I can't think if there's shit everywhere.

Suddenly, a Styrofoam container appears next to my keyboard. I stop typing to pull out two twenties from my pocket and hand the cash to the white guy standing beside my desk. Combed back auburn hair and an expensive suit, Keith looks like he's auditioning for the role of Douchebag #3.

He's a little older than me and an intern in the Cobalt magnets three times a day for me, just so I don't have to leave my desk, and he upcharges me for ten-dollar sushi.

It's worth it.

And he should be walking away right now.

But he's still here.

I point to my headphones. They're noise-cancelling, so I can't hear him past the soft beat of my music. I can't even read his lips that well, but I see his brows furrow in frustration. Okay, I don't want to lose my personal Uber Eats because I ignored him on a random Thursday. I yank my headphones to my neck.

"Abbey," he says. "This is the last time I'm doing this." He points to the Styrofoam. I grab it and open the lid, making sure he didn't spit on the tuna rolls. As far as I can tell, the sushi looks perfect.

I put the container in my mini-fridge under my desk. "Why is this the last time? Do you want more money?" I could go up to fifty, I think.

"No," Keith snaps. "I'm getting shit from the guys in my office. They're calling me your bitch." That's really not a surprise. I'm not well-liked here.

For one, I have ties to Connor, and I refuse to give these pricks an "in" with the boss. No secrets about Connor are coming from my mouth, despite numerous requests for weird shit. Like his favorite liquor and what time of day he's "least" likely to reject their proposal. Do I look like I'm a walking *Connor Cobalt Wiki*?

Secondly, I'm one of the only people who runs their own division alone in Cobalt Inc.

Connor said he'd officially title my division when I've presented my prototype. Right now, I'm keeping everything a secret—even the concept. Less pressure that way, and Connor doesn't seem to care about it.

The guys in the company—they care.

It's favoritism. Nepotism. All wrapped in one fugly looking package.

To Keith, I shrug. "I mean, them calling you my bitch is kind of a lame insult, man. Aren't we all Connor Cobalt's bitches at this point?"

Keith shakes his head and then slowly stops, rethinking. "Yeah, but you're not Connor Cobalt. You're what…twenty-three?"

"Twenty-one," I correct, probably not helping my case. "And just tell those guys to fuck off. You're making almost a hundred dollars a day off me because I'm too lazy to move my ass."

Connor doesn't do free internships, but Keith can't be earning what his senior coworkers take home.

"Exactly," Keith says. "You're lazy. You're young. You're *you*. I can't be seen with you, Abbey." He motions between us. "This partnership is over."

I roll my eyes as he walks off. There goes that one.

Focusing back on my computer, I put my headphones on and try to fix a bug in the code. I'm building the foundation of the game before I even work in the mechanics of design and more complex gameplay. It's harder not having a team of programmers, but I prefer to do it alone. At least, right now at this stage, I don't need a bunch of people in my space.

Another body arrives near my cubicle, and without even turning my head, I recognize the poised *I own this world* posture and Cartier wristwatch from my peripheral.

Connor Cobalt is gracing me with his presence, which doesn't happen every day. He gives me room to breathe and work and so far I've appreciated that.

I keep my eyes on the computer, some strands of hair falling in my face, but I keep typing. Maybe if I ignore him, he'll just vanish.

"Garrison," Connor says. I can hear his calm, assertive tone even over my noise-cancelling headphones.

I don't blink, my focus zoned in on the computer.

He waves a hand in front of the screen. Finally, I glance up at him, still typing like I'm *supremely* busy. Then I peek at his side.

Lily Calloway is here. And she looks about as out-of-place at Cobalt Inc. as I do. A casual long-sleeve black shirt and overcoat hangs baggie on her gangly frame. I don't even think she's wearing actual pants—just leggings.

There's only a handful of reasons she could be here, and I'm going to go with the most obvious. It's January 3rd, and *everyone* in this building knows what that means. It's Connor Cobalt's 30th birthday, and if you want to be on Connor's good side, you act like today is just any other ordinary day.

No fanfare. No wishing your boss happy birthday. Definitely no cake or gifts.

Apparently, Connor isn't that hyped on celebrating his age, but I'm sure his wife and sisters-in-law are planning something for him.

And all of this has absolutely *nothing* to do with me.

I return my gaze to Connor and click a button on my keyboard, turning off my music. "What do you want?" I don't know why, but those words come out a lot harsher than I intend. My muscles twitch.

"You're done for the day," Connor says, ignoring my tone. "I need you to come with us."

What?

My fingers still move over my keyboard, finishing up some last lines of code that I needed to plug in. I swing my head to Lily, trusting her more. "Is this work related?"

"Umm…" She mumbles and then shrugs.

Jesus. She's no help. And I bet she's in on this plan to kidnap me from my work.

"Will you come with us if it isn't?" Connor asks.

"No." I don't even hesitate. It's just the way it is. They're not my friends, and I can pretend all day long that they give a shit about me. But they don't. They care about Willow, and I'm an extension of her. Willow and I aren't in a great place right now, and the probability of us not working out has skyrocketed.

I'm trying to avoid a situation where I form these bonds with people and then have them all ripped away. I've been through the loss of friends before—and it's fucking painful. And I didn't even like those assholes.

It'd be infinitely worse when you actually enjoy hanging out with your friends. And I like Lily. I like Lo. I had fun at the Fright Night during Halloween. Having a good time with them scares the shit out of me. Because it's just another thing I could lose.

So…no. Whatever they're up to, it's a big capital *Fuck No* from me.

Connor doesn't miss a beat. "Then it's work related," he says. "Grab your things."

Seriously?

I wrench my headphones back to my neck with a deeper sigh. Abandoning my work. It looks like Connor's not going to let me bail on this. Plus, I'd prefer to keep my job.

To Lily, I say, "Just tell me where we're going and why."

"Ryke's house—or cottage."

I don't get why they call it a cottage. It looks like a fucking house.

She adds, "It's a surprise party for Connor."

The word *surprise* jumps out at me. I'm living in a parallel universe where words don't mean the same thing. I glance at my boss. "How

18

is this a surprise birthday if you know? And why the hell do you want me to go?"

"Surprising me is so rare that everyone uses the term loosely." He points at my computer. "You're here at six in the morning and you leave at midnight. *Seven* days a week. While I appreciate your work ethic, as your friend, it's disconcerting."

I inhale a tight breath. *Friend.* There's that word again. "You're my boss, not my friend."

"I'm both," Connor says easily, "and since you seem to be lacking in the friend department lately, I wouldn't turn my back on one, especially friendships as valuable as mine."

Believe me, I know how valuable his friendship is. The employees here can't stop reminding me about it.

Lily pipes in, "Having no friends isn't a bad thing."

I pinch my eyes. "Can you both just shut up?" It's hard to think with them in my ear. Another day spent with the famous couples: Lily and Lo, Connor and Rose, Ryke and Daisy. I should reject this forced invite, but for the sake of my job and my current sanity, there's only one real choice.

I roll back the chair and grab my backpack from underneath the desk. Lily glances at my ripped jeans, but she doesn't say anything about it.

Standing, I still have to crane my neck to look at my boss. The guy is six-four, and I swear the universe is playing right into his hand. People refer to Connor as some otherworldly being like an immortal god. He might as well be tall enough to touch the sky.

I sling the backpack over my shoulder. "If I go," I say to Connor. "You have to stop calling me your friend. We're not, okay?" I need him to understand this. I don't want him as a friend. If we're not, there won't be more collateral damage when I lose Willow.

Before Connor can reply, I look to Lily. "And I have friends…" I pause. *That's not completely true.* "One friend. She's just not here."

Willow.

My only friend.

Casually, like I didn't just offer this grand stipulation, Connor checks his watch. "Most people would be on their knees to be my friend. This just illustrates your lack of judgment."

Maybe.

I nod. "Thanks, boss." Sarcasm bleeds from my lips.

"Follow me." Connor motions to Lily and me. He saunters ahead with calm, reassuring authority. Most people love it. For some people, the arrogant superiority grates on them. After working months for Connor, I'm landing somewhere in between.

We pass a copy machine, Lily step-by-step beside me. I whisper to her, "Just so you know, you're my favorite boss." I've only ever had two. Connor and Lily.

She smiles wide, and a good feeling floods my chest.

I miss those days at Superheroes & Scones.

But I can't have them back.

The Calloway Sisters & Their Men – Fan Page

Present Day | *Followers: 75K*

It's that time! With every new year, I'm dedicated to updating you on the basics of the Calloway Sisters & Their Men. Take this as a bit of a "where are they now" post.

The Stokes
Poppy Calloway (33) & Sam Stokes (33)
Daughter: Maria (10)
Update: Not much to note about the Stokes. Like we said, this Calloway sister stays out of the media. Poppy and her husband have decided not to take part in the docuseries *We Are Calloway*.

The Cobalts
Rose Calloway (29) & Connor Cobalt (30)
Daughter: Jane (3)
Sons: Charlie & Beckett (1-year-old twins)
Update: Calloway Couture and Cobalt Inc. are both thriving, but the real news comes with a rumor that Rose might be pregnant with her fourth child!! #AlreadyPredictingBabyNames

The Hales
Lily Calloway (27) & Loren Hale (28)
Son: Maximoff (3)

Update: Maximoff might just be the cutest baby alive. We have no new baby news, but there are rumors that the Sorin-X movie is coming along. It will be the first big movie franchise for Halway Comics.

The Meadows
Daisy Calloway (22) & Ryke Meadows (29)
Daughter: Sullivan (11-months-old)
Update: We don't see much of Daisy and Sulli out and about, and unfortunately Sulli hasn't been on *We Are Calloway*. So bummed! Especially since the Meadows baby might be the most sought after for pics. Everyone wants to see Ryke Meadows dad moments. But he's the face of Ziff, the sports drink, so we are blessed with those abs.

The Unofficial Calloway Sister
Willow Hale (20) & Her Boyfriend – Garrison Abbey (21)
Update: They're still dating even though she's all the way in London for college. We've seen a little of Garrison in the background of *We Are Calloway*. But unless you're following Willow on Instagram, she's been pretty MIA online. It's possible they might not even be together anymore, despite Lily's reassurance. We'll keep tabs, and if anyone has any connections to people at Wakefield University that want to drop some tips, hit me up in my DMs.

Don't forget today is Connor Cobalt's birthday! Be sure to tweet him and wish him a happy birthday. And check out this gif set below of him and Rose in Paris!!

Love you like Loren loves Lily,
xo Olive

3

GARRISON ABBEY
Age 21

Three-year-old Jane Cobalt tosses a handful of confetti from a little pink bucket. "Happy Birthday, Daddy!"

All of their children are front and center in Ryke and Daisy's quaint "cottage"—it's definitely not a mansion or as regal as the Cobalt Estate. But it's four-bedrooms. Not a shoebox either. The outside is all gray stone with a stone-stacked chimney like they live on a pastoral English countryside and not in a Philly suburb.

The décor is like Urban Outfitters threw up in here. Boho chic or whatever. I'm not an interior designer.

One-year-old fraternal twins, Charlie and Beckett Cobalt have their own buckets of confetti, and three-year-old Maximoff Hale makes confetti angels on the hardwood, little legs and arms moving about. Daisy kneels on the ground beside her almost-one-year-old

Ryke, Loren, and Rose stand off to the side, letting their kids "surprise" Connor.

I feel like I'm intruding.

But they wanted me around. So I'm here.

Still, I need air for a second. I slip out before anyone notices me and head towards the first-floor bathroom. I've been here enough with Willow to know where it is. Gold balloons litter the ground, and I push aside a black streamer, hanging from the ceiling. They went all out for a not-really-surprise "surprise" party.

I lock the bathroom door and immediately splash water on my face. Taking out my phone, I check my messages.

None.

I'm about to text Willow, but loud laughter echoes from the living room. I want to be around them. I shouldn't want that.

Get it together. You're already here.

I swallow hard and wipe water off my face before returning to the living room. The first thing I notice is the life-sized cardboard cutout of Connor standing in the middle of the hall.

Jesus...

They really went there.

Like he doesn't already have an ego the size of a galaxy? I tilt my head, examining more. It looks so much like Connor. One of them must have bought the cutout on a celebrity site. I've seen them before. The only reason I even check out those sites is to make sure Willow and I don't have our faces on T-shirts. We're not that famous, and honestly, I hope it never happens.

I prefer the periphery where people don't have a life-sized cardboard version of me in their bedroom. It creeps me out, but I see how Lily and everyone else are laughing about it. How they try to turn this into something fun. Because it's better than dwelling on the shitty aspects of fame. It's not all bad. And I guess, it's kind of a good gift.

Which reminds me: I didn't get Connor anything. And I'm at his birthday party.

Well, whatever. He knows I didn't actually want to come.

I head to the kitchen, passing a banner that reads **HAPPY 30TH BIRTHDAY, CONNOR!** The only other people that pack the place besides the "core six" are their children. I'm literally the interloper.

Awesome.

Jane Cobalt giggles on the ground, covered in confetti. A photo of this child just smiling in celebratory streamers would be worth thousands of dollars, sold to any magazine in New York.

She's just a baby. I feel bad for her and Moffy. What kind of life are they going to have under this invasive microscope? Their parents got twenty-some years of peace before the spotlight roasted them.

They get *nothing*.

Sucks.

I shrug the thought off and slip further in the sunny kitchen, sunshine streaming through windows.

Loren pops a chip into his mouth, a jar of salsa next to him. His wife has her legs around his waist and arms around his neck in a piggyback. Lily is thin and bony and can't weigh much. He hands her a chip over his shoulder, and he's really the only person I care to greet right now.

"Hey," I nod to him and then hop up on the kitchen counter. I catch sight of a tiny potted basil plant next to the sink, and my chest tightens.

"You made it," Lo says, not surprised that I was invited.

I focus back on him. "Yeah."

He scoops a hunk of chunky salsa. "Was groveling involved to get your ass here?"

"Some."

"Good." Lo tosses another chip in his mouth. "I can't be the only one begging you to show up to birthday parties. As King Connor would say, it's *unseemly*." He tilts his head. "How's my sister?"

I'm about to tell Lo that Willow is doing great, as far as I know. She never told any of them about how I punched her college friend or the fact that I visited her in London for all of two hours.

Can this stay between us? I asked her. I was ashamed. Still am.

She agreed.

But before I can say anything to Loren, his wife cuts in. "Lo," Lily says softly, but loud enough to pull his attention.

"Hmm?" He swishes around the salsa with a chip. His other hand is planted on Lily's leg. She's still on his back.

Their embrace just makes me ache to hold Willow. My heart physically clenches, and I knock my head back against the cupboard. *Come on, Garrison.*

"Do you think Connor might be Batman or Superman?"

Lo drops her instantly.

She lands on her ass. "Lo!"

My lip twitches, almost smiling. God, I want to.

There are some things you don't bring up in front of Loren Hale. DC comic book characters might actually be number one on the list.

He waves a chip at his wife. "There are a goddamn *thousand* superheroes, and you chose two that I can't stand?"

"They make the most sense."

"They make about as much sense as calling Connor the Swamp Thing."

I almost laugh.

Lily picks herself off the floor. "That's just silly. Swamp Thing isn't even *close* to being Batman and Superman."

Willow would love this conversation. Comics remind me of her. She's the only reason I started reading them in the first place, and she still loves superheroes more than me. *I'll tell her about this.* It'll be a light thing after a lot of heavy shit.

Lo's glare sharpens and intensifies. "Please let me know where I can find my other wife. This one in front of me is a sellout."

Lily touches her heart and hurt cinches her brows. "I'm not a sellout. I just happen to not be an elitist about the whole Marvel versus DC thing, and I can appreciate *all* superheroes equally."

"You think they're all made *equally*?" Lo asks passionately. "Do you want to talk Green Lantern? We can talk Green Lantern."

"Okay, okay," Lily immediately concedes. "So I have my favorites, just like you." She's moved close, fingers in his belt loops, and she gazes up at her husband like the whole conversation is a giant turn-on. Lo wraps his arm around his wife.

I lean forward and grab a couple chips from the bag. Trying not to wish for Willow to be here.

Lo declares, "My best friend is *not* Batman or Superman." *Best friend.* That'd be Connor. It's weird hearing him say that out loud. Not that I don't know the fact. But because Connor is my boss. Loren is Willow's brother. Our connections to one another are too fucking tangled at this point.

"Then what is he?" Lily asks.

"Connor Cobalt," Lo answers without a pause. "He's Connor fucking Cobalt, and whatever powers he has, they're all his own."

I narrow my eyes, watching their exchange. Connor doesn't surround himself with people who only blow smoke up his ass, otherwise Ryke Meadows wouldn't be in this room. But pure admiration comes from Lo.

For me, I remember being a seventeen-year-old kid who vandalized a house. I remember the guy who gave me the handout when I needed it but didn't deserve it.

I don't know—Loren Hale is the one who has powers to me.

Lily's gaze drifts to a *Celebrity Crush* tabloid on the counter behind Lo, and her smile fades. "What is…" She seizes the tabloid.

I crane my head, trying to read the headline.

[POLL] Which Calloway sister has the cutest baby?

That's fucked up.

And the poll won't blow over well with Ryke, Daisy, Connor, or Rose either.

They're all insanely protective of their kids. Like they should be. Parents should protect *all* of their children. Not just the ones they like the most.

Shit, if I had a baby right now, I'd be gutted every time their name was in print. *I* can't even handle media attention. How could I expect my kid to deal with that?

And why the fuck am I thinking about a baby?

I'm twenty-one.

Willow and I are in the rockiest place we've ever stepped foot in. We may not make it to *tomorrow*. Babies are an unquantifiable part of my relationship. The more I think about the foggy future, my stomach knots.

Pain suddenly flares in my ribs as I focus more on the injury.

So I turn my attention.

Lo rips the tabloid out of Lily's hands.

"They polled our babies by cuteness," Lily explains. "They can't do that."

Lo's brows bunch. "They can do whatever they want."

"I just wish there were *some* ethical limitations," Lily says while Lo flips to the right page. Lily tries to stop him, pushing his hands. "Don't! What if Moffy is ranked the ugliest." She lowers her voice. "We'll know and we'll feel bad and it'll give him a complex."

I look around for Maximoff. The three-year-old is playing patty-cake with Jane on the carpet.

"That's not going to happen," Lo says. "We have an *adorable* baby."

"So do Rose and Daisy."

"You don't have to look," Lo tells Lily.

But I'm positive he can't help himself. I chew another chip and watch this go down.

I don't even know what I would do in their position. Maybe burn it. Stop the temptation.

While Lo reads through the article, Lily slides towards me and we chat about movies. I think it's helping distract her from the tabloid, but I haven't seen as many films as she's mentioning. Ever since Willow left, I haven't had the energy to go to the theater.

After a few minutes, Lo finishes reading the article and drifts back to us with chips and salsa in hand. "Little 'puff," he calls out to Lily.

Puff is just in reference to Hufflepuff, her *Harry Potter* house. Willow made me take the sorting quiz too, and I'm Gryffindor like my girlfriend.

I almost smile remembering how Willow spent an hour explaining *our* house to me and the history behind it. She said Gryffindors are brave, and I get why she's meant for this house—she's the most courageous person I've ever met. But I'm not sure I fit the mold. Really, of any house or secret club or thing.

Lo stands behind Lily and rests his chin on her shoulder. His eyes flit to me and then back to her. "What are we talking about?"

"Nothing," Lily says too fast and spins around to face her husband.

Lo stuffs the chip bag underneath his arm. "Nothing?"

"That's what I said," she snaps.

"Christ, when'd you get so sassy?"

Lily crinkles her nose, trying to put on a "tough" face. But she fails. Lo sticks his chip between his teeth, freeing up his hand, and he pinches her nose.

Lily playfully pounds her fist into his arm.

Lo feigns a wince and mumbles, "Ouch, love." He tilts his head back and the chip falls into his mouth.

Their love is an all-consuming thing when you're in the room with them, and my all-consuming love is thousands of miles away.

3,539 to be exact.

Why am I even here again?

To watch them flirt. To be the seventh-fucking-wheel.

So I blurt out, "We were talking about *Justice League 2*." The movie isn't coming out any time soon—the release now up in the air (which Lily and I were discussing)—but the mention of the DC property is enough to receive a Grade A grimace and glare from Loren.

Seeing him drop his own wife on the ground for talking about DC should have probably made me hesitate. But maybe I have a death-sentence.

Murder me.

It'd be easier being dead.

Lo flashes a half-smile. "Why don't you go talk about that down the street, turn right, approach a mailbox that says *Abbey*, walk up the driveway, slam the door—goodbye." He waves curtly.

Bile rises to my throat. If he even knew what walking up to my family's home means...

But maybe that's where I deserve to be.

Pressure sits heavy on my chest, and I spin an unlit cigarette between my fingers. Ryke would probably shit a brick if I smoked in here, but I could leave.

That's what Lo wants anyway.

Anger and something worse pounds against me. "You want me to go home?" I snap and then grind down on my teeth.

Home.

Let me go home and break another rib.

Let me go home and give my mom a chance to save me. Only to push me in a snake pit all over again.

Lo holds my gaze. "I want you to not speak about what-shall-not-be-named inside my brother's house, and if you can't handle that, then yeah, you can go home."

"Lo!" Lily chastises in shock, jaw dropped.

Loren pushes her chin up, closing her mouth. He almost smiles. "Lily." He mock pouts.

She pokes his chest. "You're not being nice."

"Because I'm not nice."

I release a tensed breath. He's just being a normal, raging asshole. I have to remember that Lo doesn't know anything about my home. I don't think he'd poke at this part of my life if he had any idea about what goes on there.

Lily slides her hand to Lo's cheeks and she's looking at him with intense *fuck me* eyes, so I focus elsewhere. The ceiling. The floor. My phone.

No new texts.

Willow's probably asleep.

I waver between staying here and jumping off the counter and leaving. But even with Lo practically painting neon arrows towards my house, I like it here. My other option is sitting alone in my apartment.

Being alone sounds horrible.

I've never enjoyed my own company. It's mainly why I spent my prep school years with *terrible* friends because surrounding myself with people (even shitty ones) was better than being left with my own fucking self.

Instantly, I decide to stay. I'll grab a drink—soda because Ryke doesn't have alcohol in his house—and maybe eat some cake and then leave.

The cupboards are behind my head, and I reach up for a cup.

"Garrison," Lo says with enough worry that I turn quickly.

My head smacks into the cupboard. "Shit," I curse and rub the throbbing spot. Lo stares at me with a strange amount of concern. I don't get it. "What?"

He asks softly, "Where did those bruises come from?"

Oh…shit.

Shit.

Fuck.

My mouth falls, and I shake my head. I don't…how did…

God, my hoodie and shirt must have risen when I reached for the cupboard. *Fuckfuckfuck.*

FUCK!

I dizzy, my head whirling, knowing there's no hiding this. I haven't prepared for anyone beyond Willow to know about my home life.

I glance to Lily, the only other person in the kitchen. I have zero sisters, and there's something soft and kind about Lily. It makes me want to simultaneously open up but also step back, and I don't know how to handle telling her the truth.

Lo is different.

I guess he reminds me of me. It's easier to go head-to-head with someone who wants to rip me open than someone who wants to hug me. I don't want a hug.

His question jackhammers my brain. Pounding and pounding. *Where did those bruises come from?* I look back to Lo and lean into my usual excuse. "Lacrosse. Drop it."

Lily suddenly swings her head to the living room. "Oh look— Moffy." She quickly moves to leave. Lo pinches her shoulder, and they talk under their breaths before she disappears.

It's obvious she left on purpose. Because of me. Maybe they can tell I'm lying.

I stay seated on the counter, legs hanging off, and Lo slides closer to my spot. His sharp-edged gaze drills in on me.

"Honestly, it's lacrosse," I say.

"It's been Christmas break," Lo refutes, his tone serrated. "When were you playing lacrosse?" *Never. Not since prep school.*

Air is hard to intake. Emotion that I hate to confront is compressing my lungs. "I don't know...I just was...I was." Lies die in my throat. My mouth dry.

I end up staring at a patch of sunlight on the floor. Hair hangs over my eyes, and I remember that I'm still wearing headphones around my neck. I touch the sides, the familiarity suddenly calming me. "Let me be."

I'm seconds away from pulling the headphones over my ears like a real dick. Anything to avoid this conversation.

Suddenly, Lo hands me the salsa and then digs a hand in the bag of chips, passing me one.

I stare blankly at him. "What is this?"

I don't get it. What is he fucking doing? The pressure on my chest has intensified. Smothering me.

"Chips and salsa," Lo says. "If you don't like them, we can't be friends anymore." He pops one in his mouth.

"We're friends?" I ask incredulously. A part of me still thinks the invite here was out of pity, and because I'm just Willow's boyfriend.

"Jesus Christ, do I need to make friendship bracelets for you to believe it?"

"Fuck you," I snap. Hesitantly, I dip the chip into salsa.

"Don't be pissy because I'm prettier. It's just a fact you're going to have to get used to."

I swallow the chip and the lump that's wedged in my throat. "I thought the tall one was supposed to be the prettiest." If Connor knew I called him *the tall one*, I don't think he'd love it. Too generic for the mighty god. That's why I like doing it though.

Lo starts to smile. "Shh, we don't like to tell him the truth. It ruins his allure."

I nod, my shoulders sinking forward. Into myself. *Disappear.*

Lo sweeps me in this causal way. "So what are your brothers like? You have three, right?"

Easy enough question.

"Yeah," I answer. "Mitchell, Hunter, and Davis. We're all two years apart from one another."

Me: twenty-one.

Them: twenty-three, twenty-five, and twenty-seven.

A long, tense pause strains the air, and I stare at the small scar on the inside of my pointer-finger. When I was nine, Hunter made me fish in the garbage for a *Sports Illustrated* magazine I threw away. He was pissed because he never got a chance to read it.

I sliced my finger open on a tuna can.

"Which one's the worst?" Lo asks.

It drives deep into me.

Which one's the worst. His voice is strict and sharp, sounding protective before he even knows the real issue. But he must sense the problem is with my brothers. I'm sure I mentioned them briefly before, and I couldn't have said nice things.

I look Lo up and down. "I know what you're trying to do."

"Am I right?" He motions to my ribs. "Did one of your shitty fucking brothers do that?"

My nose flares. My throat swells. I try to swallow again. I barely can. No one but Willow has ever confronted me outright. And it's like submerging my whole body into ice water. I don't know how to breathe with this type of pain. I want *out.* Out. I glance left and right, searching for some sort of escape.

It's not a physical place I want to be.

Take it away. Take this fucking pain away.

My mouth dries more. "They're just messing around." My voice is barely a whisper. But I think he hears because his jaw clenches.

Anger flares in his amber eyes.

I don't know why I defend my brothers or regurgitate my mom and dad's words. It feels easier to agree with my parents than to say what I know is true.

Silence stretches for an uncomfortable beat and then Lo says, "Can I see it again?"

I glance to the living room.

Everyone sits on couches, most aren't facing the kitchen, and their attention cements to the little kids. Not aware of our conversation or they're purposefully giving us privacy.

I rotate back to Lo, and I realize he's being really patient.

Patience isn't a quality I'd shelve under his name. That gets me for a second. So I take a breath and grip the bottom of my hoodie.

I lift the black fabric, just enough to reveal the deep purple bruise that spiders up my ribcage. I'd love to say that it looks worse than it feels. But that'd be another lie. Instead of concentrating on my own fucked-up body, I watch Lo.

His cheekbones sharpen. And he looks visibly ill.

Pale.

He skims me quickly, trying to take it all in before I shut him out, and he peers around at my back. I haven't looked there yet, but I'm betting faint bruises exist from where Davis's shins connected with my spine.

"*Get up.*" I hear his voice in my head. Not just from this week. But from so many years. Colliding together. "*You're weak shit.*"

"Let me check out your other side," Lo whispers, tearing me from my own head.

My hands shake as I lift the other side of my hoodie. *Fuck.* I inhale, and I see another black-and-blue welt along my abdomen. But this one is fading.

"I'm the little brother," I say, so soft that he tilts his head to hear. "They just pick on me. It's what older brothers do."

Stop it.

Stop defending them.

I can't. I can't. Why can't I?

My limbs tremble. I'm shaking harder like an earthquake rumbles beneath me and I can't stop it.

Lo stares at me, straight-on. His face all sharp lines. "Your ribs are fractured."

A hot tear rolls down my cheek. "Yeah, I know." I wipe harshly. *Stop crying.*

"It's happened before?"

I shrug, muscles tensed. "Whenever I see them, they like to play rough, so whatever…"

"Which brother?" Fury flames his voice.

I lift my head. *Don't cry. Don't fucking cry.* My chin quakes. "All of them."

My voice splinters.

Lo blinks something back, his eyes reddened, and so softly, so quietly, he tells me, "I'm not going to let them hurt you anymore."

Fuck.

Those words just collide into me. I try to cover my shattering face. Palms to my eyes. I slide off the counter, attempting to stand, but my legs buckle underneath me.

Fuck.

My back slips down the cabinets until my ass hits the floor, and I bury my forehead into my bent knees.

I'm not going to let them hurt you anymore.

His first instinct is to protect me. No hesitation, no second thought that maybe I don't deserve protection.

Maybe I am the sensitive little brother. Having Loren Hale know about my issues at home is this giant, scary thing. It's why I'm trembling, and I can't fucking stop. My ears ring.

Lo is seven years older than me. One year older than Davis, my eldest brother. And there are days…weeks, months that I wished I had Willow's family instead of my own. But I can't trade them in— that's not how blood works, right?

And I'm just stuck here, wanting out. *God, I want out.* I sniff hard and wipe my nose with the sleeve of my hoodie.

Without lifting my head, I sense Lo kneeling beside me. "Does Willow know?" he asks.

I nod, still looking down. Strands of hair stick to my wet eyelashes. I'm afraid they'll blame her for withholding information. They shouldn't.

It's all on me. I've been evading the whole truth. Omitted shit. And she's been here for me so much already.

I choke out, "It's not her fault…for not telling anyone. She thought it stopped. It did…for a while, but when I went back for Christmas break, they were all there…" I blink back the most recent encounter, spilt soil and a collision into wooden shelves. I shudder and exhale a sharp breath. "Forget it. Forget I said anything."

Lo's voice grows even quieter. "Will you stay at my place, at least until Willow comes back?"

My body solidifies. He's not serious. Does he even know what he's offering? I'm…*me*. And Willow isn't coming back to Philly anytime soon. She just completed her *first* semester at Wakefield.

"That's *years*."

"So?"

I glance up from my knees. Unblinking. My eyes sting, and Lo stares at me with assured intensity, like he means every word he's saying.

I don't think he understands the enormity of his offer. I'm the kid that vandalized his house three years ago. I shouldn't be *living* in his home. But here he is, passing out second and third and fourth chances like they grow endlessly on trees.

But I know Loren Hale better now than I did three years ago. In reality, second chances don't exist with him. You hurt him and he cuts you off at the knees. Why I'm the exception to that, I don't know.

Maybe I never will.

I have to think about this logically. Where I go will affect the one person I love most in this world. I think about my girl.

"Willow could break up with me by then," I remind Lo. After the shit I pulled in London, I'm sure that day is coming.

"You'd still be a part of this family." He gestures in a circle. "I wouldn't kick you out because of it."

I'm bowled over again. It's harder to breathe, but for a different reason. My eyes burn, and I impulsively shove against his offer. "I have an apartment in Philly."

"You live alone." He pauses and then gives me a once-over. "I'm going to be blunt like my brother. You look like shit. You're a little gaunt, and man, you smell like you've been spraying cologne instead of showering."

"I've been busy," I snap, not wanting that pity. "I have a job, and it's the only thing that keeps me from..."

"From what?"

I shrug, and then it just pours out of me. "From feeling like a stupid loser. Like I have no purpose, alright?" I hold back tears. "I have something outside of *waiting* for a girl. I have something... and I need to put time in it. I shouldn't even be *here*. I should be working—"

"Hear me out," Lo cuts me off just as my voice cracks. "I have this little kid who's a big pain in my ass because he keeps begging for a sibling. Every day I have to hear, 'but Jane has two brothers' and if he just saw you in the house, he'd be happy. But most importantly, you'd save my goddamn eardrums."

I let out a short laugh. "The important things."

"Damn right."

I pinch my eyes. "Stop *crying*," I mutter under my breath. *Why can't I stop?*

"I get it."

"Do you?" I snap.

"Your brothers call you a pussy for crying? They tell you you're not a real man—*suck it up, Garrison. What are you, a little pussy, a little girl?* What kind of goddamn man are you?"

My mouth falls open, shock stinging me. I almost look around for Ryke. There's *no way* Ryke could have said that shit to Lo. But I can't locate Lo's older brother because the cabinets block my view from the living room.

Lo follows my gaze, and he must register who I'm trying to find. "It wasn't my brother who told me to just *stop fucking crying.*" His jaw tightens.

I frown. "Who?"

"My father."

I ice over. Jonathan Hale is Willow's dad, too. And she didn't grow up with the man, but he's a part of her life now.

Regardless of that, I hear what Lo is saying. All this time, I've been the exception to Lo's cut-throat attitude.

Neither of us knew each other's histories, but I think deep down, we both always sensed that parts of us were the same.

The broken parts.

Maybe he's just healed before I've gotten the chance to. Maybe I won't be able to. Maybe this is it for me, you know? I'm going to live forever with this thing inside of me, bearing down on all that I am. And it fucking hurts. It just hurts.

I keep rubbing at my face, the tears not ceasing. *Please, just stop.* My body is warring with what I want. *Stop crying. Stop crying. Goddammit, stop fucking crying.*

My sleeves are soaked, and Lo scoots nearer. "You'll be okay," he breathes. "You won't see it today, maybe not even tomorrow, but one day, you'll wake up and you'll want to live."

I choke back a sob. What he's saying seems more like a dream not made for me. I shut my eyes and open them. "Are you sure?"

"I'm goddamn sure. Look at me…"

It takes me a second to raise my head, hair still falling over my eyes, shielding me like armor.

Lo says deeply, "One day at a time. Can you do that with me?"

My throat swells. Lights in the kitchen are harsh on my sensitive, swollen eyes. *One day at time.* I'd reject that fantasy under different stipulations. I'm not made to be by myself. Not wired that way.

And that's okay, I think.

Because he's not just saying *one day at a time.* It's one day at a time with him.

With someone.

Not alone.

Okay.

Okay.

Quiet stretches around us, Loren just sitting by and waiting for me to collect my thoughts. I can do this. I can accept something good for my life. Nodding repeatedly, I finally make my decision. But I still have one last thing left that connects me to my family. One thing left to claim and then I can cut ties completely.

I glance to Lo. "…will you do something for me, if I move in with you?" My stomach twists, not wanting to ask too much, but needing this.

"Yeah."

My face scrunches at his lack of hesitation. "You don't even know what it is."

"Doesn't matter."

"I want you to kill someone," I deadpan. It's a bad attempt at humor. But he's the one who's blindly trusting me. No questions asked.

Lo glares. "You joke, but have you met me?"

I narrow my eyes. Look, I don't know what he's capable of. Just like I don't try to think about what I could do. I take a breath before speaking, not wanting my explanation to come out dry and sarcastic. "Two days ago, I told my brothers that I'd never see them again. I don't know whether they believed me. They rarely take anything I say seriously, but I told them. I just don't want to talk or see them ever." I swallow hard, my throat raw. "So two days ago…I also left my parent's house in a hurry and accidentally forgot one of my hard drives there."

"You want me to get it for you?"

"Yeah…but just don't…" I take a deep breath.

"Don't what?"

"Don't hurt them. Alright. I know it sounds stupid as fuck, but they're still my brothers. Even if I never see them again, I just don't…just *don't* do it." There've been plenty of times where I've wished Hunter dead.

Where I envisioned my fist pounding his face.

But at the end of it all, I don't want a single living soul to feel the pain that I've felt.

Not even them.

I just want it to stop.

"I won't," he says, and after everything, I believe him. "Give me your phone. I'll go get your hard drive now."

I pass him my cell.

"What about your parents?" Lo asks. "Do they know?"

Goosebumps crawl along my arms, cold all of a sudden, but it's easier to talk. "I've told my mom, but she just says it's *boys being boys*..." I pause. "And my dad likes Davis the best. They don't care about anything except making money, and ever since I got a job with Cobalt Inc., they stopped hounding me about 'doing something with my life.' If I never checked in, never returned their calls, they'd just think I was too busy for them, and they'd probably be *proud*."

"Huh," he says, frowning. "They sound like dicks."

I choke out a laugh. "Yeah, they are."

He scrolls through my contacts. I have shit emojis next to each of my brother's names, which Lo can definitely see. His lips pull down, and I'm just glad that I didn't have to paint vivid portraits of all the crap they've done over the years for Lo to believe me.

He just did.

With our backs to the cabinets, he presses the phone to his ear, so I can't hear. It's better that way.

Lo's eyes flit to me. "Will they answer?"

I nod. "And miss an opportunity to pick on me?"

He glares off in the distance. My knees bounce a little, watching him. Waiting.

Someone must answer because Lo says, "This is Loren Hale, from down the street." He pauses and then says, "Garrison left his hard drive at your parent's place. He really needs it soon. Can you swing by and drop it in my mailbox?"

That's a good idea—better. That way Lo doesn't even have to confront them. Weight releases off my taut shoulders in an instant. Pressure evaporating from my chest, and I breathe easier and lean back with less tension.

Lo cups a hand over the cell and looks to me. "Where's the thing?"

"Basement table."

He puts the phone back to his ear. "Basement table." There's a long silence, and I don't know if one of my brothers is talking or if it's just dead quiet on the line.

Truth: I don't care.

I'm just glad I'm not the one with the phone in my hand.

"Do you want to say something?" Lo asks my brother.

I pick at the ripped hole in my jeans. They want to talk to me? My stomach twists again. *Stop.*

"Yep," Lo says on the phone, grinding his teeth. Like he tries not to lash out. He'd probably eviscerate my brothers with his words if I wasn't sitting here. But I think he's trying to be nonconfrontational... for me.

That means something.

Lo's eyes redden, and his glare intensifies on the cupboards. "Sure." He hangs up and lets out a heavy breath he'd been caging. He tosses me the phone.

"What'd he say?" I ask.

"He'll drop it in my mailbox. He's sorry, and he thinks you never speaking to all of them is a good idea." Lo shakes his head, confusion cinching his brows. Maybe he's wondering how easily my brother could let me go. But I get it.

I know.

"You called Mitchell, didn't you?" It's the only thing that makes sense. I remember the look Mitchell had in the greenhouse, right before I left. How he was staring faraway. Like something clicked in his head.

He's sorry.

I rub my dripping nose.

Letting me go is Mitchell's way of protecting me from our other two brothers.

"What is he—the nice one?" Lo asks.

"Mitchell could've stopped them," I mutter. He's closest in age to me. Two years older. "He never did. Does that make him nice?" I shake my head. "…I don't know. I never stopped my friends from breaking into your house. I never stopped *myself* from pranking you. We're all the same. We're all *shit*." He needs to remember who he's inviting into his home. I'm not a good guy. Doesn't he remember?

Lo leans forward, and with utter conviction, he says, "This guy in front of me isn't shit, and I'll still be here when you finally believe it too."

I inhale like I haven't taken a full breath in all my life.

I was wrong about my family—how I can't trade them in.

They may be blood, but they're not mine anymore.

I can choose my family. Lo gave me that option.

And I choose this one.

4

WILLOW HALE
Age 20

"Lo told me I could pick any room in the house that I wanted with one exception," Garrison explains as he folds clothes into a new dresser. I watch him on Skype. Boxes surround him, and computer monitors and cords litter the queen-sized bed.

Before he officially accepted Lo's offer, he called to ask if the whole thing was a bad idea. He wanted to make sure that I was on board.

My boyfriend moving into my brother's house.

In Garrison's words: *"If you become unhappy in our relationship and this makes it harder for you to break up with me—then I won't do it."*

He's always thinking about me, in most everything. Even in some strange reality where I'd break up with him, he thinks about me. By the way, that's a reality that I refuse to believe will ever come true.

During the same phone call, Garrison spilled everything about his brothers. How they hurt him during the holidays and then again in the greenhouse. How his mom did nothing.

It gutted me, but I tried to stay strong over the line for him. Towards the end, we were both crying. I wish I could've been there. With him.

His drunken anger in London made more sense, and guilt gnawed at me for not flying home with him that night. Garrison said he wouldn't have wanted me to, but I'll regret it forever.

"I regret a lot," I told him on the phone, wiping at my tears. "I could've confronted your mom or told Lo sooner—"

"No," Garrison forced out. "We were teenagers."

"I'm not a teenager anymore."

I could hear his tears and cracking voice. "What happened isn't on you, Willow. You left everything you knew to come to Philly. And you came here to meet your brother. Saving me wasn't your job. It's *mine*. And you know how many times I wanted to confront *your* mom but never did?"

He's been pissed about how easily she's erased me from her life.

"She's thousands of miles away in Maine," I said in quiet protest. "Your mom lives down the street."

"So what? I could've flown there. I have money."

I felt terrible for making this about me. "I'm sorry." I grimaced at the apology, hearing my best friend Daisy telling me not to apologize for my feelings. Even though it's hard. I sniffed back emotion and loosened my grip on the phone. "Sometimes I think that I'm a nonentity in so many people's lives—shy, timid Willow Hale," I whispered, "and I'm afraid of being a nonentity in yours." He's my guy, my only love, and it's terrifying to think that I could be this invisible shadow to the person who's been my everything.

"You've never been a nonentity to me, Willow," Garrison breathed. "From the first time we touched, you became my world and safe place. I'm so in love with you that my heart feels like it's being ripped to shreds just knowing you're sad, and I'm stuck here, sitting on this crappy floor. Wishing I could hug you."

I was sitting on the floor too. I told him that.

We laughed softly. Sadly.

I hugged my arm around my body, pretending that Garrison was with me. "Don't push me too far away that I can't ever reach you again, okay?"

"Okay." We listened to our breath over the line for a while. It sounds creepier than cute, but it felt...calming. To hear him ease and our tears dry.

So that was *the* phone call.

A big one.

All I can do is think about *now*.

How he's moving into my brother's house, and we're currently on a Skype call.

This move is a great thing for him. He'll be surrounded by people who care about him and love him. Happy doesn't even come close to what I'm feeling. I've been grinning so much these past couple days that my cheeks hurt.

"Which room did you pick?" I ask Garrison. Back on Skype, I squint at my computer screen, trying to decipher which room he chose in the big eight-bedroom Hale house.

At one time, over half of the rooms were occupied. Way back when Lily, Loren, Ryke, Daisy, Connor, Rose, and I all lived under the same roof. Hard to believe that happened at all—but it did.

Now that it's just Lily and Loren and their three-year-old son, it must be a quieter house.

"I almost picked Ryke and Daisy's old room," Garrison tells me. "But then Lo said that I wasn't allowed because it's the smallest guest room in the house and I'm not permitted to do that to myself out of guilt."

Sounds like Lo.

Garrison starts untangling his wad of cords. "And I thought about your old room, but it'd be too weird. So I chose the guest room at the end of the hall, three doors down from Maximoff's. You remember it? It's the one with the paisley wallpaper."

I nod, still smiling. "Is that the one Lo says gives him a migraine every time he goes inside?"

Garrison laughs, a real heartfelt laugh. "That'd be the one." He glances at the screen, our eyes meeting for a beat.

I push up my glasses. "I wish I were there to help you move in."

I almost bought a ticket, but Garrison told me not to miss my first week of classes for him. That we'd Skype instead.

"You are here," Garrison reminds me. His positivity is palpable, and it runs through me like a drug. "Pick a wall for my poster." He travels around the room with his laptop.

"By the window," I say.

He smiles wide. "We are two minds in one. Who knew, I was thinking the same exact thing." The way he says it—he definitely wasn't.

"Uh-huh. Sure." I match his smile. It's contagious.

"I love your choice," he says. "That's exactly where it's going and I'm going to think about you every time I look at it."

My chest swells, and I wish I had that reminder in my room. I glance at the photograph of us on my nightstand. We're both lounging on the dock at the lake house, the sun setting, and he's kissing my cheek.

PRESENT DAY

Garrison places the laptop on the dresser, the spot that lets me see most of his room. He grabs a hoodie from a box and tosses the clothing in a trash bag. He already told me he's throwing away every hoodie he owns. *New start. New look.* "How's school?" he asks.

I'm about to answer but the door opens abruptly. "Uncle Garrison!" The dark-haired toddler rushes in and belly flops onto Garrison's bed.

"Heyheyhey!" Lo calls out from the doorway. "What'd we say about knocking?"

Maximoff picks himself up from the mattress and turns to his dad. "I have to knocks before I enters," he slurs the words a little.

"Try again, bud," Lo says and then gives Garrison an apologetic look.

Garrison is full-on grinning.

Maximoff goes outside and knocks on the door. I hear Lo say, "And now what do you ask?"

"UNCLE GARRISON?!" Maximoff screams at the top of his lungs. "CAN I COME PLAY WITH YOU?!"

Garrison laughs. "Yeah, kid, come on in."

Maximoff just started calling Garrison his uncle. Even though they're not related. He'd be his actual uncle if Garrison and I got married, but we haven't really discussed that possibility. It can't be on Garrison's radar if he's thinking I'm going to break up with him.

I wouldn't.

The door opens and Maximoff bounds back inside. "Can I—can I help you unpack?" he asks with these big green eyes that are so Lily—it's impossible not to fall prey to them.

Garrison nods.

Lo notices the laptop screen. "Is that my sister?" Lo asks me, brows raised.

52

"I'm here in the…not-so-flesh," I say.

"Just a bunch of ones and zeroes," Garrison adds, and while standing behind Lo, my boyfriend winks at me. It's sexy enough that I blush.

Lo frowns and looks over his shoulder. "Are you two flirting in nerd?"

"Man, we're not nerds," Garrison snaps. "Aren't the nerd stars a few houses down the street?" Lily affectionately refers to Connor and Rose as the "nerd stars" but the Cobalts are so far from what you'd picture a stereotypical nerd. If anything, I fit the bill the most. Glasses, comic-book loving introvert.

Lo touches his chest. "Forgive me, you two are flirting in geek."

Garrison raises his brows. "That's you and your wife." Lily and Lo are the superhero-obsessed ones, sometimes even more than me.

Maximoff picks up a pillow and tosses it at his dad. Lo dodges it like it's nothing, his focus on Garrison. "Christ, you and words. Fine, you're flirting in computer shit or whatever you youths calls it."

"Binary," Garrison says.

"What?" Lo's brows knot.

"It's a binary numer—you know what, never mind."

"Good, I was thinking this was going to turn into a lesson," Lo smiles his half-smile. "You do know I dropped out of college."

"You tell us every chance you can get," I say lightly.

Lo turns back to the computer. "My sister with the jokes." He cracks another smile. "London is going well then?"

"Yeah, really well."

Lo's phone rings and he excuses himself to answer the call. Just as I leaves, I hear him say, "Hey, Dad."

PRESENT DAY

My stomach twists, unsettled all of a sudden.

Maximoff rips the tape off one of the smaller boxes, helping Garrison. It's a good distraction for him, and I need a second to myself so that I don't look like I'm about to puke.

Because I'm hiding something from Garrison. From my brothers. And if I can, I'd like to take this to my grave.

It's about that night in London when Garrison visited.

After he flew home and I stayed back, I did some damage control. Students filmed Garrison punching Salvatore, and I saw the look on Garrison's face. If that footage leaked online, he would've been prime fodder for the media. We both have been memes before, and it's only ever easy when you're emotionally and mentally prepared to handle it.

It'd destroy him, and since Connor Cobalt—the usual damage control expert—wasn't around, I had to think of different resources. I couldn't call Lo or Ryke without alerting them that Garrison was drunk, and he made me promise not to say anything.

So there was only one person left.

My dad.

Jonathan Hale.

I did what I swore I would never do after he cut me a check for school.

I asked him for more money.

He gave me a hundred grand. He knew what it was for and wanted to help. Though, he called it "pennies" which I found…a little insulting. A hundred grand is a fortune to me. And it was enough to put my plan into action.

Sheetal had filmed the whole fight, and I was able to identify everyone with cameras who recorded Garrison. Luckily, Tess knew most of the students at Bishop Hall that night. So I gave them cash in exchange for the footage. They deleted their videos from the cloud and cells.

I, *Willow Hale*, paid people off with Jonathan Hale's money.

Ryke has constantly warned me about our dad. I know he doesn't give things without something in return. Allegiance. Time. I'm not sure what he'll ask for, but I never wanted to feel indebted to him. Now...it's all I feel. And what happens when he comes to collect?

Or worse, what happens if Lo, Ryke, or Garrison find out?

They can't. *They can't.*

I practically carve those words into stone.

5

GARRISON ABBEY
Age 17

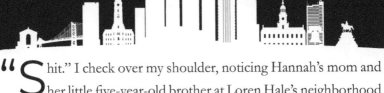

"**S**hit." I check over my shoulder, noticing Hannah's mom and her little five-year-old brother at Loren Hale's neighborhood Halloween party. Located in his overly decorated backyard. Before Mrs. Nash sees me, I pull my hood over my head.

I'm not in costume. Just my usual hoodie and dark jeans.

"What?" Willow asks, both of us loitering near the long snack table. She's filling her paper pumpkin-shaped plate with only a few kernels of caramel popcorn and two tiny bite-sized pretzels—you know the kind that people put in Chex Mix? Not like a giant soft pretzel at a movie theater.

"Just someone I know, or their mom, I mean. Not actually them." I shake my head like I'm being stupid about this. She won't talk to me. Would she? I wave Willow on. "It's whatever. Keep doing what you're doing."

58

"I'm done. So..." She pushes up her black-framed glasses. Even though they don't go with her Vega costume, I like that she wanted to be comfortable and keep them on. She tries grabbing the strap of her backpack. It's not there, by the way. So she catches air.

Willow notices me staring for a long or quick second—I'm not really sure which. "What...is it?" Her hand shakes, the paper plate rattling, and she clutches it with both to steady the thing. I spot her anxiety more than she'd probably like me to, but all I want to do is lessen it for her. I'm just not fucking sure how.

"You look pretty," I tell her the truth, "but you look pretty all days, so there's not really a difference here."

Willow pales. She does that instead of blush. "Um, thanks? You look pretty too." She winces. "I mean, you look handsome?"

I try to make this exchange as easy as possible. "Me? Nah. My dad says I need a haircut, and my eyes can't decide what color they want to be."

Her shoulders relax, and she peers close at my eyes. "I always just thought they were blue-green, which is aquamarine?"

"Maybe. I've never looked it up, which kinda shows the lack of interest I have in myself." I nod at her plate. "You really done?" I pick up my own plate. The food spread is intense. The tower of orange-frosted cupcakes alone could feed my entire lacrosse team.

"I don't have a big appetite when I'm nervous." She shrugs but stares off at the growing party, more and more teenagers, kids and parents arriving. Apples drift along the pool, water glowing orange from the lights. Torches illuminate the backyard as the sun descends.

I don't ask what she's nervous about when I'm positive it's just *this*. The party in general. The people. The *mingling*. I don't like it much either, but it doesn't bring me anxiety like her. I remember how her Tumblr questionnaire said she doesn't like large crowds.

She meant it.

I load my plate with the only thing that looks good to me. Cookies. Sugar, oatmeal—not a big fan of chocolate fudge—but I find the peanut butter ones, my favorite, and stack them high.

"I'm not really sure where to go," Willow mumbles, kind of to herself.

I stick a cookie in my mouth and point at an unoccupied haybale near the fence. "This way."

She walks beside me, passing the apple bobbing thing and a couple other games, and when we make it to the haybale she lets out a deep breath like *I made it.*

I'm not going to lie.

I want to hug her right now.

Instead though, I just sit next to Willow and chew my peanut butter cookie. I set a couple sugar cookies on her plate. "In case you're not as nervous later."

"Thanks." She starts to smile.

My lips rise too. I set a foot on the haybale and my arm on my knee. "If you could be doing anything in the world, what'd you be doing?" I ask her.

"Like a career?"

"No, just on any day, any time."

She nudges her popcorn around her plate. "I'd hang out in my room. Maybe watch a movie, read some comics, and surf the internet, nothing crazy. I know it sounds boring, but it's fun to me."

"It doesn't sound boring. Just laidback." I wonder how many people gave her shit for it—because my brothers give me shit for playing "girly" games like *Mario Party*. Which, honestly, is as much for girls as it is for boys. It's Nintendo.

"So I finished the fifth season of *Supernatural* last night…" she trails off as a blonde woman approaches us, a five-year-old clinging to her side. She's not really "in costume" like her Buzz Lightyear son. She just wears dangling ghost earrings and a tacky sweater.

"Shit," I mutter, too late to angle my body out of sight. I can't even force a fake smile.

Mrs. Nash greets me first. "Hi, Garrison."

Her daughter was my friend and part of the *"you should've been the bigger man and stood up to your friends and forced them to stop harassing people"* group. I agree, I should've done that. I should've done a lot of things that I never did, and I can't take it back.

I can't rewind time, and guess who has to live with *all* of this for the rest of their life?

Me.

It's my shit to bear.

And no matter which way people paint me, I'm still the lesser man. For ratting out my friends. Or for not convincing them to do the right thing.

"Hey," I say back, dropping my hood. I hang my head though, and my hair brushes my eyelashes.

"It was really nice of Loren to let you at his house."

"Yep," I agree. I would've never forgiven myself for what I'd done like he forgave me, but I'm not going to tell *her* that.

"You should find time to thank him tonight."

I see that she means well, but her coarse delivery rubs me wrong. I force a grating smile and say, "Yeah, I'll get on that." *Why do I say these things?*

"You're lucky you're not where your friends are, and frankly, the majority of this neighborhood thinks you should be there."

She wants me to express deep remorse, break down and maybe shed some tears, but I just—I just can't do that in front of her, in front of all these people. At this party. I can't. I know I probably should, but my defenses keep rising and rising. I don't know how to knock them down.

"Awesome," I say. "I'll be sure to pen that in my dairy tonight." I can't even look at Willow, but I sense her hesitation towards the entire situation.

I hate that my shit is making her more nervous.

So before Mrs. Nash can scold me some more, I add, "Is that all? Honestly, I don't have anything else to say about this."

"I'm so glad Hannah is no longer friends with you." *Ouch.* I just nod, and she focuses on someone else. "Willow, right?"

I sit straighter, lifting my head up because I don't want Mrs. Nash to attack her because of me.

"Yeah. I'm Willow."

I wait.

Mrs. Nash says, "Don't let him fool you. He's harassed your cousin Loren and his wife Lily for longer than he's probably told you. Just keep that in mind as he tries to make a friend out of you."

The sad part: it's all pretty much true.

Though I'm not fooling Willow. I'm not trying to, but she said that Loren told her everything that happened in the neighborhood. I never asked her to clarify which incidents, to tally off and see if he truly did recount everything to her. I didn't want to bring up my bad history.

Just as Mrs. Nash turns to leave, Willow speaks up. "He's a good person."

It gets to me. Like emotionally—it gets to me. I stay still, and I just intake that phrase that no one has ever really spoken about me.

He's a good person.

She said it so quietly that Mrs. Nash never heard. But I did. I watch Hannah's mom direct her son towards the table of food.

"Sorry," I apologize to Willow for that entire shitty conversation.

"She was rude."

"So was I," I say.

"Yeah, but..." She shrugs. "You see that you were. She doesn't see that she was. And I know it doesn't make it better, but it still matters in a way. I think, at least."

"Yeah...maybe." I'd like to believe that too.

She picks up one of the sugar cookies I gave her and takes a bite.

I feel my lips lift again. "So you finished the fifth season of *Supernatural* just last night and you didn't message me? I told you I wanted the play-by-play of your reactions. In gif form." She did it for season two, and honestly, it was the cutest thing anyone has ever sent me links to.

Most of my Tumblr posts are TV shows and movie gif sets I made, daily sarcasm, relating everyday events to pizza, and reblogs.

Her Tumblr posts are questionnaires, fan edits, fandom-related posts, and reactionary gifs as she live-updates watching episodes of TV. It bogs down my feed like crazy—and if you asked me my opinion about it before I met her, I'd say *it's dumb.*

It's not dumb. I hate that I thought it was dumb. It's really entertaining, especially when I've seen the show.

She swallows her cookie and tries to contain a wider smile. "It was 4 a.m."

I don't have the best sleep pattern, but I was actually asleep last night at that time. "Finishing the best season of *Supernatural* is the only good reason to wake me up at 4 a.m. Did we agree that the internet is the best form of communication?"

"We did, but our other option was two tin cans."

"Right." I smile at the memory. "What are your thoughts on a cellphone?"

I'm surprised when she shakes her head. *Rejected, Abbey.* Willow sets down her cookie. "I like seeing you on the internet. I mean we're not actually *seeing* each other."

"You mean my ones and zeroes aren't making contact with your ones and zeros? I thought they were dancing around each other. My ones know how to waltz but the zeros are just shit dancers. They like to step on other people's computer code."

Willow has this giddy smile that's a little infectious. "If my ones and zeroes could dance, they'd probably still choose to sit down."

I'd sit down with you. I don't say it because I'm literally sitting down with her. "What about bobbing for apples?" I ask. "No pressure, honestly."

"You say that a lot."

"What part?"

"*Honestly.*"

I hadn't noticed. Maybe I'm just scared people won't know what's sarcasm and what's sincere. "Hey, I wanted to mention something... don't take this the wrong way." Why am I broaching this now? *Don't scare her or make her feel bad.* I almost pause, but I let it out anyway—because I'm that guy. "That comic book character, the one we were talking about earlier, I looked him up again."

"Elixir?"

"No, the other one."

"Wither?"

"Yeah, him." I pause. "He kind of looks like me. For a cartoon."

"Comic," she corrects while color drains from her face. "…I like Wither, but I never said you *were* Wither."

"Yeah, I know. I just thought it was interesting." I feel like a dumbass, mostly because she can't meet my eyes. I'm about to change subjects completely and ask about her favorite part of *Supernatural* season five, but she points to the apple-bobbing tub.

"It's free. Do you still want to?"

I wonder if she was just waiting for the crowds to clear out around it.

"Yeah, definitely."

6

BACK THEN – October
Philadelphia, Pennsylvania

WILLOW MOORE
Age 17

Things I never thought I'd be doing in Philadelphia: apple-bobbing at Loren Hale's neighborhood Halloween party.

Beads of water still roll down my cheeks, and Garrison, only a couple inches away, tenderly brushes the wet strands of hair off my forehead. Everything is blurry, and he must sense my unease, so he gently fits my glasses back on.

"Thanks." I concentrate on his blue-green eyes that dance across my features. He plucks a hair stuck to my cheek and tucks it behind my ear.

My everyday nerves try to subside, and giddiness flutters inside me like confetti falling from the sky. When his other hand skims my hip, I let out a small, nervous laugh. I prefer the giddiness over anxiety, but I can't really control which comes out first. I'm just not used to touching. Everything is so new.

"Is this okay?" he asks.

I push up my glasses, hoping I can reassure him that I like this so far. "Yeah." I nod more than once.

"Can I hold you?" Quickly, he adds, "Like put my arm around you?"

I waver between a bursting smile and apprehension. I want to be on the bursting smile side of things, and I trust Garrison more and more every day. "Yes."

Garrison's arm curves around my waist—

"Hey! You two!"

I instantly jolt and become a stiff board, my head swinging towards the exclamation, but I'd recognize that voice anywhere.

Lo, my brother Lo. The one dressed like a Slytherin. The one sitting on a cluster of haybales across the pool. The Lo that everyone thinks is my cousin. That Loren Hale—yeah, he sends a *seething* glare at Garrison, one that could set the universe on fire.

I hear the warning: *don't touch my little sister.*

We both immediately tear apart, an invisible wedge shoved between us until about ten-feet separates his body from mine. Garrison rakes a hand through the side of his hair before he lifts his hoodie back up.

Lily and Ryke are next to my brother, but I can only see their lips move. My hearing hasn't reached Superman levels. Nor my lip-reading skills because I have zero clue what they're saying.

Garrison rotates, his back turned to me, and his cellphone out. I (poorly) sewed a pocket in my Vega costume, and my phone vibrates once.

"Ca-Caw!" I look up as I take out my phone. Daisy Calloway sits on the rooftop with an antler headband. She calls down to her boyfriend who's currently dressed in plaid. "Ca-Caw!"

When Ryke sees her up on the roof, she smiles and says, "Hunt me."

I don't watch them for long.

I check my Twitter message notification.

From **@garrisonwither**

Going to the bathroom. I'll be back soon. If you're back on our haybale, save me a seat?

I reply with a *will do*. As I look up, he's already disappeared. So I head towards the haybale—but I stop dead in my tracks. *It's occupied.* I swing my head to the left and right, my eyes swerving like a frantic driver behind the wheel. Where do I sit? Most haybales are taken.

I'm not good at parties.

I just don't know what to do or how to fill the time. There's a hidden memo that says: *stay off your cell.* My phone actually takes away the nerves, but then I worry about being rude. And the anxiety returns. It's not a fun cycle.

"Sorry," I apologize to a family of pirates. They try to squeeze around me. I'm in the way. I apologize to two preteen girls dressed as angels. I knocked into one of their wings—or maybe I just barely brushed it? She didn't seem that upset. I don't even know if she noticed.

Willow Moore isn't a total failure at life.

I have something going for me.

I could go talk to Lily or Lo, but they look like they're having a sweet moment on their haybale, both squeezed close together, and their tiny son, dressed like a Gryffindor-to-be, is with them.

Likewise, Rose and Connor have their daughter in arm, and they stand so near one another, their lips moving too fast to keep up. Not that I'd approach them together. I think I could grow the courage to approach Rose *without* Connor.

I push up my glasses and mutter, *"Carpe Diem."* I'm not a boy like any of the students at Welton Academy in *Dead Poets Society*, but I can Carpe Diem just like them.

I just need to…figure out where to go. I spin around, standing so close to the pool's edge that I back up and back up. Just what I need, to fall right in the—

I whack a torch.

Oh God.

I whacked a *flaming* torch staked into the grass. I go to grab the iron pole, and I fall with it onto a haybale. Where that awful neighborhood lady, Mrs. Nash, and her son sit. They spring from the hazardous area I just created, and I clumsily collapse onto the hay that begins to singe and burn and flame.

"Willow!" Lo yells.

I cough at the gust of smoke and try to stand, my cheek hot. I smack a flame off my skirt and just fall to the grass. So I can crawl away from the fire.

On my knees and hands, I quickly scuttle beyond the haybale that blazes.

Parents are already scooping water from the pool using plastic buckets and Solo cups. While they douse the flame, I stare wide-eyed, frozen in shock.

What just happened?

"Willow?" Lo squats beside me, his amber-colored eyes pinpointed with worry. He scans me to see if I'm singed. I think my confidence burned the most.

"I'm…" *sorry.* I blink a couple times, trying to push past this cold shock. As my horror meets his concern, I only hope that this flaming haybale isn't a metaphor for what I've brought Loren Hale. "I'm sorry," I whisper.

"She's in shock." I hear the icy voice of Rose Calloway. Dressed like Natalie Portman from *Black Swan*, she towers high above me. I notice Ryke and Daisy helping extinguish the fire while Lily and Connor hold their kids by the food table, distracting them from the mayhem.

I'm sorry.

I must mutter it again because Lo says, "I've done a hell of a lot worse."

I space out enough that he grows more worried. Suddenly, he scoops me in his arms.

Oh God.

Loren Hale is carrying me towards his house.

I'm being carried for the first time, and it's by my famous brother. My shock just quadrupled. Maggie, my only friend from Maine, would die in his arms.

As Loren Hale climbs the porch, Garrison is sprinting over from—well I can't really tell where he came from. Too many people are shifting around the backyard.

"Hey, what happened?" Garrison follows Lo as he brings me inside.

I don't hear Lo's response over the noise, but I can fill it in just fine: *Willow knocked over the torch and then almost lit herself on fire.*

Lo sets me on the kitchen counter, the house much quieter, and I hang my head, staring at my hands. I hear the faucet, and out of the corner of my eye, I see Rose wetting a washcloth.

"I'm fine," I mutter, but for some reason tears try to well, and I keep pushing my glasses up that slip down my nose. Only Rose, Garrison, and Loren are in the kitchen right now, but I don't release these kinds of emotions in front of people often. Even just three people seems like a lot.

Rose passes me the washcloth. "Here. This'll help."

I dab the coldness to my cheek and forehead.

Lo checks his phone. "Lily said it's not on fire anymore. See, it's not a problem."

I rub beneath my eye just as a tear threatens to fall. "I didn't mean to come into your life and set things on fire."

Lo can't help but laugh. "You think *this* is bad? Christ, Willow— I've set more metaphorical things on fire than this guy." He points at Garrison.

Garrison raises his brows in surprise. "Really?"

"Yeah, *really*." Lo, with his *sharp as ice* cheekbones and narrowed amber eyes, seems more frightening than the fire itself.

"It's true," Rose validates. "He's horrendous."

Lo flashes her a dry smile. "Says the girl dressed like a possessed ballerina."

"*Black Swan* is a *real* thing."

"Sure." Lo's gaze drifts back to me. "So what I'm saying is, you didn't ruin anything by being here, except a goddamn haybale that no one is going to miss. I'm just glad you didn't catch on fire. Because *you*—I would've missed."

My eyes fill with tears, but a different kind.

"Me too," Garrison chimes in.

"Me three," Rose proclaims.

I nod, more assured than before. *Okay.*

How I end up smiling, I can only attribute to these people, in this kitchen, who made me feel loved when I felt lost and alone.

Okay.

I smile. "Okay."

BACK THEN

And for the first time in a long time, I've felt a part of a group. A part of a family that I know is my own.

GARRISON DRIVES ME TO MY APARTMENT. AS HIS Mustang slows by the curb, I wonder if I should invite him in? We're not together, and I don't know if it'd come across as a suggestion.

"Thanks for letting me tag along with you to the party," he says first.

"Thanks for wanting to go with me at all." I take off my blonde wig and shake out my hair, a couple bobby pins were sticking into my scalp. "You're lucky that you left me for a while. I could've burned you." I'm not a smooth-talker, and in the quiet of his car, I feel more like a dork. *He knows you're a geeky dork.* And still, he wants to hang around me. That's something, isn't it?

He puts the car in park and rests his forearm on the steering wheel. We both sort of angle towards one another on our seats. I like how his hair always catches his eyelashes, and his eyes peek between the brown strands.

"About what Mrs. Nash said," he starts.

"It doesn't matter what she said." I wonder how long this has been eating at him.

"Yeah it does," he breathes. "Because…it's true, Willow. Loren can compare us all he wants and say that he did worse shit, but I did shit *to him.* I wrote on his mailbox. I put dog shit on his front porch—I even filled a bucket of…" He looks away from me, ashamed.

I know what he did.

Lo told me everything, and I told Garrison that he did. There must be a place inside of him that still feels *so guilty.* Or else he wouldn't feel the need to confess outright like this.

Garrison stares out the windshield, gathering his courage, as he says, "I filled a bucket up with liquor, so it'd pour on his head as he opened the front door. Knowing—*knowing*, he was an alcoholic and he was fighting to stay sober. I did that."

He doesn't add, *my friends were there.* I know they were, but he's not making excuses or shirking the blame. He's taking it all.

That's why he's a good person. Beneath what happened. Beneath his bad choices. He's a good person. I hope one day he can see this too.

"Lo forgave you," I remind him.

Garrison shakes his head, and softly, he mutters, "I can't forgive myself." He holds my gaze. "You shouldn't be around me, and I don't think I can be the better person and walk away from you, so you gotta do it for me. You have to tell me to stay away from you. You have to tell me to *never* come back here."

It's my turn. I shake my head vigorously. "No. I won't do that."

His eyes well. "Willow—"

"I'm not a fool." I remove my glasses, wiping the foggy lenses. "I'm just a girl from Maine who wants a friend from Philadelphia. You're my friend. I chose you as much as you chose me." I put my glasses back on to see how reddened his eyes have become. "You're the second friend I've ever had in my whole life, and I'm picky about my friendships. But I chose you."

This might be the most I've said in one sitting, my lungs filling with oxygen and threatening to burst.

Garrison tilts his head, his features twisting through so many emotions. "What kind of friendship requirements did I pass to be yours?"

"You're kind."

"I'm not."

"You're good."

"I'm not."

"You're honest."

He pauses.

"You make me feel safe."

He looks up at me, and the air tightens between us. Garrison extends his arm over the back of my seat, but he never drops it to my shoulders. He just keeps it there for a second, staring intently, thinking hard.

"Are you sure?" he asks.

"I'm sure." We're both trying to find our place in the world, at the same time. Sometimes it feels like we're floating, and we're not sure which way to land or if we even can. Before I ask if he wants to come in, his phone buzzes.

I notice the Caller ID says *Mitchell.* I think that's one of his brothers.

"I should take this. He's been calling me all night."

I get the hint, and I open the car door. Just as I close it, he rolls down the window and ducks his head so he can see me on the curb.

"Season six," he says, "want to watch it together next weekend? My house."

A *Supernatural* marathon with Garrison Abbey. His favorite show. At his house. The first invite I've ever gotten there.

"Definitely."

7

GARRISON ABBEY
Age 18

Mom: Happy 18th Birthday! Do you want anything special for dinner tonight?

I briefly look up from my cellphone. On a Sunday afternoon, the mall is packed with families. Babies cry in their strollers, and parents holler at wandering toddlers. I loiter next to a retro arcade called Galactica Arcadia and text my mom a simple reply.

Something like: I don't want anything for my birthday. Don't worry about it. I already have plans for tonight.

I basically just told my mom that my plans don't include her—which they don't. Guilt should strike me. My mom is *nice*.

Nice but completely…I shake my head, not wanting to touch any of this. Not wanting to spell out any more words relating to my parents.

While I wait for a certain someone to show up, I log into Tumblr and start digging through Willow's latest questionnaire. She tagged me in one, and I promised Willow the answers if she bobbed for apples during Halloween.

More than anything, I'm curious what questions she actually wants me to answer. It's different than the first one. Here, she's actively choosing which questionnaire I'll fill out. Whereas the first one, there was no initial intention that some guy from Philly would appear and ask for her username and yada, yada, whatever.

The past is already written, isn't it?

So here I am. In a noisy mall, filling out the new questionnaire with one hand stuffed in my leather jacket, the other gripping my cellphone.

Rules: Complete the form by answering each section truthfully. Once you've finished, tag other users to complete the task. Begin by sourcing the person who tagged you.

I source Willow using her new Tumblr account name: @ **vegablaze33**. Here we go...

Name: Garrison (It's an alright name, I guess.)

Age: 18 and surprisingly still alive

Zodiac Sign: Scorpio

Dream Home: anywhere but the suburbs.

Favorite Band: Interpol

Favorite TV Show: Supernatural. Sometimes American Horror Story.

I check my browser history for the next question.

What was your...

Last Google Search: porn. Jk, I was reading a tv recap for AHS.

Last person you told you loved: I can't think that far back.

Last time you felt jealous: not computable at this time.

After Lily Calloway said that Superheroes & Scones needed a couple more staff members, Maya hired a new employee during the Halloween weekend. One of which goes to Dalton Academy. *Ace Davenport.* Never seen him in my life—though he said he heard of me.

I couldn't really tell if he hated or liked me. Maybe he's just indifferent, but the moment he saw Willow fumbling with a rack of comics, he crouched next to her and helped re-shelve them.

They exchanged smiles.

I had a flashback.

Of me doing something kind of similar. Helping Willow pick up fallen cash from the register. It was the beginning of our friendship.

My stomach roiled at the thought of the beginning of *theirs.* I stewed silently, and Maya must've seen my irritation. She gave me a look like, *don't do anything bad.* "He's *very* valuable to our team."

Valuable. "How?"

"He's a walking Marvel encyclopedia. He knows every character, every comic line, unlike other employees." *Unlike me.* I probably won't ever be Maya's favorite, not after making her job as store manager harder, but I won't stop trying to make it up to her.

I didn't even complain when she gave me toilet duty this week. And the bathrooms were so shitty. Pun intended.

I push Ace to the back of my brain and focus on the questionnaire again.

Last time you screwed up something important: probably yesterday. Every day. Story of my life.

Currently...

What turns you on: girls with glasses.

My lips start to rise, a little surprised she asked this one.

What turns you off: anyone who's "mean" to girls with glasses.

Are you pissed at anyone: pick a brother.

Have you ever...

Been scared of the dark: never.

Cried in front of your parents: only when I was a baby

Kept a journal: nah

What do you like...

Love or Lust: only ever known lust.

Text or Call: text most of the time.

Nerds or Geeks: geeks, definitely.

Done. Not tagging anyone else, I slip my phone in my jeans pocket and then loosen my leather bracelet that digs into my wrist bone. A pack of cigarettes sits heavy in my leather jacket, but I can't really smoke inside the mall. Not to mention, I'm trying to curb the habit.

I retie my black Converse shoes for something to do, and when I look up, I see her.

Down the stretch of mall hallway, Willow spots me too, and she waves sheepishly—and her awkward smile causes my lips to curve higher than before. I skim her head-to-toe. Like I didn't just hang out with her yesterday at Superheroes & Scones.

She wears a mustard yellow shirt beneath saggy, faded overalls. Not especially trendy or something people would "like" on Instagram. Just…geeky. No makeup, but she rarely ever wears much more than eyeliner. Her light brown hair is twisted in a sloppy braid. Flyaway pieces escape, and baby hairs stick up by her forehead.

It's nice to be around someone comfortable with who they are— and who they want to be—without bowing to peer pressure. In class last week, Rachel showed Willow a YouTube video of how to braid hair after critiquing all of her loose strands.

Willow thanked Rachel for the suggestions, but she never bothered with the "proper" technique.

Closer, Willow grabs tight of the strap to her JanSport backpack, always slightly tucked into herself. Overly aware of the strollers, the bumbling people, the sheer amount of bodies, and the many hands clutching Styrofoam coffee cups.

I see her mouth a few apologies for brushing arms with people, and she glances cautiously left and right. The crowds don't cause her to fall back. She pushes through anxiety to reach me and the arcade.

I'm appreciative...more than I can even express.

"Am I late?" She nudges up black-rimmed glasses and checks her phone.

I knot my laces and rise. "Nah. I'm just early." I gesture with my head to the arcade. "I had nothing better to do."

"Oh." Willow tries hard to stifle a smile. "Yeah...me too. Sort of."

"Sort of?" I hold the door open.

As she slips inside the nearly empty arcade, she says, "I got distracted this morning."

Ace Davenport. I frown and catch up to her side. "With what?" *That douchebag Marvel encyclopedia.*

"Lily let me feed Moffy dry cereal for the first time...I mean, he's allowed to eat solid foods, but it's the first time that I fed him. It's kind of cool that she trusts me with her baby."

And it's kind of fucking cool that Willow trusts me with anything related to Lily and Loren Hale, especially Maximoff Hale. Their son is like media fodder. *Celebrity Crush* eats up any and all information about their baby, who can't be older than five or six months now.

After Halloween, I already swore up and down to Willow that I'd *never* sell a single word to the tabloids. If I ever break this promise, she has full permission to spill any of my secrets to the world, my parents—whoever she wants. When I said that, we both paused in silence, remembering when I showed her my tattoos… and bruises.

In the end, I think she trusts me because I have no reason to speak to *Celebrity Crush* editors and reporters. I don't need the money. I'm not looking for fame or notoriety. I literally want to be left alone.

I'm also no longer surprised when Willow acts like she sits on the outskirts of the Hales when she's Loren's cousin. She mentioned her mom being estranged from everyone, and therefore, she was too.

"Would you babysit if they asked?" I wonder.

Willow nods with a growing smile. "I'm used to babies since Ellie is so much younger than me. I helped my mom a lot." She stares off for a second. "I can't even believe this is my life. I can hold Maximoff Hale—do you know how many people just want to touch his pinky?"

"About forty-five thousand."

She skids to a stop in the middle of the arcade. Retro machines line star-patterned carpet, and glow-in-the-dark moons and planets are glued to the ceiling. "You saw the poll?" she asks, color draining from her cheeks.

"The one on Twitter asking a *yes* or *no* question about Maximoff's pinky finger? No, never seen it," I tease.

Willow presses her lips together, hiding another giddy smile. Something flutters in my stomach—which is lame. But whatever. I don't care. I'll be lame with this girl.

We drift subconsciously towards the *Streets of Rage* machine.

"I didn't post that poll," she says more quietly, "but I definitely entered…and it's weird, right, that I'm so enamored by a baby just because he's famous?" She frowns in thought.

"Not weird. Not when the media makes the baby seem like American royalty."

Willow mutters, "Prince Moffy," with an awkward smile, not intending for me to see. When she notices me staring, she clears her throat and touches her lips. "Uhh…yeah."

"Hey, Prince Maximoff fanfic might *actually* be a thing when he's a teenager."

"I'd read it," Willow says and adds, "but in a…non-creepy way. I'm related to him. It's just like entertainment…like television. Sort of."

"Yeah, sort of," I agree, aching to stretch my arm over her shoulders, but I tense more. We stand side-by-side in front of the *Streets of Rage* control panel: red and blue joysticks and a couple buttons each. Nothing fancy or complicated.

I strain my ears to catch her muttering, "I'm talking too much."

"You're not talking too much, trust me," I assure Willow. "You could be quiet the whole day too, and that'd be okay. I just like being with you." I want to retract that last part because she stiffens a little more.

Tension winds between us.

"As friends," I add.

She eases more.

Just friends then. Right. *Just friends.* It's easier. I know that.

Willow lets out a breath and then meets my eyes. "Before we play…can I ask you to do something for me. I mean, it's okay if you say no. It won't hurt my feelings."

I nod, curious about where she's headed.

Willow sets the JanSport backpack at her sneakers and then unzips a pocket. Retrieving a phone, she clicks into the camera app. "So you know Maggie?"

"Your friend from Maine." *Her only friend.* Before I came along.

"Every day she asks me about Lo and Lily, sometimes even Connor and Rose, and Ryke and Daisy…and I can't answer her questions. She hasn't been answering my texts in two days, which isn't like her, and she unfollowed me on Twitter."

"Damn." I rest my elbow on the control panel.

"I know, it's bad."

I frown. "All because you wouldn't talk about your cousin and his friends?"

Willow flips the cellphone in her hand. "I used to tell Maggie everything. She has a right to be mad and upset that I'm…I'm shutting her out. I'd be sad too, and I want to share my life in Philly with her. I just can't share *that* side."

It clicks. "You want to share *me?*"

Willow pales again. "Not like *share you,* share you—"

I hold out my hand to stop her eyes from widening. "I know what you meant." I see how hard this is for her to ask. We may spend a lot of time in each other's company, but she still has no idea how I'll react to new situations or where our friendship boundaries lie.

New friendships come with a shit ton of untested waters, and half the fun is testing them—but then there's the risk of drowning the friendship altogether.

With a deep breath, Willow asks, "Can I take a selfie with you?"

I think I'll always remember this moment.

We haven't really taken each other's picture. Not even during Halloween. Not alone or together. I'm not opposed to photos either. People tag me in pictures on Facebook and Instagram all the time. Most of them are of me at parties with friends.

My father scolded me about a few that "future employers" would deem disrespectful and irresponsible. Underage drinking in one picture, and about six or seven show me giving rude gestures to the camera.

Without hesitation, I hold out my hand for her phone. "I have longer arms for a selfie."

She wavers. "So that's a...yes?" Seeing that it is—even before I answer—she hands me the phone.

"Yeah." I tweak the lighting settings, and then I raise the camera towards us. She stands on her tiptoes to be closer to me, the *Streets of Rage* machine a backdrop.

I dip my head towards hers, my hair brushing my eyelashes. We're not touching, but the *not touching* thing almost builds more tension.

A good kind.

Willow smiles that awkward smile, more horizontal like a line than upturned like a U. She looks happy, and I look like the delinquent everyone believes I am.

I snap several photos and then return the phone. "What are you telling her?"

Willow texts Maggie quickly. "*This is my friend Garrison. We're playing Streets of Rage. Wish you were here! Visit when you can.* You think that's enough?"

"Maybe add emojis. Hearts, sparkles, pizza."

Willow has this look like she wants to say something, but she's mulling over her words. Thinking about them. And then finally, she says, "You know, um, if we ever fight, now I know what emojis will bring you back." Avoiding my reaction, she slips the cellphone into her backpack.

"If we ever fought, it'd be my fault, and I'd be the one to send you pizza emojis and penguins, some turtles." She's smiling. "Maybe a raccoon."

"There's a raccoon emoji?" She braves a glance at me.

I have no idea. "I'll make one." I reach into my pocket for change, but Willow is already pulling out a Ziploc baggie filled with a ton of quarters.

"No," I instantly decline. "I'm paying." *It's a date.* I haven't announced this or anything, but in my mind, it's sort of a date. Kind of.

It could be.

Willow hesitates but then opens the baggie. "You can't pay."

I shift my weight and comb back the long pieces of my dark hair. "Why not?" *She doesn't want this to be a date, you idiot.*

"It's your birthday." She pops two quarters into the coin slots, one for player 1 and one for player 2.

I was the one who sent the Twitter message: Blaze, want to kick some ass today? Galactica Arcadia, noon-ish.

Willow replied: sure, Axel.

Now we face the game with the characters Blaze and Axel, prepared to wipe crime off a city street using crowbars and broken bottles.

I never meant this arcade outing to be a "birthday thing" but my date of birth is posted on all of my social medias. So she knows.

"Hey," I say before we start playing, "do you want to hang out after this? Nothing birthday-related. I just figured we could do that *Supernatural* marathon tonight, if you want to." I keep postponing on her, and she's too nice to bug me about it.

"Yeah," she says instantly. "Yeah, of course. Still at your house?"

I nod. "Still at my house." It's weird. I've never shied from bringing anyone over to my family's place, but I like keeping Willow to myself and far, *far* away from my parent's unwanted opinions.

8

BACK THEN – November

Philadelphia, Pennsylvania

WILLOW MOORE
Age 17

laying video games with Garrison Abbey is like sharing one milkshake with two straws. I wear an uncontrollable smile that hurts my face. The kind of smile I've tried to suppress, but it's becoming fruitless the longer we play *Streets of Rage* in Galactica Arcadia.

I can only remember feeling this way one other time, when I imagined Tom Hiddleston (AKA Loki, Thor's brother and foe) running into me at Superheroes & Scones. He's never actually been to the comic book shop, but sometimes dreams are better than reality.

Except *this* reality. Right here and now, my cheeks are sore from the amount of times they've stretched towards my ears. We laugh. We curse when the game bosses arrive, and he helps me when I fumble with special combinations.

I may be better at everything comic-book-related, but Garrison is an absolute pro at gaming. I think he'd be able to work both joysticks and buttons with relative ease.

Time slips by fast, and when we run out of quarters, we come to a stop.

"New high score," Garrison reads the screen. We're second to someone who typed in the three initials: SUX.

"Not very clever, is it?" I say, pointing at the SUX scoreboard leader. It's the go-to initials for one-time players, really. Lots of machines probably have at least two *sux* in their records.

"I never really am that clever," Garrison tells me, catching me off guard.

"Wait...what?" My mouth falls. "This...is you?" I gesture to SUX, and as he nods, I want to collapse on the star-patterned carpet and bury my head. I just insulted him.

On his birthday.

What kind of friend am I?

My new eulogy: *that turd, Willow Moore, she's a "whatever" kind of friend. You should've left her while you had the chance.*

Garrison isn't looking at my downtrodden features. He's scrolling through letters to lock in the initials: GPW. I barely hear him say, "Garrison Plus Willow."

If he's not hurt over the comment, then I shouldn't agonize over it either, but for some reason, I zone in on *this* awkward part over every other great one. I wish I wouldn't do that. I rub my face beneath my glasses and then fit them on again.

"You okay?" he asks, not even noticing what threw me off. I'm making something out of nothing. Before I say *yeah*, his gaze travels to the glass entrance, and he curses, "Shit."

A scruffy older man lingers outside the arcade, his phone positioned towards us like he's using the camera. He must be playing the part of "coy paparazzi" today. I'm not sure if cameramen are allowed inside the mall or not, but I'm certain he's here because of me.

"I'll go to the bathroom," I say, "and when I come back, he'll probably be gone." I think I'm pretty boring compared to the Calloway sisters, and if I'm not with them or my brother, only one or two cameramen usually trail me during a whole week. It's not even a daily occurrence like it is for them.

"I'll wait here." Garrison keeps an eye on the older man.

I depart and find my way through the rows of arcade machines. The bathroom is lit with a neon sign that says *Relieve Yourself*. I grab the doorknob to the girl's bathroom.

"You're Loren Hale's cousin," someone says behind me, the male voice more accusatory than questioning.

I glance over my shoulder. A preppy guy waits outside the boy's bathroom. Collared shirt, khaki slacks, combed blond hair, twenty-something-years-old—he looks like a walking fraternity ad. Except for his face.

His angular features hold more contempt than I've ever personally met. *He knows Loren Hale. And he hates him.* It's the only conclusion that makes sense.

I instinctively shrink and refuse to answer the preppy guy. I just slip into the girl's bathroom. A sickening feeling descends to the bottom of my stomach.

"Nothing's going to happen," I mumble and reach for my backpack. I freeze.

I left my backpack with Garrison. *I have no phone.* "Okay," I whisper to myself and exhale a short breath. I'm making up something out of nothing again. That's what this is. At the sink, I remove my glasses and splash water on my face.

People say, *trust your gut.*

They also say, *step out of your comfort zone.*

So which one is this? Just a regular bout of anxiety or a real threat? How do I even determine the difference?

Using a paper towel, I wipe dripping water off my face, slip on my glasses, and look into the mirror. *That Willow Moore.* I've lost color in my cheeks, and my flyaway hairs stick to my forehead.

I swallow. "Step out of your comfort zone," I tell myself.

After tossing the paper towel, I exit, hoping the person has left. The minute I swing open the door, I'm met with *two* preppy twenty-somethings.

Hatred flames their eyes.

"That's definitely his cousin," the new guy says, looking from me to his cellphone screen. He must have found a picture of *Loren Hale's cousin!* from the internet.

I rush to leave, but the angular-faced guy physically blocks my path. I take a step backwards. "I'm just trying to leave," I say, much softer than I intend. "I don't know you."

"But we know Loren," the angular-faced guy says. "He slashed the tires of our car in college."

"Oh." *Oh my God.* "I'm sorry about that—"

He plucks my glasses right off my face.

I gasp and reach out for them, but I can't see. I catch air. My world is a blurry mess, especially with the dark lighting and the glow-in-the-dark shapes.

I hear the *crunch* beneath his shoe.

My heart nosedives. He…he just broke my glasses.

"You tell Loren that the public may love the person he's selling them, but everyone who *truly* knows Loren Hale still hates the fuck out of him."

I back up into the wall and reach out for the bathroom knob. I knock off a poster or something, and I go completely still.

They no longer speak. I listen for their footsteps, but it's hard to hear over the pinging of arcade machines. I think they left. *I hope they left.*

"Garrison," I say in a panicked breath. I meant to yell his name. So I try again. "Garrison." Slightly louder. Not loud enough. I crouch into a squat, feeling the carpet for my glasses. "Garrison!"

I touch the bent frame, broken in half, and the lenses are shattered. I prick my finger on the sharp glass and retract my hand.

"Willow!" Garrison must sprint because he's next to me in a hurried second. "What happened? What the hell?"

I can't see him. I can't see *anything* in here.

I start to ask, "Can I—"

He knows what I want. Garrison immediately catches my trembling hand and helps me to my feet. I edge closer to his frame, and his other palm rests on my waist. My heart beats so fast.

If I start picturing their faces, emotion threatens to well and glass my eyes. It's not even that I met real hatred for the first time. It's that they feel this boiling disgust towards someone I love.

Garrison keeps me close. "Do you have an extra pair of glasses in your backpack?"

"No, just in my room." My throat swells closed, but before he asks again, I start briefly explaining the encounter. He scans the arcade for signs of "preppy" guys, but he says it looks like they're gone.

Of course, I can't read his expression, but his body radiates with heat, angry and upset. Instead of hunting them down, thankfully he stays beside me.

My hand in his hand, he guides me out of the arcade. My backpack slung over his shoulder. (I ask to make sure he hasn't left it.) But I'm too nervous to ask if the cameraman is still looming.

"Escalator," Garrison says, pulling me back as I try to walk forward. His arm is wrapped securely around my waist.

Oh my God. Through everything that's happened, I still heat from the new touch. I can't help it. I'm stiffer than him. I'm unbending and hardly breathing properly.

Focus. I start to whisper, "I can't tell Loren what happ—"

"I hate *The Omen* too," Garrison cuts in, raising his voice. "There are so many better horror movies than that one."

I understand the hint. The older man with the camera phone—he must be right behind us. Riding down the escalator. Video-recording our conversation. Our every move.

I shudder. And this is just a taste of what Lily and her sisters deal with every day.

We both stay quiet until we reach the parking lot. Once inside his Mustang, Garrison locks the car doors. Lily dropped me off at the mall on her way to Superheroes & Scones, so my car is still at my brother's house.

The plan had always been to leave the mall in Garrison's car, but not…this soon. Not like this. I struggle with my seatbelt, unable to find the hole for the metal tip.

"Here." Garrison stretches over the middle console and helps, his hand on my hand. My nerves flutter. He guides the buckle, and I hear the *click*.

Secured.

Garrison places my backpack on my lap, and I hug the jean fabric to my chest. He pauses before starting the car. I feel him studying my features.

I replay what happened, and I go numb. My skin tingles as I try to submerge emotion like my mom taught me to do. *Don't let it out for other people to see. Bottle every last bit.*

He breaks the silence. "Did they touch you?"

I shake my head, the motion heavy. "Just my glasses." I swallow again. "I'm fine." *It could've been worse.* Partly, I think I'm in shock, throttled by the "could've beens" and the regret of not trusting my gut.

Garrison lets out a tense breath, his keys jangling like he's about to start up the ignition. He stops short. "What can I do to help?"

I open my mouth to speak, but I have no clue what to say.

"Will holding you make you feel worse or better?"

I shake my head again. Unsure. "I don't know." Tears threaten to rise, overwhelmed by everything: what happened, this moment, how nice he's being to me.

"You know I'm here for you," he tells me.

I nod and instinctively try to push up my glasses—which do not exist right now. "Thanks." We make a game plan to fetch my spare glasses at my place in Philly, and then we'll head to his house. I assure him that I'm not too shaken and that I still want to hang out.

He acts like his birthday means nothing to him, but he once mentioned that all his birthdays were spent with lots of friends. I imagine the crowds resembled the ones at Nathan's party—the one I crashed on my search for Lo.

Now Garrison is down to just one friend. Me. He has no extravagant party. No adoring crowds. He just has Willow Moore from Maine, and I hoped this would be a birthday he wishes to remember, not one he craves to forget.

I can't really replace his old friends, and I worry, in time, he'll only yearn for them more.

9

PRESENT DAY – August

London, England

WILLOW HALE
Age 21

"**W**hat'd you say?!" I try to yell over the thumping bass, a phone pressed to one ear while I plug the other ear with my finger.

I still can't hear my best friend over the flat party. Beer pong cheering, thumps of drunken bodies, and house music cranked to head-splitting levels—I'm in a noisy tunnel of collegiate pandemonium. Who throws ragers on a Wednesday at seven p.m.?

My roommates, apparently.

A little earlier, Sheetal popped her head in my room. "We're having a proper get-together, like. Need anything, a bevvie or a ciggy?" The party was already underway.

It was nice of her to remember that I'm here. I'm not invisible to my friends-turned-new-roommates: Sheetal, Tess, and Salvatore

But I would've preferred an hour's notice, and if I'm being really honest with myself, I would've wanted a full day's preparation knowing we're hosting a *house* party.

After declining drinks and cigarettes, I keep thinking it'll die down, but it's only grown. I keep hearing the main door open. More bodies piling in. More voices amassing.

"Hold on a sec!" I raise my voice over the music and speak into my phone. "I'm gonna find a quieter spot, Daisy!" I scan the small room, more cramped than my old dorm. A light blue comforter is wrinkled on a twin-sized bed, hugged against a white wall.

Most of my crap is still in a few cardboard boxes. But I've had some time to tack up a few X-Men posters and unbox photos of my brothers, the Calloway sisters, and of course, my boyfriend. I did put my *Gravity Falls* Funko Pop! collectibles on the dresser. No room for a desk.

Still, I'm lucky that I have all this space to myself, and I only share a bathroom and common area.

I eye the tiny closet.

Bingo.

I snatch the laptop off my bed before heading to the closet. It's not a walk-in. So I bend down and sit beneath hanging overalls and plain T-shirts. Wedged under the clothes, I pry my fingers under the doorframe and scoot the door towards me until it's pretty much shut.

Darkness.

And finally, some muffled quiet.

I let out a sigh.

So this is sort of what Harry Potter must've felt like. I bet he had more room under the Dursley's staircase.

I push up my drooping glasses. "Can you hear me?" I ask Daisy and open my laptop, the bright screen illuminating the closet with a blue tint.

"A ton better," Daisy tells me. "Where'd you go?"

"The closet. Maybe Skype will be louder." I'm about to ask if she has time to video-chat, but she's already dialing me on Skype.

My lip twitches in a smile, one I haven't felt much tonight. I click into her Skype call, and her radiant, photogenic face pops on screen.

"Hey there." She bites on a red Twizzler, blonde hair hanging against a crop top that says, *yeehaw!* "If Garrison wasn't coming, I'd totally fly out there and whisk you away from the madness." She tucks her long legs to her chest. "We'd ride off into the sunset away from the loud and into the quiet."

I touch my silver pinky ring, and through the computer screen, I see the identical one on her finger. My lips keep rising. "Sounds nice." I fix my glasses again. "I'm not bothering you too much, am I? I know the summer just ended, but camp stuff has to still be eating your time." She's the founder of Camp Calloway, and she's spent so much energy building this adventurous getaway for kids in the mountains.

"Camp stuff has been dying down, and I like catching up with you." She twiddles with a frayed string on her crop top, not able to sit still. "I don't want you to think...that you can't call or anything."

Daisy has a baby now, a husband, a new career, and an ocean is between us.

Sometimes it scares me too that we might drift apart, but I know, deep in my heart, that she's the friend I'll have forever. Not just because she's married to Ryke, my half-brother.

It's what she said: if she were here, she'd help me escape the party, not try to pull me deeper into it.

Daisy loves the quiet as much as me.

"I don't think that," I say softly. "I'll always call when I can."

She's about to smile, but she flinches as screaming *blasts* on my end. Screaming that usually accompanies sports games.

"I hate beer pong," I murmur under my breath.

"You can ride it out with me until Garrison gets there," Daisy suggests. "I'm just at the cottage for lunch." The cottage is her quaint stone house at the end of the cul-de-sac, down the street from Lily and Rose in Philly.

My shoulders loosen, less tensed. She doesn't pressure me to go "mingle" and try to have fun with strangers. I know who I am, and I know it's not my cup of tea. Daisy never makes me drink the anxiety-inducing concoction.

"Thanks, Daisy." I try to stretch my leg in the cramped closet, the laptop swaying on my thighs. I lift my neck, and overalls smack my face. I push them aside. "I'm hoping this party is just a first-week 'welcome back to college' celebratory thing."

Bass intensifies and vibrates the floor beneath me.

Let this be a one-time occurrence.

Please.

I'm not made for house parties. I might've found college friends in London, but I'm still the same girl who lurks in corners of comic book shops and tries not to bump into shelves or strangers. I don't want to be in anyone's way, even with my roommates.

I'm an introvert at the core, and after one big group outing, I feel like I need to recharge alone for a whole week.

Staying in and watching Netflix sounds better than hitting the bars or inviting people to throw back shots and chitchat.

The latter is…exhausting.

"Are your roommates partiers?" Daisy wonders.

"I don't think they are. I'd go with them out to Barnaby's, but that wasn't every weekend." I frown, thinking. "It was…chill. Just the three of us, and if they ever went bar hopping afterwards or met up with larger groups, I usually declined." I pause. "Tess is super popular though. She knows almost everyone on campus, and Sheetal loves staying out late. So does Salvatore…" Oh no…

Could I have really misjudged what it'd be like to room with them?

"You're probably right," Daisy consoles. "It could just be a welcome back party."

"CHUG! CHUG! CHUG!" The chanting sounds close, like a foot away.

I focus on my computer. "I can't even tell them to keep it down— I'll ruin their good time and be the stuck-up roommate." It feels unfair to ask everyone to be quiet. I'm just one person. "And I already felt badly because I didn't warn them that Garrison is coming tonight."

"They still don't like him?" Daisy asks into a bite of Twizzler.

I shake my head.

I officially moved into the flat only a few days ago, and I wanted Garrison to see where I live, even if that means running into my roommates. He's in a much better place since he's been living with Lo for eight months now. But the last time Tess and Sheetal saw my boyfriend, he was swinging a fist at Salvatore.

"We just don't talk about Garrison," I explain to Daisy. "I think they're trying to be supportive, but…it's also like we're avoiding the awkwardness of what happened."

I thought about not rooming with them after the winter party, but they hugged me and said they still wanted me here, no matter what.

Garrison was also happy they didn't abandon me over his actions, but living with college friends feels different than living with the Calloway sisters. It's starting to feel like a challenging game boss on a new console that I've never played before.

"Your roommates might warm up to him tonight. I have a theory that the worst first impressions can be the mark of a really great person," Daisy says optimistically. "So hey, there's hope yet." She swigs a water. "Are you escaping the party with Garrison once he gets there?"

I frown, realizing everything is all messed up. "That wasn't the initial plan."

"Do you plan on *ravishing* each other to the bone?" Daisy teases with the wag of her brows.

My neck reddens. "Um…sort of."

"Willow," she gasps into a bigger smile. "What's '*sort of*' mean here?"

"I want to give him a blow job tonight—the first one I've ever given. And I've already been nervous about it."

"Nervous about what?" Rose asks icily, and on the screen, I see Daisy looking off to the side, like her sister just entered the cottage.

"Hey, Daisy," Lily greets.

Make that *sisters*. Plural.

I'm just glad they walked in and not my older brothers. After a few minutes of catch-up, Lily and Rose join Daisy on a couch with boxes of Thai take-out. They fit into the Skype box, so they're visible and ready to take part in my awkward dilemma.

I'm in a closet.

Avoiding a flat party in my own flat.

And discussing blow jobs. "I already Googled how to give one, and it's not a lot of help. They just talk about being confident. I'm more worried about the mechanics of a blow job. I want to be sure I'm not awkwardly going down on him or hurting him."

"You don't have to give him a blow job," Daisy reminds me. "I don't love giving them that much."

Lily blushes a little as she says, "I think they're fun." Quieter, she adds, "It's hot." Her shoulders rise as she nods to herself.

"At times, definitely," Rose agrees, popping open a container of what she said is Pad Kee Mao. "Other times, it's a pain in the ass, and I avoid."

"I want to try," I say more confidently. "Just to see if I like it or not. Garrison won't pressure me, one way or the other, he never has."

"You should practice," Rose coaches.

"With…like a banana?" I look around the closet for something phallic.

"Just wing it," Daisy suggests.

Rose cringes at those words.

Daisy mock gasps and says dramatically, "The disgust."

Lily laughs.

My heart does a weird nosedive. I miss them. Being around them. *Living* with them. Even if they've all moved into separate houses, they live on the same street from one another.

And Rose raises a hand to both of her sisters before scooting closer to the screen. "Willow, I was a lot like you."

"You were?" Fearless, fierce Rose Calloway, who makes men shrivel and quake. I know her better than when I first moved to Philly. She's not just a face on a Forbes magazine or the star of the short-lived *Princesses of Philly* to me. She's complicated and complex, and so I'm not too shocked.

"Nervous about giving a Grade F blow job, yes." Rose loves to succeed.

"What made you feel better?"

Rose takes a breath as she says, "Connor. He was patient and made me feel…" She rolls her eyes. "Like we were practicing together and that I had nothing to prove but everything to gain. So you don't need to practice alone beforehand. You can practice *with* Garrison."

Lily pops open a can of Fizz. "That's good advice, Rose."

"I know."

We laugh.

Daisy nods. "See, even if it's awkward, it's awkward with someone who makes you feel comfortable, therefore the awkwardness is nullified, and all shall prevail." She extends her arms theatrically.

"For…" I trail off, my thoughts dying as music grows ten octaves louder. Like my door has just opened…

I stiffen.

Oh no.

"What's wrong?" Rose asks, straightening up.

"Willow?" Daisy and Lily say at the same time.

"I forgot to lock my door," I whisper and strain my ears. Floor-boards creak, accompanied by giggling. "I think someone's in my room."

"Kick those motherfuckers out," Rose snaps, yellow-green eyes pierced like she's two-seconds from crawling through my laptop screen and fighting them for me.

"What's going on?"

Oh, *shit.*

That voice, that question—it's coming from *their* end. I watch their heads swerve at the sound of Loren Hale.

My brother.

And he's not alone. He stands behind the couch with Ryke Meadows. Both of my brothers bend over to peer at the Skype session.

"Willow?" Ryke's face darkens. "What the fuck is happening?"

Daisy explains everything quickly. *Thank you.* I use the time to listen to the intruders. The music dies down, and I'm guessing they shut my door.

My pulse speeds.

Okay.

You can handle this, Willow. They're just partiers. They probably don't know that this room belongs to a semi-famous person. I'm on the periphery of fame.

They won't steal your things.

Just…let it pass.

"Willow," Lo says sharply, grabbing my attention.

"Yeah?" I nudge up my glasses for the umpteenth time

"Are they gone?"

I shake my head. "I hear…" I cringe. *No, no.* "…slurping."

Daisy's mouth falls. "They're making out."

"Abort," Lily says. "*Abort.*"

Nervous heat pricks me at the thought of a confrontation. "I can't…"

"Go tell them to get the fuck out of your room," Ryke says harshly. I'm not him. I'm not Rose or Lo.

The hot-tempered triad (Lily coined the term) could resolve this fast and efficiently.

My face contorts at the sound of my bed squeaking and *mmms*. I look up at the darkness of my closet. "Just my luck," I mutter to myself, "two strangers are desecrating my bed when Garrison is supposed to be here soon—and how can I give him a blow job for the first time on the same place where strangers just touched?" *Wait.* I freeze.

I didn't just say that out loud. In front of my brothers.

To Lo, Ryke asks, "Did she just fucking say she's giving Garrison a blow job for the first time?"

I did.

Lo shoots him a look. "Thanks for repeating that. Like I didn't need to bleach my brain before."

"I thought she's already had sex with him," Ryke says in confusion.

"Huh." Lo's brows scrunch. "Does that mean you're still a vir—"

"No," I say quickly.

Cremate me, please. I hide behind my hanging overalls.

Rose snaps, "Blow jobs don't have to come before sex."

I'm shriveling like a withering flower, and the Calloway sisters tell them to stay out of it, coming to my defense.

It's easier to focus on the strangers making out on my bed now. I want to escape the embarrassment of Lo and Ryke knowing I'm planning to give Garrison a blow job.

I tuck my laptop to my chest. "I'm going out there."

"Good," Lo says.

"We're here," Rose reminds me.

Daisy makes a heart shape with her hands.

They all watch me like this is a college-aged flick that they're very much invested in, and quietly, I push the door open.

"Right *there*, Mattie. *God*," she moans, not even hearing me crawl out of the closet.

I stand up. "Oh." I shield my face with a hand, blocking out the scene of a twenty-something dude going down on a girl in a miniskirt and floral crop top.

Should've stopped them sooner, Willow.

This is my penance. My dues that I must pay. "Um," I start to say.

She gasps at the sight of me. "Mattie. Mattie!" Bed squeaks as they shift.

"Can you please leave?" My cheeks are hot. "This is my room."

"Were you hiding in the closet watching us?" Mattie accuses heatedly, slurring some of his words, American accent and drunk-self clear.

"The fucking *nerve* of that asshole," Rose says loudly on the computer, which is faced towards my body. Not the strangers.

I drop my hand from my face.

They're staring at the computer with confusion. So they definitely heard Rose.

I try to play it off as nothing. "Uh...no," I tell them. "I was in the closet to block out the party. It was loud."

"You don't owe them a fucking explanation," Ryke growls.

Mattie makes a noise of shock. "Is that Ryke Meadows?"

I should've muted the video chat.

The girl fixes her askew skirt as she stands, ignoring her hookup buddy or boyfriend or whoever.

Mattie squints, trying to place me. "You're that girl." He sways as he rises off my bed. "What's her name, Dina?" he asks the brunette. "You know the dorky one with the glasses? She rarely talks and she's always hanging around the hot blonde Calloway?"

I'm standing right here.

I don't back up. Trying to hold my ground.

"I don't know," Dina says, putting her hair into a ponytail. "She asked us to leave, let's go."

"Thank you," I say too softly. I'm not sure anyone can hear.

Mattie holds out a hand. "Wait, hold on."

I shake my head. "The party is out there." I motion to the door, laptop in my other grip.

"Come on, don't be like that," Mattie says, sounding kind. He offers me an amicable smile. "I'm even wearing the underwear Ryke, Lo, and Connor modeled for charity this summer."

Dina snorts like *yeah right*. Like he's lying, and then she exits the room.

Leaving me alone with him.

He watches the door click shut.

My heart rate speeds. "Um…could you please go? I'm kind of busy."

Mattie smiles back at me. "Do you have time for a drin—"

"Open your fucking ears!" Lo yells so loud, my speakers crackle. "She told you a hundred goddamn times to get out of her room. So get the fuck out before I make your life a *living* hell—you'll wish all I did was break your dick in two." His voice is dripping in acid.

Mattie looks…scared, just from hearing Lo. He doesn't even see the venomous glare attached.

"I…uh," Mattie stammers. "Is that…?" Befuddlement crosses his face, and I step forward and sort of corral him out, all without touching him.

I'm lucky that he doesn't put a hand on me.

"Wait…" He gawks, dazedly leaving my room.

I shut and lock the door.

"Thanks," I tell everyone on the computer. "I have this now." They voice encouragements and "stay safes" before I close the laptop.

Anxious heat still clings to me, even though the guy is gone.

It's in these moments that I wish I took up meditation. Daisy suggested it. She's been doing twenty-minute sessions in her treehouse every morning with Sulli. It's apparently good to refocus the mind. I need some intense refocusing.

A message pings my phone.

Garrison: Landed. In cab. See you soon *pizza emoji* *smiley face emoji* *heart emoji*

PRESENT DAY

My anticipation ratchets up, and I quickly text him the apartment building's door code. I was going to meet him at the airport, but he said he'd meet me here. He knows I get anxiety at airports, but I wish I braved it for him tonight.

It would've been better than staying behind at this party. But just thinking about confronting the airport crowds made me break out in a nervous sweat for two hours.

I let out a tense breath and rest my back on the thumping wall. Music still blasting. Chants of "chug, chug, chug!" still happening.

And then I eye the smashed pillows and crumpled comforter. Gross.

Strip the bed, Willow.

I move my feet and do just that.

10

GARRISON ABBEY
Age 21

Once I'm in the apartment complex, I hear club music and drunken laughter, and I'm thinking there's no way that's my girl's place.

A house party?

On a Wednesday?

It sounds like Willow's worst nightmare. Yet, I stroll up to the ajar door where the noise booms out. Weekend-duffel slung on my shoulder, I double-check the apartment number.

This is her flat.

What if she likes parties now? I'd like to believe she hasn't changed so much that I don't know her anymore. We saw each other a decent amount this summer.

I push into the rowdy, packed apartment. About fifty students here. Already hammered. Guys are wobbling and spilling their shit on furniture. Beer. Liquor. Fizz.

I glance back at the door. Can't believe that was literally half-opened.

Any stalker or creep could just prance right on through. This is a serial killer's wet dream and the way idiots die at the start of horror flicks, before the movie title even appears.

Thinking about someone killing Willow makes me nauseous. I rub a hand over my mouth, and stepping forward, my black Converse crunches a beer can.

"Drink it! Drink it!" college students shout as a guy sucks a shot off a girl's belly button, lying on the beer pong table.

Not even one more foot forward and a familiar face confronts me. Salvatore Amadio, AKA the vampire-knockoff that I knocked out, blocks my path.

Awesome.

Here we go already.

Two button-down preppy dudes flank him. A pen is in Salvatore's mouth like he'd been scoring some drinking game, and a glass of whiskey is in his hand. His plaid pants would look douchey on just about anyone, so I try not to judge him for it.

"Hey, man," I greet. "Sorry about…" I motion to my cheek, even though I hit *his* cheek before.

He glares.

I'm so great at making friends. God, it's weird to think that at one point, I was extremely popular.

I nod. "Right. Look, you know which one is Willow's room?" I dig my hand in a pocket for my phone. Planning to text her anyway.

Salvatore takes the pen out of his mouth with arrogance, like he's the big man on campus. "You're not welcome here."

He's got to be shitting me. "My girlfriend lives here."

"Exactly." He has these annoying overprotective eyes. Like he's still trying to protect Willow from me, and it's just...

I let out an irritated laugh. "Wow, you must be *so* concerned about the safety of your roommate. Leaving the front door *wide open* for anyone and their creep cousin to stroll through, that's real smart shit right there—"

"A creep like you." He steps forward, about to physically push me out, and I move backwards on instinct, away from his hands.

My pulse jacks up. "I'm not looking for a fight, man." I stop in the doorway. Refusing to be kicked out.

Taller than me, Salvatore grips the frame above my head. "You're lucky I'm not decking you in the face after you sucker-punched me."

Sucker-punch.

Fuck, I don't think I'd call it that. I'm not that strong. Or at least, I wasn't. Now that I live with Lo, I have access to his home gym and he practically pulls me down there every night to do reps with him.

In Lo's words: *exercise is good for people like us.*

Sometimes it does pull me out of bad moods.

"Appreciate it," I tell Salvatore, "but I'm here to see Willow. She knows I'm coming."

"She didn't tell me about it."

Yeah.

I know.

Willow told me she was working herself up to it, and I don't blame her for not wanting to get into drama with her new roommates.

Agitation gathers. "I didn't realize my girlfriend needed to send you personal memos every time she breathes."

He shoves my chest, hard and quick.

I stumble out, tripping over my feet, and he slams the door in my face.

Me and my fucking mouth. My pulse is in my throat now that he touched me. I'm not a fighter.

I flee, but he doesn't know that.

Swallowing my heart rate, I try to call Willow.

The line rings out, and I send a text: I'm here. Salvatore locked me out.

Yeah, I'm throwing the douchebag under the proverbial bus. He can eat shit.

My phone vibrates.

Lo: You there yet? There's a party at Willow's flat. Make sure this prick named Mattie isn't in her room or around her.

What the fuck is happening?

Worry mounts, and I pound a fist on the door. "WILLOW! WILLOW!"

The door swings open.

And this time, it's her. Glasses slip down her nose, beer spilt on her plain blue tee and jeans. "I'm so sorry. I didn't hear your call over this…?" She winces at the party behind her and looks uncomfortable, shoulders bowed in and head ducked.

I come inside and shut the front door behind me. "You didn't know they were throwing a party?"

She shakes her head.

Fuck.

She rubs her arm. "How was the flight?" She says something else, but I can't hear her soft voice over the noise.

"What?" I lean into Willow, a hand on her waist.

She takes a breath and whispers in my ear, "Do you need to a shower, after all the traveling?"

"Yeah, that'd be good." I eye the glares from Salvatore and his guy friends.

She follows my gaze and shoots them a look like, *stop*. The force dies as the front door whooshes open behind us and more students file in with cases of beer.

Willow tries to step out of the way, but she bumps into another girl. "Sorry," she whispers, and I clasp her hand. Drawing her into my chest.

She clutches onto my waist and calms more.

My mouth brushes her ear. "Where's the bathroom?"

"Down that hall." She points to the left.

I wrap an arm around her frame, and Willow leans into me while I guide her through the party. Once we're in the small bathroom, I lock the door.

We'll probably get shit for occupying the only bathroom here, but I don't care. This is Willow's apartment too.

"This isn't how I wanted you to see my new place," Willow says softly. "With people that I don't even *know*."

I drop my duffel on the bathmat. "Like this Mattie guy?"

Her eyes bug, then realization washes over. "Lo told you?"

"Not much." I push hair out of my eyes. "Can you fill me in here?"

She does. The whole story. It takes probably ten minutes, and we're both leaning against the sink cabinets, my arm around her hips.

It's a lot to digest. "If you see Mattie, point him out to me?"

With two arms, Willow hugs me around the waist while we stand side by side, her touch still feather-light. "You don't...you wouldn't want to confront him...right?"

"I'd just like to keep an eye on him. Know your enemies and all that."

She relaxes. "If I see him, I'll let you know."

I skim her more now.

Willow wets her lips and looks nervously at the tiled floor but also, she's smiling. "You're thinking about the other part of the story, aren't you?"

I smile back. She's so cute. "The blow job part."

She talks to me, not the floor. "I thought about omitting that, but I figured it might be better to just tell you, so we can…practice."

Have I imagined Willow sucking me off? *Yeah.*

But I'd be okay with never getting head if that's what she preferred. It's not necessary inside our living, breathing soul-deep connection.

"Let's practice." I pull my shirt off my head.

"Um…do I…?" She's about to drop to her knees, but I catch her waist and pull her against my body.

Cupping her cheek, I tenderly, slowly draw her lips to mine. We kiss, consuming this trembling affection that pumps blood. Heady and electric.

Her fingers curl around the waistband of my jeans. I taste her eagerness and desire, and I track kisses down her neck. Her body bows into me. Closer, her breath shallowing.

Christ.

My dick stirs, and I trail my hand between her shoulder blades. I feel wetness from *beer*, and I pull back to ask, "Did you drink a beer?"

Willow glances at her stained clothes. "No, when you texted, I rushed to the door so fast that I knocked into someone's Guinness."

I hold her face. My heart is beating double-time for this girl. "You want to take a shower with me?"

Her lips part, then eyes widen on the tub-shower. "I, uh…"

"You can say *no*." I press my lips to her forehead. "No pressure, Willow."

She thinks quietly, her hand now in mine. She doesn't let go, and I feel her fingers tighten around mine. "Okay."

"You sure?"

"I want to," Willow says, sounding assured. She fumbles with the buttons to *my* jeans, and I undo hers. Unzipping, I see the star pattern of her panties.

I dive my hand down to her ass, and she shuts her eyes, craving. Wanting. The same physical and emotional current runs through my veins. We shed each other to just aching skin, and I kiss her deeply while I reach out and crank on the faucet.

Water pours through the tub before I flick a switch. Heat cascades from the showerhead.

She takes off her glasses, setting them on the toilet lid, and we step in together. I help Willow so she doesn't fall. Close-up, she can see somewhat without glasses, but further away, it's all blurry.

I sling the shower curtain, closing us into the small space.

Vapor cocoons us, water drenching bodies and hair. I push mine out of my eyes, and I can see Willow descending into her head. Naked and vulnerable. Her shoulders turn in.

I bring her closer to me and hold my girlfriend for a second. Hugging her to my chest. I feel her speeding heart.

"You can bail at any time," I remind Willow.

"I don't want to," she murmurs. "I want this. I'm trying not to think too much and just…*feel*." She looks up into me and goes for the kiss.

I smile against her lips, and my hand roams along the curves and valleys of her soft skin. Parting her mouth with my tongue, I deepen the kiss, drawing a gentle moan from her body. *Fuck.* I harden.

She glances down, feeling me.

I let out a rough noise between my teeth. "Fuck, I want you."

Willow smiles. "You do?"

I whisper against her mouth, "More than air." I comb her wet hair off her cheeks. "You're beautiful, Willow Hale. Inside, outside, online, offline."

"You know, you are too."

"Nah. Not as much as you."

She loosens her arms, and her knees do this weird jerky thing. Like she almost drops down, but she stops herself too suddenly.

I put a hand to her shoulder. "You'll be at a good height if you kneel."

Willow, more confidently, lowers to her knees. My build blocks most of the water spray, so she's not being drowned. She rests an uncertain hand on my ass. "I might not be any good at this."

"You don't have to be good." I hold the back of her head, more tenderly. "We're in this together."

Her lips rise, excitement flickering in her brown eyes.

I palm my erection, and I drink in Willow's body and emotion before taking her hand in mine and showing her what I like. Wrapping her hand around the base of my shaft.

She opens her mouth. Tentative. I arch my hips forward since she's not moving her body or hand.

"Wider," I instruct. "Wrap your lips around your teeth."

She does, uncertain.

I nod to her. "That's it." Her lips glide against my hardness, taking me in her mouth, and the sensitivity shoots up my spine. *Christ, that feels...* "Fuck."

She pulls back. "Did I hurt you?"

"No, no. That felt amazing."

Willow brightens, and she tries again. My muscles pull taut, just watching my erection fit between her lips.

Fuuuck. My hand tightens on the back of her head. "Willow," I groan, and her free hand descends between her spread knees. Touching herself.

I light up. On fire.

Her teeth suddenly scratch my flesh. I try to stifle a wince, but she sees and pulls back. "Sorry, did I—"

"It's okay." If I wasn't so pent-up and if I didn't want to please her so badly, I'd probably coach her to try again.

But I descend to my knees. "Will you stand up?" I ask.

Her face falls. "It was that bad?"

Shit. "It wasn't close to bad. I just want you too much."

Her breath comes short and aching, and she kisses my cheek before standing. I drape her leg over my shoulder, our gazes diving deep, and I skim my lips against the inside of her thigh before I suck her clit. Kissing her heat.

"Ahh, *I*...oh my God." She clenches my wet hair. Body rattling and twitching in arousal.

She tastes like bliss. An ecstasy I want to drown into, and she taps my shoulder, alerting me that she wants to come with me inside of her.

We've fucked enough that I know that *tap*, and I drop her foot gently and then lift her at the thighs.

Breath jettisons from her mouth. "Garrison," she cries in want.

Our lips are parted and skim, as though to kiss, but we can't catch our breathes. Tension pulled, and I bring her back to the tiled wall.

She buries her head in my shoulder. "Please."

I push into my girl. Slow, carefully, and she gasps into a shudder. Her body trembling against me. My eyes almost roll back. God, the sensation, the warmth, her wetness—it's overwhelming.

Holding her, I rock, thrusting my hips, and the friction ignites between us. Steam making it hard to breathe, and the raps on the door and drunken complaints to "hurry up" are distant.

It's just me and her.

It's been us for a while, and I'm not letting her go. Against better judgment. Against all odds. I'm not leaving this girl.

She hangs onto me, and I fill her up, in and out. Muscles burning for more and longer, but we reach that peak together.

Once I feel her contract around me, it's over. I come, groaning out her name, and she cries into my neck. Pleasured cries.

Slowly, we come down, and we end up sinking to the bottom of the tub. Water raining on us, Willow is more tucked into herself, forearms covering her chest. Head bowed down. Sometimes after sex, she gets like this. More cerebral and closed-off.

But she's across my lap, sort of between my legs, and I have my arms wrapped around her frame, holding her in the position she feels most comfortable.

She nestles her head closer to my chest.

"You replaying it?" I ask against her ear.

She nods.

"Well, just so you know, Willow Hale," I breathe, "I loved it and I love you."

Willow smiles, then looks up at me. "I loved it too."

I nod, already knowing. But it feels good hearing that she's not second-guessing anything. After a few minutes, letting our heart rates descend together, we rise, and I wash her hair. She scrubs shampoo through mine. We laugh and joke, and everything feels about normal.

Except we're not in Philly.

London.

I'm here just for now. By the time we exit and dry off, we realize the music isn't on and the chatter is gone.

"The party must be over," Willow says, knotting a towel around her body. Black-rimmed glasses back on.

I could wear clean clothes from my duffel, but I think she'd feel more comfortable if we both went out in towels. So I tie a towel at my waist.

"I'll check." I open the door, and I see a graveyard of college debauchery. Spilt alcohol, bottles, cans, and cups—so many fucking cups. "Yep, it's over." I don't see Tess or Sheetal, but I'm guessing they're in their room or maybe they went out to a bar.

I grab my duffel, and when we exit into the common area, I roll my eyes at the sight of *Salvatore.*

Willow pales, holding breath.

At least the douche is cleaning his mess, plucking bottles off the kitchen counter and shoving them in a trash bag.

We exchange a glare but no words.

He makes a show of looking from her towel to mine. He zeroes in on my tattoos. Then to my girlfriend, he says, "If you need anything, Willow, just call me."

Don't be a dick.

Don't be a dick.

I bite down on my teeth.

"I'll be fine," Willow says softly and turns more to me. "That's my room." She motions to a door past the kitchen. Her phone suddenly rings, and I can't see who calls but concern cinches her brows. "I have to take this—" She leaves quickly for her room.

Not even glancing at me.

Something is wrong.

I'm about to follow when Salvatore says, "She's been acting strange ever since December."

My jaw tics, hating how he's acting like they're BFFs and I'm no one. "Yeah?"

Bottles clink as more fill the bag. "Her whole mood changes when she gets these phone calls." His eyes hit mine. "I thought it was you that was calling."

Not me.

I'm officially freaking the fuck out.

11

WILLOW HALE
Age 21

I stare at my bedroom wall and listen, hand to my towel on my chest and phone to my ear. "All I'm saying is that the further you get into school, the more important internships are, Willow," my dad tells me.

Normally, I wouldn't have picked up his call after epic sex (definitely one of the best) and while Garrison just got here. But I missed the last two times my dad has called.

And I made a promise not to miss the third. I thought I could swiftly tell him that I'd call back later, but I've been standing here for a solid two minutes and have yet to find a space to speak up.

Garrison is leaning on the shut door in only a towel, arms crossed. He knows who called since I mouthed, *my dad.*

My boyfriend looks supremely sexy, and as I turn towards him, I have trouble not staring at his whole being. Not just his abs and lean muscles, the towel riding low, but the ink that represents him too well and the wet strands of hair that brush his ears. The corner of his lip that wants to lift in a slight smile.

His aquamarine eyes that hold our youth and early days spent together. The friendship that became an emotional lifeline and physical bond.

My heart swells.

I look away as my dad continues, "And you don't want to be in shitty fucking low-level jobs or with the Wall Street assholes who'd see you as pus—" He stops himself before saying something crude. Something I think he'd say in front of Ryke and Lo. But not me. He clears his throat. "I'm just saying, there are plenty of CEOs or even low levels who don't appreciate women."

I think about my mom.

She was sixteen when she slept with Jonathan. He was *much* older.

Was he one of those people?

If I asked Ryke, he'd tell me unequivocally *yes*. Lo would probably hesitate before also agreeing. But maybe our dad has changed.

He obviously sees the horrible side of some people in corporate power positions. My hand sweats on my cell. I open my mouth to reply, but he cuts me off again.

"So there's Harold Johnson and Patrick Nubell, both friends of the family. I'm going to give them a call. They'll have internships waiting for you next summer—"

"Dad," I say, finally interrupting him. "I'm fine. I don't need an internship." At least, I don't want him setting one up for me.

"What kind of goddamn business school are you going to? They should be teaching you that you *need* an internship. It's a fucking requirement." He mumbles something that I can't hear before saying, "This isn't negotiable, Willow. You have to have one, and you should be intelligent enough to take advantage of family connections."

I push up my glasses. "I'll be okay finding one myself."

"I can find you better ones," he says with a tight laugh. "You're so stubborn. Just like your brothers. Rejecting me on principle rather than being smart about this."

"I just want to do it on my own," I mutter. This is one of the first times I've felt his disappointment. It's a tsunami, crashing into me, especially after all that he's given me.

This is why you didn't want to take his money, Willow. I know. I know. But now I'm stuck.

I can feel the heat of Garrison's confusion behind me. But I don't confront it yet.

"I used to be a CEO of a Fortune 500 company, Willow. You don't discard the connections I have out of a need to show that you're a big girl. But I can compromise. I won't call them myself. I'll email you their contacts. Your name will get you through the door."

I can't even say much else; someone must call him because he abruptly tells me he has to go and to have a good night.

We hang up.

Goosebumps dot my skin, and I shiver. Garrison comes closer, his softened eyes asking if he can touch me.

I nod, and he rubs my cold arm. I've decided that my dad isn't a great person when he's meddling in my life.

Garrison's voice is a whisper as he says, "What the hell is going on Willow?"

My mouth dries.

"Your dad is trying to get you an internship?" He shakes his head, brows furrowed.

"He's paying for my second year," I remind Garrison, and I step out of his embrace to approach the dresser. I tug out a drawer. *Empty.*

I forgot most of my clothes are still in boxes.

And technically, my dad is paying for every semester here on out. College is expensive, and my years working at Superheroes & Scones don't even make a dent in tuition. Garrison offered to cover it, but I can't take money from my boyfriend.

"You always knew he would pay for it," Garrison says, taking a seat on the stripped bed. Not questioning the wadded-up comforter since I told him about Mattie and Dina. "But that didn't stop you from telling your dad to keep out of your career. You said those words a year ago, Willow. You said: *I'm making the decisions.* I was there when both of your brothers backed you up and shut that shit down."

That was a long time ago.

That was before December.

"Things have changed." I don't dig into a cardboard box for panties or a shirt. I want to face Garrison, so I stay standing.

"Something happened." He frowns deeply again. "Willow..." He rises off the mattress and comes forward.

I stiffen. My joints freezing up.

Hurt flashes in his eyes. I'm the one with secrets now. And they eat at me, slowly gnawing from the inside-out.

Concern infiltrates his face. "I'm not leaving until you tell me what happened. I can stand here all night."

"It may take longer than all night," I say softly.

His face breaks. "All week. All month. *Willow*—"

"I'm fine. It's fine," I say quickly. I need to tell him something. Maybe the *vague* truth will work without causing damage. "Recently, I took more of his money."

Garrison shakes his head like that doesn't make sense. "If you needed money, you could have come to me…" He stops short and then rubs his lips. "Shit." He's putting as many pieces together as he can. "There's a reason you didn't. Probably the same reason you're not telling me anything now."

He's smart and he's right.

I take another breath. "My brothers also don't know I took his money," I say. "I'd like to keep it that way."

He rests a hand on his head. "I live with Lo."

I force down emotion, my eyes burning. Telling him might hurt him. I shouldn't be asking him to do this for me—to keep a secret from Lo. Everything is going horribly wrong.

"Willow, if you're in trouble—"

"I'm not," I say, confident about this. "My dad just wants to get me an internship. It's harmless."

"For now," Garrison says. "You don't know what he's capable of."

"I think I do." And then, I think about my mom again. What does it say about me that I'm talking to Jonathan instead of her? In her mind, did I choose the monster?

I shudder.

Garrison walks closer, and this time, I let him put his hands on my bare shoulders. "Willow," he says. "You can tell me anything. Don't be afraid of hurting me with the truth. I can take it. I'm way better than last year."

My body grows cold. "Last year," I whisper, remembering.

"Last year, I punched your friend," Garrison says, "I started smoking again—fuck, I'm still smoking. I barely slept. I couldn't figure out how to go home without being…" He takes a tight breath. "You know it got bad for a while there, but I'm better now. I'm home by dinnertime because there's this kid that gets super upset if I'm not at the table."

Maximoff.

My heart ascends, and I blink back the welling tears.

He continues, "Waking up every morning, knowing you wouldn't be next to me, used to be gut-wrenching. Now it's bearable." *It's not supposed to hurt.* I know that he's not telling me he's moving on from me. Just that it's no longer this soul-sucking pain. It's what I've wanted for him. To be happy, somehow.

He keeps his hands on my shoulders, distancing ourselves so that we can stare head-on, but I keep breaking the gaze to look at the floor.

"I'm saying this now," Garrison breathes, "because I want you to know that I'm doing better. And you don't need to tell me anything *right now*, but I'm going to be someone you can confide in again. I promise you that."

I wipe at my eyes, water leaking. "You'll be mad at me," I say softly.

"I don't think that's possible."

When we were seventeen, I felt like all we did was confide in each other, and I want that now. I have to be honest and open. So I say, "There was footage of your fight last December. I paid the students to delete it."

He's frozen. Like a statue.

I broke him.

Tears spill down my cheeks, uncontrollable. "Garrison…" I choke on his name and touch his chest.

"You took money from Jonathan," he says, his voice tight. "Because of me." He shakes his head. "And now you feel indebted to the bastard?"

I don't feel it.

"I *am* indebted to him. It was a lot of money." I cringe after I say the words. *Way to drive that knife in further.*

"Hey, no." Garrison touches my cheek. "It's good. Your honesty—it's good, Willow. I'm glad you told me."

My chest rises and falls like I've run a marathon. "I just have to play along with whatever he wants until school ends," I tell Garrison. "Then I can reinstate my boundaries and things will go back to how they were." I have to believe that.

He grinds down on his teeth, jaw clenched, but his words are firm. "I'm here for you. Whatever you want."

"Ryke and Lo," I say again.

"Shouldn't know," he agrees. "They'll blow this up into an unimaginable degree, and I think you want a relationship with your dad after this."

I do.

Something less complicated. But I want one. I've already lost one father. I've lost a lot of family like Garrison, and I'm not ready to put another name on that list.

"Thank you," I tell Garrison.

"You're my girl," he says. "I've got your back. Always." He kisses my forehead, cementing this fact, and when we part to get dressed, I scan the dresser and go cold again.

"I…I swear I had photos here." I sweep my hand over the dresser, only the Funko Pop! collectibles remain.

Garrison comes closer. "You sure?"

"I'm *positive.*" Anxious heat cakes my body, and I gape at the door. "The party…" Strangers were here.

"Shit," he curses, blinking long and hard. Our eyes meet in sad realization.

134

They're gone.

My family photos are gone. Stolen. I don't even need to confirm. "People probably came into my room when we were in the shower."

"I'm sorry." He wraps an arm around my shoulder. "I should've thought about how you can't lock your bedroom on the outside."

I shrug. "It's okay. I'll print more." I frown though. "I guess we need to be more mindful of our fame." I look up at him. "I had photos of us too, and they're gone." Whoever stole the pictures— they were also interested in me and Garrison. Not just the famous Calloway sisters and their men.

His chest rises in a big breath. "Yeah. I forget sometimes that we've made it onto fan sites."

"Me too." Our fame has been a slow crawl, from small notoriety to something bigger, and I'm only afraid of it mushrooming out of control. Where there's no breathing room or escape.

12

WILLOW MOORE
Age 17

"**S**o this is my room." Garrison swings open his door. His house is abnormally large. Mansion-sized. A dream home. I'd get lost finding a bathroom if there weren't seven of them.

"Whoa." My eyes widen behind my spare glasses, vision impeccably clear. His bedroom quadruples my tiny dorm room.

With a curious gaze, I quickly sweep the area: king-sized bed, plain black comforter, a huge entertainment system against one wall (stereo speakers, multiple game consoles, flat-screen television), plush carpet, framed vintage Nintendo posters, and shelves and shelves of horror movies.

One thing is excruciatingly apparent: he is *neat*. And clean.

So clean, in fact, that I wonder if I should take off my shoes. Instead of asking, I notice that he keeps on his Converses, so I decide to leave on my sneakers.

Walking further inside, my head swerves left and right. Laptop propped on his sleek metal desk, the screen is black. No turtle, but I remember he said that Abracadabra first belonged to his brother Mitchell. Maybe the turtle's tank stays in Mitchell's room.

Garrison tosses a couple expensive black beanbags to the floor.

When he takes a seat, I plop down next to him and keep gazing at every wall and shelf.

He flips the remote in his hand and then glances at me. "What've you noticed?"

You have no pictures of your family. "You're not messy at all." No ashtray with cigarette butts. No scattered, half-opened DVD cases. No Fizz or Lightning Bolt! cans.

"That's because a maid cleans once a week," he explains.

I remember his spotless car, and I doubt the maid cleans his Mustang too. "Did she just come?"

Garrison contemplates this for a second. "No...I think she comes tomorrow."

If his room looks this picked-up after a whole week, then it proves he's neat. After two days, a pile of dirty clothes usually compounds on my desk chair.

At first I wonder if he's scared to be called neat, but after a while, I realize that maybe no one has ever pointed this out until now. Maybe he's never noticed his own trait.

Garrison switches on a DVD player for *Supernatural.* The title screen with Sam and Dean Winchester appears. I'm deeply aware that I'm currently in a boy's bedroom.

Alone. About to watch a television show.

We're just friends, I remind myself, still trying to relax and not sit so stiffly. Or else my stomach will start cramping.

More nervous than giddy, I interlace my fingers and unlace them. Unsure of where to put my hands. I try not to be suggestive.

After Garrison presses *play* on the episode I left off, he glances at me and shifts his arm close but then tenses. Pauses.

He ends up clutching his knee.

Someone knocks on the door—we both jump.

"Shit." Garrison hops to his feet, and he looks back at me with a *you alright?* expression. I nod, and he focuses on the incomer and opens the door.

For some reason, I expect his brothers, but the moment a stunning brunette woman appears, I remember they're away at college.

Standing on the other side of the doorway, his mom wears a pink dress that molds her hourglass figure. Diamonds cascade off her ears and neck, and her makeup, all pink shades, gives her a benevolent glow. Her straight hair is slightly curled on the ends, the kind of perfection I've only seen on *Real Housewives* shows. (Maybe she has a personal hairstylist.)

She's unquestionably beautiful, and if she wasn't a former model or beauty queen in her younger years, I bet people told her that she could easily be both.

Mrs. Abbey meets her youngest son's dour expression with a heavy sigh. "What did I do now?"

"Nothing," he snaps. "I'm just busy."

She peers into the room, at me, and offers a tiny smile before returning to Garrison. "If I knew you were bringing a boy over, I could've ordered pizza for you both."

Oh my God. She thinks I'm a boy? I stare down at my baggy overalls. *Don't change*, I try to remind myself. *Don't change because of his mom.*

"She's a *girl*," Garrison emphasizes, and even though I only see the back of his head, I imagine his eyes narrowing a little. "And I already told you that I didn't need anything today."

Mrs. Abbey sighs again. "Why do you have to speak to me in that tone?"

Garrison shrugs. "Sorry." His voice is entirely dry, and I try to concentrate on my cellphone to give them privacy. It's hard not to overhear.

"You're acting like I've demolished your entire world, and all I wanted to do was say *hello, how was your day?*" She seems nice.

Garrison grips the door like he's seconds from slamming it closed. "It was really good. Now can I go?"

Mrs. Abbey's blue-green eyes flit to me, then back to him, and she tries to lower her voice. I still hear her say, "What happened to Rachel?"

He groans. "We've been over this. Rachel isn't my friend anymore." In my U.S. Government class, I heard Rachel vilifying Garrison. Saying things like, *he should've convinced Nathan and his friends to do the right thing. He's no better than them.*

She hates him.

"I just spoke to her mother yesterday," Mrs. Abbey explains. "She may forgive you if you just apologize and spend a little time—"

"*No*," Garrison cuts in. "I don't care about befriending Rachel again."

"She's a sweet girl," Mrs. Abbey continues. "I always thought she'd be a great influence on you, and if you go to the same college—"

"Mom," he groans and rests his hands on his head. "Just accept that your hopes and dreams of me marrying Zeta Beta Zeta royalty are over and *move on*. It's not like Rachel and I were ever a thing. You just made it all up in your mind because you're best friends with Rachel's mom."

"That's not true," she says, offended. "I just want what's best for you."

Garrison goes rigid, and eerie silence passes. A lump rises to my throat, but I stay quiet and respect their space.

Mrs. Abbey says softly, "You should apologize to Hunter."

Garrison drops his hands and stares at the floor.

"He graciously invited you to Penn for the weekend, and he told me that you cursed at him. Every single one of your brothers is making an effort to include you in their lives, and you keep pushing them away."

"You know why," he says, almost inaudibly.

She sighs for the third time. "Boys play rough. Your father is right; you need to stop being so sensitive."

My lips part at her response, and Garrison has completely shut down. He no longer speaks back.

"All I want and hope and pray," she says, "is that my four boys will be together as family. *Please* don't make this Thanksgiving uncomfortable by hiding yourself in your room. *Please*." She looks and sounds on the verge of tears.

My stomach knots at what she's asking him to do. By being around his brothers, he risks another bruise, possibly a broken bone—his safety. Yet, she acts like *he's* at fault for the strained sibling relationship.

In the aching silence, I find myself standing up and saying softly but loud enough, "I invited Garrison to Thanksgiving with me." I didn't really, but I suppose I just did.

142

His head whips towards me, surprise opening his mouth.

I approach but not too close, and Mrs. Abbey tries to place my appearance. I seem familiar to her because I've appeared on entertainment news sites. Which is just surreal in itself.

"I'm Willow," I greet with a sheepish wave.

Recognition floods her face. "Loren Hale's cousin." *Half-sister*, I mentally correct. She touches her heart. "I deeply apologize for what my son did to your cous—"

"Mom," Garrison interjects. "You don't have to go around making amends for me. We're already friends." He gestures between me and him.

Mrs. Abbey forces a kind smile, obviously peeved by Garrison's attitude. "So you'll be spending Thanksgiving with the Hales then?"

"Um…" I hadn't thought about this. Lo has already offered, but I've been contemplating returning to Maine to spend a little time with Ellie. I've been saving for a plane ticket. "I might actually visit my little sister in Maine, but Garrison is welcome to come."

Garrison knows about my strained relationship with my mom and my little sister. Maybe that's why he says, "Thanks, Willow, but I can't."

Did I do the wrong thing by interjecting? I just wanted to give him an escape if he needed one.

Mrs. Abbey radiates with joy. As though Garrison's rejection of my offer was an affirmation that he'll try to get along with his brothers.

I drift backwards as Mrs. Abbey tells us to "have fun"—not even worried that we'll hook up. No mention of "keep the door open" or "behave responsibly"—just, *have fun.* I wonder if it's because I don't look like anyone Garrison would ever hook up with. Or if she'd categorize hooking up as a teenage expectation for her sons, so she's okay with it happening.

If she had a daughter, maybe she'd be more protective. Maybe it'd be different.

Garrison shuts and locks the door.

I return to the beanbag, and not long after, he joins me and grabs the remote. He waits to press *play*. The air is heavy and weighted.

I stare at my hands when he says, "I'm cursed. I'm fucking *cursed*, and if I spend Thanksgiving with you, I'll ruin your time with your mom and your sister—or your relationship with Loren Hale. I can't do that to you."

It's better than you staying here, I think but struggle to say. I rewind to the beginning. "Your mom knows." It nearly steals my breath again. She knows that his brothers have physically hurt him before.

He's so quiet that I turn my head. He hangs his forearms on his knees, and his solemn gaze sinks into mine. "Hunter would bloody my nose. I'd tell my parents, and they'd just say *why didn't you fight back?* To them, I'm the youngest, so being picked on is just expected. My dad said that my brothers were trying to make me tough, but..." Garrison trails off and cements his gaze on the floor. "You remember the first questionnaire?"

"Yeah." It's impossible to forget.

"Remember my answer to *any surgeries?*" he asks, unable to meet my eyes.

"I think so. You said something about breaking your wrist and leg and needing pins."

Garrison nods. "I was seven and nine. First one, my dad actually saw. Hunter was pretending to be some wrestler in the driveway, and he kept trying moves on me. I was screaming for him to stop, but he body-slammed me into concrete. My wrist broke, and the bone tore clean through the skin."

I remove my glasses, the lenses misting. "And your dad just shrugged it off?"

"Boys will be boys," Garrison says flatly.

"And your leg?"

"I was nine, and Davis thought it'd be funny to duct tape my mouth, legs, and hands and toss me in the pool. I sunk and struggled to reach the surface. I ended up blacking out at the bottom, and I was told that his friend dove in, pulled me out, and basically punched my stomach until I coughed up water."

I don't understand…how did he break his leg? And how could *anyone* do that to another person?

Garrison rubs his forehead like the memory hurts. "I stood up shaking, and Davis said, 'Why are you being such a wuss?'. He laughed and then struck my leg with a lacrosse stick. Bone fractured."

Horrified, I shake my head over and over.

"To him and his friends, it was all a joke. They were older. I was younger. I told my mom what happened, and she thanked the boy for saving me more than she scolded Davis for nearly drowning me."

I fit on my glasses, my pulse speeding at the thought of Garrison spending Thanksgiving with his brothers. Brothers that would do all of that and parents that would never acknowledge the harm.

Garrison looks over at me. "It's in the past."

Is it? I'm so scared for him. "I'd rather you…I…will you…" Why are words so difficult for me right now? I wipe beneath my eyes. "Maine is pretty, and my mom won't mind extra company. Ellie will probably like you more than she likes me."

He shakes his head like it's not possible. "I'll be fine here."

"What if you tell Lo? He might help—"

"*No*. Please don't tell him," he says, panicked. "It's not that bad anymore, Willow. Ever since they went to college, it's been easier. Hell, ever since I could *drive* it's been better." Before I speak, he adds, "Why don't you tell Loren about what happened today?"

"What do you mean?"

"The guys who broke your glasses," he snaps, not at me but rather at their invisible presences.

For a moment, I'd forgotten all about that. "I can't..." Lo will freak out. "I can't make his life harder. He has so much to deal with already."

Garrison twists his leather bracelet. "I'm scared for you," he says exactly what I feel for him. "If those guys find out where you live, I'll..." He pushes his hair out of his face. "You can spend the night here if you ever need to, you know."

I'm speechless.

He recovers by explaining, "This is a gated neighborhood. No one can get in that shouldn't be in here, and where you live, that apartment or dorm or whatever, it's not like it has a lot of security."

"I'll be okay," I say quietly, but the offer starts expelling the heavy tension. We acknowledge that we're on each other's side when other people aren't or can't be. I relax more than I did, and he leans against his own beanbag too.

"Sam and Dean?" he asks, remote braced in his hand. Ready to watch two hunters fight supernatural entities.

I agree with a nod, and he plays the episode. We're more light-hearted, and we pause the show every now and then to check Tumblr.

We scoot closer and closer on our beanbags, and four-hours in, our arms are pressed together. I'm more lying down than sitting. He clicks *play* after we paused the show and makes funny commentary about Dean eating a hamburger.

Another hour passes, and my eyes droop. I yawn, the television screen blurring.

I only notice that I fell asleep when my eyes snap open. My cheek—my cheek is on his chest.

Oh. My.

God.

I fell asleep on Garrison. I've never ever been that comfortable around a guy to do that. I gently lift my head and first glance at the television.

Sam and his lush hair are freeze-framed. Garrison waited for me to watch the rest. I feel his arm wrapped comfortingly around my back, and he watches as I sit further up.

Actually, he sits up with me. "You okay?"

I push up my glasses.

Garrison licks his dry lips. "You know I wouldn't do anything…"

"Yeah, I know." *Just friends.* My heart sinks. Do I want him to do something? Partially, maybe, but not at the cost of what we have now. "I'm just surprised."

Garrison tenses. "At what?"

"That…that I'd fall asleep on you." I'm being painfully honest, but dropping all these walls with someone has almost felt cathartic in a way. "I've never done that before. With anyone else, I mean."

His lip quirks.

"What?" I ask, his rare expression stealing my breath.

"I like being your first." Garrison almost smiles. "Ones are my thing, remember?"

"And zeroes," I remind him about the other number in computer language.

"Fuck the zeroes." Garrison balances his remote on his kneecap, and I'm more aware that he's probably been with many girls like this. It may be my first, but it's far from his. Still, he's sweet and slow with me, and I don't understand why.

"Why are you so nice to me?" I ask.

It takes him aback. He's confused, but he answers as well as he can, "Because it'd be impossible for me to be a dick to you. Is that what you're asking?"

"You just...you care about what's too far for me, and not many do."

"That," Garrison says in realization. "Yeah..." He licks his lips again, and my shyness skyrockets, tucking my arms around myself. I'm more open than usual because he's been so vulnerable with me.

Garrison retracts his arm, but we're still breathlessly close. "I understand what it's like to be pushed out of personal boundaries, and I wouldn't do that to someone. I'm not gonna do that to you, *ever.*"

My chest swells, and my smile overwhelms my face. *Stop smiling.* I try to bury my face in my hand. God, I'm such a dork.

"Can I hug you?" he asks in a breath.

I nod without removing my hand, and instantly, his arms extend around my shoulders, his biceps flexing. I reciprocate, but my arms curve around his chest much looser and lighter. He squeezes like he's mastered the art of hugging long ago.

We're still sitting on the beanbags, but the position isn't awkward. He holds me against his body like that's where he wants me to be.

My heart thuds harder.

I feel so safe with him, and I see that he feels equally safe with me. Comforted. At ease. He only draws back when I descend into my head and overthink about my actions. My limbs stiffen, and he retracts his arms.

"You know," he says, "I didn't even realize how unhappy I was with all my huge birthday parties until now."

"What's so different?"

"You." He nearly smiles. "One real friend instead of a hundred horrible ones."

I'm about to reply, but my phone buzzes in my backpack. I give him a look like *one second* and I scoot forward and dig through the backpack's contents. I find my cell and gape at the time.

Two in the morning.

Maya has sent me four texts.

Maya: Are you okay? It's getting late, and don't you have school tomorrow?

Maya: Can you respond just to let me know you're in one piece?

Maya: Not cool, Willow. If you don't answer this in thirty minutes, I'm going to have to text Loren. It's my roommate duty

Maya: Just called him

Not to mention the missed calls and texts from my brother, Lily, Daisy, Rose, and even Ryke and Connor. Maybe my backpack muffled them or most happened while I was asleep.

"Oh no," I mutter.

"What?" Garrison straightens up and stands just as I do.

"I have to go." Lo has called me *ten* times and left seven texts, which range from slightly worried, asking about where I am, to full-on panicked, saying that he's five minutes away from calling the cops to find me.

And then this text:

Loren: If someone's taken Willow's phone—if you've hurt her, I'm going to wring your goddamn neck and shove your dick inside your body, you little shitty motherfucker. You'll be peeing out of your asshole.

"I can drive you to your apartment." Garrison grabs his hoodie.

"No that's okay." I sling my backpack on my shoulder. "I need to pick up my car from Lo's house, so I'll just drive myself home. I can walk to Lo's." Before he offers to walk with me, I add, "If Lo sees that I was with you, I think he might pop a blood vessel. I've never seen him this angry." I show the text to Garrison.

He reads it quickly. "I've seen that side of him already. I'm not scared."

"You're on good footing with him though and that took a while." I don't want to ruin his relationship with Lo either.

"Yeah, but you shouldn't lie to your cousin about where you've been. Not because of me. I don't have to walk with you, but just don't lie to him."

"Are you sure?" I ask before I leave. He wants me to be honest with Loren Hale. "If I tell Lo the truth about where I've been…"

He may hate you.

"I'm sure."

13

WILLOW MOORE
Age 17

On my walk towards Lo's house, I text him and Maya, apologizing profusely and reassuring that I'm one-hundred percent okay. I also mention that I'm almost to his house, and as soon as my feet hit the front porch steps, the door bursts open.

Lo wears nothing but drawstring pants, the night air chilly, but maybe his anger heats him. His cheekbones cut sharp, and he has his cellphone cupped to his ear.

"She's here," he says to the person on the other line. "I don't know why yet. Just get your ass back home, bro." *Must be Ryke Meadows.* "I'll tell her. Okay, *okay.* Bye." He hangs up, and I stand uneasily on the porch—only an arm's length away from my half-brother.

Lo clutches his cell tight. "Ryke and Daisy have been driving around looking for you." He lets out a tense breath. "My brother said to tell you that he's 'fucking glad you're okay' and 'Daisy loves you.'"

My lips upturn at Daisy's comment to me. When I'm with all of them—Lo and Lily, Rose and Connor, Ryke and Daisy—I thought for sure, I'd gravitate towards someone like Lily. Comic book geek, resident introvert, and a lover of pop culture.

But when we're all together, Daisy keeps me the most company. She metaphorically opened her arms to me, and I walked straight into them. Life is unpredictable that way. Because I would've never predicted befriending Daisy Calloway of all the Calloway sisters.

We're the closest in age, but it's more than that. She never pressures me to fill the silence, and when I do talk, she always listens. Even if it's about superheroes and comic books that she's never heard of before.

Just three days ago, Daisy invited me to pick apples with her at an orchard.

She climbed an apple tree in the spur of the moment, and she gave me a tug and boost to the lowest tree limb. Something I never thought I'd do. She's adventurous and spontaneous, but she likes the quiet more than most people would even believe.

We sat up there and just listened to the wind.

I love spending time with Daisy, and to hear that she loves me back floods me with warmth.

But at the sight of Lo's sharp exterior, my small smile fades quickly.

"It's cold out here," he says. "Come inside." His voice is like knives.

I follow Lo through the foyer. Soft voices emanate from the living room, reminding me that Lo lives with five other people and two infants. Everyone tries to stay hushed at night because of the two sleeping babies: Jane Cobalt and Maximoff Hale.

Lo veers into the living room, a typical set-up: long couch, loveseat, and a Queen Anne chair placed towards the television and fireplace. I've hung out here enough that I'm less and less uncomfortable every time I enter.

Tonight, however, I hug onto my backpack strap and hesitate on whether to sit or stand. We're also not alone.

Rose Calloway, Lily's older and fashionable sister, looms strictly by the window, her nightgown hidden with a silky black robe. And her brown hair is pulled in a tight pony. She looks simultaneously concerned and high-strung.

To add to the sheer intimidation, Connor Cobalt, her six-foot-four, dapper husband towers beside her. His confidence radiates like the rarest, most intoxicating cologne. Just like Lo, he wears drawstring pants—and his chiseled abs…holy crap. I can't believe those are real.

Maggie would faint on the spot if she saw Connor Cobalt in his nightly glory.

I suddenly think, *can he tell I'm staring at his abs?* Paling, I whip my head towards Lo. What if Rose saw me ogling her husband?

This is so embarrassing.

That Willow Moore should've never been unleashed into the world. I hate that eulogy, but it's staying for the moment.

Lo glances at me as he walks towards the kitchen door. I'm about to follow until he says, "Stay here for a second." He rubs the back of his neck. "I need a minute." He searches the room for only one person: a gangly girl in a muscle shirt (*his* muscle shirt) that covers her thighs.

Lily hovers by the staircase, her eyes big with questions and worry. For him, I realize. They both wear this soul-bearing empathy for one another that's almost hard to stare at straight-on.

"Lily," he calls out, his voice still sharp but urgent.

Without hesitation, she bounds towards him, entangling her arms around his waist, and together, they disappear into the kitchen. Leaving me alone with Connor and Rose, two people I rarely, if ever, talk to alone.

Sure, in group settings, they exist and persist—but I still don't know them personally the way that I've come to know Daisy, Lo, and Lily. Even though they live here too, they're constantly on the go—and with the little free time they do have, they make room for Lo, Lily, Ryke, and Daisy. Not really me. (I don't blame them. I'm not that chatty or the greatest of company.)

So most of my information about Connor and Rose derive from *Princesses of Philly* and tabloids and eavesdropping (I try not to overhear but it happens).

I've read their bios on Wikipedia handfuls of times and deduced that they're two intellectually superior human beings. I mean, they *both* graduated valedictorian of their prep schools and they competed in academic competitions all throughout college.

At this point in my life, I can barely pass Calculus.

I eye the closed kitchen door, worried about Lo. I strain my ears, but their voices aren't audible at all. *I upset him. This is my fault.*

It's all I can think now.

"Let me handle this, Richard," Rose says under her breath, but her voice escalates with each syllable. "You can take a backseat."

"Are you ill?" He touches her forehead, and she swats his hand away.

Rose glares a boiling glare and perches her hands on her hips. "That is the dumbest question you've asked me this week. I am standing right in front of you, *perfectly* healthy and coherent."

"Then why else have you forgotten that your husband, me—"

"I know you're my husband," she growls.

"—never takes the metaphorical backseat in your metaphorical vehicle," he finishes without pause. Without flinching either.

My eyes grow wide, stunned that I'm witnessing their rapid-fire back-and-forths up close and not on *Princesses of Philly*. I can't remember where Lily first dubbed these moments "nerd star" flirt-fighting. Maybe in the reality show or on social media.

I can't stop watching.

I'm hooked.

Maggie would love this. I almost retrieve my phone, but I know better than to film them and send the video to my friend. I keep my cell hidden in my backpack. Where it needs to stay.

"I've forgotten nothing," Rose spouts, heated whereas he's calm and cool. "I just put you in the backseat, Richard. Stay. There."

I forget that his middle name is actually Connor, and Richard is his real first name. Only Rose seems to constantly use it. Mostly as ammunition.

Connor grins. "The fact that you still believe you can order me around like a child is partially inane and partially amusing."

"You're *fully* aggravating—and stop grinning that way." Rose covers his mouth with her hand and growls into an annoyed groan.

It looks like he's grinning more, even beneath her palm.

She drops her hand. "Why can't you just let me drive the vehicle?"

"I will, but I'm not going to be relegated to the backseat. I'm sitting next to you in every metaphorical scenario, darling." He cups her cheek, and she lets him. Softly, he says a string of melodic-sounding French that I can't even begin to translate.

Rose raises her chin, treaties in her yellow-green eyes, and she whispers French in reply. She touches his hand on her cheek, and Connor brings them down, lacing their fingers together.

Then they spin towards me.

"Uh…" I gulp, not prepared to be the center of attention when it comes to the nerd stars.

"You should sit," Rose says coldly.

She's not really ever sweet-natured. I can tell she's not intending to be harsh when she approaches the Queen Anne chair and pats the cushion.

Rose is letting me sit in *her* chair? Lo and Ryke often tease her about that chair, but their words never dissuade her from taking a seat with crossed ankles.

Walking around furniture, I lower stiffly onto the regal chair, and then, nearly in unison, Rose and Connor sit on the adjacent couch. Rose looks a bit peeved by the synchronization, but she makes no mention of it.

Connor is staring through me. With his genius-level intellect, I question whether he can interpret my body language.

I hug my backpack on my lap and risk a glance at the kitchen door. No sound, no movement—*nothing.*

"Do you need anything?" Rose asks, making this less like an interrogation. "Coffee or a blanket?"

"No…thanks," I say, still a little uneasy.

Rose nods, her posture like a wooden board. "I can't sugarcoat anything, so if you can't handle bluntness, then I advise you to cover your ears or wait for Connor to spell out everything in his *nauseatingly* smooth voice."

"She means *pleasantly*," Connor says with a growing grin.

Rose drills a glare between his blue eyes. "I hate your voice."

"You love my voice," he rephrases.

I hope they continue to digress so I can leave this conversation without saying another word.

Rose unknowingly scoots closer to him, their eyes locked together in battle. "Is your name Rose Calloway—*no*, it's not. Therefore, you shouldn't translate my already intelligible words."

"I'm reading the subtext of your statements."

Rose snorts.

He continues, "Yes, you hate my voice, but you also love my voice. Tell me otherwise, and I'll stop."

"You'll stop chiming in?" She's disbelieving.

Connor arches a brow. "Only if I'm wrong, which I know I'm not."

Rose rolls her eyes and sighs. "How can I both love and hate your voice?" She doesn't deny the fact that she does.

"Because," he says, "you're a beautiful paradox."

Rose nearly smiles, but she seems to remember me, her game-face returning. Straightening up, she says, "Where was I?"

I shake my head. I'm just as lost.

"You want to be blunt with her," Connor reminds Rose. He's firmly on his wife's side, not about to come to my defense, if I even need one.

"Willow," Rose begins, "we all feel a semblance of responsibility for you, and while that may seem absurd since you're seventeen and clearly a young adult, we're still the people that'll take care of you if something were to go horribly awry in Philly."

I nod, hardly breathing.

Rose is about to swing a figurative axe. I see the power simmer through her. "Therefore," she says, "you *have* to think about us when you're out late at night. Alone. With too many fucking perverts that know your name when you have no idea who they are. Not to mention, the rabid, foaming-at-the-repulsive-mouth paparazzi." Rose lets out a single breath, on a hot streak. "We're all you have here, and we'd break our backs for you. Leave your phone on. Text. Call—whatever it takes."

The last three words ring in my head like a cliffhanger to a story about family and friendship and love. She's asking me to embrace them entirely, even when I don't fully know her beyond the media and the encouragements she's given me in the past—but I'm not here to be a burden or a nuisance.

I've already screwed that up. Yet, I still feel myself retracting. Wanting to distance myself so I'll never ever bother them again.

In the most tranquil voice, Connor says, "We also recognize your reluctance to integrate with the six of us."

They have?

"When we go out," he continues, "you decline our invites because you're afraid to be a hassle, and you refuse to move in because you're afraid to alter Lo's life."

I ruined that tonight. Before, I was a peaceful shadow. Now I've become trouble. Someone Lo probably wishes he could return.

I'm sorry, Lo.

Connor edges forward on the couch, as though reaching towards me with his calming eyes alone. "You have affected Loren Hale." It crushes me, tears welling, and before I apologize, he says, "You have brought your brother *love*, and with love comes an unbearable amount of worry that I used to believe made people weak."

Rose is watching her husband, eyes cast proudly and affectionately on him, and I'm caught in Connor's vortex of wisdom and reverence.

"Lo isn't weak," Connor tells me. "He's just trying to figure out how to love a sister and protect a sister at the same time, all without hurting you with his *imaginative* vocabulary."

Rose nods in agreement. "If someone knows how to slaughter with words, it's Loren Hale."

"And he's afraid to slaughter you," Connor finishes.

My lips part, and they wait for me to speak. "Maybe...maybe I should stay away."

Rose gapes. "*No.* That's not what we're trying to say. We want you *here.* With us." She nearly rises out of passion, but Connor tugs her down, seeing that I'm uncomfortable. Rose continues on in a fiery rant, "You are family. *We* are family, and family fucks up and can be the biggest pains in the asses—but we're also the very best when we're together. Not apart."

I want that.

I do.

It sounds beautiful, but I can't fuck Lo up. He has a baby and a wife, and he's a recovering addict. So is Lily.

I wipe my wet eyes beneath my glasses, and then I hear the front door swing open. I go very still. Rose cranes her neck over her shoulder as Ryke Meadows storms into the house. Not acknowledging us, he sets his focused eyes on the kitchen door, his features hard, jaw scruffy and dark brown hair messy. Somehow he knows that his brother lies behind the kitchen door.

He heads straight for him.

Ryke vanishes inside, the better sibling to Loren Hale between the two of us.

I slump in my seat, and then Daisy enters the living room. "Hey, guys," she greets with a bright smile that eviscerates the lingering tension.

I breathe easier.

Supermodel tall with brown hair, Daisy rounds the furniture to head towards me. I'm used to seeing Daisy with blonde hair on the reality show, and at one point afterwards, she dyed her hair an array of colors.

She told me that this is her natural color. The brown hue makes her seem younger in a way. Then again, in fashion ads, she looks *Rose's* age, all made-up with dark lipstick, smoky eyes, and sultry clothes. I'm not sure about the true facts or timeline, but Daisy quit modeling after she was thrown into the Paris riot a couple years ago (the one that started from an overly passionate rugby championship game).

Fans on Tumblr believe she quit modeling because of the thick scar that runs down her cheek to her jaw. I can't be sure what's fabricated and what's real, but she did once mention that modeling wasn't fun for her. It'd been her mom's idea to approach agencies.

Dressed in a pair of Ryke's track pants and a long-sleeved shirt that says *wilder than the wind*, Daisy sits on the armrest of the Queen Anne.

She mock gasps at me. "You're in one piece. It's a miracle." I smile at her theatrics while she looks to the ceiling and says, "Thank you, God."

Connor arches another brow. "No." That's all he says. *No.*

Daisy wags her brows at his brow. "Thank you, Connor, my savior. My one true love."

"Don't inflate his overinflated ego by comparing him to God," Rose says, tightening her ponytail.

"I'm hardly moved," Connor tells Rose. "She speaks falsehoods and lies. Her one true love is a barking dog."

Daisy only smiles, knowing Connor is referring to Ryke Meadows.

Just now, the kitchen door swings open, and silence blankets the living room.

Lo is the first one out, more assuredness in his step, but I cower, unable to make eye contact. I stare at my backpack and listen to the two other footsteps that belong to Lily and Ryke.

Out of my peripheral, I notice how Connor and Rose stand up with the others. Only Daisy remains seated next to me on the armrest. I can practically feel every pair of eyes boring into me, and I'm too timid to meet a single one.

"It's not like anyone died," Lo says, attempting to make a joke. His tone is too razor-sharp for one. No one speaks. No one even breathes. It's like the Grim Reaper plopped on the couch to watch us all, and we're all overly aware of its presence.

The quiet tension is killer.

"Jesus Christ," Lo says, "everyone, just calm down—and I shouldn't be the one saying that. Stop role-reversaling me."

"Reversaling isn't a word," Connor says, "and I'm always calm, darling."

Ryke Meadows rolls his eyes and mumbles under his breath while Lily bites her nails, catches herself, and stops.

"I'm sorry," I suddenly and softly apologize to everyone while we're all gathered. I stare at my feet but try hard to lift my gaze. "I fell asleep, Lo. I didn't see how late it was…I'm really sorry. I'll text where I am next time. I promise."

Everyone is looking at me. My cheeks heat, and I only look up when Lo says, "It's not okay, what happened, but it will be." He very briefly glances at his brother, and Ryke glances back with a nod like *you're doing fucking great, little brother*—and I wonder how much of what he said belonged to Ryke Meadows first.

Lo can't soften his features all that much, but he clears his throat before he speaks again. "Where were you?"

"The mall and then…Garrison Abbey's house."

Connor and Rose look more than perturbed. They're not fans of Garrison, for very good reasons. I don't risk reading anyone else's expression but my brother's.

Lo repeatedly rubs the back of his neck, and then he says, "Everyone, you all should leave while I talk to my sister alone." Lo quickly adds, "I can handle it. Alright? *Go.*" He snaps at them and then shoos them away with two hands.

Rose combats, "We'll stay quiet." I think she must like to be in-the-know about everything.

Lo points at me. "Not your sister, Queen Rose. She's mine."

Surrendering, Rose huffs and then departs upstairs with Connor. Lily trots slowly and tentatively behind them. Lo looks regretful for shooing her away, but he stands by the decision, not calling her back to the living room.

Ryke waits for Daisy, and she nods to me like *everything will be okay* and then exits into the kitchen with her boyfriend.

Lo takes a seat on the couch, forearms on his thighs, and a moment passes before he collects his words. "You're just seventeen, and I get it." He stares off like he's imagining himself at that age. I wonder who he was back then. What he was up to. If he loved Lily all the same. "I get that you're old enough to do everything I'm doing now."

I make a choice and set my backpack on the ground. He just told his support system to leave, and if he's strong enough to do that, then maybe I can be strong enough to let go of a crutch.

One day, I want to feel safe and powerful without holding my backpack tight.

"I still can't drink alcohol. I'm not twenty-one yet."

Lo wears a bitter smile. "Trust me, from experience, you can still drink. It being illegal didn't stop me." He hangs his head for a second, then lifts his amber eyes to my brown. "Maybe I gave you the wrong impression."

My lips downturn. "About what?"

"About Garrison, for one," he says. "Christ, I *never* expected you two to be…" He cringes like it's painful to think about.

"Friends?"

He tries to relax at that title. "Yeah, *that*. I know guys like him. I *was* like him—it's why I'm nicer to Garrison than I am to most people—but that doesn't mean I approve of you hanging out at his place on a Sunday night. Or *any* night. No sleepovers." He pauses. "Can I make that rule?"

He's my brother, not my dad, but I see that he's just trying to protect me. "Yeah," I nod. "I like that rule." It means he cares.

Someone wants me home at a certain hour.

Someone wants me safe.

Lo hesitates and stares off again, his face a bit murderous, and I wonder if he's thinking about Garrison. Regretting giving him a hand.

"I'm glad you're nice to him," I say. "I think he needs that more than me."

Lo shakes his head once. "You're my priority."

It swells and breaks my heart. "Don't hate him because of me."

Lo runs his tongue over the bottom of his teeth, and he barely nods. It's hard to take that as an affirmation. "You should know something," he says almost inaudibly.

"What?"

"I'm petty." He flashes that iconic half-smile. "I hold grudges, and in past history, I'm not the good person. But goddamn, I'm trying to be." He lets out a deep breath. "It's hard, and I can't...I just can't promise anything, Willow."

I wipe my nose that runs before my eyes leak. "I understand."

We're all complex people with many layers and strings, and I can't sit here and pretend to know all of theirs. All of his. But in time, maybe I will see more.

Maybe I will know the kind of person they all were and maybe I'll be here to witness the kind of people we'll all be.

MY CAR WON'T START.

I'm trying to return to my apartment, but my gold Honda sits like a hunk of junk in Lo's driveway. Hood popped, Ryke tinkers with the contents while Connor points a flashlight towards the engine.

"You already checked the battery's water level," Connor says. It's not his first comment or probably his last. `

Ryke glowers. "What the fuck did I say two minutes ago?"

"I purposefully ignore you when you tell me to shut the fuck up, especially if you're wasting time *repeating* actions you've taken." Connor points the flashlight towards another part of the car and instructs him—much to Ryke's annoyance.

Our breath smokes the air, the November temperature dropping fast tonight, but we all put on coats and shoes. I cup a mug of hot chocolate thanks to Daisy. Lo is on the phone, sending work emails I think, but he's close by—and Lily and Rose stay indoors for warmth.

Daisy said Rose would probably be out here helping, but Jane started crying through the baby monitor.

"I can just drive her in Rose's car," Daisy suggests for the tenth time.

"No," all the guys say in unison. Because apparently she's a reckless driver, and I'm not even sure if she has her license beyond a motorcycle one.

"It might be a clogged fuel filter...fuck." Ryke winces, his finger caught in something, but he shakes it out.

Daisy's face contorts, a little concerned for him. He's a rock climber, after all—his hands are precious. "Maybe we should take the car into the shop tomorrow," she says. "We can let Willow spend the night. That's probably what Lo wants, too."

"No, it's okay," I interject. "I can call an Uber or something." I think everyone needs space from me for a while.

"That seems unwise," Connor tells me while shining the flashlight for Ryke. "It's late and people know who you are."

"Famous people take Ubers all the time in Los Angeles...I think. And I mean, I'm not famous like all of you. You know...?" I want to stop talking now. Thanks.

"We're not in LA. We're in Philadelphia," Connor says in a way that makes me feel dumb for making the comparison.

"Fuck off, Cobalt," Ryke says from beneath the car hood.

Daisy suddenly swings her head to the left, and I follow her gaze. Warm lamplight illuminates the neighborhood street, but darkness lies beyond.

She solidifies, eerily motionless. "Did you hear that?" she asks me.

I listen closely, but besides Ryke toying with the car's mechanisms, I can't hear much else. "Not really..."

Daisy breathes shallowly, her knuckles whitening on her mug of hot chocolate. "Something's out there," she says under her breath.

My own fear spikes, partly afraid of what she sees and partly afraid for *her*—I've never seen someone look so haunted before.

Connor watches her closely, and Ryke turns his head to Daisy. His brows furrow, intensely concerned.

"Do you hear that?" she asks again. "Something's…not right."

"Hey, sweetheart," Ryke says in a gentle tone, "you're fucking safe. Nothing's out there."

Daisy flinches, so abruptly—like someone threw something at her—and she drops the hot chocolate to shield her face. The mug shatters on cement, and no object flies her way. She's about to crouch, but Ryke immediately reaches her side.

"You're okay. I'm here." He wraps his arms around Daisy. "I'm fucking here, Dais." He hugs her tight, clutching her protectively to his chest, and his features simultaneously darken and harden.

I don't know what to do or say. I waver uneasily and just stay quiet. Daisy is immobilized by fear, and so Ryke effortlessly lifts her in his arms. Cradling her body, he carries her towards the house.

As he passes Lo, my half-brother asks him, "What the hell happened?"

Ryke doesn't answer. I think it might've been a rhetorical question. Lo knows everything that has happened to Daisy and why the dark would scare her. All I know is that Garrison and his friends didn't help with her fear.

Not when they shot paintballs at the windows, among other things.

Connor clicks off his flashlight and lowers the hood of the car. I wait to figure out what to do next while he towers above with supreme confidence.

In his presence, I feel small. I feel awkward.

I doubt he's ever felt either.

I push up my glasses and adjust my backpack straps. "I'll call an Uber."

"You'd choose the unwise option just to avoid us," he states aloud like it means little when it actually carries too much weight.

"I'm not…avoiding," I say, unable to even *look* at him.

Lo quickly finishes typing his email, about twenty feet away.

"To avoid: to keep away from or stop oneself from doing something," he defines. "You're stopping yourself from spending the night here, which is, in fact, *avoidance*."

I clear a lump in my throat. "Do you always define words for people?"

"Only for people who need definitions."

Boom. Mic drop.

Maggie would love his burn towards me. She once tweeted: All I want for Christmas is for Connor Cobalt to insult me. Please and thank you. It's supposed to be an honor. At least, to the online community. For everyone off Twitter and Tumblr, I don't think they'd appreciate being called stupid, and I doubt he'd care.

I try to nudge my already pushed-up glasses. "Do you have…an extra car I could borrow?" I risk asking him, of everyone, but if someone else stood on this driveway, I'd definitely be asking them first.

Because Connor analyzes all of my words, all of my edgy movements, and my quick glances to Lo.

"We have many cars you could borrow," he says, "but Lo will want to ride with you."

"No, no, that's okay. Never mind."

He's so *un*surprised by my reaction. It's kind of unsettling.

Thankfully, Lo pockets his phone and approaches us. "So what'd we decide?" He appraises my Honda from afar, hood closed but still broken.

"I don't know. We couldn't fix it…" I trail off as a limousine pulls to the curb and then idles. Exhaust gurgles out.

Lo swings his head to Connor. "When did you call your driver?"

Connor Cobalt's limousine. It's nearly as famous as Lily's Wampa cap. Jane Cobalt was *born* in that limo. It's like this sacred relic. I'm stunned silent.

"The same time Ryke lifted the hood of her car," Connor answers.

My brother laughs into a small smile, and he pats his friend's shoulder. "Goddamn, you make life easier."

"It's what I'm here for." Connor spins his attention onto me. "I trust my driver. I've known him for years, so you'll be safe by yourself. I've already given him your address."

It takes me a solid minute to find words. "Thank you." I say my goodbyes to Lo, and he tells me to text him when I reach my apartment.

I dazedly enter the limo, the black leather seats perfectly intact and shined. A few water bottles sit unopened in a refrigerator section.

The limo rumbles to life, and the driver takes me home. I check my Twitter messages to find a new one from **@garrisonwither**.

How'd it go? You okay?

I message back: Strange … but good, I think.

I hope.

I lean back and look around this limo, and I imagine all of them here with me. Lily, Loren, Connor, Rose, Ryke, and Daisy—and I wonder how many places they've been. How many conversations they've had right here. Days and weeks and years ago.

BACK THEN

I sit in a place that has held thousands of memories for infamous people—people that I can call family. I have trouble accepting this as reality. I feel like I'm part of someone's *Princesses of Philly* fan fiction.

But this is real life. My life. Canon.

14

GARRISON ABBEY
Age 22

"I think us being together—like sexually and not just seventeen-year-old chaste friends—is starting to finally click with your brothers," I say on the porch of the lake house. It's this huge place that the Calloway sisters and their husbands all share and use every Christmas and other holidays and generally when they want to escape Philly and the paparazzi.

I pinch a cigarette and blow smoke up in the air, my skin freezing from fingerless gloves.

It's fucking cold as hell, and I'm still reeling from my invite here. Without even knowing if Willow could fly down for the holidays, Lo asked if I wanted to join them at the lake.

Sure. I've been living with him for almost a year now, but he

Willow is bundled in a pale blue ski jacket and sits on the wooden table. She pushes up her glasses with a gloved finger. "They've known that we've been sleeping together for a while."

"Yeah, but we've been separated the majority of that time. It hasn't been in their face. Now that we're with them and also together, it's *right there*." I raise a hand to her beautiful, rosy-cheeked face.

She smiles, a giddy nervous one that lifts her carriage, like this is the first interaction we've ever had and she's bracing herself. It's magical.

It makes me smile back, and after a quiet moment that I hang onto, I say, "Honestly, I think Ryke was glaring at me this morning."

She leans closer, hands on her thighs. "He glares at everyone."

I bounce on my toes, trying to circulate blood in the cold. "This was different. His eyes said *you're sleeping with my sister. Fuck you.*"

Willow laughs. "There was no fuck you in his eyes." Her lips start to fall. "Well, if there was it *wasn't* directed at you."

She touches my shoulders, and I stop bouncing. My cigarette burns between my fingers. Even though she doesn't smoke, she joins me on most of my smoke breaks. I'm going to try and quit again—I'm going to.

Just not right now.

I think she might say something super positive, but instead her brows furrow. "I'm usually the one overthinking everything," she murmurs. "This is...different."

I nod. "I'm getting a taste of inside your head, Willow, and honestly, gotta say, I don't like it."

Her lips quirk. "They're probably not thinking about us having sex. One, that'd be weird if they zeroed in on that. Two, I'm sure they're more likely questioning whether we're going to stay together." Her eyes don't have those questions. They hold this powerful confidence.

"You don't believe we'll break up," I say, putting the cigarette back between my lips.

She shakes her head. "We've rode out the bumpy parts."

"Are the bumpy parts named Salvatore Amadio?" I wonder.

Since August, I haven't been back to London. My one weekend at their flat was enough of a hurricane between me and Mr. Dickbag. AKA vampire-knockoff. AKA Salvatore.

Willow has had a pretty rough time living at the flat. I always thought she had this perfect thing going on in London, and it doesn't make me feel better knowing it's been shitty recently.

The apartment parties are sometimes as bad as three times a week, even after she politely had a "roommate meeting" and told them house parties aren't her thing.

She was probably too polite. I wasn't there, but she rehashed the conversation. She said they sometimes remember to lower the volume of the music. But that's about it.

She still loves Tess and Sheetal, just not as roommates, and I know she'd GTFO like yesterday. But she signed a lease, and she's stuck there till May.

I don't have to love Salvatore, but I have to find a way to tolerate him while he's still her roommate. I'm trying to get there.

"Maybe one Salvatore bump," Willow says softly.

After I blow smoke up in the air, I step closer and her gloved hands wrap around me. The backdoor slides open, and Daisy's white husky bounds out, sprinting down the stairs and descending the snowy hill towards the dock.

Coconut's fur matches the white landscape, blending in with the scenery.

"Nutty!" Ryke yells and follows the husky. Heading down the deck stairs, he nods to Willow and me, and I swear there's another stern glare.

I whisper to Willow, "I'm not imagining it."

"That's his *normal* face," Willow says.

"Jesus Christ, who left the door open?" Lo's voice filters outside, and he appears in the doorway. He looks between Willow and me.

"Ryke," I answer, not caring about throwing him under the bus. He, technically, was the one who left the door open anyway.

Lo leans outside, only in a pair of drawstring pants and a short sleeve T-shirt. "Ryke, close the damn door next time!"

Ryke gives him a middle finger.

Lo is about to retreat indoors. He stays, eyes on us. "Both of you. Your room is right next to Jane's and Sulli's. Remember that tonight before you start doing things. Actually, why don't you two just not do things tonight."

Wasn't dreaming. Lo and whoever else have definitely been talking about the fact that Willow and I are having sex. Maybe because of the whole "blow job" slip-up back in August. Who knows?

Willow's eyes are saucers, skin pale.

"Do things," I say, almost near laughter. "How old are we?"

"Seven years younger than me," Lo says swiftly like he has comebacks on speed dial. "And I was censoring myself for my sister. I could definitely be cruder if you'd like. Would you like that?"

Wow, he's pissy today.

"No," I snap. "Got it. Loud and clear. All of you can have sex, but we're celibate." And I realize my mistake as soon as I say it.

"No, sweetheart, you get to be celibate just like me and Lil," Lo replies with a half-smile and all. That's right—Lily and Lo are not allowed to have sex for the six weeks after Luna was born. Since

Luna Hale came into this world at the end of November, Lo still has some time left with just his hand.

"Lo," Willow mutters, "we don't get to see each other that much." Translation: we never usually get to have sex.

Lo cringes like Willow said the untranslated version. "Fine," he concedes sharply.

"We'll be quiet," I tell him. But he's already waving me off with a hand and walking into the house.

Willow and I exchange a look before breaking into laughter. It's cut short when Ryke ascends the stairs, reaching the deck with Coconut jumping excitedly beside him.

His eyes hit Willow. "Dad was just on the phone. He said he's been trying to call you."

The air deadens, and the wind suddenly picks up.

Ryke's brown eyes carry confusion. "Why is he fucking calling you so much?"

Willow shrugs. "We talk every week about school."

I guess that's not a lie. Shit, I hate that she has to lie to them. But I am glad that she's not alone in this secret. She has me.

Ryke rubs his lips. No gloves on. But he hardly looks cold. "You need to be careful, Willow."

She nods. "I know."

His warning stays with me, even after he leaves.

15

WILLOW HALE
Age 21

Sitting against the frosted windowpane, I read a hefty *Fundamental Accounting Principles* textbook. The next semester starts in January, and I want to get a head start on the reading material. Last semester was tough enough, and my housing issues only makes studying harder.

I spend most days in the student center "quiet zones" and rarely go home. According to upperclassmen, the business courses only get more difficult from here.

Fire roars in the warm, spacious living room. The lake house feels as big as a lodge with vaulted ceilings and balconies that overlook robust leather furniture, wooly rugs, and the stone fireplace.

In the corner, wrapped gifts sit beneath a real fir tree, recently chopped. No ornaments hang on the branches because no one

178

bothered to redecorate. The first fully glammed-out Christmas tree had a hidden nest of spiders.

It was a whole holiday fiasco.

I flip a page and hear the distant cries of a baby.

Must be Luna Hale or Eliot Cobalt, both newborns. The media is rampant with "baby fever" articles about Rose and Lily. Mostly, I think they're trying to determine how many children Rose and Connor will have.

The Cobalts want an *empire*, and right now Rose is pregnant with baby number five. But truthfully, I don't know what constitutes an empire. Five? Six? Fifteen?

I mean…I can't imagine fifteen Cobalt babies. That's…a lot.

Cries grow louder.

From the other side of the window nook, Garrison lifts his head from his laptop. He glances up at the tier of balconies. Hearing the baby wails too. When he drops his head, his eyes meet mine, and his feet rub against my feet. His black wool socks caressing my mustard-yellow ones.

My lips slowly rise. Not much can beat these quiet moments with Garrison Abbey. Sharing company and doing normal everyday things together.

"Do you ever think about babies?" Garrison asks suddenly and abruptly.

"Uh…babies…like the small kind?" Oh God…

What other kind are there, Willow?

Garrison licks his lips, a smile forming. "I mean, we can talk about the *big* babies in the house, but I think Lo has already taken a lot of our time this trip."

I match his smile. "Sorry…I think all functions shutdown at the word *babies* when referring to my life. I'm rebooted now."

"And?" he asks.

"And…" I take a deep breath and nudge my glasses. "I never thought much about them before. I've just been focused on getting into college, paying for college, and now trying to survive college." I close my book and hug the hard binding to my chest, thinking. "But I want the traditional route, I guess. Marriage. Then maybe a baby."

"*A* baby." Garrison emphasizes the singularity of the sentence.

I shrug. "One seems like a good start…or end…or I don't know. What do you think about babies?" Our eyes search each other deeply and eagerly, but my body roasts from head to toe. We rarely discuss *after* I graduate and what lies beyond our early twenties. I still have five semesters left in college, and those upcoming years seem like a millennium.

"Marriage first," he says into a nod. "Then a baby, maybe."

"*A* baby," I repeat his emphasis.

"One," he says, definitive. "Siblings are…" His Adam's apple bobs, swallowing hard.

His brothers.

He's cut all three of them completely out of his life. He never talks to them. Rarely talks *about* them. They're just gone, erased from his world. For good reason. But so much pain remains. Scars on bone buried under muscle and skin.

He lost his brothers.

I found mine.

But I did lose someone, too. "My sister," I say softly, remembering. "I tried calling her this morning." Back in Maine, my family still has a landline home phone.

Garrison frowns. "I thought you were done trying."

I squeeze the textbook harder to my chest. "I guess, now I am," I mutter. "She picked up and told me not to call. She said the holidays are for family and I'm not a part of hers. That if I wanted to talk to our mom, I should call her directly."

But I wanted to talk to Ellie.

My ten-year-old sister.

I've invited her to the lake house for holidays. Lo is her half-brother, but she has no interest in ever knowing him or accepting the olive branches I've held out. Ellie blocked me on social media, and every time I dial my mom, she's short with me. After I say *I love you* at the end of the call, I wait with bated breath just to hear my mom say it back. Sometimes she does.

So there's that.

"Damn," Garrison breathes out, gaze flashing hot. He strokes the side of his foot against mine in comfort. "Your sister still sounds like a brat."

I shake my head. "I deserve it."

"You don't," he says, no hesitation.

I force down the giant lump in my throat, eyes burning. "From Ellie's vantage, I chose a famous brother over her." I blink back raw sentiments. "From anyone's vantage, I chose Lo."

"That's straight bullshit, Willow," Garrison refutes, his heated gaze sinking into mine. He wears his conviction like another tattoo, ink seeping indelibly. "You chose *answers* that your mom wasn't giving you. You chose to reconnect with a brother she kept from you." He leans forward, forearms on his bent knees. "You weren't making a choice between Ellie and Lo. And your mom should be explaining *that* to your little sister—who's eleven-years younger than you. But she won't, and that's fucked up."

I bite my bottom lip, thinking this over. I'm not sure I can release the guilt I feel.

I'm not sure I ever will.

Is my mom painting me as a villain to my little sister, so Ellie won't follow after me and leave her all alone in Caribou? Or is my mom just taking a backseat and not helping mend the burnt bridges between her daughters?

It's not my mom's job to heal the pain I've caused by leaving, is it?

That's my burden and my remorse to bear.

Garrison studies my face. "I get it," he says. "There are times during the day that I think maybe it's my fault I didn't try harder for a *better* relationship with my brothers. Because it's easier thinking you had some control in the situation. When in reality, there's *nothing* you or I could do to repair what was already fucking gone. They're gone, Willow. And we have to be okay with that."

My eyes redden, emotions battling to surface.

Garrison places his computer on the floorboards, and I set the textbook behind me. We scoot closer, my left leg dangling off the nook's seat. His right leg does the same, and we bend our other knees. Squeezing close. Only a sliver of space between us.

I rest my chin on my knee, and I whisper, "She's alive, but sometimes it feels like I'm mourning someone who died."

He presses a kiss to the top of my head and murmurs, "I know."

"No siblings," I say, agreeing with him from before.

His aquamarine eyes fill me up and he nods silently. "But our kid will have plenty of cousins."

Our kid. Hearing him say that pulls a smile out of me. "And they'll be her or his best friends."

"For sure," Garrison nods.

We look around the lake house and listen to the softened baby cries. Those children will be the cousins to our faraway future child.

As our gazes meet, his fingers dip under my soft sweater. His hands slowly skim the bare flesh of my hips. I tingle and light up from the affectionate touch, but this conversation races my pulse.

Wading into new waters with Garrison is like taking a broken flashlight into a cave. It's terrifying, but I trust in both of us to walk in the right direction.

"If you want a baby in your future," Garrison says, "does that mean you want to get married…eventually?"

Marriage…

I elbow up my glasses and hold onto my bent leg, my pulse hammering. I'm afraid we won't be on the same page for this.

"Eventually," I say, and then I blurt out something, wanting to be as honest as humanly possible with Garrison. "Or soon."

He solidifies.

I pale. "I mean, not soon *soon.*"

"You said soon," he rebuts. "You meant soon."

"I meant soon-ish."

He doesn't remove his hands off my bare hips. It's a good sign that I haven't completely scared him off. "What's soon-ish?" he wonders. "Before you're twenty-three?"

Twenty-two is already fast approaching. A little over two months away. And maybe I'll grow older and think that's such a young age to be contemplating marriage and babies.

But I left home at seventeen. I moved across the world at twenty.

My life has been a series of big challenges, and I've begun to realize that I might not be as adventurous as Daisy Calloway. I might not jump off *literal* bridges, but I have my own adventures. My own big metaphorical plunges into the unknown.

I, Willow Hale, am a risk-taker. A challenge seeker. I see that now. I feel it deep in my bones.

And I want someone with me, always, to face risks together.

I want Garrison. For as long as I can have him.

Forever, I hope.

But I'm not sure he wants those same things: Me. Forever.

Ever since I left Philly, he's opened an escape-door, something to jump out of in case our relationship goes sour. I don't blame him for that, but it's harder to know exactly where his head is at.

"Maybe not *before* I'm twenty-three," I answer Garrison. "I'd still be in school."

He glances at the textbook I set behind me.

I just ask, "Have you thought about marriage before today?"

He shakes his head, and I don't know why but that sends pain rippling down my chest.

Have I dreamed about walking down the aisle towards Garrison? Maybe once or twice lying awake in my dorm with nothing but my thoughts to keep me company. They were just thoughts though—I never went so far as to torture myself by looking up wedding dresses or rings on Pinterest. I'm not such a fool.

Garrison watches me crumple into myself. Head down, fingers grazing the threads of my mustard-yellow sock. "Willow..." My name sounds different in his voice. Almost choked. "Hey, it's not that I don't want to get married. It's just that with everything—I didn't think that far ahead."

"I understand," I say softly.

It's not like I ever thought about *babies* with him before now. Or rather, *a* baby.

His hands rise from my hips to my ribs, as though trying to reach my heart. "I thought you'd break up with me by now," he admits. "And maybe if I was a stronger person, I'd just have broken up with you last December. You deserve someone else who—"

184

"I deserve you," I snap at him. Pain in my chest radiates everywhere, clawing down my skin, but I'm holding onto his waist now, not letting go. "When will you start believing that?"

He shakes his head, eyes bloodshot. "I don't know." He removes one of his hands from my body to push away the longer strands of hair that've fallen in his eyes. "Maybe I never will, and then what?"

"Then I'll keep reminding you," I say, confident about this future.

He laughs. "Every day? Sounds fucking exhausting for you." He stares me down, straight in the eyes with this raw plea like *just let me go. For your own sake.*

I won't let him push me away.

"The only thing that's exhausting is reading this." I reach back and lift up my textbook. "Who knew accounting could be this dull?"

"That bad, huh?" He removes the other hand off my frame as he steals the book and then flips through the pages. We draw closer, our knees knocking together.

"I'd rather listen to TV static for an hour than read another sentence," I mutter under my breath.

His eyes flit up to me, able to hear my quiet voice.

He'd tell me if he couldn't.

Silence strains as he focuses on the text, flipping more pages. Snowflakes flutter peacefully outside, windowpanes frosted from the cold, and soothing crackling sounds emit from the fireplace. But nothing helps stop the tension that builds around us.

Garrison doesn't look up from the book when he finally speaks. "Maybe you don't realize how bad of a boyfriend I am because this has been your only relationship."

It feels like he yanked out a sword and wedged the blade into my stomach. My face crinkles. So what if my firsts have come later in life?

PRESENT DAY

He's never taken my innocence as naïveté. I'm *not* naïve. I understand that Garrison is my first and only relationship, but I don't need to date other people to know that this is a complicated relationship. Not a bad one.

I can't pull words from my lips. They're stuck in the back of my throat.

He looks up, meeting the hurt in my eyes, but he continues anyway. "I just want to make sure that you get what you're saying— wanting to marry me someday *soon-ish*."

"I obviously don't want to marry you, if you don't want to marry me," I say, those words almost a whisper under my breath, but he's close enough to hear them.

He shakes his head. "Of course, you're all I want, Willow, but that doesn't change things."

"What things?" I ask, my chest on fire.

"I'm the only guy you've ever kissed," Garrison says. "I'm the only guy you've ever slept with. And, fuck, there's a part of me that feels like I'm stealing you from experiencing...from doing... from..." He can't finish. Anguish lances his face.

My hands tremble, and I don't have the book to hold onto, so I hug my arms around myself. Holding on. *Hold on.*

"You'd want me to kiss other guys? To have sex with them?" The thought brings nothing but sickness and a pressure that compounds on my chest.

"Jesus, *no*. The thought of you kissing another guy..." He grimaces. "...I can't even..." His face twists more, and then he reaches for my hand.

I let him take it. He doesn't mention the trembling. He just laces our fingers together. It calms me for a second.

Garrison inhales. "All I'm saying is that I know you think I'm special because I understood that you didn't like to be touched, and I waited...and was patient. But there are other guys who'd do the same. I'm not special. I'm not the only guy who'd fall in love with you."

"Do you honestly believe *I* could fall in love with someone else?" My brows pinch, confused. So fucking confused. "You are special to me, Garrison. How can you not see that? It's not just the touching. It's who you are. Every part of you, even the parts you hate. I love those, too."

He runs his thumb back and forth atop my hand. His eyes pin to mine, carrying more worries. "I can try to see it," he tells me. "But I need to hear you say the other words, out loud. I just need to hear it, Willow."

"Which ones?" I wonder.

"That you're fine *never* knowing what it'll be like to kiss another man. To have him touch you here." He slides his free hand up my thigh, my leggings feeling thin under his palm. I breathe in, welcoming his touch, only his touch. His fingers are millimeters from my heat, but he stops short. "You'll never know what it's like to have another man's fingers in you. Another man's dick." He says those words without shying, without breaking my gaze.

"Good," I say in response.

"I need to hear you say it," Garrison says. "Please."

"I don't want to know what someone else's lips feel like," I tell him. "I'm happy never knowing what another dick feels like. Looks like. Smells like—"

His lips lift with mine.

I continue, "I don't want someone else's fingers in me. I don't want another set of eyes on my naked body. It literally makes my skin crawl even imagining these things. I only want you, and you're worthy of me. Do you understand that?"

A tear slips down out of his eye, but he brushes it away as quickly as it came. "I'm sor—"

"And you can't be sorry because I'm glad you're making me do this. I'm glad this is happening, okay? We need to *remain* honest with each other. Always."

His chest rises and falls heavily, and this is where we should reunite.

Kiss.

But tension still strains.

"What do you need from me?" Garrison asks, knowing he's wedged an invisible force between us.

"I need you to tell me that you won't leave me because you think you're not good enough," I say. "I need you to believe that you are. And maybe you can't give me that now, but one day."

"I won't ever fucking leave you," he tells me like those words are already cemented down.

But he'll push me away, force me to be the one to leave him. I know this—it's why the second part is so important.

"Do you believe that you're good enough for me?"

"Have I ever believed that?" he counters.

No, I don't think so.

I say, "Maybe you're just forgetting that I'm not as great as you think." I lower my voice. "Not only did I take money from my dad— which I said I'd never do—but I'm lying to Ryke and Lo about it. That's not exactly Girl Scout levels of good."

His lips lift into a big smile.

I pale. "What?"

"You're cute," he tells me. "You think lying to Ryke and Lo is this enormous crime against humanity, but it's fucking normal. People lie. I've done a lot worse. You wanna compare?" He winds an arm around my shoulder, and his eyes ask, *can I?*

I nod.

And he tugs me onto his lap, my legs naturally spreading open and weaving around his waist. I hang onto his shoulders and ask, "How do you know I've never spray painted someone's house? I could've had a rebellious streak back in Maine."

His brows rise. "I would have *definitely* already heard all about that." He tucks a loose strand of my braid behind my ear. "There's no way you wouldn't have gushed about spray painting houses and streaking down the roads."

"I never said anything about streaking." I blush just imagining doing something that brazen.

"I embellished your embellishment."

The fact that we're so different—his past muddled with bad deeds and mine relatively spotless—is what causes most of our friction. Whoever said opposites attract, well, they were right, but they forgot to mention how many strings are weaved and knotted between that attraction.

We're complicated, but as long as we're together, I don't care what we are.

I reroute to the earlier point. "It is a big lie, though," I say softly. Keeping this from Ryke and Lo is difficult, and I don't know what's worse: them finding out Jonathan gave me money to bury the footage of the fight or them finding out I kept it a secret in the first place.

"I know," Garrison nods, not downplaying the situation. "It's a big deal."

16

GARRISON *ABBEY*
Age 22

Two months pass in a blink. Willow and I keep the secret, and Jonathan isn't brought up much at the Hale house, making it easier.

It's also been two months since I've seen Willow in person, which is starting to get to me. We've talked about marriage and babies and begun to map out a future. Doing that has changed me a little bit. I want what we imagined together. One baby. Marriage. *Soon-ish.*

God, I want it.

But it's not going to happen if we can't see each other for months on end, so I came up with a plan.

And it could go really bad. It's what I know as I wait for 3 p.m. to hit at Cobalt Inc.

No, I'm not quitting. Willow would probably break up with me on the spot if she heard that I quit to move to London.

It's something else, but I'm nervous as hell because if Connor rejects this, then I'm not sure what I'll do. I don't have a plan B.

Maybe I should have a plan B.

"Abbey." Keith struts over and stops at my cubicle. Cobalt Inc. hired him after his internship ended, and Keith, along with his team, was awarded a humongous bonus after their Valentine's marketing push paid off. Some sort of magnet keepsake thing.

I don't really care. My job isn't in the "magnet" sector, so I don't cram my brain with useless shit. But their giant cock-sized bonus is all anyone will fucking talk about. And if he starts yammering on about it, I may just check out early.

"I'm busy," I tell Keith.

"This won't take long." He adjusts his Rolex, a gift from the CEO as part of the big dick bonus. "I heard from Diggy that you have an appointment with Connor at 3 p.m., and I need it."

I narrow my eyes. "Why in the hell does Ryan Diggins like that you all refer to him as *Diggy*?" Ryan is Connor's assistant, and honestly, I don't talk to him much.

"Because it's cool as shit, just like him, and you'd know that if you showed up to any of the company parties." He taps the top of my cubicle wall. "You're missing the point."

"Yeah, totally missed how you want my appointment time," I say, sarcasm on my tongue. "Went right over my head."

He lets out an aggravated noise. "Look, you don't even need to schedule a time to see Connor. You could walk up to him at any point. Hell, you live on his *street*, Abbey. You could knock on his door if you wanted to, and he probably wouldn't think that's weird."

He's right. Connor wouldn't.

But I wanted to do this the professional way. It's a professional matter.

"Sorry, man," I say. "It's not happening."

Keith glances at my mini-fridge. "You still need someone to grab you lunch and dinner from the caf? I've got you covered, no extra charge this time."

His offer almost makes me smile, not because I'm going to take it. But because I don't need it. "Thanks, but no thanks. I actually bring my lunch in to work now."

I make a sub sandwich every morning when I pack Maximoff's snacks for preschool. I took care of it once for Lily and Lo when they were both running late for work, and they've let me do it ever since.

I enjoy helping out, especially since I'm not paying them rent, and Lo would barely accept a check for groceries.

Keith rubs his eyes. "Abbey. There's only a short window of time I have leverage for a raise, and you have one of the only available appointment slots—"

"It's not available," I cut him off. "I have it."

Keith slowly blinks. "I've got blow."

Jesus. "Then you should be going into his office begging not to be fired," I snap. "Connor hates drugs." At least, he doesn't want his employees on them. I would know, I've had to take a fucking drug test every six months since I failed my first one. They've all been negative since.

"I didn't say I use them," Keith whisper-hisses. "But it's good leverage for the assholes who do in here." He says *leverage* and I hear *blackmail.*

I raise my hands. "I don't want a part of your bullshit." There's a reason I enjoy my division existing of one person: *me.*

"Then give me your appointment and I'll be out of your hair," Keith says. "You won't have to talk to me. Otherwise…" He reaches for the empty rolling chair, about to pull the thing over and park his ass next to me. Probably for eternity. Cobalt Inc. is infested with annoyingly persistent type-A pricks.

"*Fine*," I concede. "Tell Ryan you can have my time."

Keith grins. "You'll need to call Diggy yourself. He doesn't trust anyone in the building." *No shit.*

"Fine," I repeat. "Just leave."

He goes to pat my shoulder like we're bros—I abruptly slide my chair away. "Don'tfuckingtouchme," I snap so caustically and quickly it all slurs together.

His eyes widen. "Shit, sorry." He raises his hands. "Christ." He strolls away from my cubicle, and my pulse beats rapidly and *hard*. Like the Road Runner wields a sledgehammer inside my body.

Get a grip. I run a hand through my hair and grab my phone to call Ryan and take care of this. I'll just have to find another time to talk to Connor. But it has to be today.

LATE EVENING HAS ARRIVED, THE END OF THE workday, and I'm on Connor's imperial floor of the high-rise. The CEO is shutting down his computer. Packing up his things.

It's a huge risk to approach him right now. More than one prick has already been reprimanded for trying. I loiter near the glass office, just watching each sorry bastard get rejected. Leaving with their tails between their legs.

And Connor doesn't even yell or raise his voice. He just uses a bunch of words that makes you feel like two pounds of shit.

Still…I approach him.

Heads swing, other high-level employees looking my way. Bodies rotating. I feel more on display than when paparazzi shove cameras in my face.

Connor locks his office door behind him and notices me with a quick glance. He's casual, almost unsurprised that I'm here. Even though I go out of my way to *avoid* him at work.

Before I can say anything, his confident stride is aimed for the elevator. "Let's talk on the way home."

I think that's his way of offering me a ride.

I shake my head. "I drove here—"

"Your car will be fine in the parking deck overnight." He's still walking, brisk but casual. I keep pace beside him.

"You want me to ride in your limo with you?" I'm having a hard time processing this, but I should be able to by now. I'm living with his brother-in-law.

Connor cocks a single brow at me. "You're being impossibly daft today."

I stop short just as he enters the elevator.

He braces a hand on the door, keeping them from closing on me. "You don't want to ride home with me. Fine. But this conversation will have to take place in a home with four children under the age of five. When I say it's extraordinarily loud in there, just remember I'm not the hyperbolic one."

Now he's inviting me to his house...

An older employee passes us, eyeing the interaction. I do something really dumb and look over my shoulder. A handful of employees are craning their necks to watch us, and I'm about to get special treatment. It's fucking obvious.

Right now, I just don't care.

This is for Willow. For us. That matters more to me than whatever anyone else thinks.

I enter the elevator with him. Doors slide shut. On the way to his limo, he talks about his kids—Jane, Charlie, Beckett, and Eliot—like

I'm his friend. Happiness flows from every word like these little beings are the center of his whole world, and for a guy like Connor who bars most people from seeing his emotions, it's a privilege that he lets me see this.

It makes it easier for what I'm about to ask.

As soon as we're in the limo, he passes me a water bottle from the cooler. "We should be commuting together," he tells me. "It doesn't make sense for you to drive now that we work the same hours."

"I like my car."

"It's not a matter of like. It's called efficiency." He rests a finger to his temple and looks through me. "Let me give you an example you seem to need. You wouldn't have to make appointments with me if we have extra time to talk on our commute. And without appointment times, you won't have to worry about being hassled during your day."

My face scrunches, not understanding how he knows about my conversation with Keith today. "How did you...?"

Connor arches another brow. "It's my company. I hear everything." He uncaps his own water bottle. "And most of my employees think they're sharks. As soon as Ryan told me you had an appointment today, I knew one of them would try to bite."

I smile, realizing something. "You don't call him Diggy."

"I only use his nickname to his face," Connor says and then studies me like he's adding something up. "You remember Faust?"

Faust...

I couldn't forget that place even if I tried. I lasted a good four months before being kicked out. But that boarding school—that's the same one Connor attended, long before I graced their doors.

"*Fortunately* for me," I say dryly, "Faust is embedded in my brain."

It's an all-boys school. And I mostly hated it for that reason.

I lean my head back and stare up at the limo's ceiling. "You were something like a legend there," I add. "Everyone talked about you." And these were students that didn't even go to school with Connor. Just heard the same old stories passed down.

"I'd ask if they said good things, but I already know that answer," Connor says, confidence laced in arrogance. He sets his water bottle in the cup holder. "You flunked out of Faust for a reason, Garrison."

"Yeah," I snort. "Because I wasn't smart enough." Those guys all spoke three different languages, were tutored in math before they could talk, and had proficiency in at least one musical instrument. They were blue-blooded social climbers with something to prove, and I couldn't hack it.

"No," Connor refutes. "It has nothing to do with intelligence. More than a few idiots stood beside me at graduation." He props an arm on the seat cushion, facing me. "You flunked because you didn't belong there. That school isn't designed to uphold boys who love things other than themselves."

I loved Willow.

I missed Willow.

Every day I was there.

I think about how Faust is a boarding school, cut off from friends and family in the middle of fucking nowhere New York. Most of the guys I met seemed perfectly happy being away. No one missed for anything.

They just wanted for everything. They wanted money and prestige and that billion-dollar glory.

I just wanted my girl.

My best friend, the only friend I came to care about. Who'd turn into the single most important person in my entire life.

It's funny because if I asked Connor what he wanted when he was at Faust, I think I'd know what he'd tell me.

"I wanted it all."

I'm not sure where Connor is going with this, and honestly, I'm too in my head to even stare at his blue eyes. So I divert my gaze to the window.

Lamplight from Philly streets glows softly outside in the dark night.

Connor continues, "Cobalt Inc. isn't Faust. The things I value now are not the things I valued when I was seventeen. You belong at my company."

I know Cobalt Inc. is different than Faust. I don't feel miserable at work. The people are okay. Keith is annoying but harmless. Being around people who are driven and care about their goals is good motivation to keep going. And it's kind of nice seeing the same faces every day.

But I'm going to change that with what I'm about to ask Connor. I'm going to change everything.

My chest tightens. Maybe Connor knows something is wrong and he's trying to prevent me from quitting. *I won't quit…not unless he says "no."*

The quiet only lasts a couple seconds before I break it. "Before I ask you what I need to ask," I say, caging a breath. "I need to know something."

He waves me on.

"Your kids are cute now, but they're going to get older and not be perfect, you know. So what happens if one of your sons grows up to be something like me: flunks out of two prep schools, inks his body up, smokes and vandalizes houses in your neighborhood?"

Connor doesn't break his gaze from mine, but he's stone-faced, nothing passing through his calm, impassive exterior. And then he says, "I think we already know how that story plays out."

I just shake my head, thoughts spinning.

"You hired me because I can code," I say. "Because I was Willow's boyfriend."

"I hired you because I saw potential," he refutes. "If you believe anything else then you're wrong. Not uncommon. I'm sure it's a natural state that you're learning to live with." He runs a cool hand through his wavy brown hair. "You're in my limo right now because I like you. Despite the fact that you can't seem to enjoy your own company."

Fuck, man.

I rub at my eyes. "I have to ask you something."

He grins a blinding grin that makes me feel the size of Skittle. "So you've already said." His calming gaze softens. "I'm still waiting."

I take a tighter breath. *Let's go, Garrison.* "Willow's everything to me." Her name brings comfort and strength and I continue on. "She's more than a girlfriend. It's like code. She's the script on the program, and I'm nothing but a blank screen without her." I exhale a sharper breath. "And it's not like I haven't learned to be happy on my own in Philly and persevere or whatever. I have. I know I have, but she's still all the way in London. She'll be there for years, and the longer we're apart, the more I get in my head and ruin things. So I just need to see her more." I extend my arm to the limo window. "I can program over there. It's not a problem. I'm just asking for like *one* week every month to telecommute. That's all."

I drop my arm and massage my sweating knuckles, breath like lead in my lungs.

Connor is unreadable, brows arched. Lines crease his forehead, but I don't think they're from confusion.

I feel like shit asking to telecommute not just down the street, but a whole country away. Because I'm asking for more when Connor has already given me everything.

"So you want me to give you a week off every month when I don't even know what you're working on," Connor says. "You do know how that request sounds?"

"It's not one week *off*," I counter quickly. "I'll still be working."

"But I'll have to trust that you're working. If you're not coming into the office, I can't see you on your computer coding every day."

Shit, this is going bad. I rake fingers through my hair. "Look, I know how it sounds."

"Outrageous. Outlandish," Connor says, tilting his head. "And so you also must know that if I grant your request, it's out of nepotism and nothing more—"

"I'm okay with that," I cut him off.

Connor stares at me, still impassively, still unreadable. *Shit.*

I shift uncomfortably on the leather seat. "Until tonight, I thought I got this job out of nepotism," I admit. "It's never stopped me from going to work. It won't stop me from putting forth all my effort." Feeding on that bloated leech one more time won't bother me.

My boss just shakes his head once.

My nerves ratchet to a new degree. "Connor—"

"I won't grant your request," he says calmly, casually, like he's not just ripping apart my entire world. I also zone in on his words.

Won't.

It's not that he *can't.* Because he can. He just doesn't want to.

I look away. Out the window. As pain starts shattering my chest, my ribcage, my fucking heart. *I can't see Willow.*

PRESENT DAY

How long will we be apart? *Forever.* It fucking *feels* like forever.

Unbearable doesn't even cut it. And fuck me, for putting all my hope and desire and utter want into this one thing. Because losing something I never had shouldn't feel this devastating. This *crushing.*

"Garrison," Connor says softly. "Understand that I'm doing this for your own benefit."

That gets to me.

I swing my head and choke on a bitter laugh. "My benefit?" I say in disbelief. "Unless it benefits me to feel *miserable,* then I don't see how this has anything to do with me." I clench my knee with a shaking hand. "You know what. I qu…" I can't finish those words. They're sawed off by something inside of me.

I blink hard, pushing back more emotion.

Connor watches me with tranquility that should calm me but it's setting me on edge. "I'm not trying to push you to quit, Garrison. I don't want that. Neither do you. But if I let you go to London seven days out of the month—*every* month—you will quit."

I don't see how I will. "You don't know that."

He raises his brows. "Four words I don't hear often." His lip lifts. "I know you. I know that you lead with your emotions, not your head. And if you're in London for seven days, you'll email me asking for another day overseas. It'll turn into telecommuting for eight. Then you'll ask for another week. Fourteen days will turn into twenty-one. And then by the end of the year, you'll call me to say that you want to stay there permanently. Because given the choice between Willow and this job, you will choose Willow. So I'm not giving you the choice. I'm allowing you to have both while you still can. And one day, you'll thank me for it."

I grind down on my teeth. Pain leeches everywhere, all doors shutting from me to her. No way there. No escape or passageway.

"You don't trust me to stay seven days in London and come back?" That's what I'm getting from this.

"No, I don't. And if you thought about it more, you might not trust yourself either. Just ask yourself which would be harder: not seeing Willow for months, or having to leave her every three weeks?"

I finally understand what he's saying.

Either way I'm fucked. But at least in one scenario I get to see her. Hold her. Comfort her. But Connor already told me I don't get a choice. He made it for me. That hits me.

"This decision," I say. "It's not from my boss, is it?"

Connor rolls up his sleeves slowly. "No, it's not." He glances my way. Blue eyes hitting mine. "It's from your friend."

The limo rolls towards the gated neighborhood, slowing down. My head is heavy. Spirits dulled. I don't know what to do. How to see Willow more often. How to make this relationship work. If it's even possible anymore. I try one last thing. The good ole *guilt trip*.

"Yeah, and what happens if we break up because we can't see each other?" I ask. "You're going to be an accomplice to that, you know. If you're such a great friend, you could have helped." I feel like utter shit as soon as I say the words. Fuck, why even go there?

Because I'm me.

Because I could.

Connor stares through me like I'm made of glass. "If you break up because you can't see each other, then your relationship is too fragile to last anyway. Blame me, if you'd like. But it will be sorely misdirected."

Fragile.

I feel fucking fragile.

"How do I make us stronger?" I ask him since he seems to have all the fucking answers.

Connor smiles a soft, genuine smile. "First step is believing you already are."

The words roll around in my head for a couple minutes. Until the limo slows to a stop at Loren's house.

There's one more thing I need to ask. One more unanswered question that's going to plague me. "One more thing," I say. "How well do you know Jonathan Hale?"

Connor's expression flatlines, impassive again. "Better than you. Why do you ask?"

I shake my head, already coming up with a roundabout answer. "I just don't know him that well, I guess, and if Willow and I are going to be more serious, I figure I should start trying to." It's not untrue.

Jonathan and I have met briefly at group events—Lo usually invites him—but for the most part I don't interact with Jonathan. I always figured it was because my relationship with Willow was slow and new, but her relationship with her dad was even slower and newer. It never bothered me that she didn't want those two things colliding.

But now that I know Jonathan used to say shit to Lo that my brothers used to say to me...it changes things. I should know my girlfriend's dad better, and I want to make sure he's not going to screw her over with that loan. I can't tell Lo and Ryke about it, so I'm going to try to protect Willow myself—with everything I have.

Connor eyes me. "Jonathan Hale is a person you're better off not knowing. Especially you."

"Why?"

"Because unless you share his last name, you are collateral damage in his life. And you have the most unenviable position."

"What's that?"

"You're dating his only daughter."

17

GARRISON *ABBEY*
Age 18

"**P**lease go outside, Garrison," my mom begs from the kitchen. The smell of freshly made Christmas cookies wafts through a ten-foot archway—straight into the nearby living room where I sit.

The ornately tufted furniture, including this taupe couch my ass is on, should honestly exist in *Downton Abbey*. Not Pennsylvania.

I don't pause or turn off my game console. "Maybe later," I say, more than disinterested.

During Thanksgiving last month, my mom guilted me into joining Davis, Hunter, and Mitchell for a "brotherly" dinner in the city. Unbeknownst to our parents, they really planned some Turkey Pub Crawl thing, and with my fake ID, I could accompany them.

On paper it sounds great. Bonding time! Brothers! Beer! But I'd rather cut off my big toe than be around Davis and Hunter when they're piss drunk.

I tried to leave when Davis started shoving my head with "brotherly" aggression, but Mitchell convinced me to hang around for a while longer. I should've bailed because at the next pub Hunter waved a hundred-dollar bill in the air. The consequence, of which, gave me a bruised kidney and dislocated shoulder. For a whole week, it hurt to piss.

I still hear my brother's stupid voice and see that pub and those fucking men.

"I'll give anyone a hundred bucks to fight my brother here," Hunter decreed, smacking my shoulder hard, cash between his fingers.

I jerked out of his hold. "No," I spit. "Fuck that."

Davis laughed and chugged his beer. Mitchell hung back, texting some girl he started dating.

Hunter raised his voice to announce, "He needs to become a man." He slapped my face hard enough to leave a handprint. "You're such a little cock-sucking pussy."

I shoved him towards a high-top table, and Hunter almost flipped a switch, his eyes flashing murderously. I raised a hand for him to stay put. *Don't touch me. Don't touch me.* My heavy pulse could've busted my eardrums.

Davis laughed more. "Why are you running away from him?" he asked me. "Push back."

Fuck that shit.

"Don't be a pussy."

If I pushed back, I would've ended up with two black eyes. Hunter outsized me, and he had Davis on his side.

"Going once!" Hunter hollered at the crowds, still waving the bill. "Twice!"

Two leather-clad biker guys—way older than us—exchanged a look and then hopped up from their bar stools.

"He's joking," I said, backing up towards the exit.

"I'm not," Hunter retorted. "Come on, Garrison. Fight back!"

"Be a man," Davis shouted, hands cupped around his mouth like he was cheering me on. Pumping me up. Encouraging me. To be a man.

Bullshit. I shouldn't have to bear my fists in a drunken brawl to be called a motherfucking *man.* They're the immature ones.

I kept backing up.

The bikers followed me. Step for step. Not slowing.

Not hesitating.

"I don't want to fight!" I screamed furiously and desperately, hoping someone—anyone—would hear me.

The bikers sped up to a sprint, and I spun around to run away. I fled the pub, reached the sidewalk, and was kicked in the lower back. Right in my kidney. I fell to my hands. The man grabbed onto my arm, and my shoulder popped out as I fought against him. Freeing myself, I ran as far as I could and then spun back around to my parked car.

I offered to be the "designated driver" for that reason. I wanted an escape in case I needed one. My brothers found their own way home. Took a cab or something. And then they complained to our mom how I bailed on them.

I didn't tell anyone what really happened. Not even Willow, who was having a shit time in Maine already. Apparently, her little sister threw a tantrum about Willow moving away to Philly, and she refused to be in the same room with Willow the entire holiday.

Willow ate Thanksgiving dinner alone in her bedroom—but not totally alone. I Skyped her and ate my pumpkin pie at the same time.

In the living room on Christmas Eve, I pound harder on my game controller, crushing my score on *Street Fighter II*. My mom already guilted me into leaving my bedroom, but I'm not going to be guilted into any "brotherly" activities this time.

"Garrison." My mom says my name in a way that completely obliterates each syllable with disappointment.

I know how to fix it. How to make her happy. To vanquish her disappointment, I have to become more like my brothers, but I can't be them. I couldn't live with myself knowing I was just like Hunter or Davis or even Mitchell.

And that says a lot because I've barely been able to live with myself as is.

My mom appears in the archway, cupping a wine glass with lime seltzer. I try not to make eye contact, but she still lingers. "I know they'd love if you joined them."

They brought their lacrosse sticks from college, and they're playing in the yard, tossing the ball between the three of them.

"I'm busy," I say flatly, my stomach starting to knot. My character Ryu is knocked on his ass by Dee Jay. I lose the first round and try to concentrate on the second, but I'm overly aware of how many times I blink, trying to shake off my mom's presence and request.

I lose the second round.

In the short break, I grab the remote and turn up the volume, wishing she'd take the hint and leave me alone.

My mom struts over and snatches the remote from my hand. She turns off the TV.

I stare flabbergasted at her. Usually she stands passively off to the side and lets me be a spoiled, ungrateful shithead.

I angrily toss my controller aside and slouch back on the couch. I pull up my hood and wait for her to lecture or yell or whatever she's decided to suddenly do.

"Your brain is going to rot from these video games," she says like all moms do, but if life were different—if sports were perceived as "lesser" and video games were seen as something "more"—would I be the beloved son then?

"I have a brain?" I say, sarcasm thick. "No way."

Sadness softens her eyes, and she sweeps over my dry tone. "Your brothers are home only a few times out of the year. Why can't you at least visit with them?" It's the same question. The same fight.

The same request.

Over and over, it never changes. I don't think it ever will. "I don't like them," I tell her seriously.

"They're your *brothers.*"

I lift my foot on the couch cushion, arm draped on my kneecap. It takes me the longest second to find words. I want to shut down, but if someone can help me, I think it'd be a parent. A mom.

"Mom, it doesn't..." I shake my head and meet the confusion on her face. "Just because we're brothers doesn't *absolve* them of all the shit they've done to me."

"They love you. I know they do. They tell me all the time." There she goes, defending them again. She fights tears and cups her drink with both palms. Like she's afraid her hands will shake and she'll drop the glass.

Love. Is how they treat me called *love*? I'm not making this up, right? They truly suck. It's not all on me. *It's not my fault.*

Is it?

I hate questioning myself. I used to do this as a little kid. Hell, I do it when anyone points out a bruise. *It's just what brothers do.* Now that I'm older, I'm starting to see it's not cool or right or something I want in my life.

It's why I avoid them.

"Garrison," she pleads.

I hang my head. "You know Thanksgiving?" *I'm going to puke.* I have to tell her though. I need to tell someone. I don't want this weight on my chest. "I only bailed on them because Hunter paid two guys a hundred bucks to fight me."

I brave a glance, and she only looks befuddled. Like she's trying to figure out a defense for her three sons. Like she's their trial lawyer.

"Were they drinking?" she asks quietly.

"Yeah, but…" *What does that fucking matter?!*

"I'm sure they were just playing around. You're too sensitive about things, Garrison."

"The man dislocated my shoulder," I say, my throat burning raw. "*Mom.*"

She sighs like I'm being unnaturally troublesome.

"I didn't want to fight," I say. "I didn't want to even be there—"

"Then maybe you should try to be happier when you're with them. They won't give you such a hard time."

I'll never win with her.

After a short pause, she adds, "Your father says you need thicker skin, and you know, he's right. The real world isn't kind either."

"Whatever." I shut down now and grab my controller. As she sees me about to play my game and ignore her, she lets out this wounded noise, between a sigh and a cry.

I stare blankly at the paused television screen.

She sniffs loudly. "I just…" Her voice breaks. I *always* make her cry in the end. "I just don't know what to do anymore, Garrison."

She acts like it's her fault that animosity exists between my brothers and me, but then when she has the chance to make it better, she puts it all on my shoulders. *Go spend time with them. Befriend them. Please.*

"You could've gone to jail. Just like your friends," she starts listing my terrible decisions, bad actions, awful characteristics. "You got tattoos without me knowing. You were found drinking vodka at school."

Once.

I was caught *once*, but I'd done it plenty more times.

"You've been in trouble for vandalizing, backtalking, and cutting class." She takes a pause to wipe a fallen tear. "But thank God you didn't break into Loren Hale's home that night. Watching your best friends get in trouble—I thought that was your wakeup call. But you're still skipping school. You still won't listen to me or your father. You won't speak to your brothers. Nothing has changed."

Everything has changed.

I'm certain that I'm not the same anymore. I feel overturned. Inside-out. I'm fighting against the person they want me to be and fighting *for* the person I am inside.

The fact that she can't even see this makes me wonder who she's even looking at. Does she even know me at all? Or is she still resenting the fourth son she was given?

I shrug and turn on my game.

With the biggest sigh, she retreats into the kitchen, and I numbly scroll through *Street Fighter II* characters. Every so often, I hear her sniffle like she's silently crying. I make no effort to comfort my mom, and it's fucked up.

I realize that, but a sick part of me wants her to feel as terrible as I do. How many times have I shown her bruises from Hunter's fists and lacrosse stick? How many times has she repeated my father's phrase, *get thicker skin?*

My skin could be superhumanly thick, and I'd still get bruises and broken bones. What then, Mom?

From the kitchen, I hear the sliding glass doors swoosh open and my oldest brother's voice.

"Mom, what happened?" Davis asks. "Why are you crying?"

Shit.

I quickly pause the game and shut off the television. My brothers must file into the kitchen, one-by-one, because they each say a few consoling words while my mom blubbers something about wanting me to be *with* the family this Christmas.

"He's with us, Mom." Davis comforts her easily.

While I stand, I catch a glimpse of my mom through the archway, dabbing her tear-streaked cheeks with a dishrag.

"We'll make sure he doesn't run off to his friends," Hunter says.

My nose flares, and I find myself waiting—to listen in. I should move. I should go. I know better.

"It's not like he has many friends left around," Mitchell says with a short, uneasy laugh. Like he's not sure if anyone else will love his joke.

Hunter does. "That's right." He laughs mockingly. "What does he have, like one friend?"

"You can't be surprised he lost them all," Davis says to our mom, I think. "If he's not on his computer, then he's on his cellphone or playing video games. The kid is socially inept."

I clench my teeth so hard that my jaw aches. This is what my family really thinks of me. A socially inept, lazy delinquent. Whatever.

"Mom, don't cry," Davis says.

"I'll get him to play two-on-two basketball with us," Hunter reassures her. "You can be sure of that."

I start high-tailing my ass towards the back staircase. I can lock myself in my bedroom or crawl out the window and sit on the roof.

For how big Hunter is, he's somehow deceivingly fast. Right as my foot touches the first stair, he fists the back of my hoodie and yanks me backwards.

My pulse explodes, and I spin frantically out of his hold. But my movement forces me back into the living room.

"Where are you going?" Hunter sneers.

"To the moon," I spit back, frozen by the couch. I'm afraid to try and pass his body to reach the stairs.

Davis and Mitchell linger behind me, their irritations bubbling. All three have the same short haircut, and they wear nearly the same clothes: Polo shirts and khakis.

My oldest brother takes a couple steps towards me. "Can you please be cooperative? For once?" He lowers his voice to a whisper. "Mom is in the kitchen *crying* because you won't spend time with us. Do you even care?"

I shake my head and blurt out, "I don't care." I come across like the biggest punk ass, and where Davis and Hunter grow red, Mitchell sighs like I'm digging my own grave.

"Come on, Garrison," he says.

I'm not going to be like *Mitchell*. I'm not going to pretend that Davis and Hunter shit gold. I hate them too much to embrace that illusion.

"Let's just go play basketball," Mitchell says and nods towards the backdoor.

I pull my fallen hood over my head. "I'm not going outside."

Davis rolls his eyes like I'm being unreasonably stubborn.

Hunter pokes my back. "You need the fucking sun."

I flinch away from him, and Hunter sidles to our other brothers.

Davis scans the living room furniture, the black television screen, and my game console and controllers. "We can play video games then."

A chill rakes my arms, uneasy and hesitant. "Yeah?" I wonder, watching Mitchell grab an Xbox controller and take a seat on the tufted chair. I was playing on the Sega Genesis console, but I have different ones hooked up to this television.

"Yeah." Davis raises his brows. "Mom wants us to hang out together."

Hunter collects the remote and switches on the television. *It's a trick*, my brain screams at me.

They seem nice all of a sudden. And they want to play video games. I could suggest N64 and go really classic with Mario Kart.

It sounds *almost* like fun, which is why I move towards the couch.

"Where are all the football games?" Davis asks, fiddling with a wooden box of Xbox games beneath the coffee table. I'm about to crouch and help him—*wrong move*.

Hands grab me around the waist and throw me to the couch. Laughter pierces my fucking ears, and weight crushes my back.

Hunter *sits* on me. I grit my teeth and try to rise, but Hunter is really heavy. He braces a hand on the back of my head, pushing my face into the slit of the cushion. It smells like moldy cheese, and my lip brushes something harry or furry or whatever the hell...

All I hear is laughter.

I try to push him, and he catches my arm with his other hand and stretches my limb hard across my shoulders. Imprisoning me.

"Get off!" My voice is muffled and lost in the cushion.

Hunter pushes my head more forcefully, extending my neck. *God, my neck hurts.* I try to kick out, and Hunter goads me, "So now you want to fight? Or are you still going to run away like a little bitch?"

"Fuck you!" I yell, my face hot.

"What was that?" he sneers and purposefully sits *on* my head now. "I can't hear you, Garrison. Speak up."

I can't breathe.

I can't breathe. I can't fucking breathe. I choke for air. *Stop. Stop. Stop!*

My pulse thrashes off course, and if I can just…*not panic*, for one second. I try to tame my fear. *I'm okay. I'm okay.* My heart rate slows a tiny fraction.

I gasp into the cushion. A little air fills my lungs. I think I can breathe.

"Are you playing video games now?" My mom's voice nears the living room, and Hunter slides off my back. I immediately lift my head and then sit up, gasping for more air.

"Yeah." Davis squats beside me and rubs my head playfully. Like we're best friends.

My mom smiles from the archway and gives me a look like *see, Garrison, they'd even be willing to play video games with you.*

I shut down again, numb inside.

She says that she'll be visiting Rachel's mom a few streets over and to call if we need anything.

With that, she leaves.

And Hunter wrenches me onto my stomach again. *Shit.*

"Get off, dude," I snap, shoving and kicking him as hard as I can. Hunter curses at me all the while, calling me names, shouting his usual commentary about me needing to grow up. Fight back. *Be a man.*

I almost roll onto the floor, but Davis grabs me by the neck. So painful that I concede like a wounded animal. Hunter pushes me again, my stomach thudding to the cushions, and then he plops hard on my back.

I wince.

"Move over." Davis passes Hunter a game controller, and he makes room. Davis sits on my upper back, his controller in hand. Their weight crushes me.

In more ways than one.

18

BACK THEN – December
Philadelphia, Pennsylvania

GARRISON ABBEY
Age 18

Merry Christmas :) Meet up later to exchange gifts?

I send Willow a Twitter message and descend my staircase. Already dressed, I'm scheduled for an afternoon shift at Superheroes & Scones, and I'm dying to get there. Holiday traffic has been crazy, but on Christmas Day, I actually expect it to be slow.

Either way, I'm ready for the distraction.

A second later, a notification buzzes my phone.

@willowaIIflower: Tonight?

It's a date. I almost hit send, but I shake my head and delete those words and retype: perfect.

We're not a couple. We're still just friends, and honestly, I can't lose Willow to anything else. I'm already cursed and shit at most things, including relationships. But—I don't know. Sometimes, I think about kissing Willow.

What it would feel like. Where I'd put my hands. How I'd make her comfortable. What she'd be thinking—since it'd be her first.

Her lips look soft.

Shit. Stop thinking about that stuff. *Just friends.*

Sometimes I even wonder if we could be more. After Christmas, this next stretch of high school will be our last. We're seniors, and she's getting more comfortable at Dalton. The timing seems better than it was.

Each step down the stairs, I feel more strongly about this. About her.

"Garrison, honey, can you come here?" my mom calls from the formal dining room.

I dip into the kitchen and pass through another archway that leads to the dining room. My mom, in a form-fitting red dress, sits next to my dad at a glossy oak table, decorated with a red winterberry centerpiece and Christmas garland.

I rarely see my dad. If he's not working, then he's at home with his face in an iPad or computer. Checking stocks, making business plans—or maybe he just surfs the internet. I wouldn't know, would I?

Today, though, he has no electronic nearby. In a powder blue button-down and expensive slacks, he's seated beside my mom. My dad has always looked a lot like a fifty-something Jeremy Irons. Not physically intimidating, but his resolute expression is less friendly than my mom's gentle one.

I have no idea what this is about. Ever since my mom joined this new church when I was ten, we don't open presents on Christmas

Day. We attend church on Christmas morning, but it's always insanely packed, so we have to show up hours early just to secure a chair.

Because of that, we open gifts on Christmas Eve.

Even last night, I was reminded that I'm on the "naughty" list for my family. Good to my dad's word, he didn't allow anyone to give me a single gift. Punishment for vandalizing Loren Hale's mailbox and then squirting punch on some of Lo's roommates. His sister-in-law, Rose Calloway, was one of them.

I didn't fight the punishment because I deserved it.

Watching my three brothers open their gifts while I was left with nothing—that was the least of what could've happened.

"Take a seat." My dad points to the chair across from them.

I don't sit. My gaze falls to a white envelope on the table's glossy surface. I stuff my hands into my black hoodie. "What's this about?"

"Sit, please." He never raises his voice with me. Doesn't physically hit me. Doesn't do much of anything.

He's not a big force in my life like my mom. His million-dollar tech company leeches his time and energy, and this holiday, I only saw him smile once. When Davis asked him to throw a football outside.

He found the time to play a quick game with all three of my brothers.

I sat out, and maybe he's here to lecture or scold me. But what's with this envelope?

I teeter, stuck between sitting and standing, not knowing which to take. I decide to sit before he repeats the request.

Maybe this isn't about me. Maybe they've decided to split up or something. Uncertainty binds my lungs, and I'm not even sure how I'd feel about a divorce.

My mom slides the envelope closer to me. "This is your Christmas gift." She seems more nervous than excited.

I reluctantly pry the envelope off the table. Frowning, I haphazardly tear open the paper and find a sleek brochure inside.

FAUST BOARDING SCHOOL FOR YOUNG BOYS

I stare blankly at the photograph. A gothic New England building landscapes an upstate New York setting. Teenage guys in suits smile and hold books, some propped near a large stone statue. It looks like an Ivy League institution made for teenagers preparing for life at Yale, Princeton, and Harvard.

My stomach sinks the longer I stare.

"What is this?" I mutter under my breath, already knowing the answer in my heart.

"We've pulled you out of Dalton Academy," my dad says. "You're not excelling there, and after what happened to your friends…" He clears his throat. "Your mom and I think that Faust will provide the proper guidance you need to finish your senior year."

My brain flies a million miles a minute. Too many questions. I unleash one thing. "What about lacrosse?"

I grimace at my words. Seriously? Lacrosse.

I don't even *like* lacrosse. I pause, that sentiment not sitting right in my stomach. *I hate lacrosse.* I don't know if I really do. The thought of not playing feels strange. Feels wrong. I frown deeply. I'm not sure of anything anymore.

"Unfortunately, Faust doesn't have a lacrosse team," my dad tells me while giving my mom a look. This might've been a point of contention in their final decision.

My stomach cramps, and the brochure crinkles under my tight grip.

Mom scoots forward, hands outstretched towards me. "But Faust has a chess club and cross-country, tennis, and even swimming. You can be involved in plenty of other sports or an extracurricular."

I'll graduate at the end of May. I *barely* have any school left. It's not like I can just walk onto the cross-country team. It's not like I want to.

Why are we even discussing sports like this is actually happening? Who'd make their kid switch schools in the middle of their last year?

"This can't really be up for discussion," I say dryly.

"Of course it is," my mom says. "You can choose whichever sport you want. We won't make that decision for you."

"No," I snap. "*Not* sports. I'm talking about *this.*" I wave the brochure that's battered between my fingers, no longer crisp and pristine. "Faust. I don't get a say?" I hear my own rebuttal before my parent's launch theirs.

You're rich. You've been given everything in life. You're complaining about a boarding school, you asshole. You spoiled, ungrateful brat.

Guilt tears up my insides. I feel like I have no room to complain. No room to scream or throw shit. No room to combat, even though I'm eighteen.

"No," my dad says, voice strict. "Your opinion doesn't matter. Not after you've made this year hell for your mom and me."

I owe them. That's what I feel. I owe them for the nice clothes. For this house. For the cash, the car, the food and electronics.

For putting up with a piece of shit like me.

I hang my head and listen to my dad continue on.

"You need to leave this neighborhood," he tells me. "The friends you grew up with, this atmosphere, it's all been toxic for you. Think of Faust as a fresh start. A new school, new city, new home." My dad lets out a breath like the weight of his troubles has finally lifted. "This is a good change, Garrison."

Months ago, maybe I would've agreed. *A new start.* Away from all my ex-friends. Away from my brothers. Away from this place. It would've seemed like a lifeline, but now I feel as though my parents are cutting the only rope that grounds me to soil, to earth.

I'm doing better.

I've made a real friend, something I've never had.

If I leave Philadelphia, I'll be leaving the one good thing in my life.

Willow.

My throat swells. "There's nothing…" I swallow and start again, "Isn't there anything I can do or say to change this?"

"We've already withdrawn you from Dalton Academy," my dad explains. "You start Faust in January. You'll leave in a week for orientation and to move into the dorms. It's done."

A week.

A week.

The timeline rings shrilly in the pits of my ears.

After the shock wears off, I stuff the crumpled brochure into the envelope and wedge the thing in my pants pocket. "Is that it?" I wonder.

My mom and dad exchange a look, and then she sets her concern on me. "Are you sure you don't want to talk about it a little more?"

"What else is there to talk about?" I ask. "It's a done deal, right?" I stand from the dining room table. Not wanting to speak to them anymore. They've already proven how much power they have over my life.

Dazedly, I walk out of the dining room. Neither my mom nor my dad tries to call me back, and I snatch my blue Dalton Academy beanie off a coat rack and find gloves. I think about grabbing my skateboard from the garage, but I abandon the board and just walk.

Faster and faster.

Out the front door. Down the driveway. Past the mailbox.

I pick up speed until I jog towards Loren Hale's house. Cold rips through my lungs, and I welcome every bit of it.

Slowing to a stop, I see the red brick house and Christmas decorations. Nothing extravagant. Lights twinkle on a few trees and a wreath hangs on the front door.

As I veer up their driveway, I slip on the slick cement. My worn boots have god-awful traction, and before I face-plant, I grab onto a decorative, iron deer. My heart hammers.

Not just from almost falling.

I hope Willow is here. *She has to be.* One good thing has to happen today.

I need to talk to her. Face-to-face. Right now. Get this news off my chest.

I carefully climb the porch stairs. Crusted ice and snow covers the doormat, and I stand stiffly. Hesitantly. Not that many people in this house even *like* me. After my birthday—where Willow stayed at my house later than she intended—I can't even tell if I'm on Loren Hale's good side anymore.

And there's a *huge* chance I'll be met with anyone but Willow.

Everyone who lives here:

Lily Calloway

Rose Calloway

Daisy Calloway

Loren Hale

Connor Cobalt

Ryke Meadows

Maximoff Hale (six-months-old)

Jane Cobalt (seven-months-old)

So yeah—a lot of fucking people are inside.

Willow planned to stop by here for Christmas, so I hope she's made the drive already. No cars are in the driveway, but maybe she parked in the large garage.

I'm afraid I'll have to interact with Rose and Connor.

Loren and Lily—I don't mind as much. They're still celebrities, untouchable in a sense, but they've been cool towards me. Daisy is nice to Willow, but I don't really talk to her—and Ryke is whatever.

He says *fuck* a lot, and every time I meet his eyes, I remember all the videos I've spliced together with his *fucks* and uploaded to YouTube.

After scaring his girlfriend with paintballs, I wouldn't be surprised if he secretly despised me too.

I take out a cigarette, thinking about lighting it, but I just pinch the cig between gloved fingers. I reach for the buzzer.

As soon as my finger lands on the button, the door swings open. *Shit.*

Scorching yellow-green eyes pierce me, and I curse my luck. Rose Calloway, of everyone, has opened the door.

I stuff my fists in my black hoodie, and I watch her assess my Dalton Academy beanie. Why am I even wearing it? I'm not returning to that school. The fact sinks deeper and deeper and burns a hole in my stomach.

Rose doesn't personally know me. She probably has no idea how old I really am or that I regret *everything* I did to her and her sisters. We've shared space, maybe once, during Halloween. I didn't say anything to her directly, I don't think.

"Uh..." I stammer and glance at the thin, gangly girl trying to squeeze through the doorway. Lily, my boss at Superheroes & Scones. Right now, she's the only friendly face.

The tension unwinds in my shoulders when I spot her, but then Rose cracks the door and shifts her body into the space. Blocking Lily from escaping.

"Rose," Lily whines.

"I got here first," Rose says to her sister, but her glare remains fastened to me. Nerves rake my spine, and chills creep up my neck.

This might've been a terrible idea. I should've messaged Willow first.

I realize Rose is waiting for me to speak, so I clear my throat. "We haven't met." I outstretch my gloved hand. *Polite*, I congratulate myself. I'm doing alright.

"Yes, we have." Every word is frosted, and her grip tightens on the door.

I drop my hand.

"You and your friends sprayed red punch on my *infant* daughter and me with a water gun."

It was a joke. A fucked-up joke.

They're celebrities. Characters on television. In magazines. They weren't *real* to us. That changed for me, and I can't tell you the moment it did.

They're more than just famous. They're human. I should've seen this from the start—I'm at fault here. I know that.

I didn't break into their house because I knew there were babies and people inside, but that decision doesn't free me from all the other shit ones I made.

I don't know how to make amends for everything I've done. I'm not even sure I deserve forgiveness.

I'm not sure I want it.

But I have to say something. "It was stupid…I'm sorry…" I chew on my chapped lip. Did that sound sincere? Sickness churns inside of me. I am *so* fucking sorry.

Nothing I say will ever make it better.

So I think, *just get to the point, Garrison.* "Hey is Willow here?" I ask. "I know she's a distant cousin, or whatever…"

Please be here.

"She's coming around at two!" Lily tells me from inside.

"Lily," Rose chides, opening the door slightly. Lily's round face comes into view, and I notice how she tries to narrow her eyes at her older sister—but the glare looks goofier than menacing. Now that I think about it, I've never seen her chastise a single Superheroes & Scones employee.

"Willow and Garrison are co-workers," Lily explains to Rose.

And then Loren Hale appears. Hand on the door, he pries it from Rose's grip. The door slams into the wall. I can suddenly see everyone.

Daisy is sitting on her boyfriend's shoulders near the staircase, and she bends her head beneath the mistletoe, kissing him upside-down. They're in their own world. Thankfully not really noticing me.

Loren places a protective hand on his wife's waist, and she scoots near him. While he focuses on Lily, I wonder, *do you hate me like everyone else now?*

I wait for Loren to acknowledge my presence. Not afraid. Not afraid. *I'm not afraid.* His dark glare drives through me, and fear curdles my stomach. I can't even lie to myself. Can't even pretend like I don't care what he thinks of me.

I do care.

Loren's glower carries ten times the potency of Rose's—and her pierced eyes already make me want to run off this stupid porch.

Voice sharp like daggers, he says, "A co-worker doesn't show up on Christmas morning looking for another co-worker."

Dropping my gaze, I scrape the icy stoop with my boot. "Does this mat say *welcome* under here? I can't read it with all the snow."

"He's funny," Rose says in a way that makes it seem like I'm decidedly *not* funny. She looks one second away from seeking revenge for the punch I sprayed on her and her daughter.

"You're scary, no offense." I cough into my glove and check over my shoulder, hoping Willow will show up early. I can still wait for her here. I look back. "You're going to make me invite myself in, aren't you?"

"Yes."

My eyes flit to each of them. Rose looks fucking murderous. Loren glares like I'm the shit on his shoe he scraped off yesterday but then reappeared today.

Lily is literally the only one that smiles, but it's a weak, pitying smile. I don't deserve anything more than that.

Each one intimidates me in their own right, but I'm trying to form words. For Willow. I'm trying.

Open-mouthed, my breath smokes the cold air. "I just...I wanted to tell her that..." *I'm leaving.* I let out a weak laugh, my eyes burning. Whatever. It's all fucking over anyway, right? What's done is done. It's Christmas. I don't need to shit on their holidays too. "Never mind, it's fucking stupid..." I turn to leave.

Rose snatches my hoodie, and she physically tugs me backwards.

"What the fuck?" My heart lurches, and I spin around and quickly jerk from her hold, my pulse skipping. I frown deeply, not understanding Rose Calloway at all.

She should want me to leave. Not force me to stay.

"Are you asking her to prom?" Rose questions. "Because this is the most pathetic proposal I've ever seen. You need flowers, first of all."

"I'm not asking her to prom." My voice shakes. I can't help it. *Prom.* I won't even be at Dalton for prom. The cold realization ices me over more than the winter air. *Just let it out.* I lick my lips and say, "I came to tell her that I'm leaving, and I guess to tell you too." I nod to Lily.

No more Superheroes & Scones. Shit. I glance at Loren, but he still glares, so I avert my gaze to the ground.

"What do you mean?" Lily asks.

Rose stares off in the distance, over my shoulder. Not paying attention to me anymore. She must see something because she grabs a coat from inside and slips on a pair of boots in the doorway.

I focus on Lily. "My parents handed me my only Christmas present this morning: a white envelope." Bitterness dries out my voice. "I…*they* are withdrawing me from Dalton and sending me to this boarding school for 'proper guidance' to finish my senior year."

Rose passes me on the stoop. Honestly, I'm glad she's set her sight on someone other than me.

"Where is it?" Lily wonders.

"Upstate New York," I say. "Faust Boarding School for Young Boys."

Loren lets out a long laugh. Maybe he's happy I'll be out of his cousin's life, but maybe not. I don't know. His humor is too dry to read.

"Lo." Lily elbows his waist. "Don't be mean."

My brows furrow, not understanding either of them. "What?"

"Connor went to Faust," Loren explains, "and from the stories he's shared, you won't last a day." He flashes a half-smile.

"Great," I mutter and stare harder at the doormat. Coming here was a terrible idea. I just feel ten thousand times worse. I turn to leave, but his voice stops me.

"Hey," Loren calls out. "You want to see my si—cousin Willow, right?" He stumbles over his words, but I zone in on the Willow part. Hope floods me for a second. Will he really let me stay?

"Yeah." I nod over and over. "I just need to tell her about Faust. It won't take long."

Loren drapes his arms over his wife's shoulders, pulling her back against his chest.

I swear she kind of unconsciously grinds her ass against him, but I try not to pay attention. If Lily noticed that I noticed, I think she'd be embarrassed.

Loren appraises me head to toe. "Connor says that I'm too forgiving—that you'll probably bite my hand off if I extend it again."

I won't. I open my mouth to say the words, but a lump lodges in my throat. I feel sick.

Loren grimaces at me and then shakes his head. "Christ, I must be a masochist." He nods to me. "You want to wait for Willow, then you have to do it *outside*. You're not allowed in the house, got it?"

"Got it."

"He'll freeze," Lily combats.

"Then he freezes, Lil. It's his choice."

Lily pouts like he's being a dick.

Loren steals a kiss, and her cheeks flush bright red.

"You're deflecting," Lily notes.

"Me?" Loren feigns surprise. "Not me, love. I would *never*."

I clear my throat, and Loren's face contorts in a multitude of emotions. Landing on irritation. Lily starts advocating for me again—for maybe two or three full minutes—but it only makes Lo more and more pissed at *me*.

"I'll be fine," I suddenly say. Pulling my beanie further down, I warm my ears. "It's why God created fleece-lined pants, right?"

"Let's not give God credit for clothes," Connor says as he saunters up the porch steps. He barely glances at me—like I'm not worthy of that attention. His face is utterly unreadable, but when he leans towards Loren, he says loudly, "He's not coming in the house."

Connor wanted me to hear that.

Loren nods. "He'll be by the pool."

At this, Connor disappears further into the house. He looks back as Rose picks up her confident gait and reaches his side. Hand-in-hand, they're gone.

Lily detaches from her husband and races after them screeching, "What happened?!" Whatever that's about, I'll probably never know.

I'm lucky I've even been standing here this long.

Now it's just me and Loren Hale.

Do you hate me? I want to ask, but I'm afraid. I can admit that this time.

Another dry smile dimples his cheeks, but then he nods towards the outside. "I'll show you to the pool around back."

"I can find it myself."

"Just follow me." He shuts the door and then passes me on the stairs. His sharp glare could kill.

I trail after him. So much rams into my brain. I can hardly make sense of anything, and some of which, it's not my place to share. Like the guys at the mall, the ones that fucked with Willow because they personally hate Loren Hale.

I have no idea what'll happen when I leave Willow alone at Dalton.

It makes me nauseous thinking about it.

I just realize I'm in the backyard, and Lo opens the pool gate.

I step inside. "I know you don't like me," I tell him, "but will you make sure that she's okay when I'm gone?"

Lo freezes mid-step to the snow-covered lounge chairs. "I already do now." His expression says, *combat me. Tell me I'm wrong if I really am.*

I nod a few times. "Okay."

"If you know something—"

"Forget it, dude. I'm being an idiot." I blink rapidly and stare up at the blue sky. "You hate me, right?"

I think I'm whiplashing him with my emotions, my swift detours, and he's having trouble following my frantic mental pacing. "What?"

"You *hate* me," I say, more forceful.

He laughs once. "Most of the goddamn *universe* is on my shit list." With that, he walks off to the backdoor. Leaving me conflicted and confused again.

I'm standing knee-deep in the unknown.

19

BACK THEN – December
Philadelphia, Pennsylvania

WILLOW MOORE
Age 17

I find Garrison waiting for me by Lo's covered pool. Quickly, he stands off a lounge chair as I approach. The cold bites me through a puffy blue jacket and thin mittens, but I'd rather bear the winter with Garrison. A minute ago, I entered through the garage, and Lily said he was out back. And he had something important to tell me.

"Hi," I breathe softly, scanning his solemn features.

Garrison cracks a few knuckles, on edge. "You should sit." He brushes snow off another lounge chair for me.

My heart knots. Tension builds so rapidly, and for some reason, I feel like an avalanche looms in the horizon. I take a seat, and he sits on another lounge chair across from mine.

Garrison licks his lips and then says, "So…I saw your Tumblr post this morning."

Is that what he wants to talk about…or is he just sidetracking?
"Oh yeah." I cup my cellphone in one of my mittens. Last night
I made a post about *X-Men: Evolution*, the animated series. It was
short and went something like:

Me: *sees Storm creating lightning and thunder*

Me: *Strike me down, beautiful eternal goddess!*

I nudge my glasses. "You didn't think it was lame?"

Garrison looks like he wants to smile but can't. "Have you
checked your notifications lately?"

I slowly shake my head and remove a mitten. Fingers cold, I tap
on my cellphone screen and pop open Tumblr.

I immediately smile. "You didn't…" *He did.* Garrison made gifs
of Storm from *X-Men: Evolution* where she wields lightning with her
mutant powers. And he tagged me in them.

There aren't many gifs of the X-Men animated series to begin
with, and to have this—and know personally who made them, and
that he made them for me—means more than he realizes.

"Merry Christmas," he says. "Really, though, that isn't the present
I meant to give you."

My smile fades, remembering that I forgot my Christmas present
for him in my Honda. "I left my gift for you in my car. I didn't know
you'd be here right now, but I can go get it—"

"Don't worry about it," he says quickly. "I left mine for you at
my house, too."

So he's not here to exchange gifts then. In the lingering silence,
I fit my mitten back on, and Garrison hunches forward, winded by
his thoughts alone.

"Can I tell you what I got you?" he asks. I think he must want to
kill time before he unleashes the important news.

I nod tensely.

His blue-green eyes flit to my ears. "I know you always wear the star and the bat studs, but I thought you'd like something X-Men related."

My lips stretch into an uncontrollable smile. "You got me earrings?"

"Yeah." He pinches his fingers to try to describe them. "They're X-shaped, with a circle around them." *The X-Men symbol.*

A guy bought me a gift. A guy bought me *jewelry*. It's hard to believe. "It's perfect," I say without thinking.

Garrison tilts his head. "You haven't seen it yet."

I push up my glasses again. A nervous tic now. "I don't have to see it to know it's perfect." *Because you bought it for me.* "I made you something, so it's probably not as good, and it's sort of…"

His lips try desperately to lift. "What?"

"Dorky?" I cringe at myself. "It's a scrapbook." I just come right out and spoil it. Maggie would hate if I spoiled her about anything, and thankfully, she's been texting me again as I update her on my life with Garrison Abbey.

I have to constantly censor myself with my friend from Maine, so it's not as easy talking with Maggie as it is with Daisy Calloway. Recently, I've noticed that more and more.

"A scrapbook of what?" He takes off his beanie to rake his hair out of his eyes.

Sometimes (a lot of the time) his whole bad boy persona intimidates me. The tattoos, the skillful sarcasm, and the good looks, but he's *always* gentle with me. He has his mother's innate and natural beauty, I've realized, and of the pictures I've seen of his father, he has his hair and lean build.

"Um…it's hard to explain. I'll just have to show you later." My heart races at the sight of this person I really, really like. I can't imagine not crossing paths with him. Not becoming friends. I can't imagine my life without the company of Garrison Abbey.

He stares at me for a really long moment. His deep expression practically caresses my cheeks. My chest swells, and I find myself covering my face with my mitten-hands. I feel undone, and we're just sitting across from one another.

"Hey," he whispers, his voice low. Garrison stands and brushes off more snow beside me, and then he takes a seat next to me on the lounge chair. Our shoulders touch, but good nerves swarm me.

Nerves that shout, *"Carpe Diem, Willow Moore!"*

"I'm glad you're here," I suddenly say what I feel. Instantly, the bottom of my stomach plunges and I regret every single word.

His features contort, breaking and breaking. Then he rubs his face with his gloved hand.

I hold onto my knees. Lost for words. I can't look at him, but I feel him drop his hand and turn his head towards me, studying my anxious face and body.

"I'm leaving," he tells me abruptly.

"What?" My voice spikes, sounding strange. I feel even stranger. Like this out-of-body experience belongs to another Willow in an alternate dimension. Not me. Not here.

Not right now.

Garrison fists the beanie in a hand. "I'm leaving," he repeats, as though trying to make sense of this too. I dazedly hear his explanation about Faust, his parents, and being forced to finish his senior year at the boarding school in upstate New York.

The news pummels me. I jinxed myself. *Moments* ago I was thinking about how I can't imagine not sharing his company, and now he's leaving? I don't just need Garrison with me at Dalton Academy and Philly.

I *want* him.

And I've never wanted a friend like this. Never yearned for a person to be next to me. Never slept and smiled thinking about seeing them tomorrow.

The more he explains his fate, in a very dry but hollow voice, I slump forward. My stomach caves, and the avalanche begins to roar down the figurative mountain that is our lives. I shield my face with my hands, afraid that I'll start crying.

Crying is hard for me in front of anyone, and he needs encouragement. Strength. He needs, *it'll be okays*. Not a blubbering, dejected friend.

My throat and eyes burn.

"Willow," he whispers, his voice raspy.

I inhale deeply and wipe my running nose. "What about Superheroes & Scones? Maybe…maybe you can work the weekends."

"…maybe," he says, not entirely sure himself. "It's not like you'll be alone."

My face twists. "What do you mean?" I meet his reddened eyes.

"Ace Davenport? He's totally into you." His face is unreadable, and his voice is too flat to make sense of.

My gaze widens, and my face keeps twisting into a wince. "That's not funny." I think I might cry now. I quickly rub the corners of my eyes.

Garrison looks genuinely confused. "He always talks to you at work."

"To tell me how I stock the shelves incorrectly," I say. "And every day, after I help a customer with comic book suggestions, he makes a comment about how I'm a know-it-all, and that I'm really some poser trying to be cool." Ace is mean to me.

His nose flares, restraining hot emotion. "Why didn't you tell me he was a dick to you?"

"I thought you knew." I swallow the rock in my throat. "You always seemed irritated by him…"

Garrison stares up at the sky, tormented by this news too. "I knew this would happen," he mutters more to himself than to me.

I shake my head. "What would happen?"

He touches his chest. "I'm *cursed*…and I hung around you long enough, and I cursed you too." His voice breaks.

"I'll be okay," I try to assure him, rubbing my dripping nose as fast as possible. Pressure bears on my chest so hard that I feel physically sick. "*We'll* be okay."

His tortured gaze sweeps my face. "Then why are you crying?" A tear drips down his cheek at the sight of my leaking eyes. Water brims over my lower lids and scalds my skin.

"I'm scared," I say the truth so softly. I wipe my face again, and he rubs his bloodshot eyes.

Garrison lets out a staggered breath and then stands up. He extends a hand to me, and I put my palm in his palm. He pulls me to my feet, our boots knocking together.

Very tenderly, he asks, "Willow, can I hug you?"

I nod.

It might be our last hug for a really long while.

Garrison tucks a flyaway hair behind my ear, and then he wraps his arms around my body. I coil mine around his frame, my arms feather-light still, but his embrace carries warmth and extra pressure that dizzies my senses.

I hold tighter than before, my fingers gripping the fabric of his hoodie. *Don't go yet. Please don't go yet.* I'm picturing my life without him, and it's so much lonelier than before.

Garrison tilts and lowers his head to whisper against my ear. "You're still my girl."

And then, without a single pause, Garrison Abbey kisses my cheek. His lips leave a fiery imprint, and my body solidifies like hardened magma.

He drops his hand to mine. I'm too stunned to speak, too sad to say how much he means to me, and too heartbroken to wish for a real kiss.

"If Ace Davenport gives you shit, you'll tell me?" he asks, and he keeps talking as he sees me nod quickly. "You have my Twitter, Tumblr, and all that whatever, but…" He shoves his beanie in his back pocket. "I know we said we like the internet, but I'd really love your number."

He's asking for my phone number. It brings us closer in a different way than we both planned. "Yeah, of course."

After we exchange numbers and add each other to our contacts, he prepares to leave. Taking a few steps back, Garrison hesitates.

I wipe my fogged glasses and then set them back on my nose.

"It's not goodbye," he says to me, as though he can't bear that idea. "I'll come back here. I promise." He takes a few more steps backwards. "If not, then I guess I'll just have to find two cans and a string long enough to connect you to me."

My heart hurts, and just as he turns his back to me, I call out, "Garrison."

He glances over his shoulder.

I don't know what I planned to say. Maybe I just wanted to stop him. To see his face. I swallow hard and murmur, "Merry Christmas."

He hears my quiet voice. "Merry Christmas."

It's the saddest holiday of my life. I lost one of the most precious gifts I've ever been given. I lost my first friend from Philadelphia.

I lost him to New York. I lost him to Faust. To a boarding school and his parent's demands. I wonder if he'll return after he's graduated. Maybe we'll grow apart. Our paths that kept crossing are beginning to diverge, and I'm really scared.

The Calloway Sisters & Their Men – Fan Page

Present Day | Followers: 88K

With Valentine's Day just behind us, it's time for another update on the Calloway Sisters & Their Men! Here's the whereabouts of our favorite flower-named sisters (plus Willow!) and their sexy AF hunks.

The Stokes

Poppy Calloway (34) & Sam Stokes (34)

Daughter: Maria (11)

Update: These two were caught out and about on a romantic Valentine's date night! They did a "sip and paint" at a local studio where paparazzi snapped photos of paint brushes flying at cheeks and arms, purposefully missing that canvas. So adorable! And such a rare sighting for these two who usually keep out of the public eye.

The Cobalts

Rose Calloway (30) & Connor Cobalt (31)

Daughters: Jane (4)

Sons: Charlie & Beckett (2-year-old twins) and Eliot (8-months-old)

Update: Rose and Connor headed to Paris with their entire family for Valentine's. #CoupleGoals. Can you just imagine being a fly on the wall in their private jet?

The Hales

Lily Calloway (28) & Loren Hale (29)

Son: Maximoff (4)

Daughter: Luna (3-months-old)

Update: No photos of Lily and Loren on Valentine's. Boo! But obviously they have good reason, since I'm sure they're staying home to be with the cutest of cute babies – Luna Hale! Don't you love that name?

The Meadows

Daisy Calloway (23) & Ryke Meadows (30)

Daughter: Sullivan (2)

Update: Daisy and Ryke took a motorcycle ride on Valentine's Day, and paparazzi were given the iconic middle finger from Ryke. Check out the gif!

The Unofficial Calloway Sister

Willow Hale (21) & Her Boyfriend – Garrison Abbey (22)

Update: As far as the internet knows, these two didn't see each other on Valentine's. Truthfully, we don't have any photos of them together for like...a whole year. Some sources say they might be broken up. It would be a little odd, if that was the case, since we do know that Garrison still lives with Loren Hale. But stranger things have happened!

What do you think? Are Willow and Garrison still together? Take the poll below!

Love you like Loren loves Lily,

xo Olive

20

PRESENT DAY – February
London, England

WILLOW HALE
Age 21

glance quickly at my cellphone, regretting popping up the internet notification—or even setting notifications for entertainment headlines. Keeping up with fandoms isn't as fun when my name appears and sends a jolt of anxiety coursing through me.

Only one day has passed since Valentine's, and already, people are speculating that Garrison and I have broken up.

A random poll on a fan site has accumulated *thousands* of entries, and an overwhelming 84% of fans agree that my relationship has failed. And I'm not really surprised a credible magazine linked this fan site as a newsworthy source.

I think back, and I know I used to be the one clicking into polls about the Calloway sisters. Eagerly feeding this machine and rumor mill. Some are fun and harmless. Others cut too deep. And until I was on the receiving end, I never really understood the gravity of those cuts.

Jokes on all of them, though. Garrison and I are 100% still a couple.

But I'm not winning any Best Girlfriend awards this morning. "Maybe the time zones mixed up everything? Are you sure they delivered?" I ask Garrison on the phone while I frantically search the messy common area.

Wine glasses and empty bottles of Sauvignon Blanc make sticky rings on the coffee table, and I toss pillows off a purple thrift store couch, then peek behind the small TV. I already received an un-rate-able, out-of-this-world box of chocolates for Valentine's from Daisy—(half the tin was espresso flavored)—so I don't know why Garrison's gift is missing.

"Nah," he says. "I'm pretty sure they were already sent to your apartment last night—your time. I got an email confirmation, and someone signed off on the delivery. So they have to be there."

I woke up in a cold sweat at 7 a.m. to his text message.

Garrison: did u like the roses? You never said anything about em

My heart sunk to my knees, and I texted back: what roses?
And then he called me.

Now I'm sweeping the tiny kitchen for a dozen pink roses and wondering if I should've taken Lo and Ryke's handout.

The offer came early this month.

My brothers flew out to London ASAP—sooner than the visit they planned and booked—after Garrison made an off-handed comment about my flat being unsafe.

I don't blame him for the loose lips. He *lives* with Lo, and he said it just slipped out.

When my famous brothers arrived, the internet went wild.

SPOTTED! Loren Hale & Ryke Meadows in London!

They were trending on Twitter, but they entered my apartment dressed in workout gear—baseball caps, sweatshirts, running pants, and Nikes—appearing more like normal men in their late twenties than billionaire celebrities.

No matter their clothing, they're intimidating. Towering with overprotectiveness as I opened the door. Concern was etched in Lo's sharp gaze and Ryke's hardened jaw.

Lo bulldozed his way in. "Is this the lock?" His glare punctured inanimate objects like the doorknob already accosted me.

"Yeah," I said softly, noticing bodyguards posted up in the apartment hallway.

Ryke was full-on brooding as he sauntered inside the flat, checking on my bedroom door.

"How many people come in here a day?" Lo asked me.

"Um…" I pushed up my glasses. "Besides my roommates, it just depends." *On party nights.* "Maybe like…a dozen…or more."

Lo looked supremely more protective. He put a hand on my shoulder as he rounded my body and motioned for security to check the windows.

All three of my roommates were in class at the time, but Sheetal and Tess texted sad gifs that they missed seeing more of my family.

The living room was still a mess from a party the previous night (one that I avoided), and I'd been trying to clean up. After a short house tour, I swept up potato chip crumbs, and my brothers talked heatedly under their breaths to each other.

Lo came forward, brows cinched with seriousness. "We need to talk." He took the broom out of my hands.

"Okay." I felt really young all of a sudden.

Ryke crossed his arms, eyes darkened.

"You're famous," Lo said flatly, like I'd never been served the fact. "*Severely* famous, Willow." This wasn't the first time his fame had impacted my living situation.

But it's different now that he's an ocean away. He can't bail me out as easily, and I know Lo has always felt responsible for me.

He's my brother.

"You have to remember that," he continued. "Every day, everywhere you go." He sighed out. "For Christ's sake, *you* should have a bodyguard—"

"I don't need one," I protested, worried it'd draw more attention. I can be invisible, but that feels less likely with a muscular shadow following me.

Lo's cheekbones sharpened. "I can't leave you in a situation where you're at risk of kidnap, rape, and *murder*."

Ryke rolled his eyes. "We can add extra locks, Lo, and a fucking security alarm."

I nodded. "I'd rather just do that..." I trailed off, noticing how Ryke zeroed in on the remnants of the party. Daisy had told him about my roommate problems, so I think he was more fixated on those.

Ryke was popular in college.

The captain of the track team.

Lo was lazy at Penn and skipped class more than he attended.

I know this from what they've told me, not just Wikipedia, but I wonder how they'd be at a collegiate party in their early twenties.

Definitely not like you, Willow. Hiding. In a closet.

"Why do you want to live here?" Lo questioned.

"My lease doesn't end until May."

Ryke frowned and asked, "That's the only reason?"

I wanted to say, *no*. That I've been having a stupendous, heart-warming time living with my friends, but it's been...rocky.

Not just between me and them. Sheetal and Tess blew up at Salvatore after his hookup projectile vomited *everywhere* in the bathroom.

He said that he hired some cleaning service, but they never showed. He left the mess too long, so the three of us ended up mopping puke for two hours.

"Yeah," I said. "That's all that's keeping me here." I looked around. "It's a good location to campus. I can make it work for a while."

Lo and Ryke exchanged a look, and then they offered to cover the cost of me breaking the lease. They'd help me find a new flat ASAP and pay the rent.

I wiped the mist behind my glasses.

Overwhelmed, because their love is unconditional. They'd do just about anything for me, no strings attached.

But I couldn't accept.

It's always been hard to say *yes*.

Yet, I've accepted a worse offer before. The one from our dad that does have stipulations and uncomfortable strings.

It's not pride that stops me from taking money from my brothers.

It's something else.

With my decision set, they flew back to Philly after we put in a security system and had dinner together. We hugged, leaving on good terms.

Now I'm racing around the flat in search of missing pink roses, and I can't help but think this wouldn't have happened if I moved.

"It's okay, Willow," Garrison consoles. "They're just flowers. I can send you more."

Palms sweaty, I switch the phone to my other hand. "You put a lot of thought into them though."

"Maybe they'll turn up. Look, don't worry about it."

I turn as Tess exits her room, carrying a khaki satchel with textbooks. Pretty sapphire earrings complement her dark-brown skin, and I'd ask if they're new or from Sheetal, but on her way out, she must see my distress. "Hey, what's happening?"

"Did you see any flowers get delivered?"

Tess shakes her head. "No, I don't think Sheetal did either." She sweeps the wine bottle graveyard. "Ugh, Salvatore left his shit out again?" She sighs, then says, "I meant to tell you, we're doing a charades thing tonight. You should join us. It'll be *really* lowkey."

I shift my weight, hotter all of a sudden.

Their idea of "lowkey" isn't exactly mine. I know because the last "lowkey" flat party involved dares and tequila shots.

"Um…" I hate rejecting their invites. I can tell they feel like they're banishing me to my room.

But I'd rather be there.

I worry the longer I live with Sheetal and Tess, the more likely I'll lose them as friends. I'm the standoffish one, and I know I should make a bigger effort.

It's hard when parties are draining and my bedroom is a foot away with comic books calling out to me.

I thought we could watch *The Flash* together once a week, but no one paid attention to the TV and they always suggest other things when I bring up movies or shows.

My new eulogy: *that anxious turtle, Willow Hale, she should've taken her brothers' offer when she had the chance.*

"It'll be fun," Tess smiles and nudges my arm with her elbow.

I think about it and then nod. "Okay."

Tess high-fives me, and then says she'll see me tonight. She has a huge advertising project that's due later today.

Once she leaves the flat, I put the phone back to my ear. "Did you hear that?"

"Yeah." Garrison sounds tense. "Why'd you accept the invite?"

"I don't want to lose their friendship," I say softly, checking the bathroom for lost flowers.

"I'm gonna be an ass for a second, okay?"

"Okay." I can't help but smile at the warning.

"It feels like you're choosing Tess and Sheetal's friendship over your grades." He knows I'm a firm B and C college student now. "You've tried the whole 'maybe I'll have fun at this party, maybe it'll be different' mantra and you always end up wishing you didn't go. So don't fucking go. If they're your friends, they should understand that."

"They feel bad leaving me out."

"So what?"

I've never really cared about being invited anywhere, and now that I receive invites, I stress about how many I can reject without being alone here in London.

"I think I need to go to this one," I tell him. "I've bailed on them too many times recently." I shut the bathroom door, entering the narrow hall. "Or...I guess I could suggest dinner at Barnaby's?"

That way, they won't care if I retreat to my room early on through charades.

What I've learned: maintaining friendships offline takes work, and I just hope that in the long-run it pays off and gets easier.

"You do have to eat," Garrison says lightly.

I want to smile. It's just harder when I miss him so much. I rub my arm, wishing he was here to draw me into his chest. I just picture my cheek on his heart. And I can almost feel the warmth of his skin. I can almost hear the soft beat.

"Let me know how it goes," Garrison adds.

"I will…" My voice drifts as I glance at an ajar door. *Salvatore's room.* Pink rose petals are strewn around the bed, and a girl's ankle sticks out beneath the sheets.

My stomach drops.

"Willow?" Garrison's voice spikes. "You okay?"

"I found the flowers," I whisper. "I'll call you back." Once we hang up, I take a breath. *Confront them, Willow Hale.*

You can do this.

I step into the room and rap the doorframe. "Hello?"

Under sheets, Salvatore groans awake, stretching an arm, while the hungover girl smashes her face more into the pillow. Ignoring me.

"What is it?" he asks, Italian accent clear.

I push up my glasses. "Those roses belonged to me, and it's okay…it's okay that you signed for them but not if you planned to destroy them and give them to another girl."

He makes a face like I'm delusional. "What are you talking about?"

"My boyfriend sent those roses." I motion to the pink petals surrounding heaps of clothing.

"The card had no name," Salvatore protests.

"Where's the card?"

He points vaguely to the nightstand.

I snatch a square card from plastic wrapping. Near torn condom wrappers.

I read the card:

For my girl,
Hope these make you smile. If a whole fandom
centered on you, I'd be your number one fan.
Miss you, love you <3<3<3

I smile so much that tears brim.

Garrison might not know it, but his love is keeping me afloat here. Every time I think of him and talk to him.

"Sorry," Salvatore says, seeing my reaction and realizing the flowers were mine. "I didn't know." He sounds sincere.

I nod, accepting the apology. Maybe easier than most would, but I'm not here to cause more friction. I just want to survive this semester.

Salvatore sits up, ruffling his hair. "Can I buy you more?"

"No, it's okay."

"Yeah, let me. It's the least I can do." He glances at the sleeping girl, and then he slips out of bed. He's buck-naked.

Oh my God.

I spin on my heels. My back to the naked man.

I saw…I saw his dick.

Salvatore grabs boxer-briefs off the ground.

"Really, Salvatore, I don't need more flowers—"

"It's not a problem, Willow." Before he comes closer, I shuffle out of his room. Putting more distance between us, and for the third time, I tell him firmly that I'm okay and do *not* need more roses. And I quickly dial Garrison and find solace in my bedroom, sinking on the edge of the mattress.

My face is burning in embarrassment.

I'm dead.

I've died. I put a hand to my forehead.

"So what happened?" Garrison asks.

"Uh…I think…" I inhale. "So I kind of saw Salvatore naked and—"

"*What?*" His voice is hot and confused. "How?"

I rehash everything and thank him for the card, but Garrison is understandably stuck on the Salvatore part.

"He's a fucking douchebag, trying to buy you *flowers* when he knows you have a boyfriend. I don't even care if they're replacement flowers—"

"I know," I cut him off in agreement.

Garrison is quiet.

I swallow my mortification. "Garrison?"

"As long as you know that his intentions are fucked…"

"I do." I exhale a deep breath.

He pauses, then asks, "I have the better-looking dick, right?" His serious tone makes me smile.

"Definitely, always."

"Yeah, that's what I thought."

I lower my phone at the sound of another incoming call. "My dad is calling."

"Right now? It's two a.m. here."

"Sometimes he calls late. I think he's lonely and has trouble sleeping."

Garrison sighs, concerned. "You gonna answer?"

"Not right now." I let the call ring out. My dad has still been on my case about an internship. Especially as my second year is coming to an end and the summer is in sight.

I'm afraid unless I follow the path he wants, he'll stop helping me with tuition. He hasn't made that threat yet, but it feels like this underlying truth shoved beneath the rug. He has power over me.

Power that I can't seem to get back.

21

PRESENT DAY – March

Philadelphia, Pennsylvania

GARRISON ABBEY
Age 22

Today is going to be a good day. It's what I think when I wake up. It's the thought I bring with me into the shower.

Good day.

Today.

March 9th.

Tomorrow is Willow's birthday, and a plane ticket rests on my desk. Waiting for me. She has no clue, but I'm taking a red-eye flight tonight. I'll be in breathing distance of Big Ben and the London Eye by tomorrow morning.

And fuck, if I'm not riding on the high.

Beads of water roll down my jaw, shower pouring over me. Heat

I place a hand on the tiled wall, and with my other, I stroke the length of my dick. Tightening my fist around throbbing veins, my muscles burning, I close my eyes and imagine Willow.

I picture the moment where I wrap my arms around her body. How she buries her head into my chest, her fingers gripping my shirt. Like I'm the safest place she knows.

We hug close for a while, and after a tender, longing kiss, I lift her up around my toned waist. She gasps against the crook of my neck, feeling my hardness against her heat.

I ache to fill her, and she's pleading for me to be closer. *"Inside,"* she cries in a breathy whimper. *"Please,* please."

She's said those words in real life before. Just like that. And remembering them now does a number on me.

I grit down, on fire. I rub myself faster in the steaming shower. Muscles pulling taut in my neck and quads. *Fuuuck.*

In my head, we're magically, suddenly, naked. *Thank you, imagination.* I press her against the wall, ass in my clutch, and I push in between her legs. Warmth wraps around my erection as I nestle deep in Willow.

She hangs on.

We kiss, and I rock and rock.

Our lips break as she lets out soft, breathy noises of pure pleasure.

Fuckfuckfuck. Pressure mounts as blood rushes down south, and I feel like a twelve-year-old boy, coming so quick. That can't happen when I actually see her. *Jesus.*

Cum washes down the drain, and I wash off with soap.

"Garrison!" Loren's voice booms through the bathroom. He bangs on the door with a fist. "When you're done dreaming of my sister, I need to talk to you!"

No idea what that is about, but thank God I came already. If Lo's trying to mess with me, he should have done it five seconds ago.

But really—it's just another day living with Loren Hale.

Oddly, I do love it.

I switch off the shower, grab a towel and quickly tie it around my waist. My soaked hair drips, water sliding down my bare shoulders. I whip the door open, and Lo is just leaning against the wall.

I give him a look. "You're seriously just waiting right there?"

Lo flashes a dry smile. "You have a problem with that? It's not like you were doing anything inappropriate in the shower."

"Since when is rubbing one out illegal in this house?"

Lo grimaces. "It's not. Unless you're thinking about my sister when you do it. Then that has been illegal since the dawn of time."

I raise my brows. "So you want me to think about a different girl while I jack off?"

He glares at me like I'm the one who started this. That was definitely him. "No, Garrison, I want you to bury this conversation into the pits of hell where it belongs."

I readjust my towel on my waist. "It's buried."

"Good. Can you babysit Moffy today?" he asks. "My dad called and wants to do lunch." I already know Lily took Luna to a playdate with Rose's son, Eliot. Both babies. Both adorable but loud as hell.

My head is spinning though, stuck on the fact that Lo doesn't want to bring his own son to Jonathan Hale's house for lunch.

I have to ask. "Is it a work lunch?"

Lo shakes his head and sticks his hands in his pockets. He looks at me like he knows where I'm going. "I love my dad, but the less he's around my kids, the better."

I feel like I need to know Jonathan Hale more than I do. To understand the man that has a grip on my girlfriend's life. Lo and

Ryke still have zero clue that he gave Willow money to pay off students. To bury footage of *my* fight.

It happened a year-and-a-half ago, and I forget about it until moments like these. When it bubbles to the surface like molten tar.

My stomach flip-flops.

Lo frowns. "I'll be back in plenty of time for you to catch your flight. You don't have to worry about that."

He knows I'm flying out to see his sister.

"Yeah, no. Of course, I'll babysit."

At that last word, a toddler comes running down the hallway. Arms flailing around him. "UNCLE GARRISON! Did you hear? Did you hear?" Maximoff skids to a stop by his dad. "Mommy said I can go to LEGOLAND!" He bounces on the balls of his feet, and in his happiness, he accidentally flings the Spider-Man toy he's holding. It hits the wall and bounces off.

Lo grins—his eyes sparkling like *that's my son.*

I've never had anyone that brings me that kind of happiness. Not until Willow. Can I even imagine a kid with her?

I don't want to try. Just another thing I can hang onto and lose, right? Anyway, we have to get through this long-distance shit first.

"He's in good hands," I tell Lo as Maximoff picks up the toy. "Take your time." Honestly, babysitting is the one thing I love doing for Lily and Lo. I'm wanted and needed here. And yeah, that feels fucking good.

SO I FEEL LIKE UTTER SHIT.

Literally.

For the past seven hours, I've been sweating so much that I ditched my pull-over *and* T-shirt. The fabric is soaked through.

Maximoff lounges on a beanbag in the living room, munching on a bag of granola bites that belong to Ryke. They taste like dirt, but Moffy seems to like them.

Granola crumbs are *everywhere*. His lap, the beanbag, the rug. And I planned to vacuum before Lily and Lo come home.

But I can't move. I feel like a hundred million pounds, and on top of that, the sound, look, and smell of granola dirt has my stomach in a blender. I fight nausea and bear down on my teeth.

My phone buzzes, and I check the text.

Willow: Birthday plans tomorrow are lowkey, just dessert at Barnaby's with Tess & Sheetal. Wanna Skype later? Let me know a good time for u

She doesn't know I'm coming. But I'll be there. Even if I have to crawl my way to London, *I'll be there*.

Sheetal and Tess, I actually do like. They care about Willow, and they've given me a second chance to make a better first impression. Knowing how much I mean to Willow.

Salvatore is still a dick.

I stare at my phone, fingers hovering over the letters. I have to give her a little bit of a white lie, since it's still a surprise that I'm flying there.

So I send a few *Gilmore Girls* birthday gifs that I made for her, all with Jess and Rory. And I text back: Definitely wanna talk on this big day. Skype me after dessert when u have time *birthday cake emoji*

I cough.

Bad idea. My stomach cramps like someone is wedging a knife into my gut. Fuck, what did I eat? I cringe as another text comes through.

Willow: not that big, only turning 22

I smile through the pain and text her: yeah and we'll be the same age again. Big bold 22.

She texts back a bunch of hearts, and then the front door swings open. My duffel bag is already packed near the stairs, and honestly, I'm ready to go. I could be half-dead on the way to the airport, and I'd still find a way on the plane.

"He do okay?" Lo whispers as he drops keys in a bowl. Eyes pinpoint to his four-year-old.

Maximoff is out. Asleep with granola on his chest.

"He's perfect. Like always," I say. "Hey, I'm gonna head out." I walk past him to grab my duffel.

He frowns. "You're forgetting a shirt." Before I can reply, he adds, "Christ, you look like shit. Garrison—"

"I'm fine," I say, cutting him off and unzipping my bag. I dig through and find a T-shirt. "It's just hot in here." I pull it over my head and stand.

"No, it's not." Lo walks forward, about to reach for my forehead to take my temp. But he stops himself quickly. Quicker than I can flinch. "Please take your temperature. For me. Because I'm betting you're at a hundred-and-one, at least, and it just hurts to look at you." *Awesome.*

"I'm totally fine, man," I say. "I think the turkey in my sandwich this afternoon might have been bad or something." Pain starts jackhammering my stomach, and I suck in a tight breath. "It'll pass."

Lo grimaces. "You'd fly commercial with food poisoning just to see my sister? You're about to spend eight-hours shitting on a cramped airplane *shitter.*"

I don't fucking care. "I'm going." I try to pass, but he steps in front of me. "Lo—"

"Take my jet." He makes a surprised face at himself. "Christ, I sound like Connor."

"Rich and pretentious."

Lo lets out a laugh, a real one. No sarcasm. "Yeah."

"Why's that funny?" I ask.

"Because I've always been rich." Lo can tell that I don't fully get it, and he's not wasting time catching me up to speed. He just says, "If you're going to shit yourself, do it in the comforts of a *private* plane."

I actually laugh now, and the act hurts, pain radiating to my lower back. *Fuuuck.* I suck it down. "Sounds like a plan. See ya."

He walks ahead of me and grabs car keys out of the bowl.

"What are you doing?" I ask, my voice softer.

"Playing Jenga," he says, sarcasm on his lips. "I'm driving you to the goddamn airport. Unless you think you can make it there on your own."

Right now, I feel like I can barely make it to the door. I'll take this handout. As long as it gets me closer to Willow, I'll take whatever I can get.

We drop Maximoff off at Ryke and Daisy's, and then Lo exits the neighborhood. Paparazzi immediately tail us. The sun has set, and darkness clings to the sky. A cameraman hangs out of a Hyundai's window and starts snapping pictures at an excessive rate.

Click click click.

Flash flash flash.

The bright light is blinding in the dark. It's dangerous as fuck. Lo barely blinks, too used to it all, and he keeps both hands tight on the wheel. He'd probably be cursing them out if his kids were in the car.

"Pretty sure there has to be a law against that," I mutter under my breath. I really don't know if there is, but I'm just glad when his bodyguard's security vehicle rides up and blocks the paparazzi van. We ride side-by-side with the Escalade.

Our car bumps over a pothole, and I grimace and try my best not to vomit all over Loren's leather seats.

Fuck.

I have a high pain tolerance, built up over the years, but this is different. A part of me just wants to crawl into the fetal position and cry. Maybe then the pain will stop.

The stabbing in my stomach is a constant companion. The knife goes in and out. In and out and death seems imminent.

I'll die after I see her.

I hang my head. Arms wrapped around my stomach. Lo doesn't talk much as he drives to the airport. But I sense him glancing at me, and he slips out his phone at a stop light to text. Probably checking on his kids.

My head spins, dizzy from the pain and I blow out steady, controlled breaths.

The car starts up again, and when Lo turns the corner, I see the sign to Philly General Hospital. Ambulances pass us, and Lo pulls up to the emergency room.

"No, no, no," I say quickly. "I'm fucking *fi*..." I put my hand over my mouth to stop myself from blowing chunks.

Lo parks and quickly hops out of the car. Not sure when we lost the paparazzi but they're MIA. His bodyguard and another big burly security guy flank him immediately.

"I'm not asking," Lo tells me as he opens my door. "So either you get out of the car, or I carry you out."

I don't have the energy to reply. I'm half here. Half gone to the pain. I barely step onto the pavement before my legs buckle. Someone yells for a wheelchair. It all feels overly dramatic as hell, and I hate it. Too many eyes on me. *Weak shit.* I hear my brothers.

Fuck.

My head is off my shoulders. Up in the clouds. I don't know how I enter the hospital, but someone shoves a blue plastic bag underneath my chin. I vomit.

"Yeah, we're here," Lo says, cell pressed to his ear. "They're bringing him back now…" I lose time and focus. Lo squeezes my shoulder, I think. So I know he's still here with me.

I'm on some hospital bed and the nausea has subsided enough for the pain in my stomach to come back full-force. I'm seconds away from curling into a tiny ball, and when a doctor comes in to check on me, I can't say much but a few moans and grunts.

A nurse starts an IV, and I hear something about *oxy.* Maybe that's just in my head though. Hopeful thinking.

All I know is that I can't die here. Not without seeing her one last time.

Everyone leaves.

That's when it starts getting easier to breathe. Only for some reason, I can only do it through my nose. Otherwise I feel like hurling again.

Lo watches me. "I don't know if you heard—"

I shake my head. I heard jack shit.

"The doctor thinks your appendix might have burst. You're going to have to get a CT scan."

Panic blisters every cell in my body. "And if he's right?"

"It'll have to be removed."

Surgery. Okay, it's alright. It's okay, I convince myself. "How long will that take?" I ask. "I can still make my flight, right? The private plane will wait for me." There's that hope.

Lo tilts his head and looks at me, deeper. "You really love her, huh?"

"Man, I just want to see her," I choke.

Lo rubs the back of his neck and glances nervously to the window. Maybe he feels for me. I don't know. I can't read him. "I want to tell you something…" He shakes his head. "Never mind. I'm not gonna fuck it up. Just lie back and enjoy the narcotics." He waves me off.

I'm confused. But that confusion dies when his bodyguard slips into the room. "Mr. Hale, I just wanted to let you know that the media has been tipped off that you're here with Mr. Abbey."

Great.

Another cherry on top of this motherfucking pie.

Lo nods. "Thanks. I'll get our publicist on it." The bodyguard leaves, and Lo glances to me. "Everything's alright."

It doesn't feel that way.

"Garrison!" Willow calls my name. At least, it sounds like her voice. Faint but recognizable.

Awesome.

I'm hearing her in my head now.

"Garrison!" *What the fuck?*

I look to Lo. He's smiling. Did he hear her too?

With a wince, I pull my body up, my heart thrashing against my chest.

Lo leans out of the doorway. "In here!" he calls out.

And then a second later, I see her.

Brown hair flying out of her messy braid, she bounds close to me and catches my hand in hers. "Garrison, are you okay? Oh my God, you look so pale. And you're burning up." Worry breaches every part of her.

My hand glides to her cheek. "Are you real?" I ask. *How high am I?*

She laughs softly between overcome tears, misting her black-framed glasses. "It was going to be a surprise. My flight was supposed to get in before you even left for the airport. But it got delayed and messed everything up and then Lo texted and said he was taking you to the hospital and I rushed here. And please say something, you look like you're dead. You're not dead, right?" Alarm leeches her voice, and quickly, she takes my pulse.

"I'm so far from dead," I tell her. "And I want to kiss you, but I can't because I've been puking. So can I hold you instead?"

She glances at my IV. "Am I going to mess anything up?"

"No way." I clasp her hip and pull her onto the hospital bed, the same time she crawls next to me.

She's hesitant, scared to hurt me. Eyeing the cords and keeping her body weight off mine.

My lip lifts. I'm so in love with Willow. I tuck her closer to my chest, and she eases more.

"I'm like so fucking jacked up on pain meds right now too. I'm in-de-structable," I say, separating the syllables slowly. Okay, I feel high.

Willow smiles up at me.

I look to Lo. "You knew the whole time? For how long?"

"A month," Lo says. "I can keep a secret." He nods to his sister. "I'll give you two some privacy." He gives me a look. "Only because I know you're not going to kiss." He laughs like his joke is funny. Whatever. I'm not a kid.

"Hey, we don't need chaperones. We're twenty-two!" I yell out to him as he leaves.

"She's twenty-one until tomorrow." His voice tapers off while he walks away.

Willow squeezes my hand in hers, reminding me she's really here. In the flesh.

"It's a weekday," I tell her. "You're missing class."

She nods. "I've asked a few people to take some notes for me. It's all worked out. I'll be here for the rest of the week."

Holy shit.

"Seriously?"

"Seriously."

We're both beyond grinning. My world is lit on fire. Beautiful flames filling my heart. "I thought the universe was trying to tell me something," I say to her. "Getting sick before seeing you."

"Yeah?" she frowns. "Like what?"

"That we're not meant to be together," I laugh, a dry laugh. "And I was ready to choke the universe out to let me get to you."

Willow brushes her finger over my knuckles. "I'm glad you didn't have to do that," she says. "I'm glad I can finally see you."

It should have been me sacrificing time for her, but I bury that guilt. I don't accept it into my life. No more. I'm not going to feel bad for either one of us making time for each other. Because I choose to believe we're stronger than any force in this world. I feel it deeper than I ever have.

No separation will keep us apart. Not really.

We hold each other on the hospital bed, and I dissolve into happiness. "When you leave again," I say, waiting for the pain in those words. But it doesn't come this time. "I just want you to know something."

She lifts her head off my chest to meet my gaze, pushing her glasses up the bridge of her nose.

"Wherever you are, no matter if it's right next to me or a thousand miles away," I say, "I'm tied to you with a thread that can't break. We're connected by something stronger than time or place."

She takes a deep breath, love sweeping around us. "I've felt that for years too, even before I left for London."

"Yeah?" Tears start to crest my eyes.

She wipes the emotion beneath her glasses. "You were there for me when I first moved to Philly, and in a way, it felt like you already hugged me before we even touched."

We breathe in, and I never understood the word *solace* before Willow. But I could lie here next to her, with an inflamed appendix, not saying a thing, and feel that word too deeply.

Solace.

Peace.

We have years left apart, but it's okay. For the first time, I'm truly realizing that nothing can come between us and our love. Not even myself.

I want a career at Cobalt Inc.

I want a future with Willow Hale.

I want it all.

22

GARRISON ABBEY
Age 18

Connor Cobalt *is a god here.* A single week at Faust, and it's the first lesson I've learned.

The second: I'm in over my head. The guys here aren't just smart. They seem to *enjoy* learning. As if it's a gift given to them, and everyone supports the growth of knowledge. Translating whole passages from Caesar's Invasion is cool, and debating philosophy is just another pastime.

I know basic Latin.

Enough to chant out loud with the class, but put a sentence in front of my face and I won't be able to translate anything without a vocabulary list.

And yeah, I asked for a vocab list or a dictionary the other day. The amount of students staring at me for *that* was beyond embarrassing. And this is coming from someone who didn't give a shit if people thought I was stupid.

Here, it feels like the worst crime.

"So you have spoken to him?" my new roommate asks as I try to concentrate on translating a passage in *The Odyssey* from Latin to English. It's slow moving.

I wish this was Calculus—a language I actually am proficient at.

My roommate leans forward on his crimson bedspread, blond hair brushing his neck and brown eyes round and curious. He's asking if I've spoken to the legend himself: Richard Connor Cobalt. The moment William learned that I'm from the same neighborhood as Connor, I've been bombarded with questions.

I promised to answer them later—which was my response for five whole days. Another five days dodging these questions seems unlikely since William has already spread the news to the entire boarding school.

It's whatever.

I'm just hoping the reasoning behind *why* I'm at Faust remains a secret. These guys don't seem like they'd take kindly to delinquents like me.

I curl my hand around the book, my other hand gripping a pencil tight. "I mean...not really. Kind of. I don't know," I say to William.

I heard Connor tell Loren that I'm not allowed in his house. That's about the extent of any conversation I've had with the guy.

I can't tell him that though. I'm trying to make friends here, and the students obviously worship Connor Cobalt. Letting them know I'm barred from entering his home for spraying his wife and baby with punch would be...fucked up.

It's all fucked up.

William frowns. "Well, have you seen him around? What is he like in real life?" he asks quickly. "Is he as tall as he seems on TV?"

"Yeah," I nod. "He's really tall." This is so dumb.

"Did he or his family mention anything about all the shit that's going down on social media?" William asks, eyes glittering for more knowledge.

"Which shit?" I ask. When it comes to Connor Cobalt, there's been a lot of shit recently. Especially concerning him and his wife. Yesterday, there were hundreds of pics online with Rose's hair dyed an ugly orange color. Tumblr created a meme and literally photoshopped foxes on her head. It was weird and stupid.

"The photos of Connor going down on his wife in a parking lot," William says. I saw those too. They were dark, taken outside while they were in a car. But you could make out his head and her legs around his shoulders. It was obvious what they were doing, and when they didn't deny it, social media went nuts.

"No one has said anything," I reply.

"Can you believe he did that and basically owned up to it like it was just another day?" William says in awe. "I mean, the guy is legendary. His wife is immortally beautiful and brilliant. He can give her head in a public parking lot and not even bat an eye. Are you sure no one has talked about it?"

"I'm sure," I snap. For the love of…why are we talking about Connor Cobalt? I run a hand through my hair. I want to physically eject myself from this conversation. Would it be rude to get up and leave the room? I've never really had a roommate—besides that couple times on family vacations I had to room with Mitchell, but I don't think that counts. This is all new for me.

Being at a new school.

New place.

I itch to grab my laptop and send Willow a Tumblr message. Anything to take me away from William's probing questions about a guy that hates me.

Thankfully, a knock sounds on the door.

Guys in black blazers and crimson ties (Faust's uniform) peek inside the room, grinning from ear-to-ear.

I recognize the freckled one from my Philosophy class. Tyson. He's the kind of guy who'll argue on the side that's wrong (like literally wrong) just to have a different point of view in the conversation. Sometimes he's so convincing, he almost makes me believe he's right. It wasn't a surprise when William told me he's president of the Debate Club.

Behind Tyson and the other guy, maddened footsteps cascade across the polished floor, hurrying towards something. More doors open, people leaving.

William rises from the bed, while I remain confused and motionless.

Tyson grins wider. "The Sophist's Speech is about to begin."

"Holy shit," William smiles wildly and reaches for his black blazer. Tyson and his friend leave as quickly as they came, while my roommate slows to the door, suddenly remembering me. "You coming, Garrison?"

I frown, still not understanding. "What's a sophist?"

He laughs. "Funny. You're funny." He nods to my blazer on the desk, even though I'm already wearing a hoodie. "Grab your jacket. You're not going to want to miss this."

ON OUR WAY TO THE COURTYARD, I QUICKLY Wikipedia what the hell a *sophist* is. Ten seconds later I have my answer. *A teacher in Ancient Greece.*

Another definition I found on the internet: *a person who reasons with clever but fallacious and deceptive arguments.* Seriously? I was supposed to know this?

My shoes crunch a light layer of snow, but I'm warm with the Faust blazer over my hoodie, crimson tie stuffed in my back pocket. Wind picks up as soon as we pass through arched oak double doors. I pull the hood up over my hair and follow William's quickened foot-steps towards a large stone fountain, icicles hanging off the ornate moldings.

I expect to see a teacher heading this speech, but the person balancing on the ledge of the fountain is a student. Dressed in the same Faust blazer as most of the crowd, black hair slicked back, he commands the space without even saying a word. He can't be older than me if he's here, but for some reason he looks it.

A senior, probably.

"Who is that?" I whisper to William as we fall into the throngs of guys. Some of whom ran outside without grabbing a coat or blazer. They jump on the balls of their feet, looking more excited than cold.

"Gabriel Falls," William replies softly. "He was elected as our sophist for the term." Off my confused-as-fuck expression, William adds, "It's Faust tradition to have a senior give a sophist's speech." He grins. "Basically, it's bullshit that smells like roses. The best speech by far was Connor Cobalt's. The guy practically planted a garden with his words."

Traditions here are weird as hell. I'm used to the kind back at Dalton Academy. Which consisted of our lacrosse team drinking blue Gatorade before practice. Never the lemon-lime. And god-forbid someone even thinks to bring a Ziff on field.

I'm not even sure where the tradition started—or I guess, superstition—maybe it had something to do with the jocks hating

Loren Hale when he went to Dalton. And you know, Ziff is a Fizzle product. It's a dumb name, by the way. *Ziff.* Fizz kind of spelled backwards. Whatever marketing "genius" came up with the name for the sports drink should be fired.

Thinking about Fizzle and Loren Hale and everything just reminds me of Willow. Can't see her. Can't work at Superheroes & Scones. It all blows.

"Gather 'round!" Gabriel calls out from his perch on the fountain. And then the guy starts speaking in Latin.

I can't with this.

Cold nips at my cheeks, and just as I'm about to bail, I see someone a few yards away. Shaved head and pale skin, he smokes a cigarette between fingerless gloves and leans against a tree. With his sleeves rolled up to his elbows, I distinguish black geometric tattoos on his forearms.

He's the first person I've seen that doesn't look like he was manufactured from a J.Crew catalogue. I leave William's side and slowly make my way to the tree.

Relief accompanies each step. No nerves. I've never been bad at making friends, and this guy kind of reminds me of ones back home.

He barely acknowledges me as I stop a few feet away, his gaze latched to the fountain. But I can only make out mumbled words from Gabriel's speech.

"Hey," I say and nod with my chin. "Could I borrow a smoke?" I eye the cigarette between his fingers.

His eyes finally flash to me. Like I exist. Casually, without even moving off the tree, he sticks the cigarette in his mouth, slides a hand in his blazer, and passes me a spare. Cold whips between us.

"Thanks, man," I say as he pulls out a lighter. "I'm Garrison."

"Sasha Anders. And I know who you are." He clicks the lighter with his thumb, and I lean in. After embers eat the paper, he adds, "No need to thank me."

I step back, blowing smoke off to the side. Wind chill bites at me more, and I hug my arm to my chest. This guy is wearing less than me, and he doesn't even have a single fucking goosebump.

He stares off towards the fountain and says, "That'll probably be your last cigarette at Faust. Enjoy it while you can."

Goddamn.

I laugh under my breath, bitterness swimming in my gut. "Yeah? What makes you think that?" Maybe he's just messing with me. He can't seriously be like everyone else here? An asshole. An elitist prick who feels like he has the inability to lose.

He doesn't even look at me. Like I haven't even earned his full attention yet.

Eyes on the fountain, he says, "You walked over here. That was your first mistake." His gray, lifeless gaze flits to me for a millisecond. "We aren't the same, you and me." He looks to my tattoo, the inked Interpol lyrics peeking from my forearm, like he knows that's the reason I approached. He continues, "You could barely string four words together in Spanish class. You have no knowledge of Proust, Rembrandt, or Verdi. You're *inadequate*, but your biggest failure is your social ineptitude. The only mouse that would approach a snake is the one too stupid to realize he's in a pit of them." Sasha flicks his cigarette to the side, and it lands in the snow.

I saw that phrase in the common room, etched on a plaque and hung with other senior quotes.

The only mouse that would approach a snake is the one
too daft to realize he's in a pit of them.

- *Richard Connor Cobalt*

Sasha gives me one last glance. "Don't look for friends, mouse.
Find an exit." He pauses and his eyes dip to my fingers. "Enjoy the
cigarette."

He walks off as Gabriel's speech ends. All the students disperse,
and Sasha falls in line among the masses just the same.

Breath caged. My cigarette burns, ash falling to the snow. I don't
know what to feel. I'm more used to the kinds of insults that try to
tear me down in a single blow. *Pussy! Weak shit!*

What Sasha just did was the equivalent of taking a knife and
slashing razor-thin cuts all over my skin—and then waiting for me
to bleed out. Meticulous. Calculated cruelty.

I bite down and breathe out through my nose.

And what unnerves me the most—is that he knew I blew it in
Spanish. He knows that I stumbled over those names in English,
Art & Lit, and Music Theory. Yet, I don't have a single class with
him.

It means people are talking about me. *Amazing.* Just amazing. I'm
going to have a *great* time here.

I feel like utter shit, and there's only one person I even want to
talk to right now.

Slipping out my cell, I walk towards the pond and try to FaceTime.
The boarding school campus is an otherworldly atmosphere with
frozen, barren waters and skeletal trees. Like I've been transported
to Victorian England.

My breath smokes in the cold, and I ditch the cigarette in the
snow.

The phone clicks, and Willow pops on-screen. She's crouched down next to a rack of *Inhumans* comics. She pushes her glasses up the bridge of her nose. "Oh, are you outside? Isn't it cold?" *God.* It's nice just hearing her voice. My stomach flips, and for a moment, I pretend I'm only a few blocks down the street.

"Yeah, but that's why I've got this…" I tug my hood down further, almost shrouding my eyes.

"Your fingers look purple," she says, concerned, and then one of the comics falls from its rack. She huffs. "Stupid broken rack."

"Is that *Inhumans?*" I wonder. "I thought Loren didn't want *Inhumans* stocked in the store. Didn't he call it a mediocre version of *X-Men?* And also a comic book line that's off-limits to all *X-Men* purists and if he can help it, off-limits to everyone?" He made that whole speech during last month's meeting.

"Yeah," Willow replies, grabbing tape and fashioning the broken rack back together. "But yesterday, Lily came in and told us Loren's bias over certain lines was not going to affect the store—since it's technically hers. And that *Inhumans* is a good series and needed to be stocked. So here I am…" She realigns the comics and slides them in. "…but I think there's a reason she put it on this crappy rack. Like maybe she subconsciously agrees with him." Willow nudges her glasses again and collapses on the ground. She straightens her phone so that I'm looking at her and not the comics.

"You okay?" I ask.

"Yeah." She pins her fallen employee nametag back to her shirt. "Honestly, I like *Inhumans.* And they're pretty cool on *Agents of Shield.*"

"I don't watch it," I remind her.

She nods, remembering. "*Supernatural* is better. It starts again soon."

"Yeah," I say, but I'm not even sure I'll have the time to watch *any* TV let alone my favorites.

Faust is a big time-suck, and on my free weekends, I'm planning to commute back to Philly for shifts at Superheroes & Scones. So I can at least have an excuse to see Willow. I'm just glad Lily Calloway agreed to let me keep working part-time.

I light a cigarette. If I'd known Sasha Anders was going to be a Grade-A tool-bag, I wouldn't have bothered pretending I had no smokes. Regret hammers me. And I usually don't regret social situations that turn sour. That shit flies off my shoulders. But being here—it's different.

"So…" she says. "How's the first week been? How's Faust and your roommates?"

I shrug. "Faust is…" I glance down at my cigarette. "Unusual. And my new roommate is…well, his name is William." I smile dryly. "Which bugs the shit out of me because every time someone says it, I just think about…"

You.

The names Willow and William are too similar to not be jarred by it. It fucking sucks.

Her cheeks ashen a little, and she glances down at her shoes.

"How's everything there?" I wonder, worried. "How's Dalton?" *My friends? Are they jerks to you while I'm gone?*

She shrugs now. "It's the same."

"The same?" I frown.

"I mean, not the same. You're not here," she says hurriedly. "It's really just boring and nothing goes on. Which is better than the alternative. More tampons in the locker would be rough."

"Yeah, definitely," I say. "Boring is better than tampon pranks." But I still feel badly that she's alone at Dalton. At least she's not completely alone. She has Loren and Lily, and she lives with Maya—who is pretty cool even if she hates my lack of comics knowledge.

"You'd tell me if something happened right?" I ask. "I know I can't really do anything being out here, but I'd want to know."

"Of course, I'd tell you." She pauses. "You'd tell me if something happened there, right?"

"Of course." Sasha Anders doesn't count. He technically didn't do anything to me, except call me a mouse. In the grand scheme of things, it was nothing. Really, it was kind of stupid. I've been through worse.

Silence eats at us for a second before she says, "Garrison."

"Yeah?"

"Can you go inside? I can see your fingers again and they look really purple."

"Yeah, okay." *She cares about me.* I think she does. I mean, that definitely means she does. Right? Someone on this planet actually cares about my well-being. That thought and feeling settles in my body like falling snow.

I drop my cigarette and turn towards the buildings. An employee distracts Willow for a second, asking if she'll swap workdays. I head inside and feel the rush of warmth. Classes in session, no one struts up and down the hallways.

Empty.

I lean my shoulder against a staircase banister. Staying on the first floor, I realize I might be missing political science right now, but I don't care.

I focus on my phone and watch Willow return her attention to me. "So everyone loves Connor here," I tell her.

She smiles. "You need to tell me stories."

"I'd rather hear yours right now," I say honestly. "My whole day has been centered on Connor Cobalt, and I need a distraction. What's going on with you?"

"The media is getting kind of crazy," she says. "More so than usual. But luckily they're more focused on Ryke's surgery and Rose's new hair color than little ole me right now."

Ryke's liver transplant was heavily documented online. He gave a part of his liver to his dad, and I remember seeing the shaky video of Ryke being wheeled out of the hospital a few days ago.

I frown, thinking about something else. "I thought the media stopped hounding you when the novelty of you being Loren's cousin wore off. What's made them come back?"

"I think maybe Connor and Rose?" She shakes her head, not knowing either. "Paparazzi have been asking me why the two of them are suddenly so 'PDA-heavy' in public. I'm like the lowest person on the list of people connected to them, so they think I'll have looser lips or something. Even if I knew something though, I wouldn't say anything."

That, I know.

Willow has always been really careful around me when it comes to Loren Hale and his family. She won't talk about anything that isn't already public knowledge, and even then, I can tell she'd still rather be discussing something else. It's not new for her anymore, but it's still uncharted territory that she's trying to navigate by herself.

It's understandable.

She quickly changes the subject. "Make any new friends?"

"Nope. You?"

"Nope."

Good.

No, that's shitty of me to think. Really, I don't know how I fucking feel about her making friends, okay? Depends who they are, I guess.

The quiet weighs on us for a second, and then I say, "Hey, you know any Latin?"

"Um…just what's on the back of a dollar bill." Her eyes drop to my hand as I light a new cigarette. "Your fingers have returned to a normal color."

"A miracle." I blow out smoke.

Someone passes the abandoned hall and shakes their head at me. "No smoking inside, man."

I think he's just warning me, but then he stops a foot away and unfurls a small booklet. "I'm going to have to write you up."

"What?" I frown. *What the fuck?*

"It's against code of conduct rules."

"Are you like a hall monitor or something?" I say, confused. Aren't those only in movies?

"That's exactly what I am."

Fuck me.

Willow grimaces as I look back to the phone. "I'll let you go," she says quickly. "See you Saturday?"

"Saturday," I say into a nod and we hang up.

I wait while the hall monitor scribbles on the notepad, and Sasha Ander's words hound me. *Find an exit.*

It sounds like an easy task, but I've been searching for an exit my entire life and have yet to find it. Someone point the way. Anyone? Please.

I'm waiting.

23

GARRISON ABBEY
Age 18

reaking and entering wasn't on my list of things to do. Ever. But things change. I slide a paperclip through the keyhole of a deep navy door, scratches and dents marring the steel. Garbage stinks up the alleyway, and cigarette butts line the pavement.

Working at Superheroes & Scones gave me a lot of insight into this place. Like how the left alley door doesn't have any security cameras. Most of the employees smoke pot and suck face on this stoop. So I'm not even sweating as I take my time with the lock. The pitch-black night conceals me enough.

Honestly, I just need a place to sleep tonight. A warm floor. That's it.

Because I can't go back to Faust.

This morning the headmaster called me into his office—and I thought for sure he was going to just tell me I needed a tutor.

Because I did nothing wrong. No vandalism. No cheating. No cursing. No cutting class—except for that one time with poly-sci.

I was on my best fucking behavior.

Bookshelves towered against every wall, and the place smelled like moldy paperbacks. I took a seat in front of his polished oak desk.

"Mr. Abbey," he said, "seeing as you're a new student, I've tasked myself with looking into how you're faring here at Faust." He barely blinked. "Unfortunately, your current academic standing isn't up to par with the other pupils."

Not a surprise. I shifted on my chair. "So who's my tutor…?" My voice trailed off as I saw the expression on his face. Pure fucking pity.

He sighed heavily. "I'm afraid, we're past that stage. With your current marks, you'd have to score well beyond one hundred percent on every final to even move the needle. This is the end of the road for you and your time here at Faust. You can pack your bags. A car is waiting to take you back to…" He glanced down at a sheet of paper. "Philadelphia."

It's official. I've flunked out of *two* prep schools.

Really, I was pulled out of Dalton before I even had the chance to flunk. But I was well on my way there.

The one silver-lining in all of this, Faust doesn't contact parents by phone. Not when most of the students have moms and dads sailing the globe on yachts or too damn busy to lift their own cell. So Faust does everything by mail.

Before coming to the comic book shop, I made a quick detour at my parent's house. Stopped by for point-two-seconds. Just long enough to swipe the letter from their mailbox. The one "notifying" them that I'm a loser.

BACK THEN

The lock clicks. *Success.*

I push through the backdoor of Superheroes & Scones, and before the alarm can go off, I quickly type in the passcode. Yesterday, Lily switched the code, so Willow gave me the new one.

And yeah, I had to tell Willow I flunked. I couldn't lie to her.

I hate that she's kind of an accomplice to this whole "breaking and entering" thing. But the alternative was sneaking into her bedroom (she offered it as a place to crash) and I don't want to ruin us by being *that* guy. Willow doesn't deserve some loser crashing on her floor.

Quietly, I tiptoe through the deserted store. Not a soul or sound in the entire place. It feels like a comic book graveyard in the dark.

Dipping into the breakroom, I use a giant stuffed Millennium Falcon plushie as a pillow and lie on the hard ground.

I slide the letter out of my backpack and then flip open a lighter. Flame to paper, I watch my future—or lack thereof—burn between my fingertips.

My parents aren't ever going to know I flunked. And if I have it my way, I'll never see them again.

Honestly, that's the only future I want.

24

WILLOW MOORE
Age 18

S omeone is following me.

I know I sound paranoid, and maybe it's because of the intense paparazzi onslaughts recently. Cameramen wait for me to leave Superheroes & Scones every single shift. Without fail. I even slipped out the backdoor (the one that smells like weed) and still had this mustached man shove a camera three inches from my face.

He could have broken my glasses. That was one of my fears at least.

He did scream so loud and so close that his voice drilled into my head. "Willow! Willow! Do you know anything about Connor & Rose?! Is their marriage fake?!"

The accusations against Connor Cobalt and Rose Calloway have been horrible lately. The media discovered Connor has slept with men, before he dated Rose, and now they think his relationship with Rose isn't real. Like he's using her to hide his sexuality.

Thankfully some fans realize that Connor can be attracted to men *while* also being attracted to women. That both things can be true: Connor sleeping with guys in the past and also loving and sleeping with Rose in the present.

It just sucks that some fans aren't louder than the media.

When the cameraman rushed me, I wasn't brazen enough to scream in his face, but I felt like yelling. A big part of me regrets not saying anything. Not sticking up for Rose and Connor when they've been so kind to me.

Especially Rose.

But I'm also kind of glad I didn't say anything. Opening my mouth probably would've made the situation worse. Anyway, Ryke and Lo are yelling enough for just about everyone these days.

I did write a few supportive Tumblr posts, and I reblogged cute Coballoway gifs from fan accounts. Garrison told me to send him the links, and he did the same.

I walk down the sidewalk towards my apartment building. With the parking deck under construction, I had to park a block away. A white Volvo slowly moves on the other side of the street and keeps pace with me.

That's weird, right?

Paparazzi have never really followed me to my apartment. They lose interest in me as soon as I climb into my Honda. They couldn't care less about abandoning Superheroes & Scones for Loren Hale's boring "cousin." I've been glad about that.

But this…

Changes things.

I tighten my hold on the backpack strap and quicken my pace. The apartment complex's front entrance is inches from my fingertips, and a man jumps out of the Volvo. "Willow! I'd like to ask you some questions!"

I flinch, my pulse spiking.

I don't know why, but he sounds more serious than the other paparazzi. Like a fancy news reporter. It makes me do a doubletake, and he quickly catches up to me.

"I'm with *Celebrity Crush*—"

Oh…no. Nope! Do not want to talk. *Celebrity Crush* has been known to spout off some of the worst and nastiest rumors about the Calloway sisters.

I mumble out an *I'm sorry* or maybe it was just unintelligible words. But I say something that my brain and mouth put together before bolting into the apartment complex. My hands shake as I dig for my cell. Just as I find it in the depths of my backpack, a text pings.

Garrison: made it to S&S. Thanks for the assist. Owe you like a million. Hey, did you know how comfortable the Millennium Falcon is? Who would've guessed?

I calm just reading his text. But my heart still thrashes against my ribcage, reminding me what I have to do.

I dial his number.

The line clicks. "Willow?"

"Lo, I have to tell you something."

IF I TOTAL ALL THE DAYS AND WEEKS THAT I'VE been in Philly since I left Maine, it's been around nine months, and I'd like to think that's a long time. Almost a whole year on my own. It makes me feel better knowing that I tried really, *really* hard to not be a burden on Lo. To not accept more from my brother than I absolutely have to.

If I felt safe enough to live in my apartment, I think I could have even lasted longer than those nine months. But after the paparazzi followed me home, Loren asked if I'd like to move into his mansion-sized house in a gated Philadelphia neighborhood.

The same neighborhood that Garrison grew up in.

I couldn't say *no* this time.

I really like the Calloway sisters, Ryke, and even Connor. They've accepted me into their lives without hesitation, and I know in the beginning that acceptance originated from their trust in Lo. But I hope that now it's because they also trust me.

"We should decorate and make this space more Willow-y," Daisy tells me, rolling around my new bedroom on a skateboard. All my stuff (which isn't much) sits in the middle of the room, still packed in a couple boxes and a suitcase.

I'm officially "moved in" thanks to Lo, Ryke, and Daisy's help this morning.

They had a few empty guest rooms on the east wing of the house, and Lo let me pick which one I'd like. He didn't seem pleased when I chose the smallest of the three, but he didn't push me to choose differently.

I like how quaint this one feels. Just a bed, tin desk, and white wooden dresser. That's more than enough for me.

Daisy spins to face me as I unfold a box. She's always moving. It's kind of like watching a hummingbird flit around a space. "We could also paint the walls." She abandons the skateboard and plops on my bed. "There's a hardware store nearby, and we can buy some brushes and stuff."

I'm smiling so hard my cheeks hurt.

I have new roommates. Six adults and two babies to be exact. I'm living with the Calloway sisters and their men.

If you'd told me that's how all of this would have panned out months ago—I'd have said you were dead wrong. More surprising than that—I'm *comfortable* here. Not too nervous or skittish. I never thought I'd feel that way with people so famous and so much more interesting than me. I know it has to do with Lo. He made a lot of effort to welcome me and make my surroundings feel like home. He's my brother, but he *feels* like family now.

I follow Daisy's gaze to the walls and then I rip the tape off a box. "I have some posters in here too, and I love the new paint idea." We exchange a wider grin.

Daisy rests her feet on the skateboard, swaying them back and forth while she sits. "What color are we thinking? First one that comes to mind. Go!"

"Aquamarine," I blurt out, and then my face falls. Skin hot. Is it hot in here?

"Ooh, aquamarine. That also happens to be the eye color of a certain someone." She wags her brows. "Anything new you wanna share?"

I shake my head. "Nothing, really."

She sidles next to me with a pair of scissors, cutting open a different box. Her smile is softer and extinguishes the heat on my neck. "Nothing *nothing*. Or nothing *something*? Because I have this theory that nothing is just seven letters hiding an unspoken truth."

There are definitely unspoken truths when it comes to Garrison Abbey. But these truths aren't mine to release into the world. He's been so good about keeping *my* secrets from people—like anything I accidentally say to him about the Calloway sisters or Loren—that I wouldn't even think to share his.

And there are a lot of secrets at the moment.

Flunking out of Faust.

Lying to his parents about the boarding school.

Breaking into Superheroes & Scones and sleeping there at night.

I'm a little surprised I aided and abetted that last act, but he's my friend. And he needed my help. It's really that simple.

"The unspoken truth is…" I tell Daisy. "Besides you, Garrison is my only other friend, and so he pops up in my head a lot." I pale again. "Apparently, now with wall colors."

Daisy smiles. "Aquamarine would actually look really pretty. We can go to the paint store in a few—" She cuts herself off as her husky bounces into the room. "Hello there, Coconut." She squats down and scratches the dog's soft white fur.

A few months ago, around Daisy's 20th birthday, Ryke brought home the husky to help with her PTSD. Coconut is a certified service dog and also the cutest fluffy thing in this house.

"So are there house rules?" I wonder, pulling out a stack of hangers from the box. "It's just…I've never lived with three couples and two babies before. So I don't know how this works." Admitting my innocence causes my breath to shallow. I probably sound like a fool. Quickly, I look away before I can meet Daisy's gaze. If I can't see it, it won't be immortalized in my memory.

"Hey," she says sweetly.

I look up, and her eyes are kind and also vulnerable on me. Like she's trying to show me the sadder pieces and not just happy-go-lucky Daisy.

She tucks a piece of hair behind her ear. "I don't think many people have been in this living arrangement before."

We both look around the bare room. But it's not really the space we're feeling. It's the people, the fame, the wealth.

When our eyes meet again, Daisy says, "We're like unicorns here. Living out unique lives." She stares off in thought. "Not a lot of people will ever understand what we go through or even care, and that's partly why we've been drawing closer to each other, living together." She hugs her legs. "I wasn't always that close with Rose and Lily, but I really wanted to be."

"You weren't that close?"

And she goes on to tell me deeper things about her childhood, about being the sister left behind, and Daisy asks me more about my life in Maine.

We talk for hours and hours, and we forget about paint colors. It's a tomorrow project. Today, I just really like sharing her company. And I know I'm not going to regret moving in.

25

WILLOW MOORE
Age 18

nternal Freak-Out Status: I'm on a vacation with the Calloway sisters and their men.

Rose asked if I'd like to join their trip to the lake house.

Location: top-secret. No one online knows the destination. It's supposed to be a peaceful oasis away from the paparazzi. The fact that they're letting me in on this secret is a huge honor that I want to safekeep and protect.

The drive has been *long*. The kind that needs many pitstops and even driver rotations. Luckily, no has asked me to man the wheel. Not that I'm a bad driver. But both Jane Cobalt and Maximoff Hale are situated in car seats in the back, Connor sitting between the kids.

My nervous energy will most likely skyrocket with the responsibility of protecting the almost-one-year-old babies.

Right now, all that responsibility rests in Lily's hands, but she's undoubtably been the best driver so far. Her eyes barely even flit to the passenger seat where Rose texts on her phone.

"Is that Mom again?" Lily asks her sister.

Silence eats the car, and I wonder if whatever text Rose received is important. *Probably.* Very important people are in this vehicle. Like my brother. Lo sits next to me in one of the middle seats, an aisle between our chairs.

He gazes out the window, probably looking for the other car. Ryke and Daisy drove separately. The whole process of even leaving the neighborhood took security vehicles, diversions with an assist from bodyguards, and a lot of work before we even made it on our route.

It reminds me how secretive this trip really is.

I glance down at my cell, checking the ETA. We still have *hours* left. I wish I could text Garrison, but he handed me his cellphone this morning. It's currently stashed away in my backpack, squeezed between my shoes.

My stomach has been in a series of knots this entire car ride.

I may have…smuggled someone into this Escalade's trunk.

But he's blindfolded. (His suggestion.) He has *no* idea where we're headed, and he can't see a thing. I trust Garrison not to spill the location, but no one else in the car will trust him.

I know the blindfold might not help, but it's a last-ditch effort in case everything goes wrong and he's caught.

I haven't even been living with them long and I'm already doing something that could threaten their trust in me. My stomach tosses and turns, causing worse nausea than a normal bout of car sickness.

The alternative was worse. Leaving Garrison alone in Philly with nowhere to go. Lily installed extra security cameras at Superheroes

& Scones, so Garrison can't sleep there anymore. If I don't help him, he'll have to return home where he could run into his brothers again. That's the last place I want him to be.

I'm his only friend.

Friends are supposed to smuggle each other in trunks.

That's just how it works, right?

Before I zipped him up in the duffel bag, I handed him a water bottle and a banana. He has nourishment and fluids. Still…

I'm freaking out a little bit.

It's impossible *not* to worry. He's in a *duffel bag* right now. Bumping along with the Escalade. And since his phone is in my backpack, Garrison has no way to communicate with me.

It's dangerous.

When we left this morning, I even shoved his cell back into his chest, knowing how risky this could be. What if he has heat stroke? What if he doesn't get enough air? He could die inside luggage and I'm just sitting here with zero clue.

I told all of these things to Garrison.

But he just looked me in the eye and said, "You have to take my phone, Willow. Because if we get caught, you'll be in worse shit with your family if they know I had it." They'll think he snitched to someone about the lake house's location.

He was thinking about me.

I'm still thinking about him. I sort of hate that I agreed in the end. I mean, what's the probability that they'd even be angry if he had a phone? He's already blindfolded.

This was a *really* stupid idea.

"Rose?" Lily asks, since Rose still hasn't replied to her.

"She wants us at next week's luncheon," Rose replies, confirming that she's talking to their mom. "Which is *not* happening." I've heard about the fancy luncheons that the Calloway sisters go to just to visit with their parents. They don't sound fun.

A white Ferrari speeds up and drives next to our car; Coconut's head flops out of the open window. A big goofy smile on the husky's face. On the passenger side, Ryke clasps the top of the window frame.

Suddenly, Daisy steps on the gas, zipping off *fast*. The Ferrari must go from our speed (maybe forty?) to a hundred miles per hour in a second flat. My jaw is on the floor.

That is…terrifying.

And yet, I really love hanging out with Daisy.

"Uhh…" Lily gapes. "I'm not supposed to follow them, am I?"

Lo shakes his head. "No way. We're not driving off a cliff with Thelma and Louise."

Heat encases me, hot with worry. I dig through my backpack for a water bottle. "Do they know where they're going?"

Daisy said she planned to follow us, and I don't want her to end up in a ditch where we can't find her. Even the thought brings this wave of panicked sadness.

"Nope," Lo says. "I hope he gets lost." *Please no.*

"Knowing Ryke and Daisy, I'm sure that's their goal," Connor chimes in from the backseat.

I don't know if she'll receive it, but I quickly text Daisy. Love you. I wish I could text her the directions, but no one's allowed to share them over any electronic device. In case of hacks. Reminding her that I care is the best I can do. I wouldn't ever tell her to stop being who she is. Daredevil and all.

Leaning forward, I fiddle with the middle console air vents, trying to direct them towards the back. Even though I'm way too far away from the trunk.

But all I can think: if I'm feeling this heat, I just hope Garrison isn't suffering.

Please don't die in the trunk.

26

GARRISON ABBEY
Age 18

've done some strange shit. Drunk. High. But being curled up in a duffel bag for *twelve* hours definitely is the strangest. And I'm stone-cold sober.

By hour three, I was rethinking the sober part.

I should've taken about five shots of vodka before Willow helped me into this bag. She volunteered to load the trunk just to make sure no one would throw their suitcases on me. Grateful doesn't even cut what I feel.

A blindfold covers my eyes, the fabric soft. I'm *fully* in the over-sized duffel with just an inch unzipped for air circulation. Every pitstop when it's clear the Escalade is emptied out of passengers, I readjust. Sometimes, I unzip the bag just so I can extend my legs. But I've only done that once so far. Not wanting to risk it.

She's putting a lot of fucking trust in me.

Bucket loads.

I'm not going to blow it.

But *fuck*, it's hot back here. My shirt suctions to my skin, sweat building. A water bottle pokes me in the spine, but I haven't taken a sip. I can hold my bladder as long as I don't consume liquids.

It's been a couple hours since the last pitstop where I stretched my legs, and I'm not about to do gymnastics with people in the car. Connor Cobalt's voice sounds the closest, which makes me think he's in the backseat.

That guy is way too perceptive not to notice something rustling around in the trunk. My legs ache, but it's better than ruining Willow's relationship with her family. I'm already putting that on a razor-thin line.

"You have two miles and then you turn right." Rose's voice is faint. *Front seat.* Maybe passenger side. It's been kind of a fun game trying to pinpoint the seating arrangements. At least it's taken my mind off of being in a duffel bag.

Fuck, my life is weird.

The car starts to meander around winding roads like we're driving on mountains. The movement churns my stomach. *Don't get car sick.* Dude, if I upchuck in this duffel bag and have to sit in my own puke, I might die. Literal death.

I breathe quietly through my nose and cinch my eyes close. I drift off for a couple minutes until Loren's voice shoots me awake.

"Hey!" Lo shouts. "Crazy Raisins!"

No clue what that's about. All I know is I haven't heard Ryke and Daisy's voices in the Escalade since we left Philly. I figure they must be in a different vehicle.

Rose yells, "Follow us, please! Daisy, you don't need to be driving in the dark!"

"How many times has she driven a car?" Connor questions calmly.

Recently, Willow asked me whether my Mustang would be faster than a Ferrari. I told her it depends on the models—but I'm not a car expert or anything. I don't think she meant to tell me more. I think she kind of slipped. But off my confusion about the question, since it was out of the blue, she kept going.

I know that Daisy's Ferrari is brand new. Two weeks new. I know it's also her first car, having only really driven motorcycles before.

Information I shouldn't have.

Information I won't share with a soul. I'd die first, I think.

Rose yells louder, "Daisy how many times have you driven any kind of car?!"

I strain my ears just to hear Daisy's reply from outside. "Cuatro!"

Four.

Holy shit.

"Bro, why are you riding in the deathmobile?!" Lo yells at his brother.

"We're fucking fine!" Ryke screams from outside.

If they're going to be fine, I have to believe I'm going to be okay. Because honestly, I can't tell what's a bigger risk.

Being in a car with Daisy Calloway or hiding out in this duffel bag.

Luckily, the choice has already been made for me.

THE ESCALADE IS PARKED FOR LONGER THAN JUST a pee-break. I can tell because they're all talking outside, too casually to be in a public space.

What I infer: we must have arrived at the lake house. I can almost taste freedom out of this suffocating duffel bag. Before that, though, I have to actually figure out a way to exit the trunk without being seen.

Easier said than done.

I stay quiet. Motionless. Listening to the sound of their conversation outside.

"Is anyone else scared of bears?" Lily's voice carries loudly. *Bears.* I have no clue where we are—but I'm guessing it's somewhere secluded in the woods. Shit, I don't really want to hypothesize when I'm not supposed to know the exact location.

"Moose are scarier," Willow says.

My lips inch up.

"There are moose here?!" Lily yells in fright. "Why didn't anyone tell me about the moose?! Lo, did you know about the moose?"

With her high-pitched tone, it sounds more comical than it should. My smile pulls higher, wishing I was out there. And then, my bladder suddenly rebels against me. Fuck, I have to piss. My legs ache, and I try to rub my hamstring without causing noise.

"No, no," Willow says swiftly to Lily, "I just meant in general. There were a lot of moose in Maine, but I've never been around here, so I wouldn't know."

"No moose," Connor declares.

Someone groans. Sounds deep like Ryke's voice. It's confirmed when I hear him say, "Can we please fucking ban the word moose from now on?"

"Agreed," Rose adds.

"I like a good moose in the morning," Loren pipes in just to be *that* guy and irritate the shit out of everyone. I'd give him a gold star.

I tune them out when my hamstring starts to fully cramp. *Motherfucker.* I grind down on my teeth and press the heels of my palms to my forehead. Might as well zip up this duffel bag and toss it into a hole. Bury me in the ground where I belong.

My insides twist, and I let out a tensed breath through my nose.

"We obviously need to go over the fucking rules about bears," Ryke says to something I missed. "Unless it's hunting season or the bear is attacking you, you can't shoot it."

"Says who?" Rose combats.

"The fucking law," Ryke replies. "I can't believe I camped with you, and we didn't talk about this. Look, I brought bear spray for everyone, so it's non-fucking-negotiable."

"Let's start unpacking before it gets dark." Connor's words ignite panic in every pore of my body. Unpacking involves popping this trunk. The one where I'm currently *stuffed* inside a duffel bag. I stop breathing. Stop moving.

I might as well be a corpse.

"You guys should look at the house first," Willow interjects. "I'll start unpacking."

She's got this, Abbey. Calm the fuck down.

"You're not here as manual labor," Loren refutes. "So you should explore the house with us."

Willow clears her throat uneasily. "I…" Her voice tapers off.

I wish I were out there helping her, but that'd just blow everything to shit. Guilt gnaws my insides. *You put her in this position,* my head screams at me.

I don't want to ruin her. Turn her into someone who lies to the people who love her. But I'm sinking, and I feel myself clinging to anything on shore. So I grip her fingers, and I'm terrified I'll pull her down with me.

I'm doing it right now.

I know.

I know.

Fuck, I know.

This was a bad idea.

Willow continues, more confident this time, "I was going to call my mom—I mean, *our* mom. Or…you know, whatever she is. I just needed a minute alone."

The quiet somehow sounds tense, and I'm not even out there.

A beat later, Loren replies, "Yeah, I didn't realize you were in contact with her, but…definitely, as long as you don't tell her the location of where you are—"

"No way. I'd never do that."

"I just had to make sure." He says something else, but cramping intensifies in my hamstring. It's worse than any cramp I've had in lacrosse, and I was that asshole drinking pickle juice on the side of a field trying to eliminate tight quads.

I think…I think I have to move.

Slowly and carefully, I reach down to my thigh, my fingers kneading the muscle. I have to angle a little to touch the spot. God, that feels better. I close my eyes as I continue massaging the muscle. My elbow collides with a hard suitcase and lets out a *thump*.

Pain blooms but it's dulled under my hysteria.

My heart jettisons from my body. Out of this car. Out of this planet.

Did anyone else hear that?

I listen harder. Voices are quiet, almost distant. I have no chance at distinguishing the words. I don't know if that's good or bad. And then…

The trunk beeps, indicating that the hood is lifting.

BACK THEN

Oh fuck.

I suck in a breath, holding it. Not moving a muscle. *Please don't see the massive almost human-sized duffel bag in this car.*

"Garrison?"

Willow. I let out a breath of relief.

She whispers, "Can you...um...make sure your blindfold is on?" She adds quickly, "Don't reply. Lo is still on the stoop. I'm pretending I'm on the phone with my mom." She must have the cell to her ear. "I'm going to get you out of the trunk. Just hold tight, okay?"

27

WILLOW MOORE
Age 18

"**A**re you alright?" I whisper. "Do you need water? Food? Oh my God, your legs." I press my fingers to my lips. His calves are *swollen* the size of small melons.

Garrison rubs them as he sits on the edge of my mattress.

I've already snuck him inside the lake house, which took less maneuvering than I thought it would. All thanks to Ryke who wanted to give everyone a safety lesson with bear spray in the woods. They didn't question my phone call with my mom, so I stayed back to sneak Garrison up to my room.

Four stories, two-wrap-around porches, and giant maple trees *everywhere*, the lake house is a secluded majestic place. I feel a little badly that I blindfolded Garrison and he didn't get to see the outside. Because it truly is beautiful.

It's also *huge*.

Big enough that I have my own bedroom, and for this occasion—hiding a boy—I'm very appreciative of the size.

Garrison massages his calves. "I'm good, Willow." His voice is a whisper too. "Honestly, don't worry about me. You should go hang with your family. I'm cool to chill."

I wish we could be in each other's company for longer, and I hesitate to just abandon him here. "I'll bring up some snacks." My eyes flit to the en-suite bathroom. "If you use the bathroom when I'm not here just remember—"

"Not to flush," he finishes with a smile. "Got it. This isn't my first time being stashed away."

I pale. "Oh yeah. Of course. You've snuck into girls' bedrooms before." *Duh, Willow.* He was super popular before he met me.

"No. I mean, yes, I've done that. But not like this." He shakes his head. Eyes cinching. "I was referring to Superheroes & Scones. Although it was a stupid analogy. The place wasn't exactly packed with people when I was camping out there."

Worry pulls my face, remembering everyone I'm deceiving here.

He holds up a hand. "I promise, Willow. I'm not going to make a sound."

"I know. I believe you," I say softly. "I just want you to be comfortable." I don't want him to feel like a criminal I'm trying to hide away. Even though…that's exactly what I'm doing, isn't it? Hiding him.

He's not a bad person.

A tender smile touches his eyes. "Believe me, I'm the most comfortable I've been in a long time."

His words hoist my spirits, and we both quiet when the porch door creaks open. He nods me on with his chin. Silently saying, *go be with your family.*

What does it say about me, if I really just want to stay right here? My feet, heavy like cement blocks, shuffle towards the door.

RAIN SLAMS ON THE DECK, THE PITCH-BLACK night creating an eerie feeling in the living room. The perfect atmosphere for a slumber party—which Rose Calloway has turned into a séance. Leather furniture is pushed against wide, floor-length windows to open up the space.

I cross my legs on a red bear-patterned rug and try to enjoy the evening. It's hard with the storm outside and my brain all the way back in my room.

My mind is on a 24/7 news cycle of Garrison Abbey. It's just...I haven't had much opportunity to check up on him. At least, not as much as I'd like. And I'm trying to stay in the moment and enjoy these gatherings. Many people would *kill* to play *light-as-a-feather, stiff-as-aboard* with the Calloway sisters.

I did just that.

The game ended with Ryke (who we were lifting) crashing down on Rose. Now we all sit in a circle, candles lit in the middle. It'd be scarier if we were trying to contact a demon or something. But Rose and her sisters just want to talk to their Old Aunt Margot, so it seems harmless.

That's what I'm telling myself.

A storm rages, thunder booming. It'd tag the mood as *dramatic* and *frightening*.

New eulogy: *that Willow Moore, what a chicken—afraid of some raindrops.* Hugging my arms around my body, I watch the candles flicker.

Coconut howls from the kitchen, paws padding along the floorboards. Daisy goes rigid, and her head whips around the living room quickly. Like she's trying to mentally scan each nook and cranny.

I frown, worried that the dark, storm, and tiny bumps and bangs aren't good for her PTSD.

Ryke pulls Daisy closer to him, his lips beside her ear, whispering. She seems to relax a little at his words.

My lip nearly lifts, happy that she has someone like Ryke who cares. The thought makes me glance up towards the balconies.

Garrison.

I hope he's okay.

"Aunt Margot it is," Rose declares, pulling the attention back to herself. I think, maybe purposefully. That's just the kind of sister Rose is. She knows when to command the spotlight when others want to dip out of it. "Let's all hold hands." She extends her palm to me, and I take it.

Lily, Loren, Connor, Ryke, and Daisy complete the circle. The babies, Maximoff and Jane, are safe in their cribs upstairs.

"Close your eyes," Rose instructs.

My eyelids shut, darkness cocooning me.

"Aunt Margot," Rose begins the séance. "We're calling you, Aunt Margot." Rain hammers violently, the wind picking up. Goosebumps dot my arms. "We miss your beautiful, lost soul. Please come to us."

Lo chuckles, and it's practically contagious.

My lips threaten to rise, but I smooth them down.

Rose continues like Lo didn't ruin anything. "Fight through the barrier of the afterlife so that we may speak with you."

Craaaaaaaacccck!

I jump, my eyes shooting open.

Lily lets out a terrified, muffled squeal, her head hidden beneath a quilt.

"What the fuck was that?" Ryke asks. He glances out the floor-length window, maybe worried the lake house took damage from the storm.

"It's electrostatic discharge," Connor tells him. "Also known as lightning."

Lights flicker on and off until a bulb cracks and they all blink out. I think we might have just lost power. A chill snakes down my spine. Could this maybe not have happened during a séance? Coincidence, right?

"Ohmygod," Lily slurs in a panicked whisper.

"Old Aunt Margot?" Daisy calls out, the only one with her eyes still shut. "Can you hear us?" If I was just listening to her, I'd think she was having fun. Zero percent fear. But it's hard not to notice how her collarbones protrude like she's holding in a breath. Her knuckles whiten, gripped to her knees.

Whhhaaaaap!

Lily screams at the new noise, the one coming from upstairs. *Oh God, no.*

I shoot to my feet, my focus drilling on the staircase. I swear the sound originated from my bedroom, and maybe I'm just being overly paranoid, here, but Garrison is alone and there's a vicious thunderstorm outside.

Horrible images of tree limbs skewering windows and impaling *his* body ravage my mind. Gruesome *Final Destination* worthy fears that most likely aren't coming true, but it takes all of my energy not to run upstairs right now.

"What was that noise?" Lily asks. "Connor?"

Connor Cobalt stares at the ceiling. "An object fell."

"By a ghost?"

Unless the ghost's name is Garrison Abbey…it's no ghost.

Thuuuump! is accompanied by a long, sharp groan.

Garrison.

I don't even take account of the shocked, horrified faces around me. My ears ring, my focus tunneling as footsteps pad along the floorboards upstairs.

"Moffy." Lily bolts towards the staircase, towards her son's room, baby monitor in her clutch.

They think there's an intruder. Oh God. I mobilize, springing into action.

"Lily wait—" Lo runs after his wife, just as I sprint in the opposite direction. Footsteps gather behind me.

I'm being followed by Rose *and* Connor, but I don't stop. Not even as I hurriedly ascend another staircase on the west side of the lake house. Racing towards *my* bedroom and the source of the noise.

Without power, the second-floor hallway is encased in darkness. But even in the pitch-black, I know where I'm going. My pulse hammers in my ears. *Please be okay.*

Please be okay.

I land at my bedroom and turn the knob. Locked.

A glow from a cellphone flashlight abruptly illuminates the door—and me.

I squint from the sudden brightness. Connor holds up his cell from his six-foot-four height, and the glow bears down on me like I'm under the brightest spotlight.

Cover blown.

I don't care.

I don't care.

I only care about *him.*

I bang my palm against the wooden door. "Are you okay?" My voice cracks in worry.

"Is he in there?" Connor asks like he already knows who's on the other side. *How?* I instantly shake off my shock. I've been living with Connor Cobalt. He's perceptive.

Too much sometimes.

My mouth dries. Rose and Connor stand side-by-side, watching me.

"He didn't have anywhere else to go," I confess quickly, my chest concaving in heavy, petrified breaths. "I made sure to blindfold him here. I promise, he has *no* idea where this place is."

I've wrecked everything. They're never going to trust me again.

Rose raises her chin and takes my wrist, her touch more consoling than rough. She pulls me close to her, away from the door.

Connor reaches up to the top of the doorframe, a small key resting on the ledge. He uses it to unlock the door, and when he pushes it open, he points his flashlight cell at the room.

My stomach lurches.

Garrison sits on the edge of the quilted bed, a lamp shattered on the floor. *Blood.* I see blood. Spattered on the floor and trickling down the bottom of his heel. Garrison inspects his bare foot, a piece of glass lodged in the sole.

"Are you okay?" I ask and try to rush to his side.

Rose clasps my hand and tugs me back. "You're not wearing shoes either, Willow."

My stomach somersaults, but I stay put. Garrison avoids my gaze. Even with his head hung, I can see guilt caressing every inch of his frame. *It's okay*, I want scream and shout. He didn't mean to step on the glass. It's not his fault this secret is spilled.

Hair falls over his eyes. "I tried to turn the lamp back on. I ended up knocking it over, and I..." He winces and attempts to remove the shard of glass in near darkness.

"Don't," Connor warns. "Rose, can you get a first-aid kit and check on Jane?"

Rose is already heading to the door. "I'll be right back."

The room tenses now that it's just Garrison, Connor, and me. I scan the floor, wondering if I can Indiana Jones my way to Garrison without stepping on glass. Probably...*not*.

"One of you start explaining," Connor says casually, shoulder propped next to the doorframe and arms crossed.

Garrison mutters, "I hid in the trunk."

"He gave me his phone," I add quickly. "This entire time. He hasn't had it." I rummage through the pocket of my overalls— thank goodness they're deep. I hold up his cell. "See?" He can't contact anyone and leak the location of the lake house. I go further and explain how I snuck him into my room, while they thought I was talking to my mom.

Rose returns with the first-aid kit, her nearly one-year-old daughter in her arms, and a pair of shoes are on her feet. "I want to talk to Daisy and Lily," Rose says to her husband. Her piercing yellow-green eyes flit to me.

I've wrecked everything. "I'm so sorry, Rose—"

"I understand what it means to be loyal. But you shouldn't have kept this from us. If you wanted to bring your boyfriend along, we could've worked something out."

Boyfriend. Color drains from my face.

"Friend," I clarify. *Don't look at Garrison.*

"Would it make it better if we were dating?" Garrison asks.

My heart does a weird *thump thump* in my chest. Is he...no...I don't know. My face is numb.

Connor says, "It would make it exponentially worse."

Garrison's lips shut and his head falls again. I just want to hug him. And it's a weird feeling because I've never really *yearned* to touch anyone.

He's not alone in this. It was both of our choice to sneak him here. Guilt swims through me all the same. I waver uneasily by the doorframe. "Can I explain…I want to apologize to Daisy too…?" *Don't cry, Willow.* I push back tears and emotion. But I feel horrible for causing her distress. For her thinking there was an intruder in the house, something that I know ramps up her panic.

This was supposed to be a safe place.

Thankfully, Rose nods. "Follow me."

We leave and find Lily and Daisy in Maximoff's room. Lily bends over the crib with a rattle, softly talking to the giggling baby. Daisy lies on the ground, her white husky curled up against her. She strokes her fur in long waves.

Rose shuts the door behind me, and Lily asks, "Is everyone okay?"

"Mostly," Rose says, then plants her gaze on me.

"I'm so sorry," I begin, water pooling in my eyes. Daisy lifts her head off Coconut's fur, confusion pleating her brows. And I just burst forth like a geyser. The truth flooding the bedroom floor.

I can't stop.

Not until I've outlined, in detail, how I smuggled Garrison to the lake house. Why he needed a place to stay in the first place, which means divulging the truth about him flunking out of Faust. By the time I finish the story, my eyes have glued to the ground, unable to stare them in the eyes.

"And I don't deserve your forgiveness," I add quickly. "Especially you, Daisy. So if you'd like Garrison and me to leave the lake house, I understand—"

"What, no," Daisy cuts me off abruptly. "I don't want that."

My heart thrashes, and I risk a glance. Daisy's on her feet, light touching her green eyes. She…she doesn't seem mad?

"You're not mad?"

She shakes her head. "You snuck a boy into a trunk of a car."

"Classic Gryffindor," Lily says under her breath.

Daisy continues, "You *blindfolded* him and took his phone just so that *we*"—she twirls her finger between her sisters—"could stay safe. Why would we be mad about that?"

I wipe at the corners of my eyes. "Because I should have told all of you."

"You're not the first person here to keep secrets," Lily says, rocking on the balls of her feet. "You fit right in."

Rose sends Lily a look. "Yes, but let's not make secrets a regular occurrence."

"Agreed," Lily nods.

Pressure lifts off my chest. "So Garrison can stay?" I ask.

Daisy plops on the edge of the bed. "He just spent twelve hours in a *duffel* bag." Her eyes ping to Rose. "You can't kick him out now."

Rose scoffs. "Why are you directing that to me? I agree wholeheartedly. He's earned his spot here."

Lily frowns like she's lost in thought. "How did he survive in that duffel bag anyway?" Before I can answer, she swings her head to me. "He must really like you."

Daisy crosses her legs and puts her chin to her fist. "Yes, let's talk about the one-and-only Garrison Abbey."

Oh no. "We're just friends," I reiterate. I feel like I'm probably going to be doing this for a while.

Lily squints. "You're going to prom with Declan, right?"

"Who's Declan?" Rose wonders accusingly, like she's a little perturbed she hasn't been told all the details. I like that she wants to hear about my life.

"He's a boy," I answer. "He's a regular customer at Superheroes & Scones."

Lily smiles, knowing about him since he frequents the shop so much.

"And he asked me to prom," I explain. "I said *yes*." Declan is nice. I met him at the comic book store. He was looking for classic *Star Trek* comics. We carry more *Star Wars*, so I had to go in the back to hunt for the issues.

He talks more than me. I just kind of listen.

"You don't seem excited about it," Rose notices.

"I am," I nod. "It's just…I'm nervous because we only really hang out at Superheroes & Scones. I don't have any classes with him at Dalton."

I've never actually been around Declan *at* school. I guess he could try to find me in the halls, but he never has before. I don't know what that means. "It's also the first time any boy has ever asked me out," I tell them. "I've never even been on a coffee date, so there are more nerves than excitement. That's all."

"It'll be spectacular," Daisy tells me assuredly. "And we'll help you get ready."

"Of course," Rose says like that's a known quantity in my prom prep.

Lily is still frowning. "Does Garrison know about Declan?"

"Yep," I say. "I told him. He said that Declan sounded like a starship trooper nerd."

Star Trek, I corrected him.

Aren't those the same thing? He feigned confusion. He's been working at Superheroes & Scones too long to get them mixed up.

All the Calloway sisters exchange a look that I can't decipher. Maybe they're thinking Garrison is jealous or that he's flirting. I've questioned it before, but I know the truth—we're *just* friends.

28

GARRISON ABBEY
Age 18

G uilt has been hammering me ever since Willow left the room. No…it's been that way since the lamp crash. No, since I was born. Maybe I came out of the womb with this sour, bitter feeling rumbling around inside me. Shame swims through my bloodstream, and it's going to stay that way until I bleed out.

Ryke sweeps up the broken glass, Loren lights candles around the bedroom, and Connor sits next to me with a first-aid kit.

"I can do that," I say when I see the tweezers in Connor's hand.

He passes them over. "You need stitches, and the nearest hospital is more than two hours away."

Let me bleed out, is my first thought.

The second: I'm not going to the hospital. I can't. There's no way I'm making this worse for Willow. The hospital will blow up this situation to catastrophic levels. I've already obliterated enough.

Ryke sweeps harder, pissed off. I'm not an idiot. He's angry at me for scaring his girlfriend. The one with PTSD.

I can't breathe.

I just grind my teeth back and forth, eyes clouding and burning. Connor's gaze sears every inch of me. "Can you stop watching me?" I snap.

"I could, but I'm waiting for you to answer me."

I inspect my foot, tweezers hovering above the glass. Under my breath, I mutter, "I'm not going to the hospital."

"What was that?" Connor's tone is calm, almost easy-going.

My nose flares, emotions bubbling to the surface. Unable to swallow them down, I shout, "I'm not going to the hospital!" I jab the tweezers towards the door. "I promised her I wouldn't ruin the relationships she's made with *any* of you—and if I go to the hospital, people will see you, take stupid pictures, and everyone will know whatever nowhere-ville state we're in. So *no*, I'm not going." I suck in a strained breath and focus back on my foot, jaw tight.

"Relax," Loren snaps. "We're not going to force you to do something you don't want, but I would like to know *why* you're here."

Ryke crouches to sweep the glass into a dustpan, his expression darkening. "If he's here to get laid—"

"What?" I wince. "No." I recoil at Lo's glare. "Not that I don't like Willow." *Jesus.* This is all going wrong.

Ryke joins in on glaring at me. *Great.* I have both of them wanting to rip out my jugular. But what am I supposed to say? I like Willow. If I could ask her out today, I would. But I'm too late.

I look to Connor as I admit, "Some starship trooper nerd asked her to prom, okay?"

And anyway, Connor told me this would be *exponentially worse* if I was dating Willow, so this starship trooper nerd should be a notch in the "you didn't fuck everything up" list. Except, I'd really just like to kick the starship trooper off the list entirely. He can go be in someone else's atmosphere and ask *them* to prom.

"Declan," Lo says the name that I'd like to never hear again. "You know who he is. Lily told me that he stops by Superheroes & Scones at least four times a week."

"To try to talk to Willow," I complain. "And what the fuck kind of name is Declan?"

"What the fuck kind of name is Garrison?" Lo retorts.

I roll my eyes and sigh. "Whatever."

Connor cuts in, "As amusing as all of this is, we're still no closer to answers, and I'd like them sometime in the next five minutes."

Ryke dumps the glass into a trash bag and then disappears into the bathroom. Lo kneels beside the bed and gestures for the tweezers.

I hesitate and then surrender them.

"Is there anything we can use to sew up the cut in there?" Lo nods to the first-aid kit.

That means we're not going to the hospital. *Thank you.* My shoulders drop and muscles ease.

"We can find an alternative if that's what he really wants," Connor says.

I nod. "That's what I want."

Ryke returns and hands me a cup of water. Connor passes me a packet of Advil. I'm unbothered by the physical pain, but something pushes through me at their kindness.

I don't deserve it. Not a single bit. Yet, here they are.

And it just barrels into me, the weight of the moment. I look between them, overwhelmed, and on the verge of tears. *Don't fucking cry, man.* I suck it down by asking a stupid question. "I thought you two hated each other?" I gesture from Ryke to Connor. Tabloids say they're at odds all the time.

Ryke answers, "We're good friends."

I stare at the carpet. Lost for words.

"What is it?" Connor asks.

I shake my head and tear open the Advil packet. "I was just thinking…I don't even know where I find the kind of friendship that you three have. My friends are dicks." I let out a short, pained laugh that scratches my throat. "I'm one too…"

A heavy beat pounds before someone speaks.

"We're all assholes," Lo tells me. "But one day, you'll meet an asshole that pushes you to be a better person. Those are the ones that stick with you."

I rub at my eyes once. *Don't fucking cry.* And then I toss back the pills with a swig of water.

"We're encroaching on my five-minute time limit," Connor tells me.

I don't even make a joke about him having time limits. Swallowing hard, I explain everything. Not even leaving out the part where I broke into Superheroes & Scones and slept in the breakroom for the past month. Failure is easy to admit

When I explain how I flunked out of Faust, my anger starts to boil. Eating me. I pull my hood over my head. "And you know, it's my parent's fault." My eyes burn as I look to Connor. He went to Faust. He must know how rigorous and fucking difficult it is. "Why'd they have to send me to a new school in the middle of the year? I know…I know I fucked up, but if I even want a high school diploma, I have to be *held back*. Do you even know what that feels like?" I'm an idiot for even asking.

Connor Cobalt is a genius. He's never felt *this* before.

"What about your friends?" Connor asks, ignoring my question. "They have houses, I presume."

"You mean all my friends that broke into your house to scare you? Those ones?" My stomach twists even thinking about them. How the judge sentenced them to a year each. *That could have been me.* Some days, I wish it were.

"No," Connor replies. "Your other friends."

"I don't have other friends. No one wants to be associated with the bad guy, not at Dalton and definitely not at Faust." I shrug. "I had nowhere to go, okay? I had Superheroes & Scones and Willow, that's it."

I. Am. A. Loser.

It might as well be tattooed on my fucking forehead.

But Willow is hands-down the most amazing person I've ever met—compassionate, brave, unique, shy—and she doesn't mind spending time with a loser like me, so that's something, I guess.

There's more to tell. More to get off my chest.

"I burned the letter that Faust sent my parents before they got it—the one that said I flunked. And you know…" My voice cracks, choked. "I've never been a good person. I don't even know what some of you see in me…because I'm shit."

"You're *not* shit," Lo tells me, forceful like that's already written in stone. Carved into marble. I don't know how he sees it so clearly. He adds, "You want this glass out of your foot?"

Lo is looking at me like I'm already a good guy. I don't get it. But I want to believe it. Someday. Somehow.

"Yeah," I release a deeper breath. "Yeah, I want it out."

29

WILLOW *HALE*
Age 23

"**A**m I underdressed?" I ask Garrison quietly, right after a suspender-clad hostess seats us at Lola Vine, a cool upscale pizza place in London that I've had my eye on for months. I was so excited about the atmosphere that I forgot to investigate people's clothes off Yelp photos.

I glance down at my thin blue sweater and the unbuttoned plaid flannel I wear on top. And I'm in *jeans*. I could've selected nicer pants.

"Not to me." Garrison scoots closer to the candlelit table. "But if anyone thinks you are, then I am too. We can be underdressed together." He splays a moto jacket on the back of the velvet chair. A black tee molds his toned biceps, but I'm selfishly glad that he's

I smile more, not feeling as out of place.

Garrison adjusts his jacket for another second or two. Giddy energy flutters inside my stomach. I have a lot to be giddy about today.

The biggest one, Garrison is in London. Just seeing my boyfriend makes the weeks of dreaming about him feel real.

And we're on a date. I still can't believe he reserved a table *here*. Every time I wanted to go when he was in town, they'd been booked up for the whole week.

"What do you think so far?" Garrison asks, handing me a leather-bound menu. "As cool as you imagined?"

I realize that I've been staring at him more than the restaurant. Looking around, I soak up my surroundings: orange and purple velvet chairs and booths, swanky curved bar with fancy liquors, a mirrored ceiling, deep red carpet, and rouged drapes.

"Better." I can't stop smiling. "It feels like the Hellfire Club could exist in here." A popular comic book site named ten restaurants that reminded them of the *X-Men* films, and Lola Vine was listed under *X-Men: First Class*. I was shocked a restaurant within distance of my college made the cut.

I wait for Garrison to make a joke like *what's the Hellfire Club?* with mock confusion. After all his time working at Superheroes & Scones, I'm pretty sure he'd remember the clandestine society with Emma Frost as a member.

Garrison nods. "That's good....really good." His aquamarine eyes flit around the packed restaurant. I doubt anyone will recognize us with the lights dimmed to a dark, warm glow.

A waitress brings iced waters, tells us the specials, and leaves to give us time to order.

I peruse Garrison more than the menu. He's acting sort of weird. He keeps scooting his chair closer, perching his elbow on and off the table.

"Is everything okay?" I push up my glasses.

"Yeah, why wouldn't it be?" He takes a hefty swig of water.

I shrug. Maybe I'm overthinking his jitters, but I'd like to think I know him really, *really* well. "I don't know…are you sure nothing's going on?"

He runs a hand through his brown hair. "No, nothing's really going on." He rests his arm on the back of the chair, trying to be more cool and collected.

I mean, he does look cool.

Tattoos on his bicep, hair falling back to his eyes, and bad boy persona like a well-worn cloak—but after all these years, I know better.

Garrison Abbey is *good*.

He just has a bad reputation.

One that's been scrubbed clean by the people who love him most, the ones who gave him another chance, another shot.

I change the topic to movies after we order a margherita pizza and classic pepperoni. "I don't think anything will ever top *Avengers: End Game*." I sip my water.

Garrison is staring off behind me, then blinks to refocus on me. "Yeah, that's a good one. Jake Gyllenhaal killed it as that Mysterio guy."

Wrong movie.

We were talking about *Spider-Man: Far From Home* five minutes ago. I frown and open my mouth, about to ask if he's okay again.

But quickly, he asks, "How'd the meeting with Lily and the attorneys go?"

Lily and the attorneys.

Giddiness returns, and it's weird to think around this time, a whole year ago, I flew to Philly and ran into the hospital. Garrison's appendix was removed. I was still living in the "party" flat. I was worried about my few friendships and my slipping grades.

A lot has happened in a year. While some things have stayed the same.

My lease ended, and I moved into a studio apartment close to campus. No roommates, which has helped boost my grades up to Bs and As.

And with my new place, it's been easier keeping Sheetal and Tess as friends. They've been on-and-off as a couple all year, ever since Tess changed majors to *theatre*. But right now, they're in a "firmly together" stage.

As for Salvatore, I haven't really spoken much to him since I moved out, but we still share a lot of business classes and see each other.

It's awkward, but I prefer awkward over the discomfort and bitter anger I started to feel towards him. Especially how he kept treating Garrison like trash.

Sheetal makes class with Salvatore more bearable. She'll crack jokes before lectures, and the air always feels lighter.

But what Garrison is referencing—Lily and the attorneys—is more recent.

"I figured Lily already told you how it went," I say, since Garrison is still living in her home with Lo and their kids.

"Yeah, but it's not you telling me," Garrison says like hearing me makes all the difference.

My smile tugs higher. "Okay, so it looks like franchising Superheroes & Scones is one-hundred percent a go, and then I pitched the idea of opening up a London branch."

His mouth parts in a little shock. "London?"

I frown, realizing Lily must've left this out. "I didn't go into the franchise meeting thinking London would come out of my mouth, but Lily asked me, *'If you opened up a store, which city would you choose?'*"

He shakes his head, confused. "Why London, though? You could've said…New York City or Pittsburgh."

"I don't know New York or Pittsburgh that well," I say softly. "London has been my home for over two years, and I understand the market and the streets and people. I feel confident I could open a store here, if given the chance."

Garrison gazes at the flickering candle, his thoughts swirling.

I scoot closer now, my pulse haywire. "Even if I open a London branch, Lily said I could be in charge of opening more locations." My voice is too quiet, and in this tender way, he asks me to repeat. So I do, and I add, "She's offering me a job when I graduate. Like a corporate-level, high-paying position that I hope…I hope I can be ready for, but it sounds like a dream…"

Putting my business degree to good use while being surrounded by superheroes and comics every day—I couldn't ask for a better career.

I wait for him to reply, holding my breath. "Garrison?"

"You'll be good at it," he says, certain of this fact. "I know you will be."

"I could suck."

"No." He has so much faith in me that my heart ascends to new levels. "You're smart, Willow, and you're so passionate about business and comics. It makes perfect sense."

I scrutinize the slight dip of his mouth. "But…?" *There has to be a but coming.*

"But what does this mean for us?" He grimaces. "And I feel like a *cock* bringing myself into this and dampening the happiness of your career path."

"It's not dampened," I say with a peeking smile. "And I'd hope you'd think about what this means for us…because I'd rather there be an us to think about, you know?" *Giddiness*, a strange kind of giddy ignites.

Maybe because he's smiling again. "Alright, that's good then." He looks me over, his eyes carrying gentle affection. "What about us? You want to live in London full-time after graduation?"

"I'd rather just fly back every now and then. I know the paparazzi is nuts in Philly, but I miss it there. I miss everyone."

Garrison nods strongly, and I can tell he likes this plan. "It's not that I don't love London," he explains to me. "It's a city that'll always remind me of you. But I love Philly."

I smile. "Me too."

It's where I met my brothers, where I met my best friend Daisy, and where I met my first love who's sitting across from me six years later.

We talk a bit more about my future job. I try not to glance at my phone, but I swear we put our food orders in over forty minutes ago.

I don't care much about the pizza though.

I just like being here with Garrison.

He's gone a little quiet, and he rubs his palms, elbows on the table. He's staring around but his eyes always land on me, almost too much.

I give him a look.

He gives me one. "What?"

I shrug, waiting for him to tell me *something*. But he inhales a tense breath and licks his lips, just looking deeper into me.

I decide to talk. "Do you think they forgot our order?"

He scans the restaurant quickly, then back to me. "It probably takes a while to cook a fresh pizza." He seems disinterested in the food.

"How's lacrosse going?" I ask since he's been playing on a club team. Just for fun on the weekends. He's more resilient and determined than he lets on, or maybe he even realizes. Not a lot of people would return to a sport they have a love-hate relationship with, let alone find enjoyment in the activity again.

"It's good." He nods.

"You've been saying that a lot," I tell him.

He looks confused.

I clarify, "It's *good*, that's *good*, everything's *good*."

"What can I say? I'm a thousand-page thesaurus." His sarcasm is thick, a smile attached.

I want to laugh but my lips draw down. "Really, though, you're starting to worry me. Did something happen—"

"No, I promise, Willow, everything is perfect." His eyes grow far more tender, and he reaches a hand across the table.

I place my palm in his, and his thumb strokes my knuckles, expanding my lungs. His gaze is welling up, just looking at me.

It causes me to tear up. "Why are you staring at me like that?"

"Because I love you, Willow Hale. You're the greatest friend I've ever had, the most beautiful heart I've ever felt, and every morning I wake up, I can only hope to wake to you. Thinking of a single day without you in my life is physical torture." He takes my other hand, careful not to knock over the candle. "There was a time where I didn't even want to live till tomorrow, and now I don't ever want this life with you to end."

Overwhelmed tears roll down my cheeks, emotion that I can't conceal. Emotion that I don't try to hide.

He keeps going, his voice choked, on the verge of crying. "I want to play Street Fighter when we're too old to work the fucking controllers, and I want our kid to beat every high score we set. I want my girl, my greatest friend, to be the mother of my child, and to be my wife."

His wife.

He lets go of my hands, and my palms fly to my mouth.

Garrison.

I watch as he scoots his chair back.

"Garrison?" I croak.

Is he...?

I glance around, but of what I can see in the dim restaurant, no one is filming. People are watching, but no one has cameras out... or phones.

He planned this. He must have.

He planned this for me? For us.

"Willow." He takes a knee in front of my chair.

I'm still in tears, still stunned, and I angle towards him.

Garrison reaches into his back pocket and pulls out a black box. He wipes the wet corners of his eyes and flips the lid. "Will you do the biggest honor of my whole existence and marry me?" His voice trembles.

I cry, pinching my eyes, and I nod and say, "Yes." And then we're in each other's arms. Hugging. He brings me to a stance, to his chest, and our lips meet with so much soul and life and love that I feel like I'm soaring.

When we pull back, he slips a dainty ring on my finger, a diamond on a thin gold band with six tinier diamonds scattered like a vine. It's beautiful, but I don't have the chance to tell him.

Rouged curtains open behind me, and I hear applause and cheering before I see them.

My family.

Lo and Ryke. My dad. And Connor, Rose, Lily, and Daisy. My friends Sheetal and Tess. They're all here. Smiling. Crying.

I'm more overcome with more happiness. Seeing so many faces I love in one room. One place. In London.

I don't let go of Garrison's hand as I greet everyone.

I'm engaged.

To my guy, my greatest friend, to the someday father of my child, to my whole, beautiful future. It's going to be full of him.

PIZZAS ARE SPREAD OUT IN A FANCY, PRIVATE backroom of Lola Vine, where my family and friends had been hiding and waiting for Garrison to pop the big question.

What I quickly discover: the proposal was *months* in the making. Which means he knew he wanted to marry me months ago.

He asked me to marry him. It's still sinking in.

My face hurts from smiling.

Everyone managed to keep the secret to surprise me, and I still feel light-on-my-toes, floating and butterflies flapping—like I'm seventeen again with Garrison Abbey, about to embark on my first day at Dalton Academy.

And he's next to his car, waiting for me.

The night is winding down, pizzas devoured and a towering meringue pie picked on. I already asked Daisy to be my maid of honor. I blurted it out, and tears streamed down her cheeks as she hugged me. Instantly accepting the role.

Rose and Lily were each other's maids of honor, and Daisy never had a sister place her at the top. But she's number one on my list.

After I say goodbye to Sheetal and Tess, I take a bathroom break with the Calloway sisters, and Garrison and Connor slip into the men's room.

All should be perfectly well and good, but when we return to the backroom to grab coats, the air isn't easygoing or happy like we left it.

Lo and Ryke face our dad, all three on their feet and wielding heated glares and tense postures.

And as their eyes swerve to me, descending upon me with hot intimidation, I know what this has to be about. It's the only thing I can think of that'd elicit this intense reaction.

The lie.

My bad deed.

Years ago, I accepted Jonathan Hale's money to bribe students into deleting video footage of Garrion's fight with Salvatore, and I never told my brothers.

Every butterfly dies in my lungs, wings cut.

Garrison slips an arm around my waist. He's right next to me, but I have a feeling he won't be for long.

Rose is the first to speak. "What's going on?" Her voice is accusatory, like they're harbors of grave news on my celebratory day, and therefore, should be punished.

But it's my fault, for not telling them the truth in the first place.

"We need to talk to our sister," Lo says, his amber eyes still on mine. He seems really upset, and remorse eats at my insides.

Ryke adds, "In private."

I'm frozen, but I try to breathe.

My dad has a hand on his side, standing like he's made of importance and prestige. "If you're not a Hale by blood, you should go wait in the cars. We'll be out in a few minutes."

"I'm not leaving," Garrison retorts. "If this is about Willow—"

"She can talk to you later," Lo interjects. "We won't be that long."

Garrison's eyes fall down to me while Rose and Connor speak rapidly in fiery and smooth French to one another, filling the silence. Daisy and Lily are holding hands, and they exit the backroom first, but not before Daisy mouths to me, *you got this.*

She has no idea what I'm about to face or the truth I withheld, but she's still encouraging me. Still has faith in me. I breathe in, and I look up at Garrison. "I'll be okay."

He studies my expression and my trembling hands that I cup together. His palm glides down my wrist, to my hand, in tender comfort that floods me.

"I can stay," he whispers, and then pauses, our eyes latching like he, too, knows what this is probably about. "I should stay."

My brothers don't want him to. I whisper back, "I think I should do this on my own." I'm anxious by nature, but I'm not as nervous in the company of these three men as I used to be. At the beginning, just being face-to-face with my dad, I could barely hold a drink without water shaking and spilling out.

Ryke and Lo aren't soft, but they love me, and I know they wouldn't hurt me, even when I've hurt them.

Garrison hugs me, then stakes a glare on the room. "I know she's your sister, and your daughter." He looks to my dad. "But just remember I'm going to be her *husband.* So you fuck with her, you're dead to me."

Ryke rolls his eyes. "We're not going to fuck with our sister."

"We get it," Lo tells Garrison. "Skedaddle." He waves him off with two running fingers.

It lightens the air a little, and Garrison leaves the private backroom with one last glance at me, making sure I'm alright.

344

I nudge up my glasses with a tiny smile.

Connor and Rose reluctantly follow my boyfriend—or I guess, my fiancé. *We're engaged.* And on her way out, Rose grabs her fur coat and squeezes my shoulder with an iron grip.

Now I'm alone with just my older brothers and my dad. I linger awkwardly at one head of the table while they're clustered near the other end. A few half-eaten slices of margherita pizza are left on plates, napkins wadded on the long candlelit surface. Remnants of a happy engagement dinner.

I subconsciously touch the new piece of jewelry on my finger.

And three sets of eyes drop to my engagement ring.

Tension strains the air even more.

Ryke rakes a hand across his unshaven jaw. "Look, we're not going to ruin your fucking engagement. We just want an explanation."

"I want to give one," I say quietly, "but I don't know what you've heard...?"

Lo grips the back of a velvet chair. "Our dad said he gave you *a hundred grand,* so that you could get a bunch of students to delete some video of Garrison sucker-punching another kid. And I get wanting to keep your boyfriend's shitty night out of the press. We've all been there. Too many goddamn times. But out of everyone you could have gone to for help—your first choice was *him.*" His brows pinch in hurt and confusion. "I know you've always said you want to do things on your own. You don't want handouts. But what you took was a handout from our dad, and I don't see why you trusted him more than us."

"We would've fucking helped you," Ryke says strongly, gesturing from his chest to Lo's.

I shift my weight, trying to hold their hard and sharp gazes. "I know you would've."

Our dad narrows a jagged-edged look on his sons. "Give her a fucking break. I'm her father. She came to me for help. I *helped* her. You're both blowing this shit out of proportion."

Eyes darkened, Ryke guns him down. "Don't stand there and act like your handouts don't come with selfish fucking *conditions*."

He chokes on a hot breath. "What conditions? All I've ever wanted was for her to go to an Ivy League—not some no-name business school in *London*—but did you hear me complain about it? *No*," our dad snaps. "I applauded and sent her on her way and helped her *stay* there. And then when she called me needing my help again, I did with no questions asked."

Ryke is fuming. "What about the internship with the Nubell family she took last summer? Did she want to do that or did you push her there?"

He pushed me.

I drop my gaze, ashamed.

Nubell cookies are almost as popular as Kraft and Keebler, and I spent the summer running errands for Patrick Nubell, the great-great-grandson of the company. It was a good opportunity, just not the one I really wanted.

I had the chance to intern for a big comic book publishing company in New York. Mostly due to the fact that I was related to Loren Hale, not based on my skill or resumé. I know that, but I still would've accepted.

In the end, I had to decline.

My dad was adamant that I take the Nubell internship. *"I pulled these strings for you, Willow. It wasn't easy."*

"She wanted that internship!" our dad shouts at Ryke. "It was a perfect experience for her future—"

"For the future you want for her!" Ryke yells.

"I want the best for my daughter," he sneers back, eyes like blades. "I want the best for you and Loren. I want the best for my *fucking* children, and you're not going to make me apologize for that!"

"Stop," Lo snaps at them, often having to play peacemaker between his dad and brother. He steps between their rigid builds and focuses on me. "The one thing that just doesn't make sense to me, Willow, is that Ryke and I could've helped you so many times and you said *no* or you didn't ask when you needed it. Not just with burying that video footage, but tuition and even your flat, back when you wanted out of the lease. You didn't let us help you, so why accept our dad's help but not ours?"

Ryke faces me more now, his brows furrowed. He wants this answer too, and I know it's the biggest one.

What changed that made me go to Jonathan and not to them.

Emotion stings my eyes. "I never wanted to burden any of you." I wipe beneath my glasses. "I never wanted to come into your lives taking more than I should. You all know that; I've said as much before. But I needed the money to protect Garrison, and when I had to make a choice to burden a father or a brother, I decided to burden a father." A tear slips out, and I look to Lo. "You've taken care of me since I came to Philly, even before I knew Jonathan was my dad—but you have two children, Lo. You have a son and a daughter, and maybe one day you'll have more babies, and they're going to need your help and your support too. And the way I saw it, I couldn't take from you or Ryke because everything I take could go to your kids."

Their gazes try to soften, and I see their sadness.

"I'm not your child," I continue on. "I'm *his*." I motion to Jonathan. "And he has less on his plate than both of you." He's retired. His sons are grown up and financially independent. It made the most sense.

If they thought I went to our dad because I love him or trust him more, it's almost the opposite.

I love Lo and Ryke and their families too much to ask for more.

Lo's jaw sharpens. "I wish you didn't feel like that." He comes closer as I sniff, and my brother hugs me, a hug that slows my anxious heartbeat.

As we pull back, I wipe my running nose with my knuckles. "You've done everything for me, and it's okay that you let our dad do this."

Lo nods a few times, understanding, but Ryke looks more concerned. He'll always be worried about Jonathan having control over my life. Over Lo's life, too.

But maybe it's good that they both know about the hundred grand. Maybe I should've told them so much sooner. Because the way they turn to our dad, I know they'll never let him dictate where I go or what I do. No matter how many checks he writes.

30

PRESENT DAY – March
London, England

GARRISON ABBEY
Age 23

Last day in London before we fly back to Philly, and I'm still happily engaged to Willow. For a guy who's certifiably *cursed*, that's pretty much all I could ask for, and it's a lot to ask because it's all I want.

I accounted for some drama since I invited her dad to the engagement dinner, so no surprise there. But it's not until his daughter is gone—at a brunch outing with all the Calloway sisters—that he decides to serve his shitty opinions.

And they're all being flung on a gold platter at *me*.

"She hasn't even graduated from college yet or begun a career," Jonathan tells me in his penthouse suite, where he invited his sons, Connor, and me for lunch. "If you thought more about her academics, you would've waited. It's too soon—"

"No, it's not," I retort, leaning backward. My instinct is to draw away from bullshit, not catapult towards a fight.

Connor just went to the bathroom to take a business phone call, but the rest of us are seated at an ornate round table that looks fit for the British royal family, and we have perfect views of the River Thames, Big Ben, and Westminster Abbey.

Willow's dad is loaded. The sheer wealth of this man is literally all around me, and I stare Jonathan Hale down as I add, "Willow and I already agreed to get married *after* she graduates." She has to finish up this semester, and then she'll be a senior.

One year and some months left. That's it.

Piece of cake.

"You're too eager, and you're rushing her," Jonathan criticizes as he dunks a biscuit in coffee. "Give her time."

"Dad," Lo says with the shake of his head.

Ryke glares at their father. "Why are you always speaking for Willow? She's not fucking here, and if she were, we all know she wouldn't agree with you."

Jonathan ignores his son, his eyes on me. "You're not thinking this through, Garrison."

"I am," I snap. "Last time I checked, I have a brain."

"Use it then and let her have a fucking career first. If you're lucky, she'll still be around."

Anger punctures my eyes. He's saying that she might not want to marry me once she's established a career. "Say that in front of Willow," I sneer at Jonathan. He'd never utter half the vile shit he's been spewing if his daughter were around.

He bites into a soggy biscuit.

I can't shut my mouth. "Right." I nod. "You're a gutless fish."

Ryke and Lo go rigid in shock.

PRESENT DAY

And then Jonathan wipes his mouth with a napkin, his eyes lethal as he says, "You're a fucking cunt."

"Hey!" Ryke yells, gripping the table like he could flip it. "For fuck's sake, he's going to be your son-in-law, back the fuck off him."

My hammering pulse is in my ears.

Jonathan stands, zeroing in only on me. "I'm not skirting around you, Garrison, and you should thank me for not patting you on the ass like a goddamn toddler."

I let out a short, sardonic laugh. "Thank you, I'm just so grateful to hear that you think I rushed a proposal *after* I proposed only two days ago."

He rolls his eyes. "You're a petulant child. Grow *up*."

"*Dad*," Lo snarls, and if looks could kill, Jonathan would be butchered in a million serrated pieces by Lo. But likewise, his glare is slaughtering his own son.

I don't want to be on the receiving end of that. It scares the shit out of me, but my brain is shrieking, *fuck him*. "I am grown up. The only one kicking and screaming is you."

He swings his head to me, about to eat me alive. "You ungrateful son of a bitch—"

"Jesus Christ, don't fucking attack him," Lo cuts in, springing to his feet while I stay tilted back in my chair like the degenerate I'm sure Jonathan thinks I am.

Lo blocks his dad from me, and Ryke is standing, sort of between me and his brother. I think in case either of us need him.

Jonathan is seething, glare skewering me. "He said he's a man, Loren, so he should be able to talk to me man-to-man without you coming to his defense." He continues, "Come on, Garrison. You're all grown up, aren't you? Show me."

I grind my teeth, my stomach in knots, and my heated eyes sear the table. I'm shutting down, not wanting deeper in this shit.

I want out.

No part of me wants to prove how big of a man I am. I can't prove shit to him, so what's the fucking point?

I push back, standing up from the table.

Ryke and Lo are speaking to their dad with heat and urgency, but he's not listening to them.

"You're leaving?" Jonathan calls out to me incredulously, like our joust has just begun. He shouts at me as I walk off. "Is that how you'll be with my daughter? When the fight gets hard, you're just going to run away?!"

I will always protect Willow, but I don't need to convince anyone of that.

The hotel elevator is inside the penthouse, and as I reach my escape, Connor exits the bathroom, pocketing his cellphone. His eyes ping to me and then the echoes of Ryke, Lo, and Jonathan's heated argument.

"I leave for five minutes," he says calmly to himself, then sweeps me and then the elevator. "You're going?"

I nod. "To brunch." I'm crashing the girls' thing. Willow won't care.

"Wait here." His soothing voice somehow hypnotizes me to obey. I wait at the elevator, and he disappears. Two seconds later, Ryke and Lo are in his company, their confident strides aimed for the elevator.

I make a confused face.

"We're all going to brunch," Connor informs me, pushing the elevator button. We don't wait long for the doors to slide open, and the four of us file in.

I hang behind them. They're all fucking tall, all towering, and the way they stand like a defensive brick wall—it feels like they're shielding me. Paparazzi might be in the lobby. I think Connor is texting security.

But it's more than that.

Ryke glances back at me. "You okay?"

I can only nod.

Lo looks back next.

Then Connor.

They're all checking on me. And I have to stare at the elevator wall because something pricks my eyes. I blink a few times. Don't fucking cry.

It's okay to cry.

Lo told me that.

It's okay to cry.

I look up at the ceiling, a tear rolling down my jaw. I'm not emotional because of anything Jonathan said.

I'm emotional because I got the three brothers I always wished I had.

Connor, Ryke, and Lo—they protect me all the time. They care about me when they don't have to. These are three brothers that I'd never trade in, never swap out, and even though we're not blood related, I know they're mine.

IN THE MEN'S BATHROOM AT BRUNCH, LO AND I find ourselves alone, and I end up confessing that I don't know what to do about Jonathan.

"I want to respect him because he's Willow's dad," I say, drying my hands on a paper towel. "But I can't stand him, no offense."

354

Lo almost laughs. "None taken. I get how he is, man. I grew up with him."

I can't even imagine how he survived that verbal sledgehammer every day. But I don't say it out loud, because I know he'd say the same about me and my brothers.

He leans against the sink. "You know, way back when Lily's sex addiction leaked, he tried to push us into a marriage to save our reputations and those around us."

My brows pinch. "He tried to push you *into* one?"

"Yeah." Lo flashes a bitter smile. "The guilt-trip is heavy, almost enough to make you do things you'd never think you'd do." He stares off and shakes his head, going into a longer explanation about that time in the past.

It makes me feel...not alone.

Like I'm dealing with a cankerous sore that they've all tried to disinfect and rid.

"As much as I love him," Lo says, "he shouldn't have the power to guilt anyone into anything. Not into a marriage and not out of one."

I nod slowly and toss the crumpled towel in the trash. "You think he'll ever lay off me?"

"With my dad, just give it time, and we'll see."

PRESENT DAY

The Calloway Sisters & Their Men — Fan Page

Present Day | Followers: 201K

If you haven't heard of the *big* news and seen all the adorable pictures circulating GBA News and *Celebrity Crush*, then you're missing out on history. Our gorgeous Calloway sisters and their sexy AF men were in London for Garrison & Willow's engagement! And a little birdie around the inter-webs has revealed that Garrison *surprised* his girlfriend—how cute is that? With everyone except Willow back in Philly, here's a helpful rundown on their whereabouts!

The Stokes

Poppy Calloway (34) & Sam Stokes (34)
Daughter: Maria (12)
Update: Boo, the Stokes are *very* MIA these days. They didn't even show up to London for Willow's big day. It would've been so cool to have a glimpse of preteen Maria!

The Cobalts

Rose Calloway (31) & Connor Cobalt (32)
Daughters: Jane (5)
Sons: Charlie & Beckett (3-year-old twins), Eliot (1), and Tom (11-months-old)
Update: Rumors are floating everywhere about Rose being pregnant again! Whether it's true or not, the

Cobalt Empire deserves a confetti-blast congrats for all the lion cubs they're raising. #FamilyGoals. Have you seen a tighter-knit family? Besides pregnancy possibilities, both Rose and Connor are thriving in their companies. Cobalt Inc.'s stock has risen 31%, and Calloway Couture's boutique was packed last week (pics in the slideshow!)

The Hales
Lily Calloway (29) & Loren Hale (30)
Son: Maximoff (5)
Daughter: Luna (1)
Update: The cutest of the cute! Lily and Lo are back in Philly with their tiny superheroes, and Maximoff *loves* to dress like his Uncle Ryke. He was seen in a cool leather jacket and trying to climb onto Ryke's Ducati. No news about more Hale babies, but fingers crossed!

The Meadows
Daisy Calloway (25) & Ryke Meadows (31)
Daughter: Sullivan (3)
Update: Also back in lovely Philadelphia, Daisy and Ryke are busy, wild bees with summer approaching since Camp Calloway is a tremendous hit! It's sold out for this year and the next. No new photos of Sulli, except some blurry pics after swim lessons with her cousin Maximoff (see below!)

The Unofficial Calloway Sister
Willow Hale (23) & Her Fiancé – Garrison Abbey (23)
Update: Sweet, sweet love! After their epic proposal,

Garrison has flown back to Philly, leaving Willow behind as she finishes college in London. No one is sure about *when* the wedding is happening. Some sources are speculating early this year, others think a lot longer. Until there's clearer info, let us know your favorite Willow & Garrison ship name: #Gillow, #Garlow, or #Wilson. Don't forget to vote in the poll!

Love you like Loren loves Lily,
xo Olive

31

GARRISON *ABBEY*
Age 23

The proposal was last week, and now that I'm in Philly, I'm back to doing this thing where I try not to mope while the girl I love is an ocean away. By now, I'd say I'm proficient in the art of being okay with long-distance relationships. Productivity is key or whatever.

That's why I'm at Superheroes & Scones today.

It's weird being back and not being an employee or babysitting Moffy here. I enter the breakroom and ask the store manager where Lily is. Seeing the new face wearing the "manager" nametag reminds me of Maya.

Last I heard, Maya Ahn is still in Portland working for Image Comics.

It was a big deal when she first landed the job. Lily and Willow were really proud.

There was a whole goodbye party when she left the store, and I learned enough Korean to tell her that she'll always know more than me and she's really cool.

She smiled and said shit back in Korean that she knew I wouldn't understand. We laughed, and I hate that I'm remembering all of this—Jesus, I swear every time I walk into Superheroes & Scones, I'm thrown back into these bittersweet, feel-good memories.

The new manager says, "She's in the storage room."

I pop the tab of a Lightning Bolt! energy drink and shove inside. Boxes of merch and comics line the space. Familiarity surrounding me, and I'm honestly trying not to face-plant on Memory Lane.

I find Lily and her two kids pretty easily.

Baggy *Star Wars* tee on and phone close to her ear, Lily looks like she snuck back here for a quiet moment. Which I'm about to interrupt.

Awesome. Looks like I still have Grand Slam worthy timing.

I shut the door with my foot, not bailing.

"Lo," she says into the phone, face flushed, "you didn't tell Garrison, did you?"

"Tell me what?" I stand by an old comic stand in need of serious dusting. *Remember when you dusted the clearance merch with Willow?*

Like yesterday.

Near a life-sized Magneto cutout, Maximoff Hale leaps off a cardboard box and races towards me. "Uncle Garrison!"

The corner of my mouth lifts. Moffy acts like I'm the coolest thing in the room, and we're surrounded by crates of action figures.

The five-year-old rolls up to me, and we do a secret handshake that ends with a fist-bump.

"Never mind," Lily tells me, then listens to her phone call.

"Did you see Luna?" Moffy smiles and points out his one-year-old sister, hiding in a cardboard box. She giggles, glittering eyes peeking out at me.

"Whoa, she's getting smaller and you're getting taller."

"I am?" His smile mushrooms.

I pretend to measure his height with my free hand. "Definitely a centimeter taller than when I last saw you." Which was this morning. I still live with the Hale family.

"You think I'll be as tall as you, Uncle Garrison?" His voice sounds like he's five, but he sometimes acts older, like he's already leveled-up to a preteen in a 90s cult classic movie starring Jonathan Taylor Thomas.

"Way taller." I'm not that short, but his dad is six-two.

"Cool," Maximoff says and stares off in thought.

Lily hangs up her phone, so I walk closer, and Moffy matches my pace. Before she asks why I'm here, I tell her, "I need your help on something."

Lily tickles her daughter in the box, and Luna tugs her mom's finger with another giggle. "What can I do?"

I sip my energy drink and gesture to a few cardboard boxes labeled *The Fourth Degree*. I'm guessing each contain comics slipped in protective plastic. Here, back stock is usually just obscure issues that don't sell or extras to replenish ones that fly off the shelves. I explain, "I need every comic that has Sorin-X. There are too many issues and spin-offs now. Honestly, I don't have time to go through all of them."

I always thought Vic Whistler would continue to be the most popular superhero in *The Fourth Degree* universe. Somehow, Sorin-X surpassed the hero that launched the franchise.

It still blows my mind.

I wait for Lily to ask *why* I'm requesting this shit. She doesn't yet. Instead, Lily picks herself off the floor and glances at her son. "Moffy, there's a little Luna in a box—"

"I got her, Mommy." Maximoff goes to the box and plays with his sister, like babysitting is the equivalent of a trip to Disney.

Weird.

But wholesome.

Honestly, I like being around both.

"They're all in here." Lily guides me to *The Fourth Degree* labeled boxes. "Lo will be here soon, and he might be more help. He's read every issue about a million times."

We tear open a couple boxes and flip through the comic, setting aside any with Sorin-X.

Ones without the character, Lily gingerly slips the issue into its plastic cover. "Are you going to read these?" She motions to the Sorin-X pile.

I place another issue on top. "What else would I be doing with them?"

"I don't know." She squints at me. "You don't really read comics, not like Willow." She notes, "You had no clue who Cypher was when you started working here."

"Yeah, and none of the employees ever let me forget it." I begin to smile, remembering how Willow tried to help me learn factoids about the New Mutants so our co-workers would stop giving me shit. *Six years ago.* I swig my energy drink to swallow down the nostalgia and say, "I've read New Mutants, by the way."

Lily wears a giddy smile. "Because of Willow?" I love how supportive she's always been of me and Willow, especially since she was there at the beginning of it all.

"Yeah, because of Willow." I shake a comic back into the plastic sleeve.

"Which brings everything to Twitter. *Gillow Engagement* has been trending all day, did you see?"

My stomach nosedives, energy drink curdling.

The headlines are pretty generic:

Willow Hale Gets Engaged!
Check out Loren Hale's New Brother-In-Law!

I prepared for press to be all over our ass, but I'm worried the amount of paparazzi interested in us right now could go from "Chaotic Good" to "Chaotic Evil". I'd really love if my fame capped out here.

No more.

Lily continues, "Connor said you both made GBA Entertainment News last night too." I pegged him as a daily C-Span viewer. The guy still reads the *paper*. As in newspaper. Printed. In his hands.

"He watches entertainment news?" I say with cinched brows.

"That was my reaction."

Maybe to check himself out. He is a narcissist.

I flip another comic, recalling other trending Twitter topics. "You also forgot about *Garlow Engagement* and *Wilson Engagement*."

Fans still can't decide on a ship name, which are dumb anyway. Willow loves ships though and even owns Raisy, Coballoway, and LiLo merch. She's too kind to play favorites, so she supports all three of our ship names too.

"Does all of this bother you?" Lily asks me. "You and Willow never talk to us about the media presence."

Because *they're* the cause of our fame, and it feels shitty to complain when they've done a lot for us.

I shrug. "Being around you guys, it just comes with the territory, and we both kind of gradually stepped into it." Thank God we weren't thrown into the deep end at the start. If the paparazzi were all over me back then like they are now, I don't think I could handle it.

I tilt a comic upside-down, the panel sort of backwards. Brown hair hangs in my eyes. *Need a haircut.* It's starting to bug the fuck out of me.

My stomach is still in knots. And I know it's not about my hair.

Paparazzi.

Coming home from the engagement in London was pure hell. Fans and media bum-rushed us at the airport, and I could barely see. Barely breathe. Rabid crowds, I've dealt with before, but for maybe the first time, the spotlight was centralized on *me*.

If I think too hard, I can still feel hands scraping down my arms. Tugging my body. Pulling at my shirt, choking me at the collar until Lo's bodyguard shoved them away.

Sickness churns at the thought of that happening again.

But at some point soon, I have to go back to the airport. I have to see Willow.

And next time, Lo, Ryke, Connor, and their security won't be with me.

"Lily…can I ask you something?" I peek over at Moffy, ensuring he's not listening. Last thing I'd want is to scare him about the media. Especially when they're raising their kids to be accustomed to crowds and cameras.

He's climbed into a plushies box with Luna and chats to his sister. She baby-blabbers back.

Lily smiles fondly at her kids, then nods to me. "Sure."

"I just…" I shake my head. *Don't complain.* "Forget it. It's stupid." I chuck a comic aside.

"I bet it's not." She sidles closer.

I stare down at an issue called *Battle of the Extent* and just let it out. "The airport—I don't want to be mobbed like that when I go to London alone." I inhale. "I just…I don't want to be touched like that again."

Lily holds a breath, concerned. "Are you scared to go back to the airport?"

I shrug and then nod.

"I can ride to the airport with you when you need to go, and there's this thing we can do." She explains, "We can drive right up to the private plane and bypass the normal airport entrance?"

When Willow left for London, she did that, but I didn't think the offer would ever be extended to me.

I frown. "We can do that?"

"We've done it before. The airport gives us permission because we cause a lot of disruption. It's safer for us and for everyone else."

"But it's just me…I don't usually fly in a private plane."

"Yeah but you can take our planes alone. We don't mind. We'd want you to."

I'm already shaking my head. "It's too much for just me." I don't know what I expected her to offer—but this feels like the entire world, and I just need…

I don't know.

Air.

"Then I'll send Garth with you," she says, offering me her 24/7 bodyguard for travel. "He's the best. If it's only you, the crowds won't be as bad. I know they won't."

I have a temporary bodyguard that I sometimes use. He's okay, and I know that bodyguards who are *constantly* around the families and assigned to specific people are ten-times better. They're trained for everything. Even kidnappings.

But I don't love the idea of someone following me all day.

Even if they say nothing and just stand there.

It's creepy.

Having two bodyguards in the airport would definitely help, so I nod to Lily.

"Have you told Willow?" she asks.

"*No,*" I force out, hoping she doesn't tell her either. "If she knew, she'd start flying to Philly to see me instead of the other way around." I lick my dry lips. "Willow gets anxiety when she's stuck in the middle of crowds. I know she'd brave it out for me, but…"

"You want to brave this out for her," she realizes.

I nod more firmly. "Yeah."

Moffy shouts, "I think you're brave, Uncle Garrison!"

I smile weakly and tell Lily, "Your kid is funny."

"Or maybe he's right."

I exhale the heaviness that'd been on my chest. *Yeah, I feel better.* "So I can take Garth when I fly to London?"

"Without a doubt, no take-backs. Cross my heart." She makes an "x" over her heart and adds, "He's pretty much the family bodyguard, and you're our family."

That feels good.

I smile more. "Thanks. I appreciate everything, you know?" Again, she's helping me. Again, she's not even hesitating.

I owe so much to Lily Calloway. For her kindness. For seeing something inside me worth a damn. Because the day I walked in this store, asking for a job—it changed my life.

Lily nods again, a nostalgic smile rising.

We return to the comics, hunting through the boxes for Sorin-X, and she asks me why I need all of them.

Here we go. "I guess I have to ask about it anyway, but you have to promise not to tell the tall one. He's literally throwing hundreds of thousands of dollars at my face. I'm scared shitless he'll shut the entire thing down and fire me if he finds out."

My secret project has been on-going for *three* years. I think he's out of his fucking mind for even letting me code without evidence of what the hell I'm programming.

For all he knows, I could be pissing time away constructing a unicorn farm on Minecraft.

I'm literally a heartbeat away from purging the big secret when the storage door swings open.

Oh shit.

Loren Hale pockets his keys as he enters. He must've just left work at Hale Co. or Halway Comics, and I'm not ready to blow up this project in front of him.

Lily, yeah.

Lo, fucking *no*.

It's complicated.

I chug the rest of my energy drink, watching Moffy and Luna hide in the cardboard box to scare their dad. "Shh," Moffy whispers to Luna and yanks down a flap.

All the while, Lily and Lo embrace.

I do *not* watch their lip-lock. I've seen enough at their house, thank you. When they pull apart, Lo sweeps the storage room and nods to me.

I nod back.

But he's looking for Moffy and Luna. "Where are our kids?" Panic catches in his edged voice but quickly extinguishes as the box giggles and laughs.

I smile.

Lo is an asshole, though, so he layers on fear and panic and yells, "Moffy?! Luna?! Lily, go call 9-1-1 right n—"

"No!" Moffy shrieks, tearing up. He pops out of the box and bolts to his dad. "I'm right here! I'm right here!" He hugs onto Lo's legs, and Lo crouches, hugging his son tight. Acting so relieved to find him.

Savage.

Lily whispers to Lo, but I can't hear, and then Lo assesses Moffy's well-being. "Are you in one piece? Are you okay? Did the aliens get you?"

"What aliens?"

Lo lets out a choked laugh. "You didn't hear about the alien invasion last night? What were you—*sleeping*?"

"Yeah, I like sleep."

"No way, me too."

My smile fades into something else. It's been nice babysitting Moffy and Luna, but seeing Lo interact with his kids just makes me want to be a father.

I want a baby with Willow.

Can't believe I'm at a place where that sounds like walking into a bright horizon. Like the end credits to a movie I want to play all over again.

I tune out a bit—in a *baby* daze—but I'm back at the perfect time. Lily is about to blow up my secret project. I shake my head, trying to get her to shut up.

"We're trying to separate all the ones with Sorin-X. He said…" she trails off, seeing me finally. "What?"

I stifle a groan.

Moffy runs off to play with Tilly Stayzor action figures from *The Fourth Degree* universe.

As Lo drills confusion into me, I decide to go with the moment. "I did have something to ask you."

This isn't about work. I am worried he might say *no,* but I'm not that nervous to actually ask him what I'm about to ask. I figure it seems obvious anyway.

And so I say, "Will you be my best man at my wedding?"

His mouth slowly drops, stunned.

"You've been more of a brother to me than my brothers," I say strongly because this is the fucking truth. "I probably wouldn't be here if it weren't for you...and you." I look to Lily.

I'm not sure I tell them enough how much they mean to me.

How grateful I am and will *always* be.

Lily wipes her gathering tears.

Lo's amber eyes glass. "Of course I'd be your best man."

"Thanks," I say. "Do you think the tall one and the angry one will want to be groomsmen?"

"Connor, without a doubt, and Ryke goes with the flow." Lo laughs. "Christ, if you put him in the back row, he wouldn't even care or take it to heart."

"Okay good." I expel another long breath, until Loren grabs a comic from the growing stack.

He asks, "What's all this for?"

"I don't know," Lily says. "Garrison was just about to tell..."

I'm shaking my head with widened eyes.

She's gaping, brows bunched. "Uhhh..."

I bet she sucks at charades.

Lo glances at me. "Is this about your video game?"

My face falls. "What?" *What the fuck?*

He flashes a half-smile.

I choke out, "How'd you know?" Are there hidden cameras in his house? In my cubicle? What. The. *Fuck.*

"You're working for Connor Cobalt, man. The guy probably has fifteen brains and seven pairs of eyes. You might not know what he's thinking, but he knows what you are." Lo touches his chest. "And he's my best friend. He told me you're working on a game based on a comic book character."

I sway backwards, disbelieving. Connor Cobalt already knows I'm creating a video game on Sorin-X… "And he didn't give a shit? I thought he'd pull the plug on the project."

"He actually likes the idea. So do I."

I'm in another dimension. "What?"

"*I* own the video game rights to *The Fourth Degree* series." Halway Comics is the publisher, duh. "And Belinda and Jackson told me they'd rather eat their left arms than see a thousand people turning the game into a money-making soulless franchise."

Of course I recognize those names. Belinda and Jackson Howell are the young brother-sister duo and artists and writer of *The Fourth Degree* universe.

My head is spinning, but I gather my thoughts fast. "I have most of the technical shit coded, but I'm at the point where storyline is important. That's why I was looking through the comics, but eventually I'd need Belinda and Jackson for the art. I can only code, and what I'm making is classic, indie. I think the game style fits what the comic intended to be."

"I've been mentioning the video game to Belinda and Jackson for a full year," Lo says, "and they're interested. I know they'd work with you. I'll give you their numbers."

My jaw is on the floor.

Speechless.

In shock.

Lo has known for a full year about the video game because of Connor. He's already mentioned the project to the most important people. And they're interested.

My eyes burn, and I think for so long, I didn't believe I should try to chase after what I loved. When other people are faster and smarter, it felt pointless.

It took work to get here, but I know the first step was always belief.

Belief that I could.

Belief that I should.

And yeah…I'm happy I did.

32

WILLOW MOORE
Age 18

Dalton Academy is officially in my past. While all the seniors were ripping open their acceptance letters to Ivy Leagues and fancy private universities, they turned to me and asked where I was accepted.

With a weak, dying smile, I told them I never applied.

The shock and horror on their faces is forever engrained in my brain. But I'm happy with my decision to work at Superheroes & Scones for a while.

I'll save up money, so that when I'm ready for college, I can afford it myself. Lo offered to pay my tuition, but he's already financed my last year of high school *and* given me a place to stay. Coming to Philly wasn't about reconnecting with my brother for his wealth, and I have to be self-sufficient in order to prove that.

"Lily tried to slip me extra money in my paycheck," I whisper to Garrison in the storage room of Superheroes & Scones. I don't know why I'm whispering. It's after-hours, and we're the only ones here.

I'm supposed to be closing up, but Garrison stayed back to help me unpack the new *Spider-Man/Deadpool* issues that've been flying off the rack.

Garrison holds onto a plastic-wrapped comic, and his brows furrow. "Jesus. She wants you to go to college that badly?"

I shake my head. "She knows I want to go, and I think she feels guilty that I don't have the money for it yet. Anyway, I told her I wouldn't accept any bonus that the other employees aren't given."

Garrison smiles. "Knowing Lily, we may all have a 'surprise' holiday bonus next week." He makes air quotes with one hand.

"It's August," I say.

"Exactly." He places the comic on a stack, sorting the issues from oldest to newest. He's quiet for a second, unusually so, and I think maybe I said the wrong thing.

"Sorry," I apologize. "I shouldn't have brought up college…or lack thereof. For us both, I mean." I'm roasting.

He eyes me silently.

"It's just," I continue. "I know that it's a sensitive topic because of Maybelwood." When we returned from the lake house, Garrison finally approached his parents and confessed to flunking out of Faust.

They were angry, but they're also type-A's (as he put it), so they just went into immediate action and enrolled him in another school.

Maybelwood Preparatory. Also the same high school Ryke attended.

Garrison rarely talks about repeating his senior year, but I know his pride has been bruised. And I was the fool that just brought up college.

"Hey, Willow." Garrison leans over the edge of the box, two hands on the edge. We're a little closer now. I can smell his shampoo, a pine needle scent.

"Yeah?" I ask.

"No topics are too sensitive to talk about between us," he tells me. "Can we agree on that?"

I look him over, wondering if he likes discussing the tough parts with me—because there are so many untouchable, sensitive subjects in his life that we've been crossing together. "Yeah, definitely," I say, feeling relieved.

"Good." He smacks the side of the box and returns to sorting the stacks. "And I'm never going to college—so we can talk about it all you want. It's not a big deal."

I frown. "You don't want to go? Or you don't think you'll get in?"

"I don't want to go." His blue-green eyes hit mine. "You know when you think about something and it gives you this unsettling feeling, like you're a moment from breaking out into hives?"

Every day. "Yeah."

"It's like that. Times a billion. There's not a cell inside of me that wants to go. So I'm not going." His confidence in his decision radiates around the storage room. "Plus, there's an added benefit of getting to spend time with my girl."

My girl.

The room tenses at that term.

We glance uneasily at one another, then away. The air heavies. It didn't used to be like this. Not since *prom.*

We barely discuss what happened. How my date stood me up on the day of prom. My self-esteem leaped off a cliff into a major freefall.

That was until Garrison showed up.

He dressed in a suit and knocked on the door, ready to whisk me away and vanquish all the memories of ever being ditched.

We went as friends. That's what we both asserted *before* the limo, *during* the dance, and even *after* on the ride home. Friends.

There was no kiss.

No promise of anything to come.

Just friends.

It was a good night, but a little awkward. And tense. Like staring right at a purple elephant taking up the entire dancefloor. If I'm being truthful with myself, I *wanted* something more. Maybe not a kiss—I'm still not sure if I'm ready for that—but he could have put his hand on the small of my back or leaned in close. Instead, it felt like I was dancing with a friend.

Which is what we are. So I shouldn't be disappointed.

It's just…

He obviously didn't want to kiss me or else he would have asked like he did with hugging, right?

There was nothing standing in his way. No other boys. No school hundreds of miles up north. In fact, we're closer than we've ever been now that we live in the same neighborhood again. Plus, I confessed the biggest secret of all in the limo.

I'm not actually Loren Hale's cousin. I'm his half-sister.

"Whoa," Garrison said, but after the shock wore off, he smiled. Not mad that I lied. He was happy that I trusted him with the precious truth.

The opportunity to make a move was right there, wasn't it? But once that moment passed, awkwardness infiltrated tenfold.

And so the chance at prom came and flew by in May. Now August, we've skirted around the dance, but our friendship is solidly intact.

That's what matters.

But I can't deny the existence of this weird tension straining the room. I don't know what to do, so I just look at the first thing that catches my eye.

"Um…" I stammer before nodding to issue #6 where Spider-Man webbed Deadpool's mouth shut. "Could you hand me that? I haven't read it yet, and it looks like a good one."

"Yeah, sure." He grabs the comic from the stack and passes it over. Our fingers brush, and just as I'm about to pull away, Garrison takes my hand in his.

I drop the comic.

He drops my hand.

Oh God. "Sorry, I—" I have no words. I'm bending down to pick up the comic, and Garrison follows suit, until we're staring at each other from underneath a long wooden breakroom table that we drug into the storage area, just to sort comics.

"You don't have to be sorry." His own apologies skate across his features. "*I'm* sorry…" His nose flares.

We're both squatting, staring at one another. Unsaid things passing between us.

He shakes his head. "Dammit, I don't know why this is so hard. It's never been hard to talk to you." He rubs a hand through his hair. "But I fucked up."

"What?" I squeak.

"At prom. I fucked up," he says. "I should have asked you out then. It should have been prom. Not underneath…" He glances up, and I unfortunately follow suit. Wads of pink, white, and blue gum stick to the bottom of the table. *Ew.*

But my mind is wrapped around his other words. *I should have asked you out then.*

We meet each other's gazes.

My heart thrashes. "What are you saying?"

"Will you go out with me, Willow?" he asks. "And not just as friends. I want to be your boyfriend."

I didn't hear him right. I *must* be dreaming. This is about the same time I'd ask a friend to pinch me, but my friend is the one currently asking me out. So there's that.

"Um…" I stammer again.

Panic ascends his face. "You can say no."

I definitely do not want to say no. But still, I hesitate.

33

GARRISON ABBEY
Age 18

Willow is staring at me like I just told her we're both joining NASA together and heading on a one-way ticket to Jupiter. Maybe that sounds more realistic than the reality. Dating me.

I know I'm not a great catch, especially since I'm officially on my *third* prep school. But I just thought there's something between us.

Something more.

Unless I've been way off base.

Her mouth is ajar, eyes wide, startled like I'm a headlight that just blasted in front of her face. She hasn't said a word, and I figure she's probably questioning why we're even friends.

I fucked it all up.

"Hey, forget about it," I say quickly, salvaging what I can. "It's whatever. We can just be friends."

She reanimates abruptly. "No, I'd like you to be my…my um…"

"Boyfriend," I finish for her. My lips lift into a smile. *She'd like that.*

My excitement tapers off when she says, "Yes, that. But you should know some things before you officially ask me."

I can't help it, I'm smiling harder. "I thought I just officially asked you."

She pales a little, but her lips inch up. "Okay, true. But still, I need you to know what you're asking me."

Okay. No biggie. "Could we stand for this?" I ask. We're still squatting underneath the table. "My quads are killing me." Byproduct of Faust not having a lacrosse team, and now I'm getting ready to try out at Maybelwood's. Too much conditioning this morning.

Willow nods, and at the same time, we both rise. The box of comics is situated between us, and she skims her fingers over a cover like she's trying to take her time to gather words.

I wait. I can be patient.

A long beat passes before she lets out a tense breath. "I've never had a boyfriend before."

"I know."

"But it's more than that, I've never *kissed* a boy before." She stares at me, head-on. "And even though I like you—like *really* like you—and I want you to be my boyfriend, I still don't know if I'd be ready to kiss you right away."

Found the origin of her hesitation.

Honestly, I'm relieved. Because I figured this much out about Willow. It's not that big of a surprise. "I get that," I tell her. "I wouldn't want some label between us to flip a switch on what you're comfortable with either. We can be boyfriend and girlfriend without kissing."

"We can?" she asks like this scenario is unfounded and untested.

"One hundred percent," I say. "Honestly, I *really* want to kiss you. But I wouldn't pressure you. Whenever you're ready is good with me."

"What if I'm old and gray?" she asks.

I have a full-blown smile.

Quickly, she adds, "Not that I'm assuming we'd be together that long. Or even short." She presses a hand to her temple. "I don't know what I'm saying."

"I'm following," I tell her. "And I'm totally here for being senior citizens who only hug each other. It's not like some other dude would be making out with you or having sex with you—that I wouldn't be able to stand."

She nods slowly like she's almost in a daze. "Me too." She blinks. "I mean, I also wouldn't be able to stand some girl making out with you or...sex." She grips the edge of the cardboard box. "So you'd really be okay with waiting? Isn't intimacy like a foundation of a good relationship?"

"I mean, I'm not an expert," I say, "but I think we can have intimacy without kissing or sex."

Her eyes flit around me. "Like how?"

"Can I touch you?" I round the box to stand in front of Willow.

She nods once. I wrap my arms around her body and tuck her into my chest. My chin rests on the top of her head, and her arms kind of dangle at her sides. Her heart is a rapid, nervous organ inside her chest, thumping against me.

This tenderness doesn't exist in my life except right here.

"Willow," I whisper. "Can I be your boyfriend?" I ask again, this time better.

Her fingers slide against the belt loops of my pants. "Yeah. I'd like that." And then she adds, "So I'm your girlfriend? Does this mean I'm not your *girl* anymore?"

"No way." I close my eyes, letting my smile pull my cheeks. "You're still my girl, even more now."

34

WILLOW MOORE
Age 18

"So I need to tell you all something," I declare to too many people.

I don't love being the center of attention. Commanding a space like this is my own personal nightmare. Even if I'm just speaking to these six people in Lily and Lo's living room.

I count the heads: Lily and Lo, Ryke and Daisy, Connor and Rose.

The latter moved out of the house during the summer. They live in this regal mansion down the street, so it's not as if they're too far away.

Garrison stuffs his hands in his leather jacket, a backwards baseball cap covers his thick brown hair, and he watches me with silent encouragements in his aquamarine eyes.

Lo swings his head from Garrison to me and back to Garrison. My older brother's glare is slowly boiling. Eruption imminent.

388

And he doesn't even know why Garrison is here yet. Spilling this news might actually make it worse, but there's no going back.

I push up my black-rimmed glasses and take a steady breath. "I thought it'd be a good idea if Garrison was here too." I regret speaking the obvious detail. It causes an intense reaction.

Lo abruptly stands from the chair, and Lily clutches his leg like she's trying to keep him from confronting Garrison or maybe even chasing him out of the house.

"Is he part of your news?" Lo asks hesitantly.

Daisy suddenly wraps an arm around Ryke's waist, both seated on the couch. It's hard not to notice Lily and Daisy physically restraining their men.

Well, this is already going terribly.

"Yeah…" I grab onto the strap of my overalls, the motion a nervous tic.

Garrison slides closer to me, and his fingers thread through mine. My pulse accelerates, but I also breathe easier.

"Are you pregnant?" Lo asks me.

"What?" I choke.

"Yeah, *what?*" Garrison snaps, his face darkening. He motions to the entire room. "If anyone's knocking up anyone, it's one of you, and honestly, what the hell are you wearing?" He grimaces at Ryke.

"Underwear," Ryke says like it's just another day of being nearly naked in the living room.

"I see that, thanks," Garrison says dryly.

Do not look again, Willow. Do. Not. Look.

Since I've walked in, I've tried hard not to glance at Daisy's fiancé. (Yes, they're finally engaged!)

Me avoiding Ryke isn't just because he barely has a shred of fabric on, though that's a good reason. Mainly it's because his single

BACK THEN

piece of fabric happens to be a *tight* pair of boxer-briefs that, from a quick glimpse, look like they're five sizes too small.

Words might also be on the cotton.

I'm not about to do a double-take and stare hard enough to check.

Ryke is *intimidating.*

I thought since I've grown closer to Daisy, it'd lessen that intimidation, but it somehow amplified it. He's the fiancé to my best friend *and* the brother of my half-brother. Ryke and I don't have a personal relationship like I have with Lo or Daisy or even Lily who's my boss at Superheroes & Scones.

But I do live with him. He's around and helpful and not close to the aggressive jackass that the media likes to paint him as.

Still, Ryke Meadows is and will always be certified intimidating.

If I'm being honest with myself, most of the people in this room carry a hefty amount of intimidation with them. It makes this declaration that much harder.

I swallow a lump in my throat. "So, um…this didn't really go how we thought it would."

"Why are you saying *we* like he's a part of this?" Lo points an accusatory finger at Garrison.

"It's not what you're thinking," I stumble over my words. *This is going so, so badly.* "I'm a…" The word is stuck in the back of my throat. How do I do this? Help!

Garrison squeezes my hand, and thankfully, he finishes for me, "Virgin."

Lily peers over the couch at Garrison. "You're a virgin?"

Garrison groans. "No, *she's* a virgin. Good God, it's like tuning into five different radio stations at once when I come here. Don't you all ever get tired of each other?"

"I'm mostly tired of you," Lo refutes in his serrated tone. Even I flinch.

Garrison's lips downturn a fraction, and I can tell that missile struck him. "Whatever," he mutters.

I squeeze his hand this time.

Regret flashes in Lo's gaze for a quick second before he looks to me. "Your news can't be that you're a virgin and your friend isn't one, so what is it? Because I keep thinking you're leaving—"

"I'm not leaving," I say, confidently. "I don't have plans to move back to Maine. I promise I'd tell you if I was even thinking about it."

He nods slowly. "Is it…about something else with your parents?"

I shake my head quickly. There's no change on the parents front. My mom is standoffish whenever I call, and I haven't spoken to my dad since I moved to Philly.

"Then what?" Lo asks.

"We're together," I spit out and then lift up my hand that's interlaced with Garrison's. My heart wants to fly out of my ribcage. *Breathe, Willow.*

I realize I'm dating the same boy that vandalized their house. He was a part of a friend group that caused serious harm. I just hope they'll give Garrison a chance, so they can see what I see in him.

Lo's face is all scrunched up. Like he can't parse out what I just said. "What do you mean together?" he asks.

Connor gives a textbook definition of a boyfriend and girlfriend, and I make a mistake by looking at Ryke. His expression is ten times worse than Lo's.

Jaw set. Eyes flamed. Muscles in his biceps are ripped. He's a professional free-solo climber, ascending mountains with his bare hands. He could probably knock Garrison out with one blow.

Ryke fights with his fists, and Lo fights with his words. But I know Ryke wouldn't hit Garrison. I trust him enough in that regard, but I hate that it already looks like he's judged my boyfriend.

Written him off.

Whatever conversation I just tuned out, it ends with Lo glowering at Garrison. I have to fix this.

"It's only been a week," I explain quickly. "I know it's not a long time, but I really didn't want to sneak around, especially since I live with some of you."

Garrison watches me, still by my side. We feel like a team.

"We have rules," Lo starts.

"Have fun," Lily declares, her smile overwhelming. My lips start to lift.

"No, not have fun—what the hell, Lily?" Lo gawks at his wife.

"They're eighteen."

"Yeah, we're eighteen," Garrison echoes.

Lo glares. "Last I remember, you're still in high school." That's a low blow. I wince.

Garrison sighs heavily. "You're not her fucking father." This is true, and also a good point. I've tried hard not to burden Lo. I'm just his little sister.

"You're right," Lo says, "I'm her brother and the *first* person she should trust while she's in Philadelphia." He takes a step closer to Garrison. "She's my responsibility, and while I trust you with a lot of things, I don't want you upstairs in her room past two a.m.—and two a.m. is more than I'd give any kid of mine." Another step. "And keep the door open."

Surprisingly, I relax at his words. Maybe Lo knows I'd want the rules.

Garrison said he'd be patient and wait for kissing and sex, but I'm more worried about me. That maybe I won't be able to say *no* when he asks me if I'm ready when I'm not. That things will go too fast and I won't know *how* to slow down. Everything is new for me.

The rules will help give me an excuse to stop things before I'm ready to move forward. I can blame curfew or my overprotective brother. It makes it easier to say *no* without feeling guilty about it.

I want this relationship to go at my pace. A slow pace. Even if it's a turtle crawl.

Me staying quiet is putting strain in the air. Both Lo *and* Ryke look five-seconds away from pushing Garrison out the door.

Before I can say anything, Garrison slowly unlaces his fingers from mine. My stomach drops, but he gives me this reassuring nod. "I'll text you, okay?"

I nod back. "Will you check my gifs before you go to bed? I want to post them, but I think one isn't working."

Garrison nearly smiles. "Yeah. I'll do it first thing." He acknowledges the rest of the room with a curt wave and then heads out the door.

"When? Where? How?" Lily blurts out.

Her excitement fuels my smile, and I feel my shoulder dropping in ease. "So you're all not upset?" I linger on Lo.

"You can do better," he tells me.

Daisy steps forward. "She knows Garrison in a way that none of us do, so we should really trust her instincts." *I love Daisy Calloway.* I've never felt what it's like to have a friend so unwaveringly in my corner until her. We exchange smiles.

"You know what I don't trust?" Lo says. "An eighteen-year-old horny motherfucking guy's instincts."

"Same," Ryke adds.

"That's why there are rules, right?" I say. "So nothing should go wrong?" I hang onto this. Or else their apprehension will start to seep into me. I'm heading into uncharted territories here, and I know I'll turn to people more experienced than me for advice. I just don't want their advice to make me *more* nervous.

Who am I kidding? Garrison Abbey, the practical reincarnation of *Jess* from *Gilmore Girls*, is my first boyfriend.

Repeat that a hundred times and maybe it'll seem true.

He is so out of my league.

Yeah…

I'm nervous.

35

WILLOW MOORE
Age 18

Taco night is always the best night, and living with my brother means it's a common occurrence.

I lean my hip against the bar midway between sprinkling cotija cheese and dolloping some guacamole onto my plate.

With greasy fingers, I text Garrison back. His parents are hosting some cocktail party at his house, so I invited him over for tacos.

I slide my phone in my overalls, and glance around the kitchen. Maximoff giggles from his highchair while Lo plays "airplane" with a spoonful of yogurt.

Lily stacks tortilla chips on a plate, creating a nacho tower. The house is quiet with Ryke and Daisy out camping for the night, and Rose and Connor are busy at their own place.

"Garrison's coming over," I tell them.

Page 396

Lily immediately beams. "Oh perfect. It's a good night for…" Her voice tapers off at the look Lo is slipping her. "Tacos. It's a good night for tacos. What else did you think I was going to say?"

If I had to guess, she was going to say *it's a good night for a first kiss.* Lily made me pinky promise that I'd tell her when I had my first. She's very invested in blossoming love.

Lo's brows rise. "Every night is a good night for tacos, love." He turns to me. "And if he makes a move on you, his dick is going where it belongs. In the garbage."

It's not the first threat I've heard, so I barely react this time.

My phone buzzes.

Garrison: Hey, so I can't come over anymore. Parents are all over my ass about staying in and studying on a school night. I would argue with them but they've got friends over. Tomorrow?

I text back: Yeah definitely, tomorrow is perfect.

Lo and Lily watch me, and the air already tenses. I must wear disappointment all over my face.

But I brush it off quickly. "False alarm," I tell Lo. "He has to study."

Lo's face cinches, angrier at the prospect of Garrison *not* coming over. "He didn't seem to care about studying before he was dating you. Now he's ditching you to hit the goddamn books." He fake gasps. "Holy fuck, he's turning into a nerd." Lo accidentally whips the spoon around and yogurt flings off a little, splattering Maximoff's forehead.

The baby laughs so loud his face turns red.

"Listen up, Moffy." Lo wipes the yogurt off with a towel. "If you date a nerd, just remember that they'll love books over you."

"Not true," Lily interjects. "Rose and Connor love each other over their hardbacks."

Lo smiles bitterly. "The Queen and King are an exception." He looks to me, seriousness coating his brows. "Is Garrison okay?"

I still. "Why wouldn't he be?"

"Because it's a common line. Saying you have to study when something else is going on." He shrugs. "I can't even count the times I said it to our dad growing up." As soon as he finishes the sentence, he sees my expression and his face falls.

Our dad.

What…?

I don't understand. I'm…

Robert Moore is my dad…

Isn't he?

"Willow—"

"*Our* dad." I swallow hard. "What—what does that mean?"

"Fuck," Lo curses and drops the spoon in the sink. "Can you take a seat?"

I can't move.

He stares at me for a long moment. Maximoff lets out a small giggle. "Hey, Moffy," Lily whispers to her son. "Let's go watch some cartoons." She lifts him from his highchair and carries her baby out of the kitchen.

"I didn't find out until just recently," Lo says. "The day you told us you were dating Garrison. Right before you came over, that's when Ryke told me."

Ryke.

Ryke.

Oh…

I stagger towards the barstool, bracing the edge. Too much to process. I only think about one question. "How long did Ryke know?" I ask. "The whole time?"

Years?

Has he been keeping this from both of us?

Lo grimaces. "*No*. No way," he says. "He learned just last month. Our dad actually just found out last month, too." He laughs at that. "Bastard finally got the rug pulled out from under him."

Jonathan just discovered that I'm his daughter, which means something even worse. "My mom kept this secret," I whisper.

It's another horrible lie. Something she could have told me a year ago, at the very least, when I left Maine to come to Philly. Maybe she wasn't certain, but even then, she could have told me she had reservations about my birth father.

Instead, she stared at me point-blank and said, *"Robert Moore is your dad."*

I'm a Hale?

I grow cold all over and slide onto the barstool. Meeting Lo's eyes, I ask, "This…this doesn't change anything, does it?"

"Between us, no," he says. "You're still my little sister." He runs a hand along the back of his neck. "But now you have another big brother."

Oh.

My.

God.

Why didn't I think of that? Ryke Meadows is my half-brother. We're related. My jaw drops, my eyes grow wide. I can't even *think* of Ryke like that. He's Daisy's fiancé. He's Lo's half-brother. Ryke and I, we have no relation.

But now we do.

Lo zips to the refrigerator, filling up a glass of water. He slides it to me. "I'm more worried about our dad. He can be...harsh." He grimaces like that's not even the right word. "I'm being kind here." He exhales a sharp breath. "He's an asshole. A fucking dick. And Ryke will tell you to stay a million miles away from him."

I clutch the sides of the glass. "What do you say?"

"I love my dad," he confesses. "And even though he's done some horrible, messed-up shit, I know he loves me too." He laughs bitterly. "His love for his children is one of the few things that I don't ever second-guess. I get it, if you want to feel that again from a father...or maybe for the first time. It's your choice whether you want to actually see him, but if you do, just know that I'm going to protect you."

I think I need time to think it over.

Think it all over.

But I'm not sure I want to meet a "dad" that I'd need protection from. That sounds terrifying. Lo leaves me alone to drink my water.

I text Garrison: do you have time for a phone call?

His reply comes seconds later as the Caller ID lights up with his name. I spend the rest of the night filling him in. Saying the words out loud to Garrison makes it feel even more real.

36

BACK THEN – February
Philadelphia, Pennsylvania

WILLOW MOORE
Age 18

've been tasked with "cake" pickup for Daisy's birthday. It also happens to be a joint bachelor/bachelorette party. My first I've ever attended, but I'm not covered in a nervous sweat or anything. It's supposed to be a super lowkey gathering at Connor and Rose's mansion. Just the core six, me and…my boyfriend.

A goofy smile expands across my face, just thinking the words. Garrison and I have been dating for months now—since September—but there still hasn't been a kiss. I'm more comfortable with his touches than I've ever been.

Handholding. Hugging. Lying on the same bed together.

It's been nice, and there've been a couple times I could've seen myself kissing Garrison. Like during the summer when fireworks lit the sky.

Yet, I was too chicken to make the first move. And he didn't attempt it.

I realize I'm the one who chose the tortoise-slow pace, and I might have to be the one to *initiate* a faster one. But I don't know how to go about that without descending in my head and becoming a mess of nerves.

Anyway, I'm trying to focus on good things. Birthdays. Bachelor/bachelorette parties.

"I can't believe they ordered a dick cake." Garrison's eyes flit to the box on my lap. It indeed has a cake inside. Shaped like a giant penis.

Garrison's hand tightens on his Mustang's steering wheel, driving back from the bakery. His eyes meet mine briefly, and his brows rise. "It was a choice."

We're both near laughter. "Did you expect anything less from them?"

He shakes his head. "Not really." He glances from the box to me. "You want me to carry it in?"

"No, I can do it." Though that does cause a wave of anxiety, but I want to push through it for Daisy. It's her birthday after all. My eyes flit to the clock. We're running behind. Traffic near the bakery was a nightmare. Luckily, it's mostly cleared up now.

Garrison follows my gaze. "Hold on."

He accelerates, speeding all the way to the gated neighborhood.

"I DON'T KNOW IF I CAN EAT THAT," LILY SAYS, eyes narrowed as Ryke cuts the head of the...dick cake.

The eight of us pack into Connor and Rose's enormous kitchen, fit with state-of-the-art appliances. I've chosen a nice alcove by the expensive toaster.

It's the furthest spot from Ryke.

Ever since I found out he's my brother, I've been avoiding him. I haven't even spoken about Jonathan Hale (AKA my dad) since my conversation with Lo.

Change is hard.

But this change feels monumental, and I know I'm taking the cowardly route by dodging the reality. But we can't all be Dorothy in the Land of Oz—brave and bold. At least, not all the time.

I've let this avoidance fester so long that anytime Ryke tries to talk to me, it's this big awkward mess. Ryke Meadows is like a brooding, teeth-bared wolf, unapproachable and protectively menacing, and that's just how I felt before he became my brother.

Now that we're related, I can barely step a pinky toe in his direction without cowering. It's ten times worse.

I never saw him filling this brotherly role in my life, and since I'm dating Garrison—that's *two* brothers I have with opinions on my very first relationship.

It's a lot.

Ryke looks to Lily and says, "It's just a fucking cake."

I push my glasses up the bridge of my nose. Garrison's shoulder presses right next to mine. It's nice that anytime I'm invited to something, he's automatically invited too. We're a pair now. And even though I never felt like a seventh wheel with the core six, him being with me brings this sense of completion. Like it was always meant to be *eight*.

Garrison leans casually against the refrigerator, an unlit cigarette peeking from the pocket of his leather jacket. His eyes are on me. Mine on him. It's hard to set them anywhere else when I feel the most comfort swallowed up in his orbit.

"Why'd you take so long?" Lo asks accusingly.

Garrison swings his head to my brother. "We pulled over to fuck," he says dryly.

Oh...*God.*

I am used to his sarcasm, but not in front of my brothers. Not like *this.*

Ryke's jaw hardens. Lo's sharpens.

I choke on a breath. "We...didn't."

"They know that," Garrison tells me.

Connor makes a pot of coffee. "It's as though you want them to hate you." *That actually might be true.* I think he feels undeserving of their kindness, so he pushes them away.

Garrison pauses before saying, "That's stupid."

"You said it, not me," Connor states.

"Who wants the head?" Daisy asks, raising a plate with a slice of cake. I give her an appreciative look for the interjection and then spin towards the freezer, grabbing a tub of vanilla ice cream.

"I'm trying to remember why I like you," Lo tells Garrison, ignoring Daisy, "but it's all clouded by an image of me stabbing you, so be lucky I'm not holding a goddamn knife right now."

Garrison almost smiles. "You still like me?"

I caught that too. My spirits lift.

Lo enunciates, "*Me* stabbing you to death. Value your own life for me, so you can at least be kind of frightened."

I focus on opening the tub of ice cream—helping out and distracting myself—and then I lean into Daisy's ear to whisper, "I'm so embarrassed."

Daisy hugs my side and says even softer, "They love you, you know?"

I glance to Ryke, but the second he turns towards me, I abruptly rotate back to Daisy. My brain is singing a song on a loop. It goes something like: *Ryke Meadows is your big brother. He's your brother. Older brother! He's Ryke Meadows and you've got him as a brother! HE'S YOUR BROTHERRRRR!*

My face flames and stomach churns.

I so clearly avoided his gaze, didn't I? There was nothing smooth about it. I refocus on the ice cream. Tasks are good. Tasks keep me away from thinking about how awkward I am.

After I stick a spoon into the ice cream, I notice Rose handing Lily a middle portion of the cake. Lily shakes her head. "I can't eat the shaft."

"Lil." Lo melds his body behind hers. "It's *cake.*"

"It's a penis."

"No, love, *this* is a penis." He takes her hand and places it on his crotch.

"Lo!" A smile accompanies her squeal.

I'm used to the overly flirtatious antics and PDA, but I've been roasting since I showed up to this party. Today is on a different level. I sidle back to Garrison.

"Daisy!" Ryke calls out, standing near the dick cake. Swiftly, he scoops the chocolate cake into his palm and *chucks* the hunk at her face. It splats against her nose and mouth and eyes, pink frosting dropping off her chin.

Her smile stretches. "This means war," she warns.

"Come at me, Calloway."

Daisy digs her hand into the cake and throws a hunk at Ryke. It hits him square in the cheek.

The food fight erupts, Lily and Lo joining in. Connor and Rose sip coffee by the pot, hand-in-hand, and remain out of the battle.

I back up into Garrison's chest to avoid being pelted with a flying piece of cake. He wraps his arms over my collarbones, holding me.

406

Lo and Ryke are doing the most cake throwing, and one chunk finally pelts my shoulder, splattering my top with pink icing.

Garrison spins me around to face him. "You've got something on you," he says, lips inching up.

"That's because I was shielding *you*."

His grin explodes. "And look at that, you did such a good job." He places his hands on either side of my shoulders, and slowly, we do this dance maneuver. I follow his lead until I realize we're just walking in a circle. Until *his* back is in the crossfire of cake.

He tells me, "Now it's my turn to shield you."

Warmth ascends. I block everyone else out.

He dips his finger into the icing on my shoulder and then draws on my cheek. I can feel the shape he creates. *A heart.*

My pulse slows down like it's drunk. Intoxicated.

I swipe some icing with my finger and reach up to his cheek. He dips his head so that I can reach. I draw a star on his fair skin.

We're a breath apart, his face closer to mine.

"Willow," he whispers so softly. "Can I kiss you?"

There is no hesitation. No question.

I know in my heart I'm ready.

"Yes," I breathe. I feel the sudden flare of anxiety that comes with doing something new, but it fades as his lips draw to mine.

I close my eyes.

He's soft and gentle, and his palms hold the small of my back, pressing me close. Eagerness zips through my veins. Pulsing in places that have never really been lit up by someone. I lean closer, and he matches the movement, pinning me to the cabinet. Sparks ignite throughout every inch of my body.

But then I remember I have hands.

BACK THEN

Those pesky appendages are just dangling like noodles at my sides. My heartbeat speeds up in unease. *Where do I put these things?*

Garrison must sense my sudden apprehension, and he breaks from my lips for a millisecond. Just long enough for his eyes to caress mine.

Quickly, he just drops his hands off me and takes my palms in his. He guides them to the back of his head, and his baseball hat tumbles to the floor.

Oh…that's where they should go.

But he doesn't make me feel silly for not knowing. Instead, he presses a soft hand to my cheek and returns to my lips.

Our eyes close again, and he deepens the kiss, edging my mouth open. A soft noise catches in the back of my throat. One that I don't even know if *he* heard. But I cling harder to Garrison all the same. I follow his lead until he breaks away for breath. Forehead pressed to mine.

"That was my first kiss," I whisper to him.

He smiles. "I know." His eyes dance around me, trying to read my body language. I wouldn't even be able to translate it for him. "Did you like it?"

"Yes," I say, my body heating up from truth. "A lot. I think…I think we should do it again sometime."

"Definitely. But later," he agrees. "When we're not in a room with your brothers."

My brothers.

Oh shit.

I forgot about them. In fact, I forgot all about the other six people in the kitchen. I glance past Garrison's chest. Daisy and Ryke are lost in each other's eyes, swaying to invisible, nonexistent music. Cake stuck in their hair and covering their arms.

Lily and Lo are MIA.

Connor and Rose have migrated to the couch, backs turned to us.

No one was watching us.

I'm not sure if that's the real truth, but I'm going to the grave believing it.

37

GARRISON ABBEY
Age 19

We're huddled near the back of Connor Cobalt's limo, my laptop propped open on the trunk. Water slowly trickles from a fountain in the yard. The Cobalt Estate is made for royalty. If their mansion could talk, it'd be calling all the other houses on the street "peasants."

Cold bites my bare skin. My costume for this lovely Halloween: a red T-shirt, red slacks, and a red-horned headband.

I'm the devil.

All thanks to Loren Hale.

Halloween happens to land on his birthday. And yeah, I phrased it like that because after knowing the guy for this long, I don't think the universe put his birthday *on* Halloween. It's definitely the other way around.

As a present to Lo, we've all let him decide our costumes for the night.

Willow tucks a piece of hair behind her ear.

A circular gold wreath hovers over her head. Knee-length white dress and matching wings round out the outfit. An angel to my devil. I'm shocked. Not that Lo would choose something pure and perfect for Willow, but because he picked *matching* costumes for us.

It looks like we're a couple.

We are.

But I didn't think Loren Hale wanted to announce the fact to the world. Not like *this*. He still glares at me anytime I get within three inches of her lips. I get it. He's overprotective of his sister, especially now that I'm dating her.

Willow and I are doing well, and that's all that matters to me.

She glances at the opened laptop, an email server popped up next to a hacking software. But we haven't been talking about that.

I'm stuck on news that recently came out. "I don't get it. The artists and creators of *The Fourth Degree* must have smoked one too many joints. None of it makes sense. I shouldn't have won."

Willow moves closer to me to whisper, "You deserved to win. Your superhero was the best." She says it like it's so simple.

A while ago, Lily and Lo gave every Superheroes & Scones employee a chance to create a new superhero in *The Fourth Degree* universe.

The Fourth Degree is a wildly popular comic book series from Halway Comics. Vic Whistler (Extent) is the main character, but they're diverging to new lines and opening up the entire world for more heroes, antiheroes, and villains.

The whole thing has been plaguing me ever since the winner was announced. I just…I don't see how I won out of *everyone* who works there. People were making flow charts for this shit. It was a big deal.

If Lily was the judge, maybe I'd think she was taking pity on me, but no one in the store has ever talked to Belinda and Jackson Howell, the artists and creators of *The Fourth Degree*. It's not like they could have played favorites.

Compared to the other employees, I shouldn't have won. I barely read comics. Barely know the lore. I'm doing better than when I first showed up, but I'm not a walking encyclopedia like most of them.

My throat is dry. "I don't know. Carter had a cool superhero."

Willow's face scrunches up. "His was basically a rip off of *X-Men*. And Maya was right when she called it a Walmart Pyro. You know, Maya even said if she had a vote, it would've been for Sorin-X. So it must be good. If you don't believe anyone else, you have to believe her taste at least."

Maya Ahn would have voted for my superhero…

Damn.

That hits me. Because Willow's old roommate is the last person to feed you bullshit, and she probably has the most comics knowledge at Superheroes & Scones. More than anyone.

Sorin-X.

My creation is going to be an actual superhero. Or…more like an *anti*hero. At least, that's how I pitched him. He has teleportation powers linked to the proximity of the girl he loves. He can't teleport more than four miles away from her. And he's a recovering alcoholic.

Lo never gave me shit for it, since it's kind of obvious I drew my inspiration from him. So that's something.

I tap my computer screen. "This shouldn't take me long. Maybe just tonight." Daisy's ex-friends have been finding ways to get her phone number, even after Daisy blocked them. They've been harassing her enough that she asked me for help. Hence, the laptop.

It sucks that the price of fame can be so cruel. Like past shitty friends coming back to make your life hell. Jealously eats people up in different ways, I guess. I wish that Daisy's ex-friends could find their chill, take a hint and stop texting her.

Willow pushes up her glasses. "It's nice that you're doing this for Daisy, but…are you sure you want to? Isn't it illegal?"

"Yeah, but is it *really* illegal if I'm doing it to help someone else?"

Willow ponders this for a second. "Um…that sounds like a trick question."

Damn, she really is an angel. I lean in to kiss the top of her nose.

"Mother of dragons!" Lo yells at the Cobalt's mansion.

We've been waiting for what feels like forever for Connor and Rose.

Dressed in a navy blue, silver, red Thor costume and a winged helmet, Daisy outstretches her plastic hammer towards Lily. "You stoleth thy lightsaber, you pesky fairy."

Lily looks even ganglier in her Tinker Bell costume, green tutu dress and wings. She whips out a blue plastic beam. "Prepare to meet thy doom, Thor." Lily and Daisy are grinning as the plastic weapons make contact.

Ryke gave Lily his lightsaber, and he also lent Daisy his blackish-brown robe. So now he's just dressed in a tunic and pants. I nudge Willow's shoulder and nod towards Ryke. "He still look like Anakin Skywalker to you?"

Willow grimaces and shakes her head. "Lo's going to be upset. *But* Daisy is pregnant, so maybe he'll understand that Ryke is trying to keep his pregnant wife warm." Willow beams at the words *pregnant* and *wife*.

Daisy went through hell and back trying to get pregnant, and Willow's happy for her best friend. Hell, I'm happy for Daisy. It's hard not to want joy for someone who brings so much joy to other people.

It's why I'm confused whenever anyone wants *me* to be happy. You know, why want that?

I point to my laptop screen, catching Willow's attention. "I'm going for it."

"I'll bail you out of jail if anything goes wrong," she says softly, smiling.

My lips lift.

"Devil!" Lo shouts at me from up the driveway.

I raise my gaze from the computer screen, unsurprised that I'm being given a nickname.

"You know what happens when an angel and a devil create a bodily union? The apocalypse." *Jesus* this *is why he gave us a couple costume.* "Do the right thing and don't end the world tonight."

"That's definitely not how that works," I say dryly.

Lo looks to Ryke. "Do you hear this guy?"

"Yeah. I guess he doesn't understand the fucking meaning of apocalypse. Want to spell it out for him?"

I cross my arms over my chest and give Ryke a look like, *why do you have to be on my case too?* Man, it royally sucks that Willow now has two brothers. One was enough since his name is Loren Hale. Adding Ryke into the mix is like throwing in barbed wire and explosives.

I'm not a fucking GI Joe doll. I'm not about to run through their obstacles with a smile and *yes, sir.*

It doesn't help that Ryke doesn't trust me. I see it in every inch of his *I fucking hate you* stance and his towering, broody ass glare.

"Apocalypse," Lo defines, "also known as the end of your godforsaken, puny little life by the powers that be."

"Also known as *me*," Ryke chimes in.

"And me," Lo finishes with a half-smile. "Welcome to hell."

I barely blink. "I've seen scarier."

Ryke's brows jump in surprise. "Who?"

"My brothers." I turn into my computer, a little shocked I even uttered those words. My abdomen tenses and I roll out my shoulders. Whatever.

Lo and Ryke have dropped the whole overly protective brother routine, and Willow nudges my shoe with hers. "Sorry about them," she whispers.

I shake my head. "It's good they care about you." If it were any other guy on the receiving end of their bullshit, I'd probably be applauding. Willow deserves people to care about her enough to grill whatever guy she's with. I'm just the lucky asshole who gets her.

"They're ten fucking minutes late now," Lo complains. As soon as he says the words, the front door opens. Rose struts out first in a long, light-blue draped dress with a gold belt, along with a platinum blonde wig.

Daenerys Targaryen. The Mother of Dragons from *Game of Thrones.* It's not my genre of choice, but I've been watching with Willow.

I glance to my girlfriend. Her smile has officially burst across her face. "It's perfect," she says softly. "I never thought I'd get to see Rose dressed up as Dany." Before I can say anything, she leans a hip against the limo and angles to me. "Are you nervous about the party?"

"The Halloween party?" I ask. Lo gave us bare details. It's in the Hamptons at some famous singer's house. He annoyingly forgot the singer's name. I know this is Willow's first "adult" Halloween party that'll include more than just chaste apple bobbing.

She nods.

"Not really," I tell her. "Are you?"

"Yeah, it's just…" She rubs her arm. "Their bodyguards aren't allowed in the mansion, and what if something happens?"

"Nothing's going to happen," I say, and I don't add that if anything *does* happen, it'll probably be to the people more famous than us. That'll just make her worry for Daisy. "What are you nervous about specifically, anyway?"

"People. Lots of people. Being touched or not knowing where to go. Getting lost…lots of things."

Fuck. "I'm not going to let anyone touch you." Even thinking about it is like drilling nails into my skull. Not happening. It's not fucking happening.

WILLOW AND DAISY ARE GONE.

They left us for the bathroom, and everyone thought they were "taking way too fucking long" so we all went on a search and rescue party.

It failed.

No surprise there. I told everyone we should have just stayed at the same spot they left us. The velvet-lined coffin. The probability of them returning was a million times higher than us finding them in this maze.

But this is what happens when you have Ryke and Lo together. They freak the fuck out. I don't have a sister, so maybe I'd be the same. I don't know.

I am worried.

Just a different kind of worried. I keep checking the doorway every five-seconds. On edge. Waiting impatiently for Willow. Her words from before keep cycling through my head. *Being touched.* She's scared about all the roaming hands and bodies, and it'd be impossible not to bump into people here.

Every room in this mansion is packed except for the kitchen. Maybe because it's the least decorated area in the house. Just tiny candles set along the granite countertops.

Lo, Ryke, Rose, and Connor all congregate near the kitchen bar, agreeing to the "wait it out" method. Connor is closest to me, watching me type on my laptop that's propped up on the stool.

He's dressed in an *almost* identical costume as Ryke. Except it's all white. White robe, white tunic, white pants. Like he's some ethereal fucking immortal. If he wasn't carrying the lightsaber, I'd just think Lo dressed him up as a god.

In reality, he's Luke Skywalker.

And right now, Luke fucking Skywalker is *hovering*. When six-foot-four Connor Cobalt hovers, it feels like you're under the shadow of the tallest high-rise. It's an intense, uncomfortable place to be. I'm trying to just ignore him, but he keeps watching my computer screen as I type.

I check the doorway again.

This time Daisy and Willow walk through it. I intake a breath, and before I can get a good look at my girlfriend, Ryke rushes to Daisy, blocking my view.

"Where the fuck did you go pee?" Ryke asks. "We've been looking for you two everywhere." He sets a hand on the top of Daisy's head, his cane in his other one. After Ryke married Daisy in Peru, he had a bad rock-climbing fall, and he needed surgery on his leg.

I don't even like to think about the climbing accident. I've had bad days—but almost losing Willow's brother…yeah, that ranks up there.

"To the moon and back," Daisy answers Ryke. He looks to Willow for a better answer.

"Just the first-floor bathroom. No one was by the coffin when we came back."

"Told you," I say to everyone. Immediately I regret it because I sound like a douchebag yelling out *told ya so!* I'm a dick.

"You're either *really* embodying this whole devil thing," Lo tells me, "or it's just in your soul." He's not even looking at me. He's raiding the house's pantry with Lily hanging on his waist, trying to pull him away with as much effort as she can muster. It's not much.

"Lo, you can't," she pleads.

Lo retrieves a box of Cheez-Its. "I *can*. Maybe they should've thought about snacks, huh?" He opens the brand-new box in front of her face.

Lily whispers, "Should we write an IOU?"

"Lil." He pops one in his mouth. "Think of it as their birthday present to me."

"It could be worse," Connor tells her, but he's still glancing at me and my computer. "He could have broken into the liquor cabinet and consumed a forty-thousand-dollar bottle of alcohol."

Ryke adds, "And had a bunch of Ninja Turtles chase after you down the street."

"See, love," Lo says to her. "My worst is over."

I almost snort. *That shit* actually *happened to him?* Jeez.

Lily smiles and holds out her hand. He pours Cheez-Its in her palm, his own smile spreading across his face.

Rose sips sparkling water and paces between the doorway, hawkeyed. She's been like that since we arrived at the party, even more so since Daisy and Willow got lost.

Honestly, I'm used to Rose being in complete battle mode. She's basically the Joan of Arc of the core six.

"No one fucking hit on you, did they?" Ryke asks Daisy. The sudden question slices my chest, and my focus zones in on Willow for a split-second.

She's sliding closer to me, and when she gives me a look like *I'm okay*, I return my gaze back to the computer screen and try to relax. Willow doesn't love attention drawn to her. Us being together and showing any kind of PDA is like a spotlight bearing down telling her brothers *look here!*

I'm trying my best to make sure that light isn't so bright.

So I pretend that I'm so fucking interested in code that I don't really notice her. But I slide my hand down her arm, her skin silky smooth, and my fingers lace firmly with hers.

I squeeze her hand, and I'm close enough to hear her breath shallow. *Fuck* that causes mine to shorten.

"I'm pregnant," Daisy reminds Ryke in a tone that basically says, *I couldn't possibly be hit on.*

"Yeah?" Ryke says. "Your sister thinks it wouldn't fucking matter if you were pregnant or not."

Willow clears her throat. "We were approached…Daisy handled it really fast though."

My head whips towards Willow. "What?" My stomach tosses, and it feels like the floor caves underneath me.

Ryke's jaw hardens. "What do you mean *approached?*"

Willow makes a soured face like she's grossed out. *Please tell me they didn't…*

Fuck. I can't even think it, but I know I have to ask it.

"Did someone touch you?" I ask under my breath, hopefully soft enough that not a lot of them hear. Preferably no one but Willow.

"No, no, like I said, Daisy handled it really fast. It was just… weird, I guess. He was old."

"Fucking fantastic," Ryke mutters.

I'd like to say I'm relieved, but I'm not. I hate that Willow had to go through anything that made her uncomfortable. I hate I wasn't there to at least call the guy a fucking creep or push him away.

"It does seem like there are more guys here than girls," Lily says, munching on Cheez-Its. I did notice that, but it's a statistic that I really don't care to be reminded of.

Lo nods to Willow. "You want to leave now?"

She shakes her head vigorously. "No. It wasn't that bad, honestly."

I don't know if she's just trying to be nice and not ruin the night. Worry mounts, and I kiss her on the cheek. Hand to the back of her soft neck, my lips move to her ear, and I whisper, "I'm sorry I wasn't there. Tell me everything that happened later?"

She nods and I pull her against my side, tucking her to my body.

"How many steps are left?" Connor asks me.

I shake my head, not following, and then I remember he's been watching me on my computer all night. I lick my lips and type one last line. "That's it," I say.

"That's it?" Daisy says eagerly, edging closer. She glances at the screen, full of computer code. Her brows scrunch together.

"Whoever they had hacking into your accounts will be met with porn spam when they try again. I also increased all your security passwords, and I've written them down for you." I dig into my pocket, pulling out a pack of cigarettes and a crumpled piece of paper. I hand the paper to Daisy. "I had to add a defense to all of your accounts, by the way. No one should be able to find your phone numbers unless you personally give it out."

Daisy releases a giant breath in relief.

I motion to Lily. "And your passcodes took me thirty-seconds to hack."

Lo gives her a look.

"Whaaa…" She crinkles her nose. "It's not anything familiar to anyone, I promise."

"It is though," I say. "Your favorite movie is *X-Men: First Class*. You said it in an interview, which is public knowledge. You can't use 2011xmen as your password—"

"Shhh!" she hushes me with bugged eyes and waves her hands like she's swatting flies. "Someone's going to overhear and get into my work email."

Besides the eight of us, there's no one in the kitchen.

"If you want, I'll help you change it tonight."

She nods repeatedly.

Connor closes his lightsaber and gestures from me to the laptop. "You taught yourself code?"

"Yeah."

"Why?" Connor asks like he's actually interested. But he can't be. I'm *me*.

"I like it." I shrug. "Code makes sense to me. Does there need to be another reason?"

Connor smiles. "There could be, but the reason you gave me is the best one."

38

GARRISON ABBEY
Age 19

I collapse on Willow's bed, reeling from one weird-ass Halloween.

Willow places her halo headband on her dresser. "I still can't believe what happened," she breathes. "It's almost out of the movies."

Ryke and Lily disappeared from the group for a little bit, and when they came back, they were covered in white powder. Flour laced with *cocaine*. Apparently, a group of guys dressed as zombies flour-cocaine bombed them as they were leaving the bathroom.

"A movie we missed," I tell her.

We didn't see it happen.

She pauses. "Is it kind of bad that I wish it were filmed? Not just the flour-bomb. But the whole thing, I mean. And not for online or other people." She strolls to the bed, still wearing angel wings. "It's just, it'd be kind of nice to relive some of the good moments."

I nod, agreeing. My lips lift at that last part. "Tonight was good?"

"Yeah…besides the cocaine," she repeats. "And the emergency room." We all took Ryke and Lily to the hospital, just to get checked out.

Lily broke out into a rash, and Ryke's leg is bothering him. So they're still being admitted overnight for observation.

"So like ninety-percent *good*?" I ask.

"Ninety-nine." She smiles.

I don't want to bring up the guy she ran into then. The one who was gross towards her and Daisy. If she's not thinking about it, there's no point in rehashing something that would drop the "good" percentage.

"Come here," I say and lean forward, grabbing her wrist.

She slides onto the bed next to me. The house is empty. Everyone's still at the ER, and I can't remember who's babysitting Maximoff and the Cobalt kids, but the important part is that they're MIA.

Ever since our first kiss at Daisy's birthday, she's let me explore her body with my hands. But I've never touched her below the waistband of her panties or above the tops of her thighs. I'm careful to take things at her pace.

Don't get me wrong, I'm dying a hundred deaths waiting. Every particle inside me wants to rush through. To caress each inch of her flesh, map out her freckles and study her body so I know it expertly.

But I won't fuck everything up by pushing Willow too fast. I've fucked enough up in my life. I can't fuck up this.

My lips meet hers, and I guide her back down onto the mattress. Her angel wings crumple a little beneath her.

I cup her cheek and edge her lips open. My body stirs to find pleasure points in both of us. But most of the time, I finish in the bathroom.

I'm fine with that.

I just wish I could make her come. She's never had an orgasm in her life, other than from herself, and I, so fucking badly, want to give her that earth-shattering pleasure.

Her breath hitches as I suck on her bottom lip and then move to her neck. She's soft and hesitant and always in her head. Her hands lie next to her, not on me, because they're fisting her comforter tightly.

I suck harder on her neck, and her hips arc into me with need. I'm quick to rise on my knees, my bodyweight hoisting enough that she can't feel my erection. I don't want to pressure her into thinking she needs to get me off.

She doesn't.

I'm a fucking adult.

I'll be fine.

I barely pause, my hands sliding on top of her breasts. The fabric of her dress and bra soft under my palm. I knead her, and she lets out a raspy breath. I want to give her more.

And thank you *V-cut* dress for giving me easy access, so I graze my hand underneath her padded bra. Her nipple is already perked, and I continue massaging, my thumb brushing over the sensitive bud. Her breath staggers.

My dick throbs.

Hardening more.

With my other hand to her hips, I squeeze her flesh tightly. She squirms underneath me. *Fuck, how wet is she?* My head screams at me to check, to just slip my hand between her thighs and release these pent-up feelings that I can *physically* see coursing through her.

I clench my jaw, shutting down those thoughts.

"You okay?" I ask Willow in a whisper as my mouth glides to the other side of her neck. I press my fingers into the soft flesh of her ass, near the back of her thighs.

"Mmm," she breathes out her nose, already sinking into those cravings. And then just as suddenly, she goes rigid. Her entire body locked.

I lift up on my hands, enough that I can look her in the eyes. "What's wrong?" I ask, my gaze dancing around her body for more signs of discomfort.

"Nothing," she says so softly that I have to lean down a little to hear. "I just…I keep forgetting to touch you. It's not that I don't want to. It's that I get so lost in everything and—"

"You know where your hands are right now?" I ask her and look to her fingers, still tangled in the comforter.

"On the bed."

She doesn't get it, so I explain, "Willow, you're death-gripping the sheets like my dick is already inside you. It's fucking destroying me. In the best way."

Her lips lift slowly. "Really?"

"Really." Her shyness in bed is a literal turn-on. I never even predicated that.

She bites the bottom of her lip. "Should we get undressed?"

"It's up to you."

Her gaze flits to the top of my head, where my devil-horned headband pushes my thick hair back, keeping strands from falling into my eyes. "I like this." She touches a horn.

"Yeah?"

She nods, and then swallows hard. "We can stay dressed, if that's okay with you?"

"I'm good with that." Honestly, a little relieved too. My brothers came home from college to celebrate my dad's birthday last weekend. I'm still a little bruised and sore from their "brotherly roughhousing." Hunter elbowed me in the back when I tried to bail on dishwashing duty. I can still taste the bar of soap he shoved in my mouth.

I just don't want Willow to worry. I'll tell her about it another night.

She's quiet, still staring up at the devil horns on my head. I think she might be overthinking something else. So I just ask, "You okay?"

"Um…so I'm not ready to have sex," she whispers. "But I think I could do more tonight."

More.

Fuck. My muscles tense, head spinning. "Do you want me to make you come?"

She smiles. Like a fucking hundred-watt smile, brightening the whole room. "Yeah, I want that."

Fuck. Yes.

I roll onto my side, elbow propped up on the pillow and hand supporting my head. Willow moves like she's about to roll onto her side to face me. I press a hand to her belly. "Stay on your back," I tell her.

She relaxes where she is, but she turns her head to face me. I've come to know a lot about her. She likes instructions. It takes this immense pressure off her from feeling like she has to already know what to do.

"Can I touch your clit?" I ask her.

"Mmmhmm," she says, breathing through her nose again.

I smile and place a soft kiss on her lips. "That a yes?" I whisper against her mouth.

"Yes," she squeaks.

I pull back to stare at her beautiful brown eyes again. "Can I put my fingers inside you?"

She pauses, hesitates, and I sweep her frame, gauging her reaction. "Um…"

"That's fine," I tell her. "I don't need to be inside you to make you come."

Her mouth parts in arousal. "You can put them in me though," she says quickly. "I was just thinking that it might hurt. I've only ever had one inside."

One finger.

Fucking hell.

Blood rushes to my dick, begging me to ease into her. I grind down on teeth and bottle those urges. My hard-on strains against the fabric of my red pants, and I swallow down images of Willow fingering herself, which have definitely stormed my brain.

"Garrison," she smiles a little like she can see she's getting to me. "You okay?" She touches my jaw.

"*Fuck*," I groan and then stare down the length of her. "I want to make you come so goddamn badly."

"Then do it."

My mouth drops a second in shock and desire, and her glittering smile reaches her eyes.

"That a demand?" I ask.

Her smile falters. "No. Of course, you don't have to—"

Fuck. I kiss her again, stopping her from overthinking this to death. When I part from her lips, I say, "I'm going to make you come, but I'm only going to put one finger in you. How does that sound?"

She nods and relaxes more. I scoot closer to her, our legs tangled. But I'm still lying on my side while she's on her back. I have a better view, and she has less chance of feeling my erection.

Our lips continue to explore each other, deepening, and while she loses herself to the moment, I skate my hand underneath the waistband of her panties.

Holy…

My fingers immediately dip into her wetness. Soaked. I skim the top of her swollen clit, and she shudders instantly. I barely rub her, and she breaks from my mouth with a soft cry. *"Garrison."*

Fuckfuckfuck.

She buries her head into the crook of my chest, breath heavying as I make soft circular patterns over her sensitive flesh.

Moans breach her lips, and her eyes snap shut like her senses are overloading. Reboot and restore are not going to be in progress any time soon. Not until I give her the best orgasm of her fucking life.

I can't believe she's this sensitive with nothing inside of her.

It's blowing my mind.

I press my thumb more firmly onto her swollen bud.

Her thighs tremble, and she lets out a whimper.

"I have you," I say. "You're alright."

She starts thrusting against my hand. Arching her hips.

I don't think she even knows what she's doing because her eyes are closed, and she looks gone. But it's like her body is calling out for a release. Calling out for me to fill her completely with my length and bring her to that peak. It's like her body knows what it wants faster than her head.

But I'm listening to her head on this one.

Still, I watch her hips lift and lower in small throbbing waves. My body is set on blaze, and I ache to reach down my pants and release my one pent-up need.

I'm not there yet. But I've got to end her torment.

I slide a finger through her slick folds and inside her. Beyond tight, she immediately clenches around me. *Christ.*

Her legs vibrate, and her forehead presses harder into my chest. "Garrison. Ah…"

I pulse inside of her a couple times and continue circling her clit. It happens so fast. Her abdomen spasms and her cries bleed into the air. Her hand whips to my wrist to stop my movements. Too sensitive. Too gone.

She curls up on her side, even with my hand still against her heat. Like she's cocooning herself against me. My head is floating, a billion miles in the sky. So wrapped up in this girl.

Her flesh glistens with a light layer of sweat, and I brush back her hair so that I can see her face. "You okay?" I ask.

"Mmmhmm." Her breathing is still heavy.

I can't last much longer. I remove my hand from her panties, my fingers slick. "I'm going to the bathroom. I'll be right back. Promise—"

She catches my wrist to stop me.

Veins pulsate in my dick. "Willow," I whisper. "I have to go jack off."

"I know," she says, still out of breath. "You can do it here, though."

Here?

"In your bed?" I lick my lips. "You sure?"

"Yeah. I want to…um…watch you."

I smile. "Seems fair." I just got to watch *her* orgasm. I lie on my side again.

She smiles back. "Do you need—"

"Don't offer it, if it's just because you think you have to," I say, stopping her. "I don't need you to touch me if you're not ready."

Hesitation fills her gaze. "You sure?"

"Yeah. This is enough." I didn't even think I'd be doing this tonight. I slide my pants to my ankles and kick them off. Just in my boxer-briefs, I slip my hand down the fabric, gripping my rock-hard dick. Unlike her, I don't close my eyes.

I keep them open and attached to Willow as I stroke myself.

She watches me with parted lips.

She looks at me like I'm an otherworldly thing too good for this Earth, but I'm lying next to her jacking off while literally wearing a devil's costume.

In my soul, I know, hell is where I'm from.

39

WILLOW HALE
Age 19

On one of the best days of my life, it has to be pouring. Rain pelts the roof of the courthouse, and I guess it should feel ominous. But I couldn't be happier sitting in the first row beside Garrison and my dad.

My dad.

I've been referring to Jonathan Hale as my father for almost a year now. He reached out to me, *wanting* to have a relationship. Wanting to get to know me.

Our first real meeting as father and daughter was accompanied by Ryke and Lo, but it told me what I needed to know.

Jonathan Hale isn't perfect. Not in the slightest. But I've never had a parent fight to spend time with me. My mom let me run off to Philly like she was tossing feathers into the wind, and long before that, Robert Moore rejected me just on the assumption that I *might* not be his daughter. Maybe deep down he knew.

And he's here.

In the very back row.

He's the only part of the day that clouds the happiness. I don't peek over my shoulder again to check if he's still in the courtroom. I know he has to be.

Garrison holds my hand tightly, giving me encouraging nods. The fact that he's here with me through these giant moments in my life—it brings about this wave of comfort and longing. For a future. One that lasts forever with him.

Lily leans over Garrison, at the end of the first row with Lo, to whisper to me, "They're here."

Okay, I have to glance back this time. Sucking in a breath, I rotate a little. But four bodies block my view from Robert Moore.

Daisy, Ryke, Connor, and Rose walk down the aisle, and Daisy rings out her sopping wet hair, drenched from the storm. Her other hand rests atop her round belly, baby due any day now.

They came here just for me. It's an overwhelming feeling knowing that so many people care. This isn't a birth or a wedding. It's just one of those unique pivotal moments in my life that I didn't think would matter to other people.

But I see that it does.

My glasses mist, and I quickly rotate to face the front. Not wanting them to see me cry. I take my glasses off, wiping the lenses with my shirt.

When I turn back, they've already slipped into the second row. "Thanks for coming, everyone," I tell them.

"Wouldn't fucking miss it," Ryke says.

I put my glasses back on and hold his gaze, which has been easier these days. My relationship with Ryke isn't so awkward anymore. And I couldn't tell you the day that it changed. It was a slow, gradual process to accept that this intimidating force in my life is also my big brother.

"I meant to give you this." My hand shakes as I pass him an envelope. *Willow, you fool, stop shaking.* "You can open it now or later. I already gave Lo and Dad his."

"Are we doing presents already?" Lily asks.

Daisy stands. "I left Willow's in the car."

"No, it's alright," I tell her. "I can wait until later. The time just presented itself to give them theirs, so…"

Daisy gives me a smile. "I really want you to see it. I'll be right back, and I'll be really fast." She holds out her palm to Ryke, asking for the car keys. Daisy's enthusiasm is contagious, and I find myself grinning.

Rose and Lily stand like they're accompanying Daisy, and Ryke passes his wife the keys, despite the torrential downpour outside. Daisy jingles them in excitement before ambling out with Rose and Lily.

Just as they leave, Ryke tears open the envelope.

My heart beats faster. Gift-giving always has that effect. What if the recipient hates it? And then there's the worst scenario: the recipient hates a gift but pretends to love it, *and* it's so obvious that both parties partake in this quasi lie.

But luckily, I don't think Ryke would lie.

All worry washes away when Ryke pulls out a photograph. It was taken in a candid moment during Christmas at the mountain lake house. Lo, Ryke, and I sit on the patio around a fire. We're

438

all drinking homemade, non-alcoholic Butterbeer that Lily and I concocted together.

All three of us are smiling.

Ryke doesn't say anything as he stares at the photo, but he has this faraway look like he's remembering that day. He flips it over.

I wrote on the back.

Ryke Meadows (Gryffindor), Loren Hale (Slytherin), Willow Hale (Gryffindor, like Neville Longbottom).

Thanks for caring about me, even before we were family.

I could have probably said more, but the photograph wasn't big enough. Anyway, I don't think there are enough words in the dictionary to describe what my brothers mean to me. What Ryke means to me.

He takes a deeper breath. "You changed your name?" he asks, his voice splitting.

Tears threaten to rise. "It's pending, but yeah." My eyes burn, fighting off the waterworks. "I just hope everything goes right."

I guess, there's still a possibility that things end poorly today. But I've tried not to believe that. I glance anxiously at the judge's bench. Empty. Once she arrives, all will either go smoothly or horribly.

Even though Jonathan Hale is my biological father, Robert Moore has legal claim, since he was my dad at the time of my birth. It's all really complicated, and I hate that there are hoops to be jumped through just so that Jonathan can be my dad on paper.

The biggest hurdle: Robert has to give consent to Jonathan.

I may be eighteen, but Jonathan wants me on his health insurance, and I'm willing to accept *some* financial help from him. Maybe not a lot. But I don't want to be drowning in debt when my dad actively wants to be involved. I figure it's easier accepting this than a twenty-grand medical bill from an accident or surgery or some unknown thing happening to me.

"I need to talk to you," Connor says, abruptly capturing everyone's attention.

His gaze isn't planted on me though.

He's looking at Garrison.

My boyfriend frowns. "Me?"

"I am staring at you," Connor says, expressionless and calm.

Garrison turns to me for answers, just as puzzled as I am.

I shake my head. I don't know what this is about.

"Let's not drag this fucking out, Cobalt," Ryke says, but his brows are furrowed in confusion. I think that Connor might be the only one who's caught up to speed.

Connor says to Garrison, "I've been looking for a new investment, and I want to invest in you."

Garrison laughs like it's a joke. I want to whisper to him and tell him that I don't think it is, but his face quickly falls when he sees Connor is just waiting patiently for him.

"You're serious?" Garrison's brows shoot up. "You want to invest in *me*?" He pauses. "You do know who I am, right?"

"Garrison Abbey, proficient in tech and coding. You like Tumblr, gifs, hacking, Final Cut, classic video games, and the girl sitting next to you."

Wow…he's good.

Garrison shrugs off his leather jacket like he's hot with frustration. "I'm unreliable. I was kicked out of two high schools. I have no fucking plans to go to college—"

"You lack confidence, so I'll give you some right now. You're talented, self-motivated, and driven. If you don't see that in yourself, open your eyes and look at what you can do. All I'm asking is for you to create something, anything, and I'll back it."

Garrison blinks for a long beat. Stunned and shocked. "Why?"

"I value everything I just listed, and you need someone who believes in you. Create something brilliant, Garrison, or don't create anything at all. That's your choice."

Garrison stays quiet, processing. I'm doing the same. It's a lot to digest.

Lo says, "Take it, man. The god has spoken."

Connor grins.

Ryke groans. "Come on. He's a fucking six-foot-four human being with good hair."

"At least we've established one thing," Connor says. "Ryke loves my hair."

"I think you want to be fucking punched in a courthouse."

Connor's grin widens, but he plants his deep blue eyes back on Garrison.

My boyfriend's brows are furrowed, still thinking over the offer, and he keeps glancing at me. The second time he does, I realize why. It didn't really hit me until now, but if he accepts Connor's offer, we may not see each other that much anymore.

At least not for the next four years.

My stomach is already churning, but there's no desire to stop Garrison from this. Not for me. When he looks to me for the third time, I tell him, "Take it." Our eyes lock in a heady beat. "You can do *anything*, Garrison."

I truly, truly believe this.

Garrison looks back to Connor. "I'll have to stay in Philadelphia?"

"Yes," he says. "You've never done a start-up of any kind, and while you're creative, you need me to teach you about business."

Connor isn't the type to just blindly invest in a *person*. This isn't a normal job offer, and anyone receiving it would be jumping head-first at the chance. No questions asked.

Garrison angles towards me, confusion still pleating his forehead. His eyes carry raw, hard truths.

I've been accepted to Wakefield University, and I'll be leaving for London in August.

Different countries.

Different continents.

A whole ocean separating us. And I see that he wants to keep me close. I want him by my side, too. That was the plan when I chose this college. But he can't come to London and leave behind an opportunity as great and big as this one. Working at Cobalt Inc. is the road that will lead him in the right direction. I know it.

"Take it," I repeat, sucking in a tight breath. Pain lances me. "I just want the best for you." *This is the best.*

"The best for me is to be with you." His nose flares, restraining emotion. "I'm a better fucking person when I'm with you." He rubs his face a couple times, trying to stop himself from crying.

Our lives are about to split, fissure, and fracture by this one decision. But I think it'd break worse if he didn't choose the job. I think we'd both resent each other in the end.

I lean closer to him, a breath apart. "Don't be afraid," I whisper. "You can do anything on your own. I know you can." *But can I be without him?* The question rips through me, and my glasses fog up.

I take them off.

His reddened eyes meet mine, and he's a little fuzzy in my vision now, but it's not too bad. He clasps my hand, threading his fingers. "I love you," he says.

Tears crease my eyes.

"No matter where we are," he tells me. "You're always going to be my girl."

THE FUTURE FEELS DIFFERENT NOW THAT GARRISON and I are planning to live apart. More somber and up in the air. But I try to push the reality behind me to focus on what's before me.

The courtroom quiets as Robert Moore approaches the bench. My dad and I already stand in front of it. I hold my arm to my chest, nervous that everyone is looking at me. *Because everyone is.*

I try not to glance at Robert. Not wanting to have my earth shattered today with a mental image of his expression.

The judge looks to him. "Since the means of Mr. Hale outweigh most, I wanted you here in person. I need to make sure you haven't been coerced, threatened, or swayed by financial means to give consent."

The court reporter's fingers move quickly, capturing the judge's words.

"This is what it's come to. I'm not surprised." Robert's words are a battleax to my heart.

He did raise me. Before the divorce, before things soured, he raised me.

"Are you in agreement surrendering your parental rights, Mr. Moore?" the judge asks.

I glance over at that.

Wrong move.

Robert shrugs. This nonchalant, *I don't give a shit* shrug. "All along, I think I knew that she wasn't my kid. It's not just about looks, but no one in my family needs glasses."

It feels like a hole is being chiseled through my chest. I'd have loved going the rest of my life not hearing Robert's opinion about me.

But he crosses his arms and keeps going. "She doesn't act like any kid of mine. She's practically mute half the time." *I can't breathe.* "She dresses more like a boy than a girl." *Please stop.* "She has no friends."

Feet clatter behind me, and I glance over to see Lily, Lo, Ryke, Daisy, Connor, Rose, and Garrison all standing to their feet. All silently saying *she's my friend.*

Tears stream down my cheeks. When my eyes land on Daisy, she mouths *my one friend* and makes a heart with her hands, smiling.

My best friend. Daisy Calloway. Her friendship is the rare, beautiful kind, and I'm never letting it go.

My smile matches hers, and I rub my wet face. I notice Lo's cheekbones sharpening like he's grinding his teeth. Ryke looks equally pissed. Just when I think they might explode in the courtroom, my dad's voice cuts in.

"Can I say something, Your Honor?" He raises his hand. His face is creased with severe, strict lines.

The judge nods. "Yes."

My dad narrows a malicious glare on Robert. The tension in the room seems to amp with that one look, setting ablaze any fake congeniality. "Don't ever insult my daughter again, you microscopic prick—"

"Alright, Mr. Hale—"

"In the seventeen years that she was with you—did you even talk to her?" my dad asks. "Did you know she's charismatic when you discuss things that interest her? Maybe you should've seen a goddamn movie with her—"

"Mr. Hale—"

"—instead of sitting around on your ass, you scum of this planet." He fixes his suit, as though a fistfight just ended with Robert Moore bloodied on the ground.

"Mr. Hale," the judge snaps, banging her gavel forcefully.

"I'm done," my dad says.

And I can breathe again.

Robert has taken five steps back like he's been physically pushed, and his beet-red face is coated in a sheen of sweat.

I think about something my dad said. How Robert should've seen a movie with me. In the first few weeks of even talking to each other, Jonathan Hale asked to watch a film of my choice. I picked *Doctor Strange*. And even though he hated the storyline and characters in the first five minutes, he still finished watching it with me.

"Let's continue," the judge declares. "Robert Moore, do you wish to give up your parental rights as Willow's father to Jonathan Hale?"

Without hesitation, he says, "Yes."

"Then the court recognizes Jonathan Hale as Willow's legal and biological father. Thank you all for coming today, and congratulations Willow." The judge's eyes flit heatedly to Robert before she leaves the courtroom.

I almost can't believe it. I'm…a Hale.

"Ca-Caw!" Daisy calls out to me, making the bird noise.

I laugh a tearful laugh as I turn around, and everyone in the room starts clapping. My heart has grown outside my body. Too big to fit inside me. Love. It's all just pure, unadulterated love.

Daisy squeezes out of the row, aimed for me. Robert passes her, leaving in a hurry and probably sensing my brothers' glares on his back. I make sure to watch this time.

I want *this* to be my final image of him.

Shuffling out of the courtroom with the realization that the daughter—the one he didn't really ever want—is loved. And I never needed him.

Daisy lands beside me at the first row and passes me an envelope. "This is for you, and I'm totally kicking myself because it would've been awesome if you had it before…all of that." She waves towards the judge's bench like it's already old news.

I carefully open the envelope. A simple silver pinky ring inside.

I immediately recognize the black square carved in the center. I gave her an identical pinky ring a long time ago when her ex-friends were harassing her.

I told Daisy, "*My favorite superhero wears this ring. It protects Tilly Stayzor from anyone outside of the Fourth Degree, basically her personal enemies. This ring is just a reminder that there are people who have your back. And we all need protection at some point. I want you to have mine.*"

She's still wearing that ring on her pinky, which means…she bought me a matching one. We're both crying. Tears flowing down my cheeks and hers.

We smile together as I fit the ring on my finger.

"We all need a little protection sometimes," she says, so she must remember what I told her. That crashes through me and I push back more raw sentiments. She adds, "And there are a lot of people who love you here."

I have to take my glasses off to wipe them. "This means…so much to me. Thank you." I fit my glasses on again.

"There's more," she says with a bigger smile.

More?

With a trembling hand, I inspect the envelope and take out a photograph. On the picture, a tiny little willow tree is freshly planted next to a cabin. The sign hung over the door says, *Green Willow.*

I immediately know what this is, and my eyes flood once again.

"You're now officially a girl's cabin at Camp Calloway," she tells me. "You didn't think I missed you, did you?" When Daisy started building her camp, she named cabins after her sisters. Pink Lily. Yellow Rose. Red Poppy.

I just never thought about myself in the equation.

Never would have assumed I'd be included.

I knew I was going to have monumental moments today, but I didn't expect for this to be one. Feeling Daisy's friendship and love and sisterhood wrap around me so tightly and protectively—I'll never forget it.

She holds out her palm for our friendship handshake, but I wrap my arms around her shoulder, light as can be since she's pregnant.

Daisy hugs me back.

Afterward, I search the courtroom for Garrison, and when our eyes meet, a bittersweet realization passes sadly between us.

London.

Philadelphia.

We're going to split apart. *Not yet.* We have some months left together before I leave for college, and I hang onto those like a lifeline.

40

GARRISON ABBEY
Age 24

"Oh no, I'm dying, I need health—I need health," Willow says in panic, punching buttons on a Sega controller with skill.

"Knock over the steel drum—*fuuuck*." I rock back as my health meter depletes to zero. "I just died."

Willow laughs, and then Blaze, her *Streets of Rage* character, kicks ass for another five minutes, gaining health, and not long after that, Blaze perishes too.

We take a food break, and I flip open the pizza box on the floor—where we've thrown down plush blankets, bed pillows, and set up our TV with a few game consoles. Move-in boxes surround us in the large, open space. Sharpie scrawled over the cardboard sides, most labeled *Abbeys – living room* and *Abbeys – kitchen*.

Willow was happy to sell all her textbooks. Not needing to pack any since she *officially* graduated college with a shiny business degree. She'll open up the London branch of Superheroes & Scones soon.

And eventually, Lily wants to hire Willow as the Chief Brand Officer. Which is big.

I'm really proud of everything she's accomplished.

Earlier, we dug into a few boxes to find the N64, so Styrofoam popcorn packaging litters the ground too.

I lost at Diddy Kong Racing like fifteen times in a row.

"You're killing it tonight," I say while tearing into a slice of pepperoni.

Willow smiles, brown hair wet in a messy braid after a shower. "Must be the new place," she says softly, just wearing blue cotton pajamas. "Maybe I'm lucky here."

My lips rise.

Yeah, I like that idea. Our new home together is a place of good fortune for Willow, and me too. It feels that way, at least, and tonight is only our first night here.

She scoops up a cheesy piece of pizza, and I smile at the bathing suit tan lines on her shoulders, visible outside the spaghetti straps of her PJs.

"What?" She nudges up her glasses, seeing me staring.

I lick my lips, feeling my smile expanding. I shake my head at first, but then words come easy. "It just dawned on me that when I look at you, it means that I'm looking at my wife."

She has trouble chewing pizza, her smile uncontrollable. "Stop...I can't..." She laughs.

I laugh.

Willow chokes on the food.

Shit. "You okay?" I place a hand on her back and pass her a water bottle.

She nods repeatedly, then swallows. "Thanks." She sips the water. I keep my arm around her waist.

We spent our honeymoon in Hawaii. Seven beautiful days under the sun. Hence, our recent tans.

My chest swells. Remembering it all.

Feeling.

Because before that, I married Willow Hale in a small garden wedding, mostly just family attending. Right here in Philadelphia.

The quiet, intimate ceremony on May 31st was perfect, but I think we both loved the honeymoon more. Just us. No crowds, no one to greet or try to please.

Being back home, we've mostly been dealing with the new move. We wanted a place of our own, just not in Philly suburbs.

An industrial factory in Philly was converted into premium lofts about a year ago. Seriously *premium*. A doorman is posted at the entrance, and so far, Barry seems cool.

But living in the city comes with *privacy* issues.

We asked for help testing the "tint" of the massive window in our open living room and kitchen. On the fifteenth floor, we have a pricey view of a cool park and eclectic shops.

Worth the money. I'd rather not stare at a brick wall.

Lo, Connor, and the Calloway sisters came over earlier to determine whether paparazzi could see into our loft from the street.

The verdict: *a little bit.*

A little bit is too much, so we'll need to increase the tint level. Until then, Willow and I hung curtains that are drawn shut.

Willow notices me staring at the shrouded window. "You think if we were Lily and Lo, paparazzi would've taken pics of us by now?"

"For sure." I swallow the crust of my pizza. "Give it a couple days though, and I bet we'll see headlines like: *Newlyweds Move into*

Coolest Loft Ever. The article will call me a high school dropout with connections, and you'll be Loren and Ryke's awesome little sister, of course."

"Of course." She smiles into a sip of water and then stares faraway in thought.

"Are you still worried about it?" I gesture to the window. "The media finding us?"

Willow shrugs. "I know it's unavoidable…I guess I'm just scared of what we talked about before." She turns to face me. "Chaotic Evil."

Yeah, we've discussed the probability of our fame piquing to monstrous, catastrophic levels. "We're still at Chaotic Good," I tell my wife—*still love that.* "Media isn't printing any cheating rumors or making up fake scandals. They're just obsessively relishing in our wedding and honeymoon. Next, it'll be our new place."

Willow looks around the loft, all metal and concrete. I can see us living here for a long time.

She agrees, "We haven't been cannibalized. Not yet, but when we have a baby…what if they say that I'm a bad mom or butt into our parenting style?" She's seen the Calloway sisters deal with public criticism raising kids.

Pretty sure they could breathe and the media would say they're not inhaling long enough.

My muscles tighten, just picturing Willow going through that bullshit.

I place a hand on her bare ankle. "Is there more?" I wonder since she intakes a tense breath. "Willow?" My chest hurts.

"I just—I want to not care what happens, if the worst comes, but I've seen so many shippers and fans *turn* on Lily, Rose, and Daisy at a single headline. They go from love to hate with the snap of a finger. It feels like they're Thanos—"

"They're not," I refute, knowing the *Avengers* reference. "They can't 'dust' your universe."

But I won't be the one attacked. I'm a dude. Media and so-called fans harass the girls twenty times more.

So, it's a misogynistic Thanos snap.

Her eyes downcast.

I edge closer, my hand ascending to her calf, and all I'm thinking is that I need to protect my wife from Chaotic Evil. Since we were seventeen, making Willow feel *safe* and at ease in any given situation meant everything to me.

It still does.

Maybe even more now, if that's humanly possible.

"It's just a fear, I guess," she says quietly.

"Hey, your fear is my fear, Willow." My hand travels to her kneecap, and our eyes meet as I tell her, "Fans either don't care about us or they somewhat like us. We're like the underrated gems. I know that could change if we're too overexposed, and maybe we've gotta figure out ways to stay under the radar so no one burns us down."

Fandoms almost always self-implode.

Very few things are loved forever. And we've been sitting inside a beloved thing that's detonated multiple times. Calloway sisters going from *adorned* to *scorned*, back to adorned, then scored and the cycle starts all over again.

Truth: Willow and I haven't even been on Tumblr in months, maybe a solid *year*. If I make gifs, I just send them to her through text.

We'll always love the internet, but our relationship with it has shifted. It had to for our health.

I don't want to stumble on hate posts about Lily or Daisy or Rose. People we love. It sucks the wind out of our sails. Punches a fist through our guts.

Fuck that pain.

We deal with enough already offline.

Willow suggests, "Maybe we shouldn't do interviews on *We Are Calloway* anymore." The critically acclaimed docuseries won an Emmy last year for the fourth season, and we don't make *large* appearances like the core six, but we've done interviews for the show.

We exchange a deeper look. Because I know why she'd propose tossing this out.

I've been quoted *everywhere* after episode twelve aired where I said, *"I married someone much braver than me."*

It's true, but Christ, I didn't expect to become gif sets and video compilations. And yeah, the irony isn't lost on me.

I did the same shit to Ryke for his f-bombs.

Years ago.

Years ago. Time carries my thoughts in a drift.

Knowing what I know now, I wonder if I still would've made the videos. I'm not sure if age has changed me more or just the events and circumstances of my life.

Maybe I'll never really have the answer.

"That's probably the best idea," I nod. "Do you still want to appear on the docuseries, even if we're not doing interviews?" We're often spotted in the background.

"Yeah." She doesn't waver or hesitate. "If we leave Philly where paparazzi is or if we try to avoid cameras, then I feel like we're also avoiding my brothers and Daisy and Lily...Rose." She takes a deep breath. "I never want to subvert the spotlight so much that we draw away from our extended family."

Our extended family.

My eyes burn, but I push back emotion for a second. "Same."

We make a pack to never avoid the media at the cost of our relationships with the Hales, Meadows, and Cobalts.

She smiles more. "You think one day we'll reach Chaotic Neutral? Where we're like flies on the wall to all the madness?"

I stand up. "Let me ask the all-knowing one."

Willow grabs her half-eaten cheesy slice. "You're calling Connor?"

"Uh, *no*. He's still the tall one." We both laugh, and I wash my hands in the sink, then rummage in the game box near the TV.

There it is.

I shake a Magic 8-Ball to Willow. "You ask the question."

She rises to her feet, biting into crust. "Will we be a fly on the wall to all the madness?"

I shake the ball and then steady it, the triangle floating up in the dark-blue dye. I read, "*You may rely on it.*"

Willow is closer, only a foot away from me, and my eyes roam her soft features and the curve of her waist, affection and desire heating my blood. Her eyes travel just as yearningly along the ridges of my abs and the ink along my tanned skin.

I near my wife and she walks backwards to the kitchen, a bashful smile playing at her lips.

I shake the ball as we move. "Will we have a boy, eventually?" I'd rather raise a girl, but I'll be happy no matter what gender.

Her back meets the island counter. "What does it say?"

I press my muscular body up against her soft frame. Her breath shallows, and I whisper, "*Outlook good.*"

Willow holds onto the counter behind her, breastbone rising and falling. "I'm going to ask it something."

"Okay." I run my free hand up her pajama top. Fingertips brushing the flesh along her hips, her ribs.

Love and want flood her brown eyes. "Will Garrison Abbey kiss me?"

I smile and rattle the 8-Ball. "*Reply hazy, try again.*"

She wets her lips, smiling an overwhelmed smile. "Will Garrison kiss me?"

Shaking the ball, I dip my head closer to Willow, our eyes diving deep before I shift them to the results. "*Concentrate and ask again.*"

We laugh.

"Concentrate," I coach.

"Okay, hold on." She shuts her eyes, and in the heady beat, I just look at my girl and our home—and my bright smile conjures tears.

Happiness, it never felt in reach.

But I woke up today, and I love who I am. And I'm forever in love with the girl who fell asleep next to me.

Very softly, eyes still closed, Willow whispers, "Will my husband kiss me?"

I gently cup her cheek and bring my lips to hers. Our tender affection alive and quiet, like a firefly in the summer night.

41

WILLOW ABBEY
Age 24

My lips sting beneath his, lit a billion ways, and I want more, so much so. But… "I need to wash my hands," I whisper after I pull back.

He already wiped off the pizza grease, but I haven't.

The thought keeps disturbing *the* moment: our new house, a flirty make-out. I've been pulsing between my legs, but the "hand washing request" could've just punctured the sweet and hot mood.

My face is on fire.

Garrison smiles and draws back. "Yeah, go ahead."

I wash my hands in the sink, and I find my phone on the counter, near a liter of Fizz Life. Maybe music will help reset the tone.

I brave a glance back at him. He rests against the island, bare-chested with low-riding drawstring pants. Inked and cool, he waits

His lip upturns.

Garrison Abbey is my husband.

I realize my eulogy will now say "wife"—I'm someone's wife. *Here lies Willow Abbey, loving wife…*

My pulse races, heart on a tilt-a-whirl, and I dry off my palms and scroll through Spotify for a specific song.

Our marriage reminds me of our wedding, and how we invited my mom and my little sister to the ceremony. Before that, they ended up changing their phone numbers and never gave me their new ones, so it's been harder to stay in contact.

But when they didn't RSVP at all, I knew they'd eradicated me from their lives with more permanence. I don't blame them. My dad was invited to the wedding, and I'm sure my mom didn't want to be anywhere near him.

In the end, Garrison and I both lost our families. He left his, and mine eventually left me. I grieve the loss at times. Like an ocean rising above me, it swells up in random moments. When I see a princess crown in the kid's aisle of a store, reminding me of Ellie.

But I have a lot of love to pull me to the surface. Garrison and I gained another family. Not just with the Calloway sisters, but with each other.

I've never felt more loved than by him and with him. He's my comfort and home.

My lungs are light, and I return to the island with my phone in clean hands.

Garrison clutches my hips and lifts me onto the counter.

I nearly drop the phone, breath caught in my throat, but he steadies my wrist. His other hand travels up my thigh. My legs are split around his waist, so he fits as close as possible against me.

We consume one another by sight alone. Not needing to say much to feel a lot. I click into a song, and as soon as the first few notes play, Garrison smiles more.

Interpol's "Rest My Chemistry"

A few of these lyrics are tattooed on the crease of his forearm and bicep, along with a black skull.

I glance at the Magic 8-Ball beside me on the kitchen surface, then up at him.

"I have another question about our future." I push up my slipping glasses.

He grabs the 8-Ball. "Ask it." We're almost eye-level, his lips skim mine with a light, longing touch.

I hang onto his waist. "Will we always be this happy?"

Our eyes well up. We're finally together in the same city, same house, same room, same bed.

Sharing everything.

A life.

Love.

Garrison stops shaking the 8-Ball and sets the plastic sphere on the counter. "We don't need that to know the answer."

I smile with him. "*Without a doubt*," I say our answer, my chest elevating with a big breath that we both take.

His forehead touches mine, our mouths an aching distance away. "*It is certain*," Garrison whispers, and we kiss with slow, yearning passion.

We're twenty-four, but when we're together, I feel blown back. It feels like we're only twenty, then seventeen. Distance, time, miles and hours are intangible, metaphysical things, all woven and jumbled in an invisible tapestry, and like my favorite comic books, the beginning is really the end and the end is just the beginning.

42

BACK THEN – August

Philadelphia, Pennsylvania

GARRISON ABBEY
Age 20

Candlelight bathes Willow's bedroom, rose and vanilla scent strong. Music plays softly from a playlist. It feels like I'm living a dream—and tomorrow I'll wake up in my tattered, damaged reality.

Until then, I'll stay here.

I'll never wake up.

Willow is tucked close in my arms, her heartbeat slowing as we both let the night wash over us. I just took her virginity. Filled her in ways I never have before.

It's been one of the best nights of my life, but it ends soon. And I really haven't come to grips with that.

"What time is it?" Willow whispers, cocooned by my body. I have the better view of the clock. It's that weird time period, what some people call morning and other people call night. 3:10 a.m.

I know what she's really asking. "We have to leave in twenty-minutes."

Her suitcase is already downstairs beside the door. We've even showered, dressed, and returned to bed, lying on top of the comforter. I don't want Willow to leave my arms because there are parts of me that wonder—maybe this is it.

This is the last time I get to hold her.

She's moving to London.

She's starting a life over there.

I'd be an idiot to think there's a good probability this can last. But Christ, I want to believe it. I want to believe this is just a roadblock, a setback—not the end.

Never the end.

I swallow hard and kiss the top of her head. We're quiet in the stillness of the room, letting the moment pass.

"Maybe I should stay," she starts.

"No." I rub at my dry, raw eyes. "Let's just head to the airport. We'll have more time in the car together." I need to get moving because the longer I lie here, I'll do something stupid. Like agree to her suggestion.

She wipes her nose with the back of her hand, and I see that she's been crying.

"Hey." I pull her into my chest. I need to be the strong one here. Even though I'm being ripped open. "We're not apart yet." I brush her tears with my thumb. "And when we are, I'll be all over you with my ones and zeroes."

Her lips lift in a quivering smile. "Me too."

We all drive to the airport together, the private plane sitting on the tarmac. Willow's not taking commercial this time because Lo wanted to say goodbye at the airport and not back home. Paparazzi aren't allowed here, and it gives Willow enough peace to talk to everyone.

Wind whips around us. The sun hasn't risen yet, but the airport lights illuminate the area. I watch as each of Willow's family hug her goodbye. Her dad, her brothers, Lily, Rose, and Connor. She bends down to put her arms around three-year-olds Maximoff and Jane. The toddlers sniff loudly, sad about their Aunt Willow and favorite babysitter leaving them. Nearly one-year-old twins, Charlie and Beckett smile as Willow kisses the tops of their heads.

When she moves to Daisy, it's harder.

Everyone falls hushed. In Daisy's arms is a six-month-old baby, Sullivan Meadows, who almost didn't make it into the world. Willow lets Sulli wrap her little fingers around her pinky, the one with the friendship ring. And Daisy and Willow break into sobs.

I stand off to the side, watching each goodbye through a sickness that tosses my stomach in awful knots. My throat swollen. My whole body tensed up in terrible ways.

Don't go! I want to scream.

Stay!

PLEASE!

My soul is fighting with myself.

I have loved her for longer than I have loved myself. I found her when living seemed like a worse choice than ending it all.

And now I'm losing her.

To London.

Fucking London.

Willow wipes at her wet tear-streaked cheeks, her olive-green shirt makes her warm, brown eyes glow even more in her sadness. Daisy backs away, crying and sniffing loudly, she walks into Ryke's arms.

And then Willow looks at me.

We're five-feet apart and that already feels like the biggest fucking distance in the world. *It's about to be a million times worse.*

Kill me.

Just fucking do it already.

I've been waiting all my life to die. She leaves, maybe I'm going to finally be ready. Maybe it's just time.

I can't tell her this. I can't tell her how hard this is going to be for me. Because if she stays for a loser like me, I'll never survive that.

Each step closer to her is a knife in my chest. It feels like my brothers are here. Standing off to the side, sliding in the blades.

One after the other.

Step. Cut. Step. Cut.

Step…

I'm bleeding out.

But I touch her. Hand to hers.

She's a mess of tears. She's *my* mess. "Willow." My voice cracks.

Her chin quakes. "I don't want to go. I change my mind—"

I bring her into my chest, tucking her close, hand on the back of her head. Tears stream down my jaw, but I face the plane, not her family.

I swallow the pain.

Swallow it down.

Down.

I pull back to look her in the eyes. It's somehow easier to speak. Maybe because she's right here. Like my brain knows she's not gone yet. "We're going to make this work," I tell her, trying to sound confident. "I'm going to text and Skype." I cup her wet cheeks between both my hands. "We're going to make this work, Willow. Because you're my girl, and that's not going to change."

Please…don't let that change.

She cries into my shirt, soaking the fabric. We stay like that until she has to board the plane. Until I have to watch her physically leave me.

I'm cut open on the ground.

Nothing without her.

Epilogue

PRESENT DAY – June

Baltimore, Maryland

GARRISON *ABBEY*
Age 39

irt tracks, bicycle tires, and a familiar announcement projected over a rowdy audience, "riders ready…watch the gates"—I smile, taking it all in.

Summer.

I've lived through thirty-nine summers, and before I met my wife, before those long drawn-out summer days in a comic book store, the few hot months out of school were hell.

I hated every summer.

My brothers were home more, and I'd do anything and everything to stay away.

Now, I hunger for the summer days, for the sticky heat and dirt under my soles. And I know with certainty—at thirty-nine—that

Standing behind a wooden fence, I'm among the noisy crowd who cheer on racers. Sun beats on an outdoor BMX track, a little bit outside of Baltimore.

I run my palm back and forth over my head, hair buzzed short. I prefer nothing in my eyes. Not needing to hide anymore.

I haven't for a long time.

My parents never tried to reconnect. Not even when I was in my early twenties and first left. They released me from their household like a crow who flew through the window and found its way out.

I never had to attempt to pull away twice or a third time. Once was all it took. And I'm grateful for that.

All three of my brothers ended up working for our father's tech company. I never see them. Never speak to them, and like my parents, they're gone from my world.

"Let's go! Let's go!" people shout from the sidelines, pumping up the teen racers as they catch air over dirt hills and skid along the curves of berm turns. Pedaling towards the finish line.

I drop my left arm, while my right arm remains loosely draped over my wife's shoulder. And I smile as my eyes graze Willow and her fingers that are laced with my hand.

My gaze keeps traveling across the event. Competitors in full-face helmets, visors, and long-sleeved jerseys line up with their BMX bikes and wait for their *moto*, what Lo still calls a "heat" even after the tall one corrected him a hundred times.

Loren Hale is still *that* guy.

The corner of my mouth rises, and I glance down the fence. Where Lo has his arms around Lily while they watch the race. Lo is smiling, and in a quiet beat, he catches my gaze and we exchange something pure and happy.

Something I think only guys like me and him can ever truly understand. How long it's been and how far we've come. To peace around us and to peace with ourselves.

I nod.

He nods back.

Johnathan Hale died twelve years ago after his many years of alcohol abuse finally caught up to him. He started laying off me after my kid was born. And by the time he passed away, we were on better terms.

Close by Lily and Lo, Rose spritzes water on her neck and collar. Connor says something to his wife, inaudible over the crowds. She glares up at him. He grins down at her.

My office is still inside Cobalt Inc.—so that weird back and forth between Connor and Rose is too commonplace.

Willow always thought they'd have like eleven children. Enough to fill out a football team. They didn't end up with *that* many. But all the Cobalts are at the BMX track today, and their *seven* kids make up a large portion of our group.

An empire.

Literally the media calls them the *Cobalt Empire*, and Willow and Lily own too much Cobalt Empire merch. I love the T-shirts and water bottles. Hate the snow globes.

"Oh…no, I'm out of storage," Willow says beside me, and I glance back as she untangles our hands and quickly tries to free up storage on the DSLR camera strapped around her neck.

Keeping my arm splayed over her shoulder, I use my other hand to hold the camera and help Willow.

Daisy notices the dilemma after Ryke drops her on her feet. He had her upside-down. Even after all these years, Ryke is a beast.

Physically able to climb any mountain and also toss his wife over his shoulder. Paparazzi aren't allowed in the event, but I bet their telephoto lenses captured that shot.

Media loves a flirty *Raisy*.

"I still have the video camera." Daisy holds up a newer digital camcorder, Velcro-ed to her hand. "We won't miss a thing."

Everyone also has cellphones. No matter what, the competition will be recorded a billion times over by the core six.

Willow smiles at Daisy, who smiles brightly back, and they let me fix the DSLR. My eyes skim the women as they talk and laugh.

Their friendship has only strengthened through the years. Even as work pulls everyone away at times. Willow is the Chief Brand Officer for Superheroes & Scones, and every now and then, we'll return to London. We always make a point to time meetups with Tess and Sheetal. They live in Atlanta, but they visit Sheetal's family in Liverpool about twice a year.

We went to their wedding in London.

And currently, Tess is an actress on a medical TV drama that we tape every Tuesday night, and Sheetal is a producer on the same show.

I click into the camera settings. Two clicks later and the *no storage* warning sign disappears. "Got it."

Willow grins up at me. Rising on her toes, we kiss and she whispers, "Thanks."

My lips upturn more, and I cup the back of her neck in tender affection. "Anytime, anywhere." Still, to this day, my heart belongs to Willow.

At the sound of a familiar whistle, my gaze drifts. Near us, twenty-two-year-old Jane Cobalt has two fingers in her mouth, whistling the way her Aunt Daisy taught her.

Bright smile, freckled cheeks—Jane cheers on other teens, basically strangers, while we wait for the next moto.

She's smart. Like genius intellect. In a minute flat, she calculated the points needed for the top ten racers to qualify for the Grand Nationals in Tulsa.

And I thought I was good with numbers.

While Jane lives in Philly, she's been seen out with some douchey bro. Connor acts like it's not the worst thing in the world, but I see how his face twitches whenever Lo and Ryke bring up the subject. Connor has run about ten different background checks on the guy and was even a heartbeat away from asking me to hack into the bro's computer.

I don't blame him.

Jane is severely famous.

The five oldest kids are.

I glance over my shoulder at our tent. Coolers surround pop-up chairs under the shade. Maximoff Hale has a few bottles of Ziff in arm, on his way back to everyone. Athletic, kind-hearted, unwavering confidence is in his entire demeanor.

I feel fucking old. Because next month, he'll turn twenty-two, and I look at him and still see the little kid I'd babysit.

The one who made me feel alive when being away from Willow seemed like certain death.

His thick brown hair is dyed lighter and blows in the wind.

Moffy smiles as he stops beside me. "Is it time yet?"

"Should be next." As he passes a blue flavored Ziff to Willow and limeade to me, I notice a wet piece of paper in his hand. "What's that?"

He makes a face and stuffs the paper in his back pocket. "A guy gave me his number." His eyes briefly flit towards a group of twenty-something racers before landing on me. "I didn't want to reject him in from of his friends."

I glance between the smiling guy and Moffy, a lot more coolly than his dad would be. Lo has no chill when it comes to his kids and dating. "You're not interested?"

He shakes his head. "He's cute, but..." Moffy stares off in thought. He's bi and considered a top "eligible bachelor" in the nation. He's never been in a serious relationship, and I think whoever ends up with Moffy will probably need to be tough as hell.

As new riders reach the gate, we all face the track.

Willow squeezes my hand in excitement and then starts snapping pictures.

"Let's go!"

"You got this!"

Everyone shouts around me.

I cup my hands around my mouth and yell, "Ride smart! Stay sharp!" My pulse ratchets up.

USA's BMX East Coast Nationals has been in full swing. Day three, and my kid already raced six motos to qualify for this Main.

Every time I watch my thirteen-year-old, I'm fucking nervous. It's not a safe sport, and we've already dealt with a broken arm at age six. Lost control of the bike during a district championship.

Crowds cheer, "Come on! Let's go!"

Eight competitors grip their handlebars. My thirteen-year-old among them. In the blue and black jersey and full-face helmet.

Let's go.

I keep my arm over Willow.

"Set yourselves," the announcer calls out. "Riders ready...watch the gates." *Beep beep beep.* The gates drop, and I hold my breath as tires descend on dirt track. Speeding and flying over hills.

I clap and yell, and when the last lap comes, Willow grips my shoulder.

Our kid is in third and shooting for first.

"Wait, wait…" Willow says and then we wince when two competitors pass at the turn.

Shit.

We see the standing.

Sixth place.

"Good race!" I shout and clap. This year, our thirteen-year-old came in first at the East Conference Championships and needed to place fourth at this event to have enough points to attend Grand Nationals.

Have to wait till next year.

Willow and I meet the competitors at the end of the track.

"Awesome job," I say with a hug and tap of the helmet. "You did great out there."

"Except I *screwed* that turn."

"You'll get it next time," Willow encourages with a loving smile.

And then our kid grips the helmet with two gloved hands. Taking it off and shaking out a loose sandy-brown braid.

Our daughter smiles a gap-toothed smile like she won the race, even when she lost. "I did better than last year, faster start out the gate."

"Yeah, for sure," Willow says, passing her a water bottle.

"Thanks, Mom." She takes a swig. "So I can go to Arcadia Galactica tomorrow, right?"

I lift my brows. "You're still grounded, Vada."

"Aw, come on." Her voice is light, knowing she shouldn't get a reprieve for biking after dark. A rule she constantly breaks. We still live in the city, in the same Philly loft.

Vada is brave like her mom. And she's also nonconfrontational, in a way like me. I rest easy knowing she walks away from fights.

"Next week," Willow reminds her, "you can always go then, unless you get grounded aga—"

"I won't," she says quickly, walking her bike back to the tent with us. "I'm having Pac-Man withdrawals like so bad." Her aquamarine eyes flit to me. "Literally, Dad."

I hate that game. She knows I hate that game, and honestly, I can't believe my kid loves playing for hours upon *hours*. Vada pulverized Willow's high score when she was four, and not because her mom is bad. Willow is fucking good at that one.

While we keep walking, Vada talks and smiles over the pics that her mom captured.

They both laugh.

And my chest rises in a light breath. In happiness.

Vada Lauren Abbey was born from love, and we named her *Vada* after the character in the movie *My Girl*. Lauren after the guy who changed our lives.

As soon as we enter the tent, Vada is rushed by family, by her cousins, three of which are girls around her age—and also her best friends. They pour ice water over her head. Laughing. Congratulating.

I extend my arm back around Willow, sharing a gentle smile with my wife. Summers are my favorite part of the year, always full of family.

And with this family, these people who protect and love without question, sixth place can feel like first.

Video Game Reviews

Sorin-X 5

Overview: 9.5 IGN.com, 5/5 Trusted Reviews, 94% Metacritic

Developer: Abbey Game Studios

Publisher: Cobalt Electronics

Creator: Garrison Abbey

Director: Garrison Abbey

Designer: Garrison Abbey

Programmer: Garrison Abbey

Writer(s): Garrison Abbey, Jasmine Lang

Artist(s): Belinda Howell, Jackson Howell

Composer: Anya Rhodes

Series: *Sorin-X*

SALES: *Sorin-X 5* sold 1.6 million copies within 24-hours of release and sold through its 15 million first-run shipment order to retailers.

AWARDS: *Sorin-X 5* received high critical praise and gaming awards from publications, including awards from GamesHighlight and Game eVolution. It also won the Game of the Year for innovative gameplay and story, and the *Sorin-X* series continues to dominate the gaming landscape. Working under a small team with an emphasis on originality and character-connection, the creator has been lauded since the first iteration of the game fourteen years ago. Garrison Abbey is considered one of the greatest video game creators in modern history.

Thank you so much for reading *Wherever You Are*!

We hope you enjoyed the conclusion to

Garrison & Willow's romance.

CONTINUE FLIPPING FOR A BONUS SCENE

Grown-up Maximoff Hale, now twenty-two, talks to his

Uncle Garrison about Vada, bodyguards, and more!

The Abbey Loft

Bonus Scene

2 Weeks Before Damaged Like Us

Maximoff Hale
Age 22

I ride up a graffiti-painted elevator inside an industrial factory, which was converted into premium lofts.

And my uncle's loft is here.

He's one of the few people in our family that lives outside of a gated neighborhood. His level of fame hasn't amassed like my parents, but I still see Garrison Abbey pop up on a magazine or two. His name isn't immediately recognizable to the average person.

So chances are, you don't know about him. Not unless you've dug into our Instagram photos and clicked on the tags.

His wife is my dad's sister, but in all honesty, our family history is so complicated that it fills multiple paragraphs on Wikipedia.

The elevator slows to a stop at the fifteenth floor. I left Declan in the lobby level. My bodyguard isn't my bodyguard for long, and

Losing him.

Only two more weeks and someone else will be a huge part of my life.

But I'm trying not to worry about that.

I have other things to do.

Elevator doors slide open to reveal a distressed metal door. I use my keys and unlock, stepping inside—

"Watch the bike!" Garrison shouts at me from across the loft.

Sure enough, I almost trip over a bright orange dirt bike. My knee ends up knocking over the helmet that'd been hanging on the handlebar. I bend down and pick it up. Carefully hooking it back.

"Sorry about that," my uncle tells me. He's standing at the kitchen island with a screwdriver and a laptop, the entire casing open. "I'm doing this thing where I've stopped picking up Vada's crap."

I smile and squeeze past his bike by the door. His thirteen-year-old daughter is best friends with my little sister Kinney. "How's that working out for you?" I ask.

"Her shit is now everywhere." He grabs a pair of plyers and removes a chip from the computer. "So...not well."

His brown hair is buzzed, and wayfarer sunglasses are hooked on the crew-neck of his black shirt. At thirty-nine, he's the youngest of my uncles, and I have memories of him living with my parents when I was just a little kid.

Good memories.

We'd wake up early and I'd watch him play Mortal Kombat on Sega Genesis.

Add in the fact that his job is literally creating and developing video games, and he's probably the coolest person in my family.

Right behind my mom and dad.

I near the kitchen island. His artsy loft has huge windows that landscape a wall, and the entire floorplan is open. The bookshelves are my favorite part of Uncle Garrison and Aunt Willow's loft. Each one is filled to the brim with comics and old retro video games, preserved behind glass doors.

"Hand me that flathead," Garrison tells me.

As I reach the island, I find the green flathead screwdriver among his tools.

He takes it from my hand with a *thanks*. "So I looked at your proposal for the updated security hardware," he tells me, still focusing on the computer.

Yesterday, I sent him an email about my plan for a Christmas gift to everyone. Hopefully something that can be completed by this year.

I want to update security on all our tech.

Phones. Computers. The whole works. I haven't always felt safe texting people, and I know I'm not the only one. And I want that safety for my family, for my cousins and siblings. Our tech hasn't been updated in a few years.

And now that Jane and I moved into the city, I know she'd like to sext her Asshole With Benefits without fear of being hacked or leaked.

Garrison has an extensive background in coding, and so he usually runs point with our tech team.

My proposal was pretty simple, but the timeline may be too short. "I can still tweak some things if it's asking for too much by Christmas," I tell him.

"No, you're good," Garrison replies casually. "I can have it rolled out by then." Before I can thank him, he nods his chin to a box on the kitchen table. "Got that yesterday if you want to take some."

I already know what's in it before I even cross the room. A couple years ago, Garrison was photographed at one of Vada's races. He was biting the end of his sunglasses and cheering.

The headline: **Sexy Dad Cheers on Dirt Biking Daughter.**

It went viral and ever since, he's been sent free sunglasses from a ton of companies. All hoping he'll wear them in public.

My assumptions are confirmed after I flip open the flaps to the box. Three rows of designer sunglasses stare back at me.

I take out a pair of bronze aviators. "How's the new game coming?" I ask him.

Garrison glances at me with cinched brows. "That's seriously what you want to talk about, Moffy?" He screws the backing onto the laptop.

"Let me guess." I lean my ass against the edge of the kitchen table. It's gray marble shaped in an octagon. "My dad said I was freaking out."

I'm calm.

But I've been thinking. A lot. Drifting off, wondering and contemplating this colossal change in my life. I feel in flux.

Like my head isn't on my body, and I'm wondering if this new bodyguard will make me feel like I'm spinning out of control at a million miles an hour in an unnamed galaxy.

Or whether he'll just be like Declan.

A silent companion that I forget is even there.

And then I think.

I think that sometimes I'm not even sure I know what I want. And that terrifies me too.

"Your dad said," Garrison starts. "And I quote, 'Maximoff is acting like someone stole his childhood Batmobile bed.'"

I laugh.

It was a fucking awesome bed. But if my dad were here, I would have to respectfully disagree with him. I'm not acting like a petulant child. I just want details about the new bodyguard.

That's it.

"He would say that," I reply and slide the sunglasses over my eyes. The room bathes in a warm orange hue. "But I'm surprised he didn't convulse when he uttered the word *Batmobile*."

"He did admit to puking in his mouth," Garrison says.

My eyes flit to the tattoo on Garrison's neck. It's of the Bat-Signal—something that I've been thinking about inking on me but I know better.

I ask, "You still thinking about getting it covered?"

Garrison looks up from his laptop, trying to figure out what I mean.

I tap my neck where his tattoo is and say, "The *battoo*." That's what my mom calls it.

"50/50," he tells me. "On one hand, it reminds me that I can be a real shithead—which is a good thing sometimes. On the other, it reminds me that I'm a shithead." Garrison shrugs. "Life lesson, Mof, don't get revenge ink."

He's not really into Batman that much. Aunt Willow is the comic book reader in the Abbey family, but *she* doesn't even read DC comics.

Garrison's tattoo stemmed from a bad night fueled by anger. A few years ago, he started smoking again—he'd quit years back—and my dad was all over him about it.

I think my dad sent Garrison a picture of a burnt, charred lung almost every day. The way Garrison tells the story is that the photos were a joke at first, but when my dad didn't let up, something snapped and it just got to Garrison. So he went out to the tattoo parlor, and in retaliation, he inked something he knew would piss off my dad.

The next day, he regretted it *and* stopped smoking.

"Upside," I tell him. "My dad is still alive, so maybe there's a chance I could get a Batman tattoo and he'd survive."

Garrison looks at me like I'm insane. "I'm not his kid," he reminds me. "And your dad doesn't just hate DC tattoos. He hates *all* tattoos. He's a petty asshole." Garrison smiles. "But we love him."

We do.

I return the aviators to the box and pick up a pair of white way-farers. "So do you know anything about my new bodyguard?" I ask him, slipping the sunglasses on. "No one will tell me anything about him…or her." I realize I don't even know that simple detail. Jesus.

"Probably because the transfer isn't set yet," Garrison says. "There's still a couple weeks." He types on the laptop keyboard and then glances at the clock.

"I can go—"

"No don't," Garrison says quickly. "Willow and Vada won't be home for another hour. I'm supposed to be cooking dinner, but I'm thinking about just ordering pizza." He types on the keys again. "And you're one of the few people I like."

He's selective about who he hangs with. Kind of like my dad.

They have a lot in common.

"Vada's at her eighth grade orientation, right?" I ask him and near the island again and slide on a barstool. My little sister has orientation today, too, and Kinney texted me her schedule and asked if I've had the teachers. When I told her Mrs. Korrie is tough, she replied with coffin emojis.

Garrison cringes at the word *eighth grade*. "You know when she was born, I almost thought she'd stay little forever." He stares off and shakes his head. "She's *thirteen*. Fuck." He rubs his eye and then nods to me. "I'd like to just freeze time so she doesn't go to high school." His eyes meet mine, and I remember being a little kid and seeing this sadness in those eyes.

A sadness that I couldn't quite understand back then, but I felt it pour over me like a cold bath that steals your breath.

He seemed lost, but God, I loved him. I loved every second that he spent with me, and I thought he was one of the coolest people in every single universe. Like an older brother I didn't have.

And I didn't need him to smile at me. I just liked that he wanted me around him, and later, I found out that he just liked that I was dying to be near him.

Right now, staring in his eyes, I don't see that sadness from years past. But I see him recalling some part of it, and he tells me, "I know you didn't have a bad time in high school, but it was shit for me. Worse for your aunt. Teenagers generally suck."

I slip off the wayfarers. "She has the girl squad."

Garrison rolls his eyes at the mention of them. "Yeah, love the girl squad, except for the fact that they're acting like this year is their last year together on planet Earth." Since Winona and Vada are in a grade higher, they'll be going to high school before Kinney and Audrey. It's a big deal for the four of them.

I've witnessed a lot of group hugs and death emojis. My sister is usually the one delivering the latter.

My phone buzzes.

Janie. Texting me back. I asked her to grill her brothers and parents for information. See if they know anything about my new bodyguard.

Sorry, old chap. They're all too tight-lipped. Or they don't know anything. —Jane

I reply: its hard too believe your dad doesn't know anything
My grammar is all fucked up, but I don't really care. I just send.

True. But then he's been sworn to secrecy. — Jane

I glance up at Garrison. His fingers fly over the keyboard and it makes noises. "You really don't know who my new bodyguard is?"

He doesn't look up.

"If you think I'm covering for someone, I'm not," he replies. "I'd snitch on Connor and Ryke in a heartbeat."

"My dad?" I ask.

He wavers for a second, and then his eyes meet mine. "To you, maybe."

It's not a yes or no.

But I'm certain that I'll still leave here knowing nothing.

Two more weeks without details.

Christ.

SPECIAL THANKS

The biggest thanks to our mom for continuing to be in our corner and putting up with our intense deadlines. We love you to the moon and back. When we call, you're there. No questions asked. We always say you're our very own Rose Calloway, and it's never been more true. From the bottom of our hearts, thankyouthankyouthankyou.

xoxo Krista & Becca

READY TO SEE HOW THIS STORY CONTINUES?

You can find out how Maximoff Hale's bodyguard comes into his life. Oh...and this maverick, know-it-all bodyguard just so happens to be Maximoff's childhood crush!

Read their epic love story in *Damaged Like Us*.

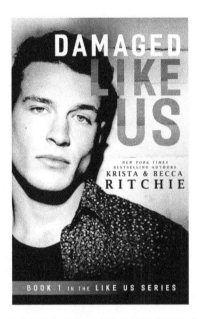

WANT MORE BONUS SCENES LIKE THE ABBEY LOFT?

Join Krista & Becca's Patreon at www.patreon.com/kbritchie

Joining Krista & Becca's Patreon will give you access to over 100,000 words of bonus scenes. Plus new content and extras release every month! Patreon is a great place for readers who love behind-the-scenes posts and all the extra goodies.

CONNECT WITH KRISTA & BECCA

www.kbritchie.com
www.facebook.com/KBRitchie
www.instagram.com/kbmritchie